DEMON
FORSAKEN

DEMON ENFORCERS, BOOK 2
JENN STARK

A Sin so great it cannot stand...

It's not easy being the wittiest, sexiest, most devilishly handsome member of his elite team of Demon Enforcers, but Finn of the Syx has worked it his entire existence. The existence he can remember, anyway. While his fellow demons can recall their lives as Fallen angels--and the sins that got them condemned--Finn's memory is a blank slate.

Which means his Sin was so horrible, not even the mind of a demon can handle it. Outstanding.

Now Finn is given his last chance for redemption: twenty-four hours to find an encrypted list of mortals marked for death. Unfortunately, the only person who can help him is Dana Griffin--the gritty, passionate, fiercely independent security expert who's far more than she thinks she is, and definitely more than Finn deserves. Not to mention she's being hunted by the worst of his kind.

Finn knows Dana is the key to his future and his past, but she'll also be a dead woman if he can't remember how to save them both before the clock strikes midnight on Christmas Eve. No pressure, though.

The life you've lost is all that can save you when you're a *Demon Forsaken.*

OTHER BOOKS BY JENN STARK

The Demon Enforcer Series

Demon Unbound
Demon Forsaken
Demon Bewitched

The Immortal Vegas Series
(series complete!)

Getting Wilde
Wilde Card
Born To Be Wilde
Wicked And Wilde
Aces Wilde
Forever Wilde
Wilde Child
Call of the Wilde
Running Wilde
Wilde Fire
One Wilde Night *(prequel novella)*

The Wilde Justice Series

The Red King
The Lost Queen
The Hallowed Knight

For Kathy Holzapfel,
Love and Light to you

CHAPTER ONE

Moeller Mfg. Distribution Center
Kansas City, Missouri
Dec. 21

Finn of the Syx, ultimate Demon Enforcer, hit the ground in the perfect superhero landing. One of his knees and one hand rested flat on the concrete floor, his other knee was bent, and his right arm was raised in a mighty thrust to ward off the ravening horde of demons who were ruthlessly poised to attack in all their howling, slobbering glory.

No one paid him any attention.

A quivering mass of bodies surrounded him, all right, but they were all undeniably human. Big, burly, poorly washed humans, pressing toward the front of the large warehouse room. They shouted and chattered excitedly, their beer-soaked laughter ricocheting off walls painted the color of despair.

Finn stood, wincing as some blowhard with a bullhorn started shouting over the raucous throng. "Climbing into the ring now *isn't* Mack the Truck, as planned, but someone even *better*. Someone that will *rev* your engines and rock your *worrrrrld*!" boomed the powerful bass.

Beside Finn, Stefan of the Syx stood ramrod straight, hands on hips, his lean, muscled form tense and his scowl fixed. He also wasn't paying any attention to the impressively flourished magnificence of Finn's arrival. Instead, the slightly older, certainly prettier, and unquestionably more mature demon enforcer surveyed the assembly with an expression of chilly disdain. "Tell me this is a joke."

"Which part?" Finn asked. "It's not like we could say no."

When a summons came for one of the members of the Syx, they went. As many of them as were required for a particular problem, with only the barest whiff of information to prepare them for what they were about to face. In this case, said information had been beyond sketchy. Finn squinted around the bleak space, trying to get his bearings, but he was as confused as Stefan.

"I thought this was a fight. A UFC fight." Stefan's eyes glinted red, betraying his irritation. "Like the one at the arena last week. With Kanye and Pitbull taking selfies and the women more bloodthirsty than the men—every one of them dressed to kill."

"Yeah, well. This ain't that," Finn said. "These guys are maybe dressed to meet their parole officer, max." He scanned the high ceilings and bare walls and stained concrete floors, the lights set up on rolling dollies blanketing the space. It barely resembled the mixed martial arts match they'd seen not two weeks earlier in Las Vegas, complete with high-tech screens and gleaming cages and easily ten thousand screaming fans hanging from the rafters of the glittering arena. No. This fight looked like it should be outfitted with prison wardens and body bags.

And that wasn't the worst of it.

"How many demons we got here, by your count?"

Stefan exhaled a long breath, his gaze sweeping the room as well. "Not as many as the humans, I can tell you that, but they're all crowded around the ring. And they're definitely freshly hatched, which is interesting."

Finn snorted. "Not all that interesting. This is exactly the kind of place that would appeal to a demon on his first day out of the slammer. Lots of low-hanging fruit."

"Fair enough."

There was no question these demons were new to Earth either; the glamours that allowed them to appear human were almost harsh to behold. They were also too eager, too stupid. No wonder they'd tripped some mortal's trigger hard enough for that human to pray to God for help.

Those kinds of prayers were exactly the kind the Syx answered.

Finn and the rest of the Syx had been demon enforcers for going on six millennia, charged with taking out the worst of their kind. A good job even when it sucked, really, since it allowed the team to hang around Earth more often than not, rather than rotting in their cell-like bolt-holes on the other side of the veil, which was where they should be serving out eternity in payment for their sins.

Humans had their own first line of defense when it came to demon hunting, of course. But despite all the good press exorcists got, it still took a demon to kill a demon, and archangels couldn't be choosers when humans got desperate enough to pray for help. So, a human begged, the Archangel Michael heard, and on or more of the Syx were dispatched for cleanup.

Recently, however, the game had changed. Due to a series of deeply unfortunate events, a new horde of demons had been dumped onto the planet, as pervasive and deadly as trash in the Pacific. And unfortunately for Earth, demons were the plastic straws of celestial refuse: damned near indestructible.

Which explained why Finn and Stefan were standing ankle-deep in a particularly foul-smelling horde this fine solstice night in the heartland of America — along with a couple of hundred humans who had no idea how much danger they were in.

Just another day in paradise.

Finn watched as Stefan's gaze locked on the human women in the group. Of all the members of the Syx, Stefan was most attuned to females. He connected with them, understood their needs, their desires, their states of mind and body —

"They're drugged," Stefan murmured, the first tremor of concern coloring his deep, resonant voice. "Voluntarily, I think. But they seem happy enough underneath the narcotics. They're not who called us."

Finn took in the laughing women, surrounded by dozens of grinning men, every one of them redolent of cheap beer and skittering adrenaline. "I don't know. You should probably plan on saving a few, anyway. Gotta keep up your skills and all."

Stefan chuckled, his mouth easing into a sly, determined smile. He not only was attuned to women — he genuinely adored them. The more of them, the better, in fact. "I think I can manage that." He glanced toward the darker knot of demons surrounding the ring. "But these new guys aren't behaving right. They're fixated on he fight, not the humans. At least not any of the humans

10

who're outside the ring."

"Forty of 'em, you figure?"

"Give or take." The makeshift octagon at the center of the room was blocked by a thick knot of spectators that was growing by the minute. "They're too keyed up, wild. Stupid with their newfound freedom. I don't think we'll need any backup. Hell, they're one head butt shy of dropping their glamours and revealing themselves to the crowd by mistake."

"Agreed." Finn gestured to the ring. "So let's see what all the excitement's about."

They moved forward carefully, keeping their own glamours strong. Since he and Stefan been summoned here by one of the humans, the demons couldn't pierce the their illusion that made them appear human to any who happened to glance their way. It was the same type of glamour that any demon adopted around humans, only the Syx did it better.

They did a lot of things better. Even if they were currently outnumbered by forty to two.

Despite all that, Finn tried to avoid the direct glance of any of the demons as he passed them. It was a superstition of his, but he'd always been sure he'd see the worst of himself reflected in their eyes. Or, worse, he'd see an image of himself as a Fallen angel—still glorious, still right, still whole. He wasn't sure he could take that, no matter how many millennia had passed.

Fortunately, he didn't have much cause to stare a demon in the eye. Most of the time, they were too busy trying to kill him before he killed them back.

It hadn't always been this way, of course. First there'd been only humans and angels. Then came the Fallen—angels who'd wanted to bridge the gap between the celestial and mortal planes. Being a Fallen wasn't a bad thing, in theory—God had allowed it, had wanted some of his own to teach the sprawling crowds of humanity.

In practice, however, the temptation to sin had proven a deadly siren song for far too many of God's celestial choir. And once a Fallen committed a sin against humans...they were judged, by God and His righteous angels. Those Fallen whose sins were considered sufficiently heinous were then condemned to become a demon, abruptly shut off from God's grace, His forgiveness, His love.

"Water under the bridge, my man," Finn muttered beneath his breath. Right now, he needed to worry about killing whatever piece-of-crap demon was ruining some human's day.

"So who's our guy?" Stefan asked abruptly, sliding his gaze to Finn. Finn had gotten the call first, so by all rights, he should know.

Finn grimaced. He *didn't* know, though. He never did. Not only was he shit for remembering details of his own past, he was the worst at tracking down the humans who cried out for the Syx's help. It was as if he blocked their 911-demon calls instinctively. While this probably was connected to his own personal sin, it was a colossal pain in the barbed tail. He hated it when he got a direct summons.

"That way," he said with a confidence he didn't feel.

"Agreed." Stefan's voice was steady, certain; that made Finn feel a little better. And, as they approached the ring, he couldn't deny the quickening of his blood. This was all that was left for him, after all: to fight the worst of his own kind.

As they edged closer to the howling spectators, he felt more certain too. "Our summoner still breathes, but he's in deep. I doubt he even knows how deep."

"Then let's get this over with," Stefan said. Together, they started worming their way through the crowd.

The throng of spectators was surprisingly robust for an unsanctioned fight, most of them knotted around the fenced-in octagon that looked sturdy enough to hold livestock. Which it probably had at some point.

When he and Stefan finally broke through the last line, however, Stefan muttered a curse. "No. Just no."

Finn looked up to where he was staring and sighed. "Fantastic."

Their most likely summoner was standing in the ring, pressed against one corner of the octagon…and he was little more than a teenager. His eyes were the biggest thing on him, and they were pinned to his opponent—not so much in fear as dread. And though he had his elbows up in a fighter's stance, his fists shoved into the kind of low-profile boxer's gloves favored by mixed martial arts practitioners, he clearly wanted to be anywhere but here.

"That's right, ladies and gentlemen, standing in for the Mighty Mack MacElroy, we have Mack *Twooooo*! Mack's oldest boy, and a national champ of welterweight wrestling, come home for Christmas and fresh out of college."

"Fresh into the meat locker, you mean!" someone called, and the crowd jeered, shoving closer. Finn glanced to the other side of the octagon, knowing who Mack Two's opponent had to be.

Yep.

"Definitely a recent arrival," Stefan commented drily. "Not a very pretty one either."

Finn swept his glance over the slavering demon, who was so excited that her glamour was beginning to falter—at least for those who knew how to look. And since Finn did… *Ew.*

"At least you know why you're here," he grinned, waggling his brows at Stefan. "One smokin' hot chick, comin' right up. You guys will get along great."

"Funny."

The demon on the other side of the octagon had the affectation of a male, the glamour most demons assumed when walking the earth. But the creature beneath that glamour was definitely female. As members of the Syx, both Finn and Stefan could see her true self, or the self she'd been transformed into when she'd been condemned to an eternity as a demon after she'd fallen. And that transformation had been a doozy. The head and neck of a long-beaked bird, four arms that stuck out from a waspishly thin torso, and the lower body of something between a snake and a millipede.

Finn recoiled when he took in all her…legs. "Good *God*, she's gotta be the ugliest one yet."

"Finn," Stefan breathed in warning, but it was too late. As if hearing their words, the demon turned—or the human she was impersonating did, all ham-hock jowls and beefy arms and clenched fists. But Finn wasn't worried about being outed—not by this chick, anyway. Another perk of the Syx, their glamour was ironclad— and only made stronger by the proximity of the summoner.

And there was no question that the boy in the octagon had had something to do with their summons, though Finn remained a little curious about that. Despite the sick look on his face, the kid didn't seem like he backed down from too many fights. Focusing on the human, Finn reached out, filtering through his thoughts with long-practiced ease. One picture held firm above all others. An older version of the boy, huddled in a back corner of this very room, hollow-eyed, bruised. Sick…or beat up. Something.

The kid's dad, Finn had no doubt. And judging from the crucifix clutched in the man's hand as he tried to force his battered fingers together in prayer, their summons here was starting to make a lot more sense. There must have been money on this fight if the old guy'd thought he'd had a chance. He'd probably tried to fight himself, until his son had stepped in. Merry Christmas all around.

The announcer's next verbal assault confirmed Finn's suspicion. "For the final bout tonight, with a prize of three *hundred* dollars, Mack Two will be taking on The *Destroyerrrrr*!" Another howl from the crowd, and the demon in bulky-meat-sack clothing raised her fists. The Destroyer gave the crowd a grin that displayed several replacement teeth gleaming with chrome. The crowd's clamoring ratcheted up another notch.

Stefan stiffened, worry tightening his features. "What in the hell is she *thinking*? She won't learn anything from this fight. And three hundred dollars isn't worth attracting the archangel's attention."

"Yup." Finn watched as the two combatants edged toward each other, a fight that was destined to go south for the human almost as soon as it began. But that was only part of the problem. "Except maybe she's not the one going to school. Look at the way the others are watching her. They're way too tight, almost mimicking her. It's like they don't know what they're doing. They're going to take out this whole room just for practice, I'm thinking."

"Practice." Stefan nodded. He stared first at the shining faces of the demons, then at the completely clueless faces of the men and women around them, and cursed. "She's teaching them — and they're letting her. They're latching on, working together. That's...unusual. And by unusual, I mean not good." He shook his head. "The archangel should have warned us about that."

"The archangel should've warned us about a lot of things." Before Finn could say anything else, however, the boy in the ring suddenly rushed forward, getting in a jaw-shattering uppercut to his opponent as the crowd roared in approval.

"Here we go," Finn muttered.

They plunged into the knot of demons, and chaos reigned.

"It's this way, Ms. Griffin, exactly as ordered. We haven't touched it."

Though they'd be outside the weather station for only a few minutes to visit the site's storage facility, Captain Landreau of the Royal Canadian Air Force wore a thick jumpsuit of shiny, vaguely metallic fabric, which Dana Griffin appreciated. Her own gear was equally warm and equally bright. She'd made sure of it before she'd boarded the last leg of her chartered flight to Alert, Canada, which was deep in the middle of its polar sleep cycle. That meant it wasn't merely thirty degrees below zero before wind chill was factored in...it was also completely, mind-numbingly dark.

"Watch your step," the man continued gruffly.

She followed the captain away from the snowcat toward the supply building, where Lester had told her she'd find the box he needed her to recover — her alone, he'd insisted. Not her team. The RCAF were touchy about interlopers, and her uncle had gotten Dana clearance solely because she was a blood relative to him. That made her the only one either side trusted to carry out the small set of artifacts uncovered by Exeter Global Services' engineers while they'd been installing a new weather station annex as part of a joint scientific research initiative between the US and Canada.

As it was, Lester was being allowed to step in and whisk away the unfortunate discovery primarily because the RCAF wanted those artifacts gone. If the conservationists got wind of them and declared this patch of bleak, frigid dirt some sort of historical site...well, the Canadian military needed that like a hole in the head. Lester had agreed to take the problem off their hands.

Lester was good at that. Especially when he could send Dana in to do his dirty work for him.

"Through there." The man stood aside, back straight, face inscrutable. "Small box, about two feet by one foot. We would have brought it out for you—"

"But my uncle insisted no one else touch it, I know. Don't worry, I'll find it." Dana Griffin squeezed between two narrowly spaced pallets in the storage hut, which was colder than it really should be, even for northern Canada in mid-December.

"Whaddya got for me, Max?" she subvocalized.

Her headset crackled. "It's to your left, or it should be," Max Garrett, her head tech at Griffin Securities, murmured additional directions in her ear, his voice low, focused. This far north, the security wasn't tight, and no one had thought to frisk her. Despite her uncle's insistence, however, Dana wasn't going anywhere completely alone up here. "The electrical signature is off the charts. Whatever Uncle Fester has stored in that box, it's packing a punch." Max paused. "You think it's aliens?"

Dana's mouth twitched. "I'm pretty sure it's not."

"Last time, it was aliens."

"Last time, it was an empty crypt."

"*Exactly.* And the only way it could have been empty is because of aliens, I'm telling you."

"Max…"

"I'd checked its energy signature the day before. The day! Then we get there and we got nothing but an empty chamber and a hell of a lot of static. That wasn't the first time either. You know it wasn't. We were absolutely killing it until, what? A year ago? Maybe more."

"Eighteen months," Dana muttered.

"Eighteen months. Thank God, Lester eased up on his artifact search, or we'd have been ash-canned for supreme suckage. And it wasn't our fault! It had to be—"

"Aliens," Dana finished for him.

"Exactly."

"Okay, hush," Dana said, tightening her coat against the cold. "I need to focus."

She slid around a pallet, the movement causing a sliver of pain to shoot up her right shin and dance around her kneecap. *Sweet mother, that hurts.*

It'd been over seven weeks since she'd been shot while providing routine security protection for Lester on Halloween night, and she still hadn't fully recovered.

"Hushing," Max chirped back, thoroughly happy to work on his deep-ops vibe. Truth was, Dana didn't mind these assignments Lester sent her on either, especially this one, with its multiple flight legs up from Cleveland to this northernmost outpost in the Canadian tundra. Traveling solo, she hadn't had to fake being completely healed, completely pain-free.

Because she wasn't pain-free, not even close. And there was no way she should be having this much trouble with a through-and-through gunshot injury sustained nearly two *months* ago, for heaven's sake.

Nevertheless, facing the utter dark of Canada's long winter's nap seemed a hell of a lot more appetizing right now than facing the streets of her hometown after what she'd sworn was an all-out attack on the old man. No matter how many times he denied it.

Dana couldn't quite remember exactly what'd happened after she'd stepped in front of her uncle that night, though her nightmares had tried to fill in the blanks: the flash of rage after she'd been shot; her fists pounding flesh and breaking bones. But Lester had told her a million times over she'd done no such thing. She'd been shot. That's it. She'd lost a lot of blood, sure, but everything else she'd thought happened after that…simply hadn't. He'd flatly rejected that she'd beaten back four grown men after taking the bullet to her leg, explained to her that she'd collapsed — like anyone would have collapsed after such a frightening injury.

He'd then dismissed her nightmares by telling her she was suffering from post-traumatic stress disorder, imagining things that were simply never there. Her leg had been flayed open with superficial wounds of flying shrapnel along with the bullet that'd pierced her, and she also sported a scar the size of a quarter on her forearm, where they'd injected some supercharged antibiotic or special healing thingamajig that Lester had the patent for. But after all that, according to her uncle and all his doctors…she'd healed. Faster than anyone had expected her to.

Sort of.

Dana grimaced in the frigid room. Maybe Lester was right, maybe all the pain she'd endured had been a function of a traumatized mind, not a traumatized body. And she wasn't going to get any different answers from him, that much was clear.

Besides, what mattered most was that despite the doctors' initial dire predictions during that night of a long and fraught healing process — predictions that changed within hours to a bright prognosis of a complete and rapid recovery — Dana was now wide-awake and standing, and not in a hospital, screaming in her sleep.

She shifted again, wincing at the renewed shot of pain in her leg. Then again, maybe flying so many hours in cramped airplanes hadn't been such a great idea after all.

"Sorry to harsh your Zen again, little grasshopper, but you're getting close." Max's voice had grown scratchier, and Dana didn't need his monitors to explain why. The box the captain had described was right in front of her — and it was glowing. Flat-out glowing.

"Max..." she whispered, but got back nothing but static in return.

Dana edged forward. *What is this thing?* According to Lester, the artifacts stored here had been excavated out of the arctic permafrost under heavy security not six days earlier. No one knew anything about the discovery in the scientific community or the historical community. They'd picked up a few whispers in the black-market community — but that'd died down too, after Dana had asked Max to anonymously post pics of bogus artifacts showing mastodon tusks and leg bones. The box had been stashed in the frigid back room of the weather station awaiting transport out via Alert Airport. She was that transport.

Now the thing was practically on fire. She stared down at the plain, unadorned case for a moment, then squatted. The moment she touched the lid, the iridescence surrounding the box faded. Interesting.

The case was secured with only the most basic of padlocks, and she unlatched it easily. Inside, as Lester had described, were a few random trinkets along with the big prize: a chunk of rock carved with a group of winged figures. The *Anunnaki*, her uncle had told her, his breath catching with excitement. A relic that had absolutely no business being in the northern hemisphere, let alone snugged up against the Arctic Circle.

"You got it?" Max was back, his words barely whispered.

"I got it." She relocked the padlock, fitted two more locking mechanisms around the case, then lifted the box, surprised at how light it was. Its glow was now almost completely doused. "You'll love it. Best winged-god images I've ever seen."

"Aliens," Max corrected her somberly.

"Aliens." She thought about the weird, dying light. "Maybe."

She emerged out of the back room to find Captain Landreau already at the door, his face stern, wary. He looked up as she approached. "Good. I was going to come get you if you took any longer."

"Oh?" Dana glanced to the front door. "What's the problem?"

"I don't know." They stepped outside, pausing beneath the small covered porch as the wind whistled around them. "The snowcat driver said he thought he saw something outside the vehicle but couldn't be sure.

He flipped on the lights, made some noise, drove off a bit to see if anything followed him. Nothing did, but something doesn't feel right. I told him to get back here and we'd return to the weather station."

"But…" Dana frowned into the darkness, seeing nothing but the oncoming lights of the snowcat. "What would be out there? Surely everything's in hibernation."

"Most everything is," the captain said, the tension in his voice drawing her focus back to him. "We've seen some wolves, of course, but that's about it in terms of predators. And we're pretty far north for them to be roaming when it's this dark out. Not worth taking any risk, though. Here we go."

He waved to the vehicle as it approached, only to stiffen, his hand frozen midair. "What the…"

Dana turned, then took a faltering step back, clutching the box to her chest. Something broke the light of the snowcat's headlights, once, twice—then a dozen times. The vehicle lumbered to a halt, its driver laying heavily on the horn, but the flickering shadows didn't stop. Then the banging started.

"Um, are they attacking the vehicle?"

"That's exactly what they're doing. Son of a bitch." Captain Landreau unholstered his service weapon and took several strides toward the vehicle, but it wasn't a long-range rifle. Dana hustled after him. Though her brain was nearly frozen, she began working out the details as he cracked off a shot.

"Wait—!" she shouted.

The creatures scattered at the unexpected sound. Then they started running.

Toward them.

"Back, get back!" They stumbled toward the storage hut, Dana spinning around, but it was too late. A wolf blocked their path — *no, it can't be a wolf, it's way too big for that*. But whatever it was, it leapt between them and the hut, cutting off their route to the door, almost as if it knew what it was doing. Which was crazy.

"What the hell is going on?" she demanded.

"Shoot to kill," the captain ordered. He blasted off a few more rounds into the darkness, but Dana's weapon was securely locked up at the weather station. *Stupid!* The snowcat driver was also too far away, trapped. The wolves — they *had* to be wolves — had stopped their immediate assault…but they were circling ever closer, growling low and fierce.

Dana blinked, shook her head. There was something almost familiar about them, the way they moved in the darkness, staring at her. Shivering. Hungering —

They leapt.

Dana's scream was cut off sharply when a man dressed only in street clothes barreled past her from the side of the storage hut, then raced straight into the pack of wolves, shouting at the top of his lungs. "*Wolves?* Are you kidding me with the wolves?"

Dana turned to the captain, but Landreau was simply staring, his eyes wide, his mouth slack — apparently stunned immobile. Meanwhile, the man in the middle of the pack grabbed one of the beasts by the midsection and hurled it into a second.

"Hey!" Dana fought past the clamor in her mind to shout. She struggled to take a step forward, to help the man fight, but her legs weren't working right.

"Wha — sweet blessed Lord!" The man glanced back to her, then faced the wolves again. "Can I not do anything right?" He seemed genuinely annoyed as he punched a wolf in the face, then flicked his hand back, hard. The beast yelped just as something exploded in

Dana's mind, and she staggered to the side.

Run! I have to run!

Her mind fogging over to anything other than that imperative, Dana turned, grabbed the captain, and, hugging Lester's box to her chest, started racing for the lights of the snowcat, everything else forgotten.

Completely forgotten.

CHAPTER TWO

Treasure Island Casino
Las Vegas, Nevada
7:00 p.m., Dec. 23

Finn's head was still ringing as he scraped himself into the empty conference room, where he'd been summoned to meet with his Asshole Excellency, the Archangel Michael. Beyond all the other things he was in this world, Michael had the power to dictate the ultimate fate of the Syx, which made him Finn's boss. When the archangel called, Finn came — or went, as it happened, like he had the other night.

A night he was still paying for.

Still, at least so far, the archangel of God had allowed the Syx to live and fight and make the world a little bit more demon-free for the past six thousand years. So he wasn't a total waste of feathers. And with the recent influx of demons, Michael had further made the Syx an offer they couldn't refuse.

Do what the archangel said, undergo his Ultimate

Demon Warrior test of redemption, and maybe—just maybe—the Syx would remain on permanent assignment on Earth. No more bolt-holes beyond the veil, no more wondering if their lives would be cut short merely out of spite. They'd still be Fallen, but they'd at least be that.

Which would be quite something, especially for Finn. Because unlike the other members of the Syx, he had not one freaking idea what he'd done to merit God's fury—not one. Like all former angels, he couldn't recall his time in God's presence; that slate was wiped clean for demonkind. But Finn also couldn't remember any of his time as a Fallen. It'd all been obliterated the moment he'd become a demon.

Which meant being a demon was all he'd ever known.

He'd told the leader of the Syx that once, when Warrick had asked him to join the demon enforcer team. After Warrick's reaction—a mixture of horror and pity—Finn had never told another soul.

Now he drew in a ragged breath. Normally, he recovered from demon battles in two shakes of a succubus tail. Then again, normally he didn't pull a doubleheader, going straight from the smoker fight into the ass edge of the polar ice cap to confront demons who'd crawled inside honest-to-God wolves.

Dire wolves, the Syx's leader, Warrick, had explained to him after he'd thawed out. For the record, possessed dire wolves were a lot harder to kill than they should be.

"You okay?" Stefan was at his side again, probably because he'd been the one to punch through the layer of ice coating Finn when he'd blown back into the Missouri warehouse. Thank God there'd been nothing much left but one freaked-out kid and a lot of black demon goo by that time, because Finn had barely been able to walk. They'd hung around long enough to give Mack Two enough scratch to keep Mack One from ever fighting again, then they'd peeled out of there for points west. Finn had passed out again almost immediately.

"I've been better."

"You know, if this'd happened to me, you'd have assembled a pack of wolf cub stuffed animals and piled them on my bed," Stefan said wryly. "And you'd only be talking to me in howls."

Finn smiled, then winced. "I don't know why this hurts so much."

"It's a side effect of the Possessed you encountered. And who commanded them."

They both turned as a new voice filled the room. Not the archangel, but close enough. The other celestial bigwig atop their organizational chart, Death, had entered the building.

Death, as it turned out, was one of the most formidable beings on Earth at the moment, a member of a council of sorcerers that the archangel also sat on. But though she was technically named after a card in the Major Arcana of Tarot, Death wasn't merely her stage title. She was truly commissioned with ushering souls into the afterlife, and she also had some sort of overseer's role with the Syx that only now was getting revealed, bit by bit.

A role that apparently included acting as welcoming committee.

"Dire wolves are an ancient creature, one harkening back to the dawn of history, but they can't be possessed by demons unless someone more powerful commands it," Death said. She stood with her back against the far bank of windows, her form lean and muscular in a black

T-shirt and ripped jeans, the harsh fluorescent light of the room making her shock of white-blonde hair and piercing blue eyes appear starker than usual. "Someone also from the world's earliest days."

Finn kept his face carefully neutral. "A Fallen." He knew that, in theory, there were Fallen angels who *hadn't* become demons, who merely continued to walk the earth, relics of a bygone age. But he'd never encountered one before...not in all the millennia he'd been a Syx. "And the archangel chose me to go up against one who'd co-opted his very own kennel of sled dogs. Why?"

Death shrugged. "I suspect he wants something."

"From me?"

"From you." This second voice was different—louder, more resonant, and worst of all...closer. Finn flinched away, but he wasn't fast enough. The being that suddenly stood beside him burned bright enough to melt through another layer of hoarfrost that seemed to have wrapped itself around Finn's bones. As the ice fell away, the pain returned.

"Dammit," Finn gritted out.

"It would seem you've done enough of that, demon," Michael said, in what Finn suspected was an attempt at a joke. The dude was a walking pile of laughs.

Finn forced himself to look more or less into his boss's face, though it cost him. The archangel was tall, slender, and dressed in a plain white suit, his skin so pale as to almost be translucent. His hair was the fairest blond, his eyes barely blue, and his lips were bloodless.

"But Death speaks true," the archangel continued. "A Fallen has emerged at a most inopportune time. And, as it turns out, you don't have any preconceived notions of what being a Fallen means."

Finn stiffened, which didn't improve his pain level any, and slid a glance to Stefan. The demon gave no indication that he'd picked up on the archangel's inference, but Finn sure as hell had. The archangel *knew* that Finn couldn't remember being a Fallen.

What else did he know?

Michael held his gaze steadily. "You're wondering why I suspect a Fallen is walking the earth with grave intent."

"Not even close."

"The answer is simple. Only a Fallen or an angel can command a demon to possess a dire wolf. Or command a demon at all."

"And, what, you didn't see any new angels hanging out at the last Elks meeting?"

The archangel shifted, and another wave of pain lay down on Finn, making him wince. "Okay, okay, so it's gotta be a Fallen, got it. A bad Fallen." He paused. "Wouldn't that just make him a demon?"

"Not if he hasn't been caught," the archangel said. "For him to take such a risk now…"

Finn forced himself to straighten again. "It's because of the horde of demons that just made landfall. He wants to…do something with them. Not something good, I take it?"

The archangel smiled. It wasn't a happy smile. "Not something good. I can tell at least that much by the Fallen's decision to command demons to achieve his goals. It puts him at risk for discovery, so there must be a purpose for it. He wants something, something he can't get at directly. He's circling close, but he's not quite there. Which gives you your opportunity."

Finn heard what the archangel was saying, but the words simply wouldn't come together in any way that made sense. "It does?"

At the far end of the conference room, a door slid open and two figures emerged. Finn glanced their way, then stiffened his spine. He hated looking weak in front of humans, even ones at the tippy top of the psychic pyramid.

Death and Stefan turned as well, both of them seeming far more satisfied with the new arrivals. "Sara, Nikki," Death said. Stefan merely glinted at them. It was what he did.

"Yo." Nikki Dawes, as usual, spoke first, though her best friend Sara Wilde was far more psychically gifted than she was. What she lacked in psychic ability, however, Nikki made up for in sheer attitude. Today, the six-foot-four bombshell had added three inches to her height, and she was dressed like...well, a superhero, Finn decided. He took in the skintight red bodysuit, black thigh high boots and elbow-length gloves, and the sweep of bouffant red hair. The costume's bright red fabric was interrupted only by a brilliant yellow-and-black shield stretched over Nikki's ample chest, highlighting the letter "i." He blinked rapidly, forcing himself to look away, but not before she gave him a knowing grin.

Nikki turned to Death and the archangel. "You gave us the heads-up to shoot over, but as we speak, there's a Christmas cosplay contest going on at the Mirage that Elastigirl here is totally going to rock, so make it snappy. Whaddya need?"

Beside her, Sara smiled, looking a little weary around the edges. She was deceptively slight, maybe only five foot seven, with her hair pulled back in a messy ponytail and her body encased in a scuffed leather biker's jacket, tank top, and dark jeans.

"Hey, Finn," she said, her gaze lighting on him with concern. He felt the impact of that gaze immediately. Of all the psychic humans he'd ever encountered, or Connecteds, as they were called, Sara was the strongest. He suspected she didn't even know how strong.

"Hey." He thought about raising a hand, decided against it.

"What happened to you? You look like a demon popsicle." She edged forward, and he let her come. Sara Wilde had a way of getting in your personal space without setting you off, and he was so damned cold…

The archangel folded his arms, watching Sara approach. "I didn't invite you."

"I did," Death said. "She can help. She certainly knows artifacts better than Finn does."

That stopped Sara. A brief, avaricious gleam lit her eyes. "Artifacts?"

The archangel flicked his gaze again to Finn. "Your mind picked up the thoughts of the woman. She held an artifact that shouldn't have been where she was." He gestured, and an image appeared between them, a chunk of stone carved to depict a line of men with wings, several of them carrying objects—a large ring, a wand, a feather.

"The Anunnaki," Sara said, sounding surprised. "That's a nice relic. How'd I miss it?"

Beside her, Nikki snorted. "You've been a little busy, dollface."

"And this was—where you were?" Sara continued. "It couldn't have been someplace that cold unless, what, were you in Tibet?"

"Canada," Finn said. "Very northern Canada. Definitely not Tibet."

"No way." Sara shook her head emphatically,

cocking her gaze at Death. "That kind of artwork has never been found intact anywhere outside Mesopotamia, at least not in that condition. I don't care how much crazy the ice melt is revealing, there's no way that intact rock would ever have made it that far north on its own."

The archangel ignored them, focusing on Finn. "Who sent the woman to recover the artifact?"

Finn answered without hesitation—he'd picked up the human's thoughts easily. It was what demons did. "Her uncle. Lester Morrow. He's the one who sent her on the assignment. He's her boss in some way. Or she thinks of him that way." He paused, another detail coming to him, shimmering in his memory. "Her name is Dana Griffin."

"The wolves, what were they there for? To claim the artifact, or to kill the woman? Is she psychic?" Michael gestured dismissively. "One of the Connected?"

Finn's eyes widened. He hadn't realized he'd captured the thoughts of the wolves he was dispatching as well...but once again, the answer was right in front of him. "No," he said. "No, she's not Connected, not psychic. And the wolves weren't supposed to kill her. Merely incapacitate her until she could be taken. She was supposed to be bait. The artifact...that was a lure too. To get the woman out in the open, exposed. She...she's the quickest route."

"To what?" the archangel pressed. "What did the Fallen seek?"

"Wait, what?" Sara interjected. "We have Fallen running around too?" She swiveled her gaze to Nikki, then to Death. "Shouldn't I know this?"

"Focus," the archangel intoned, staring at Finn. "What was the desire behind the order? What was the—

"

Pain burst through Finn's mind, but incredibly, the word was there. *How is that possible? How can I connect so closely with a Fallen?* It didn't matter. The archangel said something else, and the word was driven out of Finn on a spike of agony.

"The list!" he gasped. "A list her uncle has. Of something. I don't know what. There was only that thought. Only that. The rest…" He swayed on his feet. "Merely jabbering. Take the human holding the stone, get the list from Lester Morrow. Then a lot of wolf-flavored screeching-wailing-gibbertyjack. That's all."

"The list…" the archangel said thoughtfully. "Why not go directly to this Lester Morrow for it?"

"No idea." Finn waved vaguely at Sara as another wave of pain washed over him, the echoes of the dire wolves chanting in his head. "You want to find something, send your flunky out for it."

"Watch it, Winter Warlock," Sara retorted, though her tone was wry. Among her many skills, finding things was totally her jam. "You're a little frosty to be calling anyone names."

The archangel shook his head. "Not Sara. You. You'll go after the woman, find her uncle. And get this list."

Finn thought about arguing, decided against it. "The list, not the stone?"

The archangel snorted. "Not the stone. The stone is worthless."

"Whoa, whoa, whoa," Sara interjected again. "*I* want the stone. That's the best execution of an Anunnaki ceremonial ritual I've ever seen. And I've seen a truckload of them."

Michael kept his gaze pinned on Finn. "I want the

list. And you're going to get it for me. Consider it your test. If you succeed, the next step in the Syx's path to redemption will be secured."

Finn swallowed. The Syx were being granted a chance for permanent residence on Earth...but each of them had to do their part to secure it. Even the one who had shit for memories. "And if I don't?"

"You don't want to know," Michael said, though his face had taken on a faraway, distracted expression. "But to have even the chance at success, you need to be on an even playing field with the rogue Fallen. Anywhere he can go, you must be able to. Anything he can do, you must be able to do as well."

That at least sounded interesting. Finn squinted at the archangel. "Meaning?"

"Meaning you will — temporarily — become a Fallen." The archangel hesitated for only the barest of moments. "You should enjoy that, I think."

"Become a Fallen," Finn said flatly. He had no idea what that meant. "Uh, sure. But why me?"

Michael shrugged. "Apparently, God has a sense of humor."

Ass. "And what's this list about?"

"Also unimportant. Your task is to recover it, not understand it."

"Uh-huh." For a list that was so unimportant, both Michael and this mysterious Fallen guy were awfully interested. "So why do you want it so bad?"

Michael narrowed his pale blue eyes. "You ask a lot of questions."

"It's part of my charm." Something else was nagging at Finn, though. "Why now? You said the Fallen — a guy who's been lurking in the shadows since Atlantis deep-sixed — was only acting now, and in such a way that he could totally get caught. Why? There was a lot of urgency in those wolves, for all that I took them out. They fought back. Hard."

That made the archangel pause. He turned away, stared down at the city. "It's Christmas Eve," he murmured.

"Well, not quite," Nikki put in. "It's technically still Christmas Eve Eve. Which means I have only a few more minutes to get to my costume contest, so choppity choppity."

The angel refocused on Finn. "You want answers? I'll give you this one: your assignment has a deadline. You have only twenty-four hours to be a Fallen and accomplish your mission. Then, at midnight on Christmas Eve, *if* you have done what I've asked, if you've earned your redemption, then perhaps you will be given an additional gift." His lips twitched into another brittle smile. "A Christmas bonus, if you will."

Finn's brows shot up. "Wait, was that another joke? Did you seriously—"

But Michael was no longer there. Not so much as a feather floated in the empty space in front of Finn as he sagged forward a faltering step. "Um, what just happened?"

"Hang on there, buddy," Suddenly, Sara was at his side, her hand on his shoulder. "I suspect Death wanted me here for reasons other than my crack archaeological instincts." She squeezed. It took only a second for a river of healing warmth to pour through every inch of Finn, making his knees go weak.

"Whoa," he managed, the word little more than a groan.

Sara grinned and gave his shoulder another pat. "You're welcome. But, you know, if you happen to see it lying around anywhere, you could maybe get me that Anunnaki carving…"

Finn nodded, slightly dazed, feeling better than he had in longer than he could remember. "I—I'll try."

After a round of goodbyes—and a complicated hand lock with Stefan they'd been perfecting for the past three hundred years or so—Nikki, Sara, and Stefan left. Finn knew he might as well stay where he was. If the archangel was giving him only twenty-four hours to get this job done, Finn would be spinning through the sky soon enough, en route to wherever he'd find this Dana Griffin person. Hopefully, she was somewhere warm.

To his surprise, however, Death remained beside him. After a long moment, she spoke as well.

"So, to answer the question Michael conveniently ignored," she began almost casually. "The timing of this *is* important. Midnight on Christmas Eve is a moment of remarkable power. Power for this Fallen, and, it should be said, power for you."

Finn stared at her. "What kind of power?"

"For a Fallen? Only this: at midnight on Christmas Eve, whatever you ask for…you get."

He narrowed his eyes. "You mean like from Santa?"

Death quirked her lips, but her eyes remained serious. "There's a reason why certain superstitions have endured through the centuries. But no, not because of Santa, this time. All you need to know is, because of what you were—what you are—when the clock strikes midnight, you'll have the chance to ask for anything."

Finn glanced away, not wanting Death to guess at the thoughts running through his mind. What did he want? His memory, most definitely. But also, if he was honest, understanding…and restitution, maybe. A chance to be forgiven for a sin he couldn't remember committing.

A chance to return.

Finn's thoughts ground to a halt, and he realized his heart was racing, his hands sweating. *Would it…could it be possible?* He licked lips that suddenly had gone dry and met Death's stare. "You're kidding me, right?"

"I'm not." Death's expression was unreadable, but her eyes remained intent. She leaned in close, her gaze not leaving his. "So whatever you do, Finn of the Syx, if you do get that chance…be careful what you wish for."

CHAPTER THREE

Ritz Carlton Ballroom
Cleveland, Ohio
12:27 a.m., Dec. 24

"You've got five minutes, Margaret. Then I'm breaking out of this stupid cage myself."

"Now, dear, you don't need to look like you're *really* in prison," Margaret Pettiman said breezily in reply as she waved her thick ring of rhinestone-studded keys in the air for emphasis. "It's all in good fun and for a wonderful cause, so why not make the effort to appear as if you're having, you know, fun?"

"Who put you up to this, specifically?" Dana asked, narrowing her eyes. "Mom or Uncle Lester?"

"Between the attention you'll receive in here and your company providing security for the event, you should garner several new business opportunities!" Margaret beamed in apparent excitement, her skin tensing up in brief alarm at what would have been a wrinkle-inducing movement on any other face.

Not Margaret's, though. Platinum-haired and carefully preserved, the chairwoman of the Founder's Circle Charity Ball had been nipped, tucked, lifted, and lasered in nearly every way imaginable, to the point that the rest of her skin knew better than to crease or fold without express permission. "Your mother will be *so* pleased you agreed to your uncle's suggestion to participate in this little fund-raiser. And again, it's so much fun."

"Right." Dana grimaced, trying to regain her patience. Mrs. Pettiman was her mother's oldest and dearest friend, and that counted for something with Dana. "So where is Mom, anyway? I've been trying to talk with her all night."

"She offered to see the mayor's wife home. Didn't she tell you?" Margaret turned back to Dana, her delicately arched eyebrows caught in a permanent state of mild surprise. "She said she planned on coming directly back."

"Uh-huh," Dana said. "Holding my breath. Starting now."

If it was one thing Claire Griffin was good at, it was avoiding her daughter. Especially these days. Since Dana's injury on Halloween night, it was her mother who'd officially ghosted. Most of the time, she didn't care—it wasn't as if the two of them had ever been close. But between the nightmares and the pain and Dana's own debilitating doubts…a little motherly attention would have been nice. But, apparently, not going to happen, not even on Christmas Eve.

"Now, Dana, enough with the grim expression. You should smile! Enjoy your moment in the limelight." Margaret fluttered her gloved hands. "With both your mother and your uncle in such prominent roles tonight, you'll truly be living the Founder's Circle motto: 'With a strong family, you can save the world.'"

"Right." *But who'll save me from them?*

As Margaret leaned over to air-kiss an eighty-year-old man in a sixty-year-old tuxedo, Dana shifted back away from the bars, her knee sending up a bolt of annoyance at the sudden movement. *Dammit.* Her fifty-yard dash to reach the snowcat in Alert had earned her high marks with the RCAF captain, but she'd been paying for her enthusiasm since the moment her adrenaline had drained away. The weather station crew had been beside themselves at the unexpected wolf attack, and no one could figure out what'd happened to scare off the creatures.

But something had scared them, thank God.

The pain in her knee grounded her, but that didn't make it any easier to bear. Biting back the string of foul language that would definitely *not* earn her high marks as a charity prize, Dana brushed her hip to convince herself her gun was there, then turned her attention to the world outside her cage.

Glittering pinpoint lights dripped from graceful chandeliers, illuminating a dozen fully decorated trees that stretched above the crowd like proud ballroom sentinels. A silver-haired band looked ready to belt out every Christmas standard from the last seventy years, and everything seemed appropriately merry and bright. She even caught sight of Max determinedly weaving his way through the crowd, technically operating as security detail—never mind that the most vicious attacker he'd ever dispatched was a computer virus. Still, it was good to have him here. He'd been with her since she'd opened Griffin Security with its dual focus on tech security and on-the-ground protection, and that mattered too.

Almost unconsciously, Dana raised her hand to her lapel, touching the heavy pin that Lester had given her the year before. Her uncle had a habit of acquiring bright and shiny things—especially if they were *old* and bright and shiny. And he never denied her anything, if she was truly honest.

Dana leaned against the bars, guilt stealing through her. She needed to talk with Lester, finally. She knew she should've told him about the wolves in Canada showing up out of nowhere, then suddenly running away—but she hadn't. And she didn't know why. Ever since the attack they'd both sustained in October, she couldn't shake her uneasiness about her uncle. She hated that. She hated even more that she hadn't been able to get her mom alone long enough to finally ask her questions about Lester either.

She sighed. She'd had such a noble plan in place for tonight too. She'd show support for her mother's favorite charity. She'd convince Lester that she was a hundred percent healed from her injuries, so he would stop with the twenty-four seven questions about her recovery process. She'd reach out to her mom again.

But now she was here, and her mother was AWOL. Again.

"Ladies and gentlemen…" Dana jerked upright as Pettiman's voice wheedled out over the AV system, and she glanced to the front of the room, her hand falling back to her side. "It appears that Dana Griffin, one of Cleveland's rising young entrepreneurs, has gotten herself in a bit of trouble. We owe it to her to set her free, don't we?"

Dana inwardly winced as Margaret directed the audience to stare at her standing in her makeshift cage.

Dutifully, she gave a little wave and what she hoped was a charity-worthy smile. *Lester is so going to pay for this.* Her uncle might be her firm's number one client, but this kind of public humiliation went way beyond her usual rates.

"After all, Dana and her family have given so much to the community." Pettiman's tone oozed pomposity and the sort of self-righteous cheer that people dredged up when they talked about saving orphans and homeless dogs. Dana looked back at the woman, startled at Margaret's melodramatic turn. She began to feel the cage shrink around her, was suddenly afraid of what was coming. *Not Dad*, she thought. *Please don't pimp a dead man for your charity, Margaret.*

Then Pettiman opened her mouth again, and Dana's blood pressure spiked.

"That's right, ladies and gentlemen," Margaret sang on. "Caught behind bars is none other than the daughter of the late, beloved Cleveland police officer, Walter Griffin, who served our fair city for more than twenty years before he was cruelly cut down in the line of duty."

Dana held herself carefully straight as the crowd oohed their admiration. The minute she got out of here, she would perform a citizen's arrest on the woman for harassment. Common Decency violations. Something. Then she would go find Pettiman's stock of Mary Kay cosmetics and set it on fire. With no other option at the moment, however, she gave her best Miss America smile and scanned the room again. No Lester. No Claire.

"As some of you know, Dana has recently rejoined her firm after recovering from injuries sustained in an assault while valiantly protecting Lester Morrow, CEO of Exeter Global Services, who is generously sponsoring tonight's event."

"Put a sock in it, Margaret," Dana muttered as applause greeted that announcement. Her shooting had been in the news, of course. A cop's daughter shot in a parking garage on Halloween while protecting a male executive was titillating information for a slow news day in early November, even if the man she'd been protecting was her own uncle. But to hear Lester tell the story, the attack had been a mugging gone awry, nothing more. He was the target, and she'd gotten in the way.

He had that part right, anyway.

"We'll open the bidding on Ms. Griffin quite high," Pettiman continued, her voice devolving further into a singsong, sugary ooze. "And remember, all the money goes to support the Founder's Circle Society in our fight to help fund pediatric cancer research. Ms. Griffin's bail amount will drop every fifteen minutes, so don't wait to get premium billing as a supporter of all our many children in need. The bidding will start at ten thousand dollars!"

Dana blinked, forcing her expression to remain steady in the face of such abject madness. *Dammit, Lester.* Ten thousand dollars? She'd be stuck in here till New Year's Eve.

After the surprised murmurings drifted away and the stalwart smiles dimmed, Dana cast a glance around the fastenings of her cage again. Actually, it wouldn't take so much for her to unscrew the wires…

She placed her hands on her bars again, trying to keep from rattling them. Briefly, she toyed with the idea of bailing herself out, but decided against it. Griffin Security was full up with clients, nearly all of them Lester referrals. But nobody needed to know she was flush with cash. Least of all the Founder's Circle Charity committee.

Then Margaret's leering face swam into Dana's vision again, and in a flash, she understood why inmates would reach through the bars to strangle their captors.

"Try to look pretty, Dana dear," Margaret said, warming to her role as jailhouse matron. "Perhaps you can find yourself a young man this way. Your father would thank me, I'm sure."

Dana felt her hands begin to itch. "Actually, I think my dad would be happier if you—"

"I apologize for interrupting."

The words were not so much spoken as brushed over her skin, and Dana turned abruptly to the edge of her cage closest to the corridor. The shadowy side. Appropriate, because the man standing there looked like he belonged in the dark.

Holy crow.

Lounging in front of her cage was an unreasonably tall, powerfully built Adonis, a heart-wrenchingly dark angel, with sleek black hair and penetrating blue eyes and a face so chiseled that he looked almost frozen in time... Frozen, except for the full, curving, heartbreakingly lush lips that—

Dana blinked, struggling to refocus. "Do I know you?" she managed. He looked...almost familiar. Didn't he look familiar?

A smile played over the man's lips as if he could follow the trail of her thoughts. "Do you want to know me?"

Margaret spared Dana the need to reply by laying her stubby, satin-clad fingers on Mr. Gorgeous's arm. "You look *so* familiar, dear," she cooed, and Dana's brows shot up. So it wasn't only her. "Are you a member of the Founder's Circle?"

Dana watched as the stranger took in Margaret with his come-and-get-me smile, his manner as smooth and seductive as if Margaret was a starlet in the first blush of youth and not a scheming harridan out to bilk him for every dime he carried. Unaccountably, Dana felt irritation cut through her lust. The woman was a billion years old! *Have some self-respect, both of you.*

"Actually, I'm looking for a gentleman you may know," Mr. Sizzle said to Margaret, in an unreasonably sizzling way. "Lester Morrow?"

"Why?" Dana asked sharply as Margaret's mouth moved into a girlish "Oh!"

The man's gaze swung back to her. "You know him?" he asked. Gone was the smolder, replaced with cool, keen attention. Dana felt the flames of her budding desire collapse into rapidly cooling ashes.

"Yes, I do. I'm his personal assistant," Dana said smoothly.

"His…assistant." The International Man of Mystery studied her as Margaret openly gaped. Dana flicked the woman a hard glance, and for once the woman got a clue. She nodded, wild-eyed, then scurried away without another word. Thank heaven for small favors.

Dana turned her all-business smile back on the newcomer. "Mr. Morrow has stepped out, I'm afraid, and I'm not sure if he's going to be back tonight." Dana reached into the interior pocket of her suit and pulled out her phone. "Do you have a card? Or a number where I can reach you?"

"Where has he gone? It's important I see him as soon as possible."

The man stepped forward, and Dana's breath

hitched, her arm falling uselessly to her side. His eyes glittered, cold and blue in the soft light, and she suddenly felt dizzy. There was something wrong with his eyes, she thought. Or maybe she was jet-lagged. Could you get jet-lagged flying from Canada? Either way, she couldn't understand what was happening to her body, the warm rush of heat that coiled in her belly, making her legs weak and her heart pound.

She needed to get herself back together. She licked her lips and tried again. "If you don't have a card, I can give you one of mine."

"I don't need your card. As you can see, I found you easily enough."

Dana lifted her brows. "So you did." So much for lust. All Mr. Crazy Eyes incited in her now was irritation. "Can I take your name and have Mr. Morrow get back to you?"

"Or perhaps you can take me to him."

"I'm afraid I'm a bit tied up here."

"I can get you out easily enough."

"Thanks, but the place has kind of grown on me. I'm thinking about decorating, maybe inviting over a few friends."

"Really." He cocked his head, those maddening eyes focusing on her once again. "And yet I wonder what you would give me for loosening your restraints?"

Inexplicably, Dana felt a resurgence of heat flood through her, her breasts tightening beneath her silk suit and her lips tingling as his gaze came to rest upon them. Her brain stutter-stepped another second before annoyance surged forth again, banking the unexpected fire. *Chill,* she ordered herself. "Nothing that would make it worth ten thousand dollars, sorry."

"I'd appreciate the opportunity to find out." He

watched her try to master her reactions, and his smile deepened into a sensual grin. "You're thinking about it."

"Nope, simply memorizing your features for the police report."

The man leaned forward, and Dana nearly whimpered. Her body suddenly felt flushed, wobbly, and she swayed forward against the bars of her cage. Something was going terribly wrong. Sweat threaded its way down between her breasts, and her breath seemed stalled in her lungs.

"What do you want, Ms. Griffin?" Bobby Blue Eyes asked. "Are you sure it's not something I can give you?" He lifted his hand to graze her fingertips as her hands clutched the bars, and Dana's throat tightened, her mind skittering into dark and forbidden places.

"I want answers," she gritted out, surprising herself with her candor. "A lot of them."

"Which means you've decided what you'll give me in return? No." He raised a hand as Dana glared at him. *Who is this jackwit?* "I prefer to savor the possibilities."

He looked to the front of the room. "I'll be right back."

CHAPTER FOUR

Ritz Carlton Ballroom
Cleveland, Ohio
1:05 a.m., Dec. 24

No. Touching. The humans.

Finn turned sharply away from his target, his physical reactions completely outside normal bounds. He'd been a demon for more than six thousand years, and had been among humans a good portion of that time but this — this was different. Everything felt fresh, new, and, well...*his*. Like he was walking through a miracle of inestimable proportions, and he was a part of that miracle.

He took two long strides through the crowd before he brought his heart rate down to an acceptable level, but his breath was coming too fast, too unevenly. Around him, the mortals parted with open mouths and startled eyes, and he smoothed his passage with a gentle touch to their minds, their surprise turning to pleasure, their confusion shifting into a kaleidoscope of comfort and reassurance. They murmured to him as he passed, a lilting cadence of warmth and contentment.

He wished he could convince himself so easily that all was right in the world.

It wasn't, though. He had less than twenty-four hours to complete his mission; there was no margin for error. For the sake of the Syx, he needed to be more careful.

Finn felt Dana Griffin's gaze tracking him across the wide hall, and he frowned anew. When he'd first heard her shout in the freaking North Pole, realized she was going to try to help him—a mortal, helping *him*—he'd been drawn to her. At least long enough to impress on her mind to get the hell away from danger. Now that strange attraction was happening again. A human female! He wasn't that guy. Stefan was that guy. And some of the other demons too. But he—he simply couldn't. Mortal females were not for him.

But when he'd seen Dana Griffin in her cage, when he'd *spoken* to her...his body had responded almost before he realized it, his blood flush in his veins, his skin warming, his hand reaching out to touch—

Forbidden! The ancient edict rang in his head with horror and indignation. The children of Earth were not the playthings of his kind. He more than anyone knew—

A crack of pain shattered across his senses, and Finn tightened his jaw. Time to get this party started. The human was important to him, but strictly to help him accomplish his mission.

Finn moved toward the auction table set up in the corner of the large ballroom, cataloguing his impressions of Dana Griffin.

She was what most humans would consider

beautiful: tall and lean, with long dark hair and expressive features — large eyes, a gentle mouth, and fair skin that easily showed emotion. But the softness ended there. She seemed almost unreasonably capable, harshly efficient. Her eyes betrayed both intelligence and wariness, and her aura shone far stronger than those of the mortals around her.

She could also clearly suppress her reactions with a skill to rival the demon horde, which was troubling. Not only was she ignoring a significant level of pain that he could sense was racking her body, she was also resisting her physical and emotional response to *him*.

Which shouldn't be possible. Mortals were normally oh so manageable.

Most importantly, the woman was highly protective of Lester Morrow, though she definitely wasn't his assistant. More like…

He frowned. More like she was his security detail. But while she'd had no thought in her head about this list everyone seemed so hot for, she almost certainly remembered Finn in some small way from the wolf attack, even though she shouldn't.

How was that possible? Dana Griffin wasn't warded with a blessed icon, and she wasn't Connected. But…what was she?

His blood fired, even as caution whispered in his ear. If the archangel suspected for a moment that Finn could be distracted from his assignment, he'd be hauled out of this ridiculously frigid city and back to Vegas in a heartbeat, instead of being given this opportunity for redemption. But he would not miss this chance. He'd get what Michael wanted, this list that apparently Lester Morrow had. And then he'd get out.

"Champagne, sir?"

JENN STARK

Finn stopped, turning to a serene, white-jacketed older woman who proffered him a tray of tiny glasses filled with sparkling liquid. "I'm sorry?"

"Champagne. With our compliments, sir. As long as you're not driving, we're not carding." She smiled at him as he picked one up, his fingers closing around the slender glass stem as gently as if it were a baby bird. He lifted the flute to his lips, felt the sweet slide of liquid roll over his tongue, and it hit him—as it still too often did.

Earth.

A place of light. Of magic. Of pleasure and pain and endless possibility.

As if for the first time, Finn turned to take in the sweep of people surrounding him—the joyous cacophony on the small stage, as glowing horns and rich wood instruments shifted in the bright ballroom light. The rustle of expensive satins and lace, the hiss and rush of whispered voices, sudden laughter, and carefully phrased taunts and invitations. The wafting perfumes and colognes, the aromas almost too much in a confined space to someone with his sensory capabilities, vying for precedence over each other. The views from the towering windows of a city alight with expectation. And over it all, the delicate, bubbling froth of a drink meant for the gods.

Finn made his way through the crowd, soaking it in. Was this what it had meant to be Fallen? To be able to sense what humans felt, experience the power of their bodies, the tumult of their emotions? At every turn, he knew their pain, their passion. Their endless, thrumming desire. Gone was any hope of peaceful contemplation, gentle detachment. Now, in its place, was the thrusting, clamoring, soul-consuming pulse of *life.*

In the cold, remote bolt-hole where the Syx had been banished after every job, he'd wondered what it was that he had lost. It had been this...*this!*

"Fallen," he whispered. And he could remain one permanently. Every one of the Syx could, if what the archangel said was true. If he didn't fail.

Finn's pulse started thrumming again. He'd find Lester Morrow and secure his list, and deliver it to the archangel. Even if it required him to use Dana Griffin to do it.

He frowned, recalling the woman's initial response to his appearance in front of her makeshift cage. She'd appeared...distressed, even before he'd begun working on her. Distracted. Uncertain.

Dark temptation stirred in his veins, and his mouth curved into an involuntary smile. Perhaps he could find some way to put her at ease.

No.

"I want to free that woman," he said tightly as he reached the auction table. He reached out with his mind as the sticklike young woman with a halo of yellow hair blinked up at him, her glossy lips parting in a startled moue of surprise.

"You wish to m-make a donation?" she stuttered, and Finn eased up further. Like any of his kind, he could influence mortals subtly, planting suggestions in their minds that they thought were their own. But modern humans seemed far more susceptible to his touch than he realized. Too pliant, too...open to manipulation. He'd nearly knocked out the doorman who'd given him the information he needed about the gala. He'd have to be more careful with Dana Griffin.

His lips twisted, recalling the delicate flute he'd

cradled in his fingers. So simple, so precious. So fragile and perfect. It had been a long time since he'd needed to be gentle about so many things at once. But, such was the beauty of Earth.

"Right, yes. A donation," he said. "To release the…to free Ms. Griffin." Finn gestured back to where Dana stood eyeing the roof of her cage, her entire body radiating suspicion and anger.

And then…something else. Finn straightened. A shiver of darkness rolled through him, and he tensed, suddenly aware. He wasn't alone here.

Demons on the dance floor? No, not quite. Finn's eyes narrowed as he took in Dana Griffin again. No one was around her, unless you counted the small knot of human males that had drifted toward her cage, which he didn't. Nobody of any strength was in this room. Outside these four walls, however, it was a different story. If the rogue Fallen the archangel had pitted him against had a brain in his head, he'd have seeded every back alley of this frozen city with demons.

It didn't matter. Dana would take Finn to Lester Morrow, and he'd complete his mission. Then, at the crack of midnight, he would ask and he would receive. Within a mere twenty-four hours, he could prove his worth at last…and maybe, finally, be forgiven of a sin so dire, he couldn't even remember it.

He was not going to fuck this up.

"Ah, in case you didn't know…" The woman in front of him blushed. "Ms. Griffin's bail is currently at ten thousand dollars."

Finn smiled. If she led him to both Lester Morrow and the rogue Fallen, Dana Griffin was worth far more than that.

While the brittle blonde fumbled through her

papers, Finn pulled out a checkbook thoughtfully provided by the mortal in Room 304. His abrupt arrival at the hotel had stunned the room's only occupant, a doctor who'd given up his ID, his money—and his night, as Finn had convinced him to fall into a deep and blissful sleep. Lee Schaeffer would wake up with a dream no one would believe, minus one healthy donation for which he would be reimbursed with change, but he would survive Finn's visit to this frozen metropolis.

The rogue Fallen and his demons would not, if Finn had anything to say about it. Which, for the next twenty-three hours or so, he did.

Finn bent down to write out an amount that had nothing to do with the number the woman pointed at with trembling fingers. He handed her the check.

"Oh! That's very generous of you," she breathed, her voice still tremulous. Finn sighed. Despite his best efforts, his very presence had succeeded in frightening this one too.

Poor humans.

At least Dana Griffin had managed to hold her own with him. So there was some hope.

As he turned away, Finn's mind returned to the mortal's full lips pursing in annoyance and her unyielding, wary eyes. Dana Griffin, it seemed, bore many secrets.

He wondered how many she would share with him when he finally had her alone.

CHAPTER FIVE

Ritz Carlton Ballroom
Cleveland, Ohio
1:15 a.m., Dec. 24

"Wow, you're a real American hero."

Dana jerked her gaze to the front of the cage, taking in Max Garrett's lanky, loose-limbed body that always reminded her of a newborn moose. He grinned at her, his lantern-jawed face irrepressible beneath the shock of golden-brown hair that he wore a little too long for respectability. He was young, but he was good — and very little caught him by surprise.

She narrowed her eyes. "Did you know they had this stupid cage thing planned?"

"I had my suspicions after Pettiman asked me for, like, the fifth time where you were. Which, actually, was a good question. Where were you? We were expecting you here at eleven thirty."

"Why, was there a problem at the slushy machine?"

"No, but if you recall, the last time you didn't check

in, you ended up in pieces. And then there was that tiny problem of you getting attacked by *wolves* up in Canada. On solstice. Not to mention you getting shot on Samhain."

"Halloween."

"Tomato, tomahto. It's a trend of holidays, and not a good one. Because I'm not sure if you've noticed, but we're officially at *Christmas Eve*. You ever hear of Yule? It's a thing. And we're in the middle it."

Dana stifled a sigh. Max didn't even know the whole story about what had happened in Alert. She wasn't about to clue him in either. Not until she'd finished processing it herself. "I figured you would call me if there were any issues, so I took my time. I hate these things."

More or less true. She did hate fundraisers, of course. Who didn't? But the real reason for her delay tonight was that the walk from her apartment had taken longer than she'd anticipated.

Ever since the night she'd been attacked with Lester, the streets of Cleveland had seemed — unfamiliar. Almost threatening, which aggravated the hell out of her. Her father had been a beat cop in this city, and he'd taken Dana up and down these sidewalks more times than she could count. Still...something simply hadn't been right tonight. A weird energy had filled the concrete canyons. She'd been so keyed up by the time she'd arrived at the Ritz, she could barely stay inside her skin.

"Well, just so you know, you've got major resting-assassin face," Max said, drawing her attention back with a wide grin. "You'd probably get more cash if you smiled or something."

Dana bared her teeth. "How's that?"

"Still not good. You look like a piranha."

"I'll keep that in mind. How's the AA patrol going?"

"I've ordered more drivers, and we have a block of rooms on hold for those too plowed on candy-cane cosmos. We also made the announcement we'd comp anyone's parking fee who had to spend the night."

Dana snorted. "We're nothing if not conscientious here at Griffin Security. Remind me to post that tab to Lester's bill. Now, do something else for me, if you would." She nodded toward the front of the room. "You see that guy over there? At the auction table."

"The big dude?" Max asked, straightening up to squint over the crowd. "Dr. Doom in a tux?"

"Yeah, him," she said. "I need you to run a routine background check on him, but keep it low-key. He's asking about Lester, and—"

"Roger that," Max interrupted her, his entire body trembling as he went into full secret agent mode: hands loose, jaw tight, feet set wide, brows drawn together. *Oh, geez, not this again.*

Max wanted nothing more than to be a secret agent or possibly a superhero, but she couldn't bring herself to call him on it. Back when she'd been strung out on pain meds after the attack on Lester, Max had been one of her most constant visitors—filling her in on new clients, current accounts, and the Cleveland PD's complete lack of progress in finding her uncle's assailants. One day, in a moment of weakness, Dana had suggested that Max might poke around on her behalf, see if he could find anyone with a reason to hurt Lester. He'd jumped on the task with far too much fervor, ridiculously eager for any security assignment that took him far away from coding and hardware. He'd first zeroed in on Sal Morelli, the closest thing to a godfather personality Cleveland had these days. Then he'd moved on to the FBI, secret societies, and international terrorists. The fallback, of course, was always aliens.

Now the guy was one comic book shy of a complete fanboy meltdown, and it was all her fault. Even as she watched him, he stared at her mystery man and released his breath in a soft hiss, dropping his voice to a strained whisper. "You think he might be tied to the attack?"

"No, I don't," Dana snapped, her tone not even fazing him. "And stop with the 007 crap, will you? The guy bugs me, that's all."

"Don't worry about it." Max nodded, still serious. "I'm on it."

"I mean it, Max. I want this under the radar. If he's some new prospect of Lester's, I don't want to piss off either one of them."

A staccato tap of the microphone drowned out Max's affirmative. "Ladies and gentlemen…Ladies and gentlemen, your attention please," Margaret said, color high in her cheeks. "I'm delighted to inform you that we've received a most *generous* donation for the Founder's Circle charity efforts."

"Well, whaddya know?" Dana murmured. "He actually did it. He posted my bail."

Max pulled out his cell phone, surreptitiously taking pictures of the mystery man as he stood scowling up at Margaret, his arms crossed, shoulders tight. The man really did look good from a distance, Dana thought. Frankly, she wanted him to stay at that distance.

"Dana Griffin," Margaret continued, squinting down at her clipboard. "Is officially released on bail to Dr. Lee Schaeffer, for the donation of…fifteen thousand dollars!"

An appreciative gasp went up from the crowd, and

Max whistled low beside her. "Looks like Dr. Doom has a crush on you," he said, tucking his phone back inside his jacket. "You're, like, Invisible Girl, I guess."

Dana ignored the comment, waving at the applause and forcing a polite smile to her face. She suspected she still mostly resembled a piranha, but there was no helping that. "Call Lester for me," she said through clenched teeth. "Make sure he's got A-1 security on him, wherever he is. And find out if a Dr. Lee Schaeffer means anything to him."

"Got it," Max said, but he continued to stare at Schaeffer, transfixed. Dana stepped over, poking him in the shoulder through the bars.

"So *go*," she said.

"I'm going, I'm going." Max melted back into the crowd, and Dana watched as Margaret swanned off the stage, all but throwing her keys at Dr. Schaeffer as she pointed in Dana's direction.

Dana stared hard at the man walking toward her, arrogance curling off him like faint smoke. He sure as hell didn't remind her of any doctor that she'd ever seen.

"You're free," he said, placing a hand on Dana's cage as she stepped away from the bars. He could probably rip the thing apart without ruffling his dinner jacket.

Dana glared at him. "A man of your word, I see," she said.

"Always." His dark gaze met hers, a hint of a smile on his face. "I apologize for keeping you waiting."

"I'll try to recover." Resolutely, Dana shifted her eyes away from his face. She couldn't afford to be attracted—*distracted*, she meant. Distracted. Her alarm system was still going full tilt. The man was *some* sort of threat, dammit. To her or to Lester, she wasn't sure which.

After turning the key in the lock, he pulled the cage door open and gestured her out. "Ms. Griffin."

Ignoring his outstretched hand, Dana stepped out of the cage. "Your donation was very generous, Dr. Schaeffer," she said. "The children of Cleveland thank you."

"Call me Finn," he said, watching her as she shifted away from him another inch. "And you can thank me by taking me to Lester Morrow."

Dana burst out in a startled laugh. "You don't give up, do you?" she asked. "Please let me be clear, then. Mr. Morrow isn't taking any further meetings tonight. You'll have to contact his office tomorrow. And I thought your name was Lee."

"I never said it was, Dana." He full-on grinned this time, and Dana's temperature went up another ten degrees. He'd used her first name, she realized, and she felt her focus wobble dangerously. Had she given him her first name?

Oh, wait. They'd said it in the announcement; that's how he knew. Of course. It shouldn't feel so awkward.

"Pose for a picture!"

Lights flashed in front of them, and Dana blinked in surprise as her benefactor took a sharp step backward, his gaze swinging around as if he expected the gala photographer to bash him in the head with his Nikon.

So, the good doctor didn't want his photo taken. Interesting. With a reaction like that, she'd bet the Christmas bonus she planned to give herself that the man had a record. But if so, why the public donation? What did he have to gain from this? And why did he need to see Lester so quickly?

"Closer together, please." Another society-page

photographer, this one from the *Plain Dealer*, moved into position. Schaeffer glared at the cameras for another moment, then stepped toward Dana decisively, sliding his right hand behind her to rest on her lower back. Dana found her left hand had nowhere else to go other than high up on Finn's shoulder — and she clamped her lips into a tight smile to keep from falling down on film.

Dr. Schaeffer was on fire. Or she was. Beneath her palm, the muscles of his broad shoulders bunched together in a thick knot, his possessive hand on the small of her back making her feel claimed, almost wanton, the plaything of a god. He smelled of cinnamon and sex, the heat of his gentle touch twisting within her and flushing her cheeks as the camera lights flashed, a chorus of photos taken and retaken.

Dana suddenly began to feel claustrophobic, aching to get away, but Schaeffer leaned down close to her as the photographers changed position. "Would you care to get a drink?" he asked.

"A thousand percent," she said, her eyes fixed solidly ahead. "Just not with you."

He chuckled and replaced his hand on her arm. "I get that all the time."

Doing her best to ignore the hand scorching her through her silk jacket, Dana gazed blankly through another wave of photographs and tried to unscramble her brain. Her uncle's business had been her number one priority for more than five years, and it had become an obsession since the Halloween attack. She had dossiers on all of Lester's business partners, his employees, his golf buddies, his charity connections, his clients, and his *clients'* clients. Since early December, she'd had Lester's calls recorded, his movements tracked, and every one of his contacts scanned for ties to international terrorists. Her uncle couldn't buy an ice-cream cone without her shaking down the Good Humor man. So how come she didn't know this guy?

What've you been up to, Lester?

Still, every time she looked at Dr. Lee Schaeffer—Finn—she *wanted* to give in to an overwhelming sense of well-being, an instant opiate of calm. It was only when she turned away that the anxiety returned.

Dana grimaced. She was probably thrown off because she was attracted to him. God knows that hadn't happened in a while.

Pushing back her misgivings, Dana turned to Schaeffer as the photographers moved away. "Look," she said, forcing a smile. "You mind telling me why you're so interested in Mr. Morrow that it requires an immediate audience?"

He took a moment to glance out the far windows at the brightly lit city, a king surveying his domain. "As I said, we had an appointment, and I'm only in town for the day."

Uh-huh. "Then I'll call him tonight and set it up," she said. *We'll have a nice cozy breakfast, all three of us.* "How about eight a.m. tomorrow morning, at Ritz's restaurant on the first floor? Would that work for you?"

Schaeffer looked back at her, surprise and concern in his gaze. "You don't need to be afraid of me, you know."

Dana's chin firmed, anger overriding caution. "There are many things I'm afraid of, Dr. Schaeffer—"

"It's Finn."

"What?"

"My name is Finn. I'd prefer if you called me that."

"Fine, then, *Finn*," Dana said. "My point is, there's nothing further we need to discuss until tomorrow. So why don't you run along and try your luck with one of the lovely trust fund babies roaming around, okay? We'll see you tomorrow. Eight a.m. sharp."

He lifted his brows in a soft, sensual invitation. "Do you always fight this hard against your instincts?"

"Actually, my instincts are right onboard with this one, thanks," Dana said. Now her anxiety was running in lockstep with a desire that was way too strong to be legitimate, and the pairing wasn't a pleasant one. Yet another reason why this man was off-limits. Her heart was jackhammering against her ribs, her head hurt, and even her eyeballs ached every time she looked at him. *So much beauty. So much challenge. So much disaster waiting to happen.* Sometimes, her life really sucked.

She held out her hand to end their conversation civilly. "Your plaque commemorating your donation will be shipped to you within the week. It's truly been a pleasure."

"Yes, it has." Finn reached for her hand and brought it to his lips, the movement so effortlessly careless that he looked like he'd been performing it for hundreds of years.

But the moment his lips touched her fingers, Dana's world spun off its axis.

A river of soul-defying warmth flooded her body from head to toe, concentrating with a bolt of hot bliss immediately south of her right kneecap. "Oh—my God," she gasped, her heart swelling in her chest at the sheer visceral amazement of simply *not being in pain*. She looked up at him, dazed, her hand gripping his so hard that her knuckles were bone white. "How are you doing that?"

"Doing what?"

Dana blinked, fighting to stay upright for the second

time in an hour. "There's...there's no pain."

Finn stiffened in surprise, and Dana, realizing that she was practically clinging to him, yanked her hand from his fingers.

And nearly shrieked as the pain came thundering back.

Dana staggered to the side before Finn shot out his hand and grabbed her once more. Instantly, the wash of healing energy flowed through her again as their hands touched, but she still felt physically ill. She sucked in a deep breath that was little more than a moan. *You mean I have to be touching you to make the pain stop?*

He chuckled, squeezing her fingers gently. "There are worse fates."

God, had she said that out loud?

"Yeah?" Dana managed, her breath tight in her lungs as her body lit on fire. "I can't think of any right now."

"Be still, Dana. This will only take a moment."

She blinked as Finn squeezed her hand again for one long breath, then straightened, stepping away from her and releasing her hand. Dana's leg felt whole, even without him touching her. He'd taken the pain away from her.

"What did you do?" she whispered, staring at him, unable to understand — to focus —

"Consider it an energy transfer. An apparent perk of my new job," Finn was saying, but his words barely registered. Dana's breath was quick and uncertain in her throat, her skin crawling with energy, her heart skittering in an unnatural cadence. All she could see was Finn's smile, soft and inviting. Wanting her. His gaze warming her to the roots of her hair. And her leg felt whole in a way that she'd never imagined would be possible again. Like it had never been torn apart. Like it was as fresh and new as the energy pounding through her, demanding release. Like she'd been reborn as a creature of light and fire and endless, soul-filled longing.

But something hammered at her, right below the surface. *I shouldn't trust this man, I can't trust him, I won't.* "I—I really do have to go," she heard herself saying, as if from far away. She needed to leave, immediately. That was all she could focus on, all she really knew.

"What do you know, Dana?" Finn asked. "What do you want to tell me?" His gaze drilled into her, heavy and insistent, and Dana shook her head, fear clawing up in her throat again. Fear of death, somehow. Of loss, of obliteration. *No, no, no.*

Finn reached out to grab her, and she yanked her hand away.

"Dr. Schaeffer! Dr. Schaeffer!"

From the center of the ballroom, a delighted Margaret Pettiman was towing every single female member of the Founders Circle board of directors toward them, matchmaking commandoes out for first blood. Dana stepped back quickly as Finn was surrounded by the halo of glittering matriarchs, his eyes remaining on her, daring her to stay, to talk to him, to tell him what he wanted to hear.

No. Dana took another step back, her brain finally catching up with her body. Something was happening here—and had been since the moment she'd first seen this man. He was playing on her senses, creating a reaction that was completely out of place, impossible to justify.

Dana spun away as the crowd converged, blindly heading for the lobby. She had to get out of here, had to breathe — to *escape*. She blew in and out of the coat check in less than ten seconds, but the lobby space in front of the elevator seemed crammed with people. She blinked several times, her eyes watering with the effort to see. Suddenly, everyone around her seemed surrounded with a thin film of light, their faces shimmering like double-exposed photographs and their bodies moving too slowly as she rushed by them, then wheeled into the stairwell of the fifteenth floor. Not two hours ago, the thought of running down the stairs on her still-injured leg would have turned her blood to ice.

Now she barely felt the impact of her boots hitting the smooth marble as she raced toward freedom.

What did he do to me?

CHAPTER SIX

West Third St.
Cleveland, Ohio
1:40 a.m., Dec. 24

Finn stepped into the frigidly cold night, the rush of wind exhilarating him. He never got used to this either — the walls that mankind erected to stifle the very air that surrounded them, the lights they burned to hold back the night. Even after so many thousands of years, they battled their own world, counting it as enemy, not friend. Now, two thousand years after the birth of Christ, mortals had begun to harness electrical waves, magnetic fields — and their own highly disciplined brains. But there was so much more they could do.

So much he could teach them.

He blinked. *Where'd that thought come from?*

Finn breathed in the pollution-choked air to ground himself, feeling it burn as it entered his lungs, electrical pulses rushing through his system with equal parts pain and pleasure. Deliberately, he refocused, centering again on the human.

He would follow Dana Griffin.

She was his easiest point of access to Lester Morrow, since the man had never returned to the ballroom. And Finn would absolutely reach her before the rogue Fallen did.

He grinned. He'd rout whatever demons he'd sensed up in the ballroom, subdue the rogue Fallen, and hand over both the Fallen and the list by midnight to the archangel. That should be more than enough to earn his keep.

Then there was the matter of his Christmas bonus…

Forcing himself to relax, Finn sucked in more of the foul air and turned his head to catch the imprint of Dana's passage. He still didn't feel quite right, but he'd only been a Fallen for about ninety minutes. Maybe there was an adjustment period. Either way, his body was too tense, too tight, his emotions too close to the surface.

And as his mind focused on Dana, he felt the stirring within him again. His response to the mortal was dangerous. *Forbidden*. And yet…

Finn rubbed his eyes, remembering it all. The woman had practically burst with light, unlike anyone else around her, her body calling to his with a power he'd never experienced in a human. And, though he'd merely sought to give comfort, he'd been able to completely eliminate her pain with a touch.

Moments later, she'd fled from him in horror, her eyes wide with the knowledge of what he'd done, her body full and strong again, shimmering with energy. And he'd felt her departure like a physical blow — a crushing loss.

He shifted in the darkness, frowning. He simply

needed to adjust, he told himself again. The mortal was not the problem; he was.

Still, she had reacted to his touch too strongly. Mortals had never been *that* sensitive. Even Warrick's human, the cop, had been helped along by her blessed cross. The ornate pin Dana had been wearing at the gala was nothing more than a trinket in the hands of anyone other than a high priestess.

Unless she'd already encountered the rogue Fallen in some fashion, and he'd made Dana stronger—more open to being healed?

An unexpected surge of fury raked through him. He'd had no *right*.

But then neither had Finn. Yet he couldn't forget the way Dana'd felt beneath his hand, her reaction to his touch, to his kiss on the back of her hand.

Finn grimaced. He needed to get moving.

He glanced up and down the short access street, his breath steaming out in a curling white cloud. Though humans had upgraded their methods of transportation over the centuries, he was much faster on his own. He allowed his senses to point the way.

Dana had departed the ballroom nearly ten minutes ago, but she'd left her mark on the very air as she'd moved through it. She'd stopped here, at the entrance to the Ritz Hotel, then had left the hotel at a fast, steady pace. He could still pick up her light, exotic scent as he stepped out onto the sidewalk. It had been buried in the chaos of powders and perfumes in the ballroom far above, but here, in this moment, he could almost taste it, whispers of jasmine and vanilla blending together in a sweet, intoxicating swirl. Her scent was richer than those of the other women he had been surrounded by, and far more memorable.

Everything about her, in fact, had been burned into his brain. Her strength, her passion. The unadorned beauty of her full mouth and flashing eyes. Reliving every sensation he'd felt in the last two hours, Finn nearly groaned at the memory of the mortal's fingers against his lips. Dana Griffin felt more real to him than anything he'd touched in more than six thousand years. So vibrant, so angry, so excited, so…alive. She was fully, gloriously mortal.

And she'd been horrifically damaged.

All too recently, a bullet had caught her leg at an excruciating angle, exploding her tibia into a dozen fragments. Mortal surgery remained barbaric, so after the bullet had been removed, the real violation had begun. A steel plate and screws now held together her bone as her muscles knit together furiously to bear the weight not only of her body, but of the work she forced herself to endure. She'd added new muscle as well recently, the flushed pink layer hanging boldly over the old. A cry of determination against her own weakness.

Finn's own ungainly heart seemed to enlarge in his chest cavity. From what his senses told him, Dana had received that injury within the past few months. No human in the world could heal that quickly, that cleanly, without outside help.

Focus on the prize, buddy. Dana isn't the goal, the list is. Finn's orders from the archangel had been clear. If he didn't complete his mission and stand before the portals of heaven at midnight, he'd lose his freedom for good. As would the rest of the Syx. He needed to bring his A-game. He owed that to his team. To himself too.

Finn followed the curve of the street, pausing in the shadows as he saw Dana's willowy form silhouetted against brighter lights in the distance. His need surged again, hot and insistent, but something else cut across his reaction as he moved down Prospect Avenue—the unshakable awareness that he wasn't alone on the streets of Cleveland.

"Here, demon, demon, demon," he murmured.

He hadn't been mistaken in the ballroom when he had felt their presence. There were demons here—maybe even the bad seed Fallen as well—all of them coming to take him down. Finn's jaw hardened. *Bring it.* If there was one thing he was good at, it was tossing demon asses back across the veil.

Finn deliberately slowed to let the demons catch up with him. He projected his senses forward, draining his energy as he scanned the city streets within a solid half-mile radius. The shadows ebbed and flowed on the far side of Dana, but there were many streets through this city, many paths for the horde to find Finn.

"C'mere sweethearts." Resisting an urge to goad the pack with a sharp whistle, Finn moved onto the balls of his feet. Dana ranged farther away from him, and he focused more heavily on the horde. Their thoughts, their fears. These weren't straight-up demons, he decided, but possessed humans. Totally had to be the rogue Fallen at work. Finn hadn't fought a Possessed since the Dark Ages, but he imagined the process hadn't changed all that much. True, demons could be torn out of humans and thrust back into their own plane while preserving the lives of their human hosts. But such "exorcisms," as mortals termed them, took too much time. Incapacitating their human hosts was quicker.

Finn made no effort to hide his presence, and he could tell by the shift in energy the moment both the demons and their possessed humans finally realized he was there. On the faintest whisper of wind, he could feel the creatures stirring, somewhere deep within the concrete canyons. Then the coiling, jibbering force of their excitement heightened, keening on the wind, and they gathered together as one quivering being before bursting apart again, slipping into the darkness. He waited, his body charged and ready for the fight.

But no one came for him in the still of the night. No one attacked in the shadows, far away from human eyes.

And in that moment, Finn knew.

They weren't coming for him.

They were coming for Dana.

CHAPTER SEVEN

Prospect Ave.
Cleveland, Ohio
2:03 a.m., Dec. 24

Dana settled into her usual long, loping stride, forcing herself not to turn around for what seemed like the fifteenth time. She was *not* being followed, she told herself. Merely suffering from melodrama, her mind racing faster than her legs could carry her.

She'd tried calling Lester again, but he hadn't picked up. Probably just as well. If he'd arranged on the side to meet with this Finn, Lester had violated every freaking protocol they had. Dana felt hot anger crawl up her cheeks again, searing against the frigid cold outside. The old man had *always* acted as if he was some kind of retro Hollywood kingpin, rather than the CEO of a simple Cleveland-based engineering company. Especially since the recent attack, her uncle wasn't even supposed to go to lunch without leaving Dana's team a detailed schedule, let alone set up private midnight meetings with unsecured business contacts. She could only hope, wherever he'd snuck off to, that Lester had brought his own security guys with him, even if they were mostly night watchmen. *What had he been thinking?*

And who—or what—was this man he'd arranged to meet in the middle of the night? Assuming Finn's story was even true.

Finn.

He'd dropped fifteen thousand dollars on her charity bail to get to Lester more quickly. He'd set off every instinctual alarm Dana possessed.

And he'd healed her with a touch.

Her leg wasn't simply better. It was *perfect*. After she'd left the ballroom, she'd even hopped up and down on it in the stairwell for good measure. No pain. Not even a twinge.

His touch. He'd called it an energy transfer. She called it... What? A miracle? Sure, if you believed in such things. At this point, she didn't know what she believed anymore.

So what exactly did Mr. Touch want with Lester?

She texted her uncle again, telling him to contact Max, that a very strange man she'd met wanted to meet him. That would get the old man's interest, she knew, and then maybe she'd get answers.

That sent, Dana hurried down Prospect toward home, punching her hands deep into her jacket pockets. The street was brightly lit past Ontario, with both Flannery's Pub and the Ultralounge going strong. Of the two, Flannery's was more her scene, just as it had once been her father's. She'd stop in for a minute, she thought, reconnect with her own people on Christmas Eve. There were no smartly dressed waiters bearing champagne flutes there, no glitter-wrapped guests wearing a year's honest salary around their necks.

Instead, there were all-you-could-eat peanuts, fifteen different Irish beers on tap, and WWE Smackdown parties every Friday night, where the regulars could happily dissect the legends of Hacksaw Duggan and Gorgeous George, then deliberate for hours between Ric Flair or Rick Rude. *Everything a girl could want.* Even at this hour on Christmas Eve, the tavern's homey warmth reached out to her as she neared, tattered holiday lights winking from the wrought iron fence, a familiar knot of smokers huddled in the door front. Christmas. It was her father's favorite holiday, and the poinsettias in the window of the pub she knew had been placed there by its owner in homage to her dad. They still remembered him, after all these years.

The older men raised their voices in greeting as Dana ducked into the pub, suddenly feeling better than she had all night. Bob was working the bar, and he came right over as soon as he recognized her.

"Coffee?" he asked, already reaching for the pot.

"Only if you spike it with something good," she said, taking a seat.

"Sure thing." Bob grinned.

It was good to be back among people who knew her, Dana thought, and she felt more of the anxiety of the last two hours melt away. She gave the older men at the counter beside her a nod, absurdly happy when they nodded back, their faces ruddy beneath worn fedoras and faded snap-brim caps. For as long as Dana could remember, these same men had shared their stories and grins over gleaming bartops and half-empty mugs. Nearly two decades ago, her father had often joined them after hanging up his badge for the night. They were louder then, she recalled, their eyes more vibrant, their laughter booming. Now, they just shuffled to the pub each night with their little-old-man steps, every year a little slower, but never failing to show.

"On the house." Bob set her drink in front of her. "We'll charge it to your old man, same as the flowers. Merry Christmas, doll."

"Thanks." She inhaled the decadent aroma of Baileys and coffee and ran her finger over the top of her mug, glancing up at the bank of TVs rehashing the day's bowl games. *All those wannabe superheroes buried in padding,* she thought. What was the point? Now, a gold lamé headband, designer leopard-print tights, and a giant steel cage? That was entertainment. A guilty pleasure her father had brought home from Flannery's that the two had once and always shared.

Dana worked to chase away the bittersweet memory as Bob paused in front of her. "Someone was asking about you today," he said, collecting half-emptied snack bowls from the bar.

Hope and new apprehension slivered through her. *But how can he know…?* "Was his name Finn?" she asked, keeping her voice light. "Well-dressed, big—European? Maybe a doctor?"

Bob shook his head. "He didn't leave a name, but he didn't strike me as European, no. And certainly not a doctor type. More of a thug, you ask me." He shot her a worried look. "I told him I'd never heard of you before."

Dana raised her mug to him. "Then here's to friends you can't remember."

He nodded, his worried expression easing in the face of her dad's favorite line. "And nights you can't forget."

Dana barked a short laugh. "Thanks for looking out

76

for me." She warmed her hands on her mug, as the old man closest to her caught her attention.

Willie, she thought as he leaned toward her a bit too quickly, jostling his drink. One of her father's favorite bar mates, once upon a time.

Now Willie's rheumy eyes were wide with concern as he turned to her. "You in trouble, kid?" he asked, his tone roughened by decades of whiskey and cigarettes. He swayed a bit more than usual, and Dana's heart tightened.

"No, Willie," she said, watching the foamy head of his Guinness spill over the side of his glass. "Just business." She smiled easily, inviting confidences. "Why, have you seen this guy who asked Bob about me?"

The old man harrumphed. "I don't see much of anything anymore."

Dana bit her lip. "You see plenty," she said, her heart twisting. "You always have." *They're all so much older now.* While her father had been caught in time, never changing in the precious focus of her memory, each of his friends faded a little more each year. "You having a good Christmas this year?"

Willie scowled, pointing a thin, knotty finger at her. "He's *watching* you," he said sternly. "He is, and you should never forget it. He told me he'd watch over you forever. He loved you that much, Dana. As much as his own flesh and blood."

Dana looked at the old man worriedly. *C'mon, Willie, snap out of it.* Despite her wildest childhood assertions that she'd been adopted, stolen at birth, switched by fairies, maybe even genetically engineered...Dana was a Griffin. With Lester's help, she'd unearthed her birth certificate back when her dad had died. She hadn't known what she'd been expecting, exactly, but it didn't matter. As oddly matched as they sometimes seemed to her, Walter, Lester, and Claire were her family.

"Well, I was sure proud to be his daughter," she said. She patted Willie's arm in reassurance, shocked at how frail the old man suddenly seemed beneath his heavy wool sweater.

Willie shook her off him, his eyes suddenly mirror bright. "He's watching you," he said again, hunching over his Guinness. "And he always will. A proud, proud papa."

Dana exchanged a look with Bob, who gave her a "whaddya gonna do?" smile. Sighing, she returned to her Baileys and coffee, her hands shaking only slightly as she wrapped them around the mug.

I miss you so much, Dad.

The joy she'd reclaimed had faded again from the night, so Dana quickly finished her drink and wished them all a Merry Christmas, patting Willie on the back again. All she got was a grunt in response. She'd have to check in on him more frequently, she thought. Willie was an old friend of her father's, and that made him family.

Margaret's words came back to her. *With a strong family, you can save the world.*

Dana scowled. She didn't need her family to save the world. She simply wanted it to be safe. Thoughts of her uncle assaulted her again, and frustration sprang up anew. If Lester would simply follow the security rules she'd laid out for him...

Tightening her coat, Dana stepped back into the night, heading for home. She leaned into the breeze that swirled along the street until she finally reached Ninth, turning left into a whole new burst of wind. The street ran straight as an arrow to the lake, and the gusts here always blew right through your bones. Head bent, shoulders hunched, Dana huffed out a breath, then suddenly felt a quick uneasiness pass through her. She slowed a half step before forcing herself to walk normally.

It was back again. The sensation of being watched.

"He's watching you," Willie had said.

But whatever was out there, it sure didn't feel like her dad.

Keeping her head down, Dana scanned the street. Without the cheery light of the bars' Christmas decorations to balance the night, the shadows seemed murkier here, more dangerous. Adding to the ominous atmosphere, the right side of the street was a construction site, the sidewalks torn away, the buildings half-shrouded in mismatched scaffolding, plywood, and ripped plastic sheeting. Only St. John's Cathedral glowed in the distance ahead, a welcome beacon of safety. She wondered what Father Franks was doing right now, in the untracked early morning hours before the storm of Cleveland's grandest Christmas Eve celebration. Probably sleeping, which she would be doing soon. *Almost home,* she thought, moving forward again.

She felt the prickling sensation deepen.

Dana swallowed, walking a hair faster, the muscles in her injured leg beginning to throb again—no longer in pain, but *awareness*. Something really felt wrong here.

She eased opened her jacket to provide easier access to her gun. She didn't want to spook herself into doing something stupid, but she also hadn't spent nearly two months in rehab only to get jumped by some street punk on her first night out.

The lit cathedral was only a little ways up the street, but home remained the technically closer refuge. Only one more block to go. She cut across Euclid at an angle, staying well away from the construction debris as she picked up her pace again and the deserted buildings' plastic sheeting snapped and fluttered in the stiff wind. She passed an open section of the construction site, the graffitied plywood on the other side of the street suddenly giving way to eerie, complete blackness.

That's it, she thought. *There's something in there, watching me.*

She felt it as clearly as she felt the butt of her gun, even if she couldn't yet see what lurked there in the darkness. *Who* lurked there, she corrected her rushing mind. Not *what.* She had to believe it was a who. Maybe she'd interrupted a vagrant rifling the construction site. Or maybe it was the thug who'd asked about her at Flannery's.

"Okay, so we've got company," Dana murmured to herself. "No problem." She pressed the alert button on her phone to notify the on-call tech at Griffin Security. If she didn't check in with another call in a mere two minutes, the tech would notify Max and the police with an urgent distress call, and one of Cleveland's finest would be dispatched to her precise coordinates, sirens blaring.

A brand-new fail-safe measure at Griffin Security, instituted after the attack on Lester. She'd never actually imagined having to use it, though. Certainly not this soon.

Dana paused, unable to resist the urge, and stared straight into the absolute darkness across the street. If these were the same men from before, men with guns, her alert probably wouldn't matter anyway. Either way, it was time to pound the pavement. To really test her newly healed leg.

But it was already too late.

Directly across from her, in the open black maw of the construction wall, the darkness erupted. Four figures burst from the opening, forgotten shadows springing to new life.

And the shadows were racing toward her.

Dana reared back as the night surrounding her literally screamed, all the half-remembered nightmares of the past two months rushing back into her brain with a paralyzing hailstorm of fear and terror.

She knew these men. These *things*. These were the same attackers who'd come after her eight weeks ago. And just as it had then, her world was suddenly going red, the landscape coated in an odd, shifting crimson haze. She recognized it; she understood it. There was nothing she could do to stop it.

And, most frightening of all, a part of her almost *welcomed* it.

"Get back!" she yelled, waving her gun, struggling to recapture reality, even as her legs somehow carried her several yards down the street, only to realize that some of her attackers had slipped past her, cutting her off.

Now they all came toward her, panting and snarling, and Dana opened her eyes even wider as she tried to make sense of what she was seeing. Their bodies were distorted, misshapen in odd angles. Too large in places, too twisted. *Not normal men at all.*

It was Halloween all over again, and Dana now understood why she'd blocked so much of that first attack out. As they had been that horrible night, these men's faces were also swollen, broken, their eyes wild with lunacy, jaws gaping with hunger.

Not only Halloween either. There was something in these men she'd seen in the wolves too, from the other night. The wolves and...something else. Someone? She couldn't remember.

Focus! Her confusion was a trick of the shadows, of her own panic and fear. What else could it be? This wasn't a world of actual demons or monsters.

Whatever her attackers were, they'd completed the circle around her to block off any hope of escape. One of them laughed, a rough, urgent sound, and they pressed inward, snuffling with excitement. Fear shoved an icy spike into her chest, and —

And then it was suddenly gone.

Dana straightened as warmth flowed through her, a swift, unexpected support. As if she wasn't alone. And she drew on that new strength, channeling it, as the circle closed around her and the men reached out to her with grasping, pulling fingers —

"Back. *Off.*" She aimed her gun and pulled the trigger.

A voice rang out beside her. "No! Get back — no!"

As her pistol fired and the closest man hurled himself forward, someone broke through the circle, knocking Dana's arm up and shoving her back. The gunshot cracked like thunder between the empty buildings, exploding the silence.

Finn jumped in front of her. He slammed his right fist into the closest attacker's face, and the creature plunged sideways to the street's curb. Something dark sprayed across the sidewalk across Dana's boots, and even beneath the echo of her gunshot, she distinctly heard the sound of several teeth clattering into the gutter.

Finn stood directly between her and the others, bending down toward the thing in the street. All she could see was his broad back and shoulders, but she knew it was him. This wasn't a man she'd soon forget. Or a *feeling*. She'd sensed him, she realized. She'd simply known he was there.

Finn.

This was all…extremely familiar. Way too familiar.

Her head pounded in sudden pain as Finn yanked up the fallen assailant, then tossed him out at the others who'd already stopped dead in their tracks. Why was he here? And how —?

Finn braced himself, apparently preparing for another attack, and Dana briefly checked him for some evidence that he'd just taken a man out with a single swing. But Finn wasn't even winded. He shouted in strange words she couldn't understand, his voice filled with rage and warning. She wanted to believe the words were something European — *Polish, maybe, or Czech?* — but she didn't think so. This was something else. Something ancient.

Beyond Finn's imposing bulk, the other men had regrouped into a loose half circle, their comrade at their feet. Gibbering quietly between themselves, barking sounds similar to Finn's back at him. Threats. Curses.

They were afraid of him, she realized. As if they knew why he was there, what he was capable of. As if they *recognized* him.

"How'd you find me?" she demanded, taking a quick step forward. "Who are these men?"

Finn turned and scowled at Dana, and in that smallest space of his hesitation, one of the men lurched out at them, his grapple-like hand punching past Finn and knocking Dana off her feet.

She crunched down hard on her newly restored right leg, a wall of white flashing across her vision, blinding her anew. Staggering, she collapsed face-first to the concrete.

And suddenly, she remembered even more. The pain first. A shrieking, shocking agony in her leg, and then the memory of men like these beneath her own fists, as she pummeled and ripped and tore at them with her own hands. Nausea and rage heaving up within her, violence singing in her veins.

She tasted the cold, briny pavement for a moment more, then rolled over to see Finn brutally knock away the man who'd touched her. As that man slumped in a pile at Finn's feet, two more took his place — and the closer of the two wielded a glinting blade.

What happened next took only a second or two, Dana knew, but it played out in slow motion before her eyes. The long knife came low, aiming for Finn's stomach, but he'd shifted downward with the attack, crossing his arms in an X to stop the man's upward thrust, and shooting his hips back and away from the driving blade.

In the same fluid movement, Finn's hand slid up the assailant's arm to the elbow, twisting it awkwardly and forcing the man down, so that the frenzied attacker was hunched over with the knife pointed into *his* back. Finn moved to drive the blade in with his free hand. All he had to do was punch the hilt down, and Dana half closed her eyes, her blood jumping with expectation —

But he stopped. Instead, he snatched the blade away and twisted the man's elbow up until there was an audible pop. The man fell forward, and Finn used his right knee to finish him off, *then* dragged his knife across the man's throat. Snarling with anger, the attacker geysered with blood that was black as tar, and she flinched away as Finn turned for the other men. *So many*, she thought…

"Get up," he ordered to another man on the ground. "You're free. Stay that way."

Dana scrambled upright as Finn used the knife to keep the men at arm's length, then she watched as his face lifted, and he stared down the street. Suddenly, the sound of a car's screeching tires tore through the street.

"Go," Finn shouted at her, half pulling, half shoving her up Ninth.

Dana whipped her head around, staring at the oncoming car. Several things imprinted on her at once, with an immediacy she'd never experienced before and couldn't doubt. *Dark Lexus, Pennsylvania plates, license number 074332, speed. Danger!* And with eyes that had gone hypersharp with fear and adrenaline, Dana saw the gun shoved out the window, the barrel aimed at Finn.

"Watch out!" she screamed, surging up with such force that Finn fell back.

A bullet ripped between them.

Dana felt her hair blow back as it passed, the heat of the bullet scorching her cheek. *Faster than a speeding bullet,* she thought, the words hysterical in her mind. She brought her gun around for another shot, fired once, twice, and the car swerved enough for her to turn again, to ready herself for flight. She couldn't even feel her right leg anymore. She had to escape, had to get them inside, out of harm's reach.

"This way," Dana yelled as she started up Ninth toward Superior.

The cathedral.

She could go there; she could *always* go there. Her

father had told her that endlessly and Father Franks had reminded her every year since her dad's death. She even had a key to the building on her keychain, never before needed — or used. Tonight, that was going to change. She picked up her pace as Finn fell into step with her.

"Where?" he asked, and she felt his arm around her, protecting her, supporting her while urging her on. He wasn't even winded, she realized, while she could barely form a sentence.

"Up there," she managed, and then her breathless words were cut off as more bullets peppered the sidewalk beside them. Somewhere, a siren started, but it was too far off, and the wind began to scream again as Finn practically lifted her off her feet and they raced on, moving at a speed Dana wouldn't have thought possible in light of her battered leg, whether it was recently healed or no.

They ran up Ninth and took a hard left at the cathedral's grand entrance, Dana shoving her hand deep inside her jacket and wrenching her keys free. Behind them, the sedan bounced over the sidewalk and screeched to a halt, doors slamming just as they reached the rear door to the church.

"Get inside," Finn growled. As the keys slipped in her hands, he cursed in the same strange, guttural language he'd leveled before at their attackers. Guiding her aside and away, he slammed his shoulder once into the thick wooden door.

It crashed inward, banging off the wall.

"Inside," he barked again, and the sound of uneven footsteps in the street behind her jarred her, shouts coming closer. "I'll stay out here. They'll scatter once inside the church."

"No," she gritted out. "I won't leave you."

Another burst of gunfire shattered the night. Clutching at Finn wildly, she grabbed a fistful of his jacket before falling inside the doorway, and finally, he came with her. He'd no sooner pushed the heavy wooden door closed behind them, securing it with two heavy padlocks set high in the wall since the main lock was broken, than she heard the sound of a police siren cutting through the night. Dana staggered against the wall, then painfully lurched around until her shoulder blades rested against the cool, cream-painted walls of the cathedral's side entryway.

This wasn't even the church proper, merely a half-lit corridor between the main church and the administrative building. But given what they'd left behind on the other side of the door, she definitely felt like she was on holy ground.

She wiped the sweat from her forehead and glared at Finn, who now stood with his back against the door. The look of ashen resolve on his face deflated her anger.

"Hey," she managed, not recognizing her own broken voice. "You okay?"

Finn straightened. "This…isn't the church," he said slowly, looking around in confusion.

"Not technically, no, it's the admin building behind the church. But…" She stared at him, lost. *What's his problem? Had he endured the same military-grade nuns she'd had in grade school?* "Finn, I don't underst—"

"Dana! What's happened?"

Finn silently withdrew into the shadows, pressing himself back into the alcove as the robust figure of Father Leo Franks burst into the hallway.

"Father, I'm all right, really." Dana let the tall, stoop-shouldered priest take her by the arm, glad he was distracted from Finn, who still looked shell-shocked from his brush with Christendom. Father Franks leaned down to search her face with his worried brown eyes, the flush of his skin unlike anything she'd ever seen in the normally placid, contemplative old man.

"What did they do to you?" he asked. "Why were they here?" His gray hair hung wildly around his ears, and his hand shook on her shoulder. "Should you sit? *Can* you sit? Your leg…"

Dana breathed out her explanation in a rush, moving deeper into the hallway and away from Finn. "I'm fine, Father, I'm so sorry to wake you. There were men out there — thugs, lunatics. I was caught off guard, walking home, and I ran. I hate to burst in on you, but I — I had nowhere else to go."

"Of course, of course," Father Franks said, his mournful eyes searching hers. "You were right to come." He smoothed his black priest's shirt, clearly shaken. Concern knifed through her.

"Father, are you —" she began, just as the priest stiffened.

"You're not alone, are you?" he said, the words more a statement than a question.

Before Dana could speak, Father Franks turned and looked straight back at Finn, who stepped forth from the doorway's shadows into the half-light of the hall.

To her shock, the priest's face blanched, his eyes going wide like those of a man seeing his own death.

"God in heaven protect us," he breathed, his words barely a whisper. "Dana, what have you brought?"

Chapter Eight

Cathedral of St. John the Evangelist
Cleveland, Ohio
2:47 a.m., Dec. 24

Finn straightened to his full height, staring down into the holy man's outraged face. The world had gone quiet around the cathedral, waiting for the confrontation that must play out, that had to play out, when demons crossed the paths of Earth's prophets and priests.

It had always been this way. This strangeness, this *recognition* by anointed mortals that he and his kind were not of this world. Fallen angels had been considered gods in ancient days. Heroes and sometimes monsters, sent from the sky. And those who'd stayed had fueled the legends of six thousand years.

Demons, of course, had occupied a far uglier position in those legends.

Only…Finn wasn't a demon anymore. Not exactly. Though apparently, he still had enough of the demon within him to trigger the priest's alarms.

"Good morning, Father," he murmured. "I didn't mean to disturb you." No more than the truth. He had no quarrel with God's emissaries on Earth. And he couldn't afford to give Dana any reason to keep him from Lester.

"How *dare* you defile this hallowed ground," the priest hissed back, his words quivering with intensity. Franks was a tall, rangy man with wiry gray hair that flared wildly around his ears, his slight stoop shaving a few inches off his height, and a face that looked as if it would be far more at home with easy smiles and gentle shrugs. But now the human's gaze was flat and angry as he took another step toward Finn. "You haven't been summoned here," he said. "Get out."

"Um, Father?" Dana's cautious voice dipped between them. "What's wrong?"

"I haven't come to harm you," Finn said, his voice carrying over her question. "Or her."

"What are you talking about?" Dana's tone sharpened, and her gaze shot back to Finn. "How do you know each other?"

Finn looked at her for a moment, deciding, then turned back to Franks. "Whoever, or whatever, you may believe I am," he said. "Know that I am an ally."

"No, you're not," Franks snapped back. "You are a liar, the father of lies. And you're not welcome —"

"Father, please, stop," Dana cut in, laying a hand on the priest's arm. A hand the priest ignored, and her words came more quickly, more urgently. "This is Finn Schaeffer. A — a doctor I met tonight. He helped me when those men outside attacked me, and —" She slid a look at Finn. "I probably wouldn't be here if he hadn't come along when he did."

Father Franks frowned, turning to her. "He helped

90

you? How?"

She grimaced, as if trying to put it together herself. "He—scared the men off, most of them. When others followed we…ran here." She looked away from the priest, and Finn could see her mind stumble over the improbability of their escape. They'd outrun a car racing toward them at full speed. They'd outrun bullets. "We ran…really fast," she ended faintly.

Franks's brows rose. "He led you to a church?" When Dana didn't respond, the priest snorted, shaking his head. "His name isn't Schaeffer. His kind have no last names." The priest tilted his head, his smile calculating as he stared hard at Finn. "But since you are here as a friend, *Finn*, come. A tour of our Lord's house is in order."

Franks turned sharply away from them, striding deeper into the building. In his wake, the walls closed in, pressing down on Finn. Stifling him. Still, if he wanted to reach Lester tonight, he had no choice but to follow. If he turned and fled, as every muscle and nerve in his body was imploring him to, then Dana's trust would be lost to him. The hours wasted seeking out Lester without her could be enough to ruin the entire mission. There was no choice here.

He took one step toward where the priest beckoned, then another. *I have the blessing of the archangel,* he reminded himself. *I'm a Fallen, not a demon. For the next twenty-two hours, anyway.*

Dana stepped close to him. "What's the hang-up between you two? Why doesn't he like you?" she asked, her words a tight whisper. "Are you a Baptist or something?"

"No." Finn slanted her a quick look. "He thinks I'm a demon."

She snorted. "Well, don't take it personally. We get a lot of those in Cleveland."

He stopped to consider her. She really didn't know who or what he was; not yet, anyway. He didn't know if he should envy or pity her. It was probably best that she remained in the dark, though. Humans were so frail…

Speaking of…

"You've stopped bleeding." He gently touched the side of her head, but Dana jerked away.

Too late, he realized his mistake. Energy arced between them, a tangible spark that leapt from his body to hers, seeking to finish the process he had already begun. She clearly felt it too and briefly touched the wall to steady herself.

She'd been injured again in the fight, he thought. She was only human, after all.

"Are you all right?" he asked, knowing the sensation of his touch still moved through her. Millennia of pent-up energy that clearly couldn't be contained. He'd have to be more careful.

"I'm fine," she said, unwilling to meet his gaze. "Shaken up a bit, is all. And the cut — wasn't deep." She wiped her palms on her pants as Father Franks paused at the door to the sanctuary, watching as he pulled a set of keys away from his belt like a man about to unlock a torture chamber. "Seriously, how does Father Franks know you?"

"He doesn't," Finn said. "He only thinks he does."

The door to the church boomed open, and Franks looked up from the end of the dark hall, his lips twisting into a sneer. "He cannot hide what he is before God. No one can hide here." He gestured grandly with his arm. "After you, 'Finn.'"

Finn met the human's glare, every instinct in his body crying out at the thought of entering a house of God. He'd done so before as a demon a handful of times, always under duress, and always at the request of humans, who didn't so much care about the pain their demand would bring, who cared only about ridding themselves of *other* members of the horde who were strong enough to defile sacred ground.

That took a pretty strong demon.

But for all the injuries Finn had endured at the hands of his foul brethren, none of it could compare to walking into a church. Much less a fully consecrated cathedral.

He knew what was to come. The radiance of this holy place, built by faith alone, would arrow through him, flaying open his skin, laying his spirit bare for punishment. The focused energy of a million devout souls — present, past, and future — driving into him, seeking to destroy him. For he was a creature forged without hope, with no beginning and no end. He was a creature that knew no being greater than himself. And for his pride, for his emptiness, he must pay the consummate price whenever he walked among the true believers of this world.

Finn stepped past Father Franks, and through the cathedral doors.

Light exploded around him. The church was still, slumbering in anticipation of its holiest of days, but the blaring of illumination that assaulted him came not from man-made fixtures, not from the candles wavering in the sterile, frigid silence. It came from the very stones of the cathedral, from the wood of the carved frieze that he stumbled past on his way to the grand altar, and from the thousands of panels of richly stained glass trapped within huge vaulted windows. The luminescence rained down on him, the glass alight with the memory of the arcing, piercing rays of sunshine that showered the blessed with purples, reds, and blues.

And…there was no pain for him here.

The cathedral didn't hurt him.

It welcomed him.

Under the cathedral's radiant fire, Finn forced himself forward, half-blind with wonder, taking in the majestic rose window blossoming above the Hand of God, the Madonna portrait deep within the opposite alcove, surrounded by the stars of heaven. He cast his gaze skyward, and the images of Revelations opened before his eyes, peeking out from the elaborately carved arched ceiling, shining down on him in beautiful, glorious relief.

Behind him, he knew that Dana and the priest had also advanced into the room, could hear them speaking in hushed, angry tones, but he could not yet face their curiosity, their questions, the poking, prodding inquisition of children at the zoo. Despite his shock at his own reaction, despite the faint, twisting horror of the demon lurking in his soul, Finn spread his arms, reveling in every last mote of wonder and awe that this sanctified place of God would spare him.

He drew in a long, shuddering breath, then straightened, forcing himself to focus.

"You have a lovely cathedral, Father," he said, turning to the priest, burying the demon far beneath the impermeable layer of his Fallen status. "I'm glad it has you to care for it."

Father Franks, it appeared, wasn't wholly convinced.

The old man strode forward, words of ancient Latin spilling from his lips as Dana's eyes flew wide, her hand rising to her mouth. In his right hand, the priest brandished a crucifix, and Finn managed a short, brutal laugh. All these millennia later, and the tools of the priesthood remained the same. "What, no surplice?" he asked. "No stole?"

"The arrogant have risen against me; the ruthless seek my life." The priest's voice lifted, the Latin incantation rich and fulsome in the cathedral's hushed beauty. He held out the crucifix, and Finn narrowed his eyes.

"It's not your words that can harm me, priest," he said, though pain pricked at him, deep inside. "Not in the way you believe. Not anymore."

Franks didn't condescend to reply, and Finn almost smiled. Catholic exorcists never gave in to a demon's tendency to chatter: that was the way of the rabbis. Different lore, different tools.

But Finn did not have time to placate Father Franks, especially when the priest lifted the crucifix even higher, like a weapon, and stepped closer to Finn with fire in his eyes. To Finn's heightened senses, the crucifix glowed with the power infused in it by its makers, and by the holy men and women who had carried it ever since. Believing in it, trusting it. Transferring their energy to it.

Even as a Fallen, this was going to hurt.

Slowly, deliberately, Finn reached out with his left hand to grasp the golden cross, knowing the effort would cost him—but that it would cost the good father more. With a quick, decisive movement, he pulled the crucifix from the priest's fingers.

Franks's face flamed red as the cross jolted Finn with a screaming hiss of energy. "Blasphemer!" Franks cried, and with the speed of a trained boxer, the priest pulled his arm close into his body, then released a vicious uppercut that caught Finn squarely on the chin, forcing his head back with a snap.

Dana shouted in surprise, and Finn gaped at the priest, for a moment not even fully registering that the old man was swinging at him again.

But only for a moment.

As Franks completed his motion, Finn's right hand lashed out and stayed the priest's fist with no effort at all. The mortal was strong, determined, but his faith held more power than the thrust of his arm. Fortunately, humans never seemed to figure that out.

"I am *not* who you think I am," Finn repeated tightly, the pain in his left hand dialing up, channeling the cathedral's energy currents through him like a lightning rod. "I have the blessing of the archangel of the Lord. I mean you no harm."

"Father!" Dana was between them suddenly, pulling on the priest's shoulder until he faced her. "*Stop* it, seriously. Finn is a friend. That's what's important here. He saved me from some seriously bad guys out there. And you" — she turned on Finn, her gaze hard and implacable — "are clearly not a doctor or a priest. So you can start explaining the whole 'blessing of the archangel' business this second because I am *all* ears."

Dana's voice rang off the walls, but even as it echoed, Finn and the priest locked eyes again. Neither of them moved as they glared at each other. Neither spoke. Finn's eyes bored into the priest's bitter, lost face, so much emotion raging across it that Finn knew this was not the only battle that the priest had fought. There was darkness in those eyes. The darkness of betrayal, loss, and boundless, unbearable sorrow.

Not all of the priest's demons resided in the world around him.

"Reveal yourself, then," Franks spit out, staring fiercely into Finn's eyes. "Reveal yourself as what you are, an angel of the Fallen, and I will stand down and let God wreak his vengeance upon you." Franks's entire body shook with a combination of fear and rage, but his face was resolute. The priest fully intended to land another punch, then another. As many as it took to bring Finn down.

Finn grimaced. If every mortal gave him as much trouble as Dana and this priest, he'd never get the list delivered.

"I'm not here to harm you or any of your kind," Finn said again as the priest's eyes raked over him. "I'm a messenger."

"So you're, ah, an angel?" Dana interjected, though it was clear she didn't believe that was possible.

"Not exactly."

"Oh, not exactly." Her tone was measured, skeptical but not unkind. Probably the way she'd talk to a child, Finn thought. Or someone on drugs. "A demon, then."

Finn grimaced. "Not exactly that either."

"Right." She peered at him, her eyes narrowing. "Do *not* tell me you're an alien."

Finn opened his mouth to respond, but Father Franks's horror-struck gasp cut him short, the priest's gaze riveted on Finn's wrist, which had edged out of the pristine French cuffs of his starched white shirt.

"Heavenly Father, *no*," the priest breathed. "You bear his mark."

Finn pulled his hand away sharply, stepping back from Father Franks as the old man stumbled forward. Dana was there to catch the priest, her arms going around him even as he looked at Finn with newfound dismay.

Finn glanced down, then up again, glaring at the priest, whose entire demeanor had changed. The man looked miserable, stricken at what he'd seen on Finn. And, sure enough, there was something there on Finn's skin. On his interior right wrist, a mark had appeared, one he'd never seen before. A kind of cross and circle design, with the four arms of the cross extending beyond the edge of the circle at differing lengths, like a poorly drawn Sun Cross or a ragged crosshairs mark. He had no idea what it was—but the priest clearly did.

"Who?" Finn practically growled, instantly thinking of the rogue Fallen. Probably made sense that there was a way to identify Fallens to humans, though he'd never considered it before. "Who else do you know who bore this mark?"

The priest blinked at him, his eyes haggard and confused, the flush of his cheeks fading to a dull gray. "He was…a holy man, they said, once upon a time," he said quietly, as if from far off. He leaned against Dana almost unconsciously, and she held him up with an equal abstraction, as if she was born to the task. "His name was Bartholomew. And I—I've felt his presence again recently. Here in this city. I believed…hoped I was mistaken." He swallowed, half shuddering, then turned his sorrowful gaze on Finn. "I see now that I was not."

CHAPTER NINE

Cathedral of St. John the Evangelist
Cleveland, Ohio
3:20 a.m., Dec. 24

Father Franks shrugged off Dana's hands, and she stepped back, wary and vigilant. Her career had taught her when to shut up and watch, and this was one of those times. She'd also known, vaguely, that the priest served the diocese as an exorcist, but she'd never seen him haul out a crucifix and accost someone. He and her father had been best friends, and he'd never mentioned the priest doing anything like that. Of course, he'd never talked about the priest at all, so maybe they'd been out fighting demons together all those nights her father had left her alone in the apartment, watching reruns of the WWE, while her mother was out with her tennis friends.

Dana took in Franks's disheveled clothes, his wild hair, and haggard eyes. He'd clearly thought Finn was a demon or at least some seriously effed-up angel, and given Finn's bizarre responses to her questions, she couldn't fault the priest for that one either. She'd encountered two separate people who'd thought they were possessed since she'd started working in security, and both had been seriously scary souls.

Finn didn't give any indication that he was about to start foaming at the mouth, and he didn't have a tail, but she clearly needed to be more careful around him. Her mind went instantly to her leg and how he'd seemed to almost magically heal it...then to their unreasonable speed in evading attackers who *had* looked like demons. Creatures who'd bled black goop instead of blood.

Yeah. She was going to need to be a *lot* more careful.

But Father Franks now stood hunched in on himself, a criminal forced to the point of confession. Dana's nerves hummed with the pressure in the room, but she couldn't speak, couldn't think. She could barely draw breath.

Finn held out the slender gold crucifix, and Father Franks took the cross, his eyes cast down, his shoulders slumping as he cradled the sacred object. Dana shoved her hands into the pockets of her jacket, grateful for the reassuring feel of her cell phone. So if Finn wasn't a demon or a straight-up angel...what the hell was he? And who was this Bartholomew character who was distressing Father Franks so much?

A headache thrummed behind Dana's eyes, tiring her further, but she pulled her phone free, swiping it on. Someone had aimed a gun at them from a limo. Someone who hadn't been one of the slobbering creatures in the streets. Barely looking at the device, she keyed in the name Bartholomew and sent the text to Max. First-name-only searches were a nightmare in a city the size of Cleveland, but it was Christmas, after all. And she'd been a very good girl this year.

She replaced the phone as Franks turned and placed the cross on the altar, resting his palm flat on the cool marble for a moment before lifting his gaze heavenward, staring up at the enormous wooden screen behind the altar. The saints glared back down at him, unrelenting. Then he spoke, his powerful voice calm, almost eerily flat.

"I hadn't been a priest for very long when I received the call from Rome. It happened to many young men who showed an aptitude for learning, they said, for languages and history. New priests who fit a certain profile. I had become a servant of the Lord with such zeal, determined to make a difference, convinced that I could succeed where so many others had failed." He shook his head at the memory. "I was told my service in Rome would bring me great spiritual reward. I would study ancient languages, assist the Vatican in matters of clerical importance for a few years, then return to run a parish of my own in some large city, wherever the need was greatest."

Franks's voice strengthened as he spoke. "When I arrived in Rome, it was much as they said for the first year. I studied constantly, translating texts, learning and relearning Greek, Hebrew, Aramaic. I memorized arcane rites, ancient arts of spiritual healing, incantations to return evil to its hell. All for the supposed purpose of cataloguing these instructions to fill the Vatican library with yet one more research text. It seemed a colossal waste of time for me. I yearned to preach God's word to the people, to guide a flock of my own. I knew I could turn them from their paths of ruin, help them find the way to the Father." His lips twisted. "It was my arrogance that had drawn their attention, you see."

"Who?" Dana asked, but the priest went on. She thought of Franks with the crucifix, his bold confrontation with Finn. His bent but still-powerful frame. The way his hands had held the holy relic. This man had been her father's best friend, yet she hadn't known him at all.

Something clicked inside Dana, a door unlatching. She gripped her hands tight, willing her mind to be quiet and listen.

Franks lifted his eyes to the ceiling, as if he was tracing the patterns of stars tucked into the shadowed archways. "And then it came—a new summons, to a new cathedral. Not so very far away from Rome, barely over the border and into France. A special meeting for me, I was told. A special test in Lyon."

"Lyon?" Finn asked sharply. Franks turned to him, his eyes bright with unspilled emotion.

"There was a man they kept there in the crypt—an insane man known only by the name Bartholomew," he said. "A man who'd been kept alive for hundreds of years."

The tension in the room deepened. Finn didn't move a muscle, but his focus on the priest was all-consuming, as if he could will the words out of the old man. Franks turned away from him, his voice trembling and low.

"He'd come to the gates of the church in rags, the story went, in late May of 1527."

Dana's mind seized, stumbled. She'd heard that wrong, she thought, and her brain reordered the numbers, restated them into a date that could be real, could be possible. Not one that was nearly five hundred years ago.

"The man's body was strong, his voice pure, but his mind had been fractured. His eyes burned pure gold, and he was filled with rage and fire. That first day, it had taken a dozen men to subdue him, and he screamed at them in languages they could not decipher until he passed out from apparent exhaustion. They brought him to the cathedral, and he seemed crushed. Defeated. Until he saw the clock."

Finn frowned. "The clock?"

"The astronomical clock of Lyon." Franks sighed. "He made them understand, eventually. That he knew the clock and all its inner workings. He convinced them he'd made one similar to it, and they were overjoyed. The astronomical clock of Lyon had a complexity that had been lost in the many years since its creation. He would tend it, make improvements, and remain within the church walls, even though—" He paused, shooting a glance at Finn. "Even though he could not fully reclaim his mind."

"He arrived in 1527." Finn spoke as if to a ghost. "After the sack of Rome."

"He told me that, yes, but I soon learned that part of the story had not been shared with the current generation of priests at the church. To them, Bartholomew wasn't a refugee from one of the greatest crimes against the Holy See and its defenders, he was simply…a miracle, a gift from God who'd been possessed of a demon. Their challenge was to release the demon while sparing the angel." He shook his head. "They'd been trying ever since."

Finn's scowl grew ominous as Father Franks continued. "I'd been brought in to drive the demon out of the poor man once and for all. I was locked in the room with him for three days, watched through a slit in the door." His lips twisted bitterly. "It was my test as an exorcist."

"And did you pass?"

"Well enough. I did not—could not—drive the demon from him. He laughed when I made the attempt. But he gave me words to share with my superiors, to convince them I had, somehow, reached the spirit behind the devil that caused him such agony. But he told me more, words that I was not to share. What he'd seen in Rome. His name. The mark on his wrist and its purpose. That he was no demon...but also no human. That he was a Fallen angel, beloved of the Lord. He also told me how..." Franks swallowed. "How much power he still possessed."

"Why you?" Finn asked.

The priest shrugged. "My arrogance must have caught his attention too. But when I said I would return to help him again, he said no."

"No?" Dana asked, and this time, Franks did look at her, and she took a step back, struck by the misery in his eyes.

"He believed he deserved the pain he was in, that he had failed in his mission and should be punished. That he could never trust himself." Franks's mouth trembled, and Finn winced, knowing that sorrow, that belief. "The Church thought him an angel, and at the time, he had decided that an angel was the only thing he could be, or everything else they believed would be held suspect. But he was very different from any angel I would ever expect. He was...deeply damaged." His gaze swung back to Finn. "I heard nothing more of him, and after the years passed, I let myself forget about Bartholomew. But I have felt his presence strongly these past few weeks. He is *here*. And now, so are you. Bearing the same mark. But you are not mad."

"Not yet, anyway." Finn grimaced.

Finn's words galvanized Dana, and she forced her hands down to her sides, her mouth to work again. "So what exactly is going on, Finn? Who are you?" she asked in a low voice. "And why do you want to see Lester?"

That shook Franks out of his own troubled thoughts. "Lester?" he asked. "Tell me he hasn't endangered Dana yet again."

But Finn was looking at Dana, not the priest. "I'm not what this Bartholomew guy was, or whatever he's become. Because clearly...something broke inside him." *Broke, and is a serious problem.*

"And it hasn't broken in you. Yet."

He quirked a smile. "Not that I know of."

"How about some honest answers here?" Dana snapped, anger finally breaking through her sense of dread. "Let's recap. Father Franks is an exorcist. Years ago, he was called to exorcise a demon out of a church prisoner named Bartholomew, only he couldn't. He did, however, see Bartholomew's cool ink, listened to his story of being an angel on Earth, and got the impression that the dude had lived a really, really long time. Fast forward to tonight. You show up, also tripping Father's demon Spidey sense, and you've got the same ink. You want to tell me you're also several centuries past your expiration date? And that you've got feathers?"

She didn't know how she was asking these questions in her normal-person voice, but when Finn stared back at her, refusing to answer, another synapse snapped. "Jesus Christ," she muttered. "What the hell are you?"

"He's a Fallen," Franks said simply, his voice low, defeated. "No more or less than that."

Dana curled her lip, trying not to snarl at the priest to pull it together. "A Fallen angel. Great. And you've floated down to Cleveland on Christmas Eve—why, exactly?"

"I need to speak to Lester," Finn said implacably.

"So you keep saying," Dana said, watching Franks's shifting emotions with interest. Franks wasn't denying Finn's words anymore. He'd accepted Finn, which was its own circle of crazy, but there was too much she needed to know. Starting with: "Why do you need to see Lester, again? And why tonight?"

"Because he's expecting me," Finn said smoothly. He smiled, and every sense in Dana's body went on high alert. She hated it when he smiled. "He has something to give me. I honestly don't know anything more about it. If I did, I'd tell you."

Dana blew out a long breath. Lester had a penchant for collecting the odd and the crazy, and he was, admittedly, a little bit of a nut for religious antiquities. So if Finn was part of some group of people who could convince even straight-up priests that they were, ah, angels or demons or whatever, she could see such a group appealing to her uncle. Secret societies and ancient artifacts and arcane lore were the old man's catnip.

So okay, but...there was still Father Franks's reaction to contend with. And her own apparently healed leg.

Which once more raised the question: who was this guy?

Dana's attention fractured as her phone buzzed, and she turned away from the two men. Max would be texting her. About time.

She flipped to her texts.

Got the name, running the search. Also, L called me. I told him about Dr. Doom. Turns out he's expecting him — and he's

106

massively geeked. Wants to send his goon squad to get you both. Good?

Dana sighed, resigned. That solved at least one mystery, then. Lester might be one fruitcake short of a full bakery, but he was both her client and her uncle. And Finn—so far—hadn't proved dangerous so much as protective. "Good news. He wants to see you," she said to Finn. "He'll send a car."

Finn nodded. "Excellent. The sooner I can finish this, the better. Those men out there aren't the last of your problems. There will be more, and until I have what I need, they'll also be looking for Lester. If they can't find him…they will find you."

The half-forgotten nightmare assaulted Dana again, distorted faces, misshapen bodies. "What were they?"

"Demons, some of them. Others were Possessed, which is almost as bad—and worse, in some ways," Finn said. Father Franks shifted beside them, his face closing down, the secrets of the Church locked within it. "But the important part is, they'll only get stronger. They'll strike again before midnight tonight. You can count on it."

"Uh-huh. What do they want from Lester?" she asked. *Demons.* He said the word like it was God's own truth, and Franks wasn't contradicting him. *Great.*

"The same document I've been sent for, I told you," Finn said, eyeing her as if he was trying to see if his words meant anything. They didn't. "Once I have it in hand, the attention of these things that were following you will turn away from you and your uncle, and fix on me."

She narrowed her eyes. "That's it? They'll leave us alone after you get this document? How do you know Lester hasn't made a dozen copies of it?"

Finn's gaze arrowed through her. "I don't. But if he gives it to me, whatever it is, he'll be safe." She sensed herself being almost physically pushed back by the force of his gaze, surrounded by it. "You'll both be safe. I swear it."

The moment felt heavy, ominous, a fire stinging along Dana's nerves that hadn't been there before, Finn's dark eyes blazing with heat and intensity. "All right," she said, keying another message to Max to unleash her uncle's hounds. "I'll take you to Lester. But I'm not letting you out of my sight."

The smile on Finn's face flickered dangerously. "I also get that all the time."

Dana rolled her eyes. The phone buzzed again in her hand, and she glanced down at it. *Goons en route. Be there in five.*

CHAPTER TEN

Public Square District
Cleveland, Ohio
3:45 a.m., Dec. 24

Finn watched Dana as she slid into her uncle's limo beside him, taking note of every twitch of her muscles, every nuance of her tone as she gave her orders to the driver. He could practically hear her questions as they formed themselves in her head, but to her credit, she didn't speak right away. They set off down the street, the expensive vehicle purring into the night. Dana watched the streetlamps pass by for one block, then two.

Then she turned to him.

"Seriously? You're…" She slid a glance to the driver. "What Father Franks said you were?"

Finn weighed his options, wondering how to play this conversation. Dana was still trying to convince herself there were no demons in the world, or angels either. But at least by his count, she'd already been attacked three times by representatives of the demon horde. Ignorance was no longer bliss, it was sheer stupidity.

"I'm what he said I am, and that means I can kill what attacked us tonight. *I* can. You can't. Because of what they are."

"What they are," she repeated, her eyes hardening.

"I know you don't want to believe it. I don't blame you. But that doesn't make it untrue. And right now, Lester's in danger. So are you."

"And this Bartholomew? What's his relevance?"

Finn shrugged, not wanting to scare her more than she already was. "I have no idea. Father Franks recalled him because he shares the same tattoo that I do. That's it."

"But you said—"

"You'll find I say a lot of things when I need to. At the moment, I need to get to your uncle, and to do that, I had to get the priest on my side. I'm obviously not the only one interested in reaching Lester Morrow, but as to whether the guy behind tonight's attack is the Bartholomew that the priest encountered or someone else, I don't know."

"Bullshit," Dana retorted, catching him up short. "You're both the same kind of whatever, and you're both here. And so far tonight, you've shown up at a charity event, ingratiated yourself with a complete stranger, spent fifteen thousand dollars to make a statement, and foiled an attack by some seriously disturbed souls on the streets of Cleveland at three in the morning, then played hot potato with a gold crucifix and damn near made a priest cry. And you mean to tell me that a holy man who may or may not be possessed— but who is definitely deeply broken—and is also a known associate of both you and Father Franks doesn't have anything to do with it?"

"Bartholomew is no known associate of mine," Finn said, but even as he spoke the words, he hesitated. He didn't at all recall the sin that had brought him to his demonic status. He didn't remember anything at all about being Fallen. Had he known this Bartholomew? Did the rogue Fallen know something about what had caused Finn's disgrace?

"What is it?" Dana demanded, and Finn blinked, surprised to see her staring at him. Humans weren't supposed to be able to see anything a demon didn't want them to see, including their changing expressions, and Finn was currently a Fallen. He should have more protection against the curiosity of mortals, not less.

"Nothing," he said. When she made a face, he felt compelled to continue. "Okay, something. I don't know anyone by the name of Bartholomew, I don't know this man or what he's done, or if he's interested in your uncle's document. But yes, I will grant you, it's as reasonable a theory as any that he might be involved. And if that's the case, you must be even more careful. Because if he *is* the agent behind these attacks you've experienced —"

"Attacks?" she asked sharply. "There's only been one. Tonight's."

Now it was his turn to watch her with skeptical eyes, and Dana scowled at him. "You have no way of knowing about anything else. Unless you were behind them."

"I wasn't behind them," he said. "But I know that you were attacked two months ago, I know that you were attacked three nights ago as well. I'm almost certain that the first attack was connected, and I can tell you for sure that the second one definitely was."

"What do you know about what happened in Canada?" Dana winced as she spoke, lifting a hand to her brow. "Damn, that hurts," she muttered.

Finn hesitated, then lifted a hand as well. It might help, he reasoned, if she knew a little more. She might count him more as a friend.

Never mind that he suddenly *wanted* her to count him as a friend. It wasn't his place. This fierce, lost, driven woman had a life and a purpose in this world, while he would be gone in less than twenty hours. But for this barest moment in time, he didn't so much care.

With one gesture, a haze dropped between the seats, separating them from their driver. To the man in the front seat, they would appear to be staring out the window, no longer talking. It was the easiest of illusions, and it was one he knew Dana would instinctually appreciate — if she could have noticed it.

Which, insanely, she did.

"Oh, so now you drop the cloaking device?" Her eyes were bright, alert, and she reached out, touching the air. Nothing was there, of course. Nothing visible to ordinary humans, anyway. "Couldn't we have started this conversation that way? All of Lester's goons have recording devices."

"It's not just a soundproof barrier. It's visual as well."

Her brows shot up. "Really? How?"

Despite himself, Finn smiled. "Really. And how doesn't matter. You're safe, Dana," Finn said. "No one can see you, so let me do this. Let me help."

Without waiting for her to respond, he reached out both hands to brush Dana's hair with his fingers, pressing lightly against her temples. She froze beneath his touch as he took the pain away from her, her eyes wide as she stared at him. In that glance, there was fear, worry, even a little anger. But there was also...hope. And it was the hope that tore at Finn, made his own breath ragged in his throat. Hope was an emotion he had never understood.

What was it that Dana truly believed he could give her? Whatever it was, she was bound to be disappointed. But not...not yet, he decided. Not yet.

"It was me," Finn said quietly, holding her gaze as her dark eyes flared. "I was there three nights ago, when you were attacked by the wolves. I fought them off, got them to scatter. Stayed until I knew they were gone."

"But — how?" she managed. "You were following me?"

"I was following you," Finn said. Or the archangel was, more to the point. Which meant that Michael knew a lot more than he was letting on. Did he also know what this list was? He certainly wanted it badly enough. But why the cloak and dagger? Finn and the Syx were bound to the archangel's service. It wasn't as if there was any reason for subterfuge.

He shook off his uneasiness. Dana was staring at him, waiting for him to continue. "At that point, my goal was merely to keep you safe, not to approach you."

"What changed?" she asked, and he looked into her eyes, for a moment forgetting anything but how close she was to him, how real, how vital.

"You did." The words were out before Finn could stop himself, and he flushed, the unexpected surge of emotion warming him in a way that even Sara Wilde's healing energy hadn't been able to. He could see Dana's lips part, sense her instinctive twitch away from him, but he pushed on. He had only this second, this moment. Life was so fragile and fast moving, in a blink,

Dana's life would end, her soul would pass, and he'd have missed his chance. To say...to say...

"I don't understand," Dana whispered, but her eyes were on his, dark and intense—and a little desperate. "Help me understand, Finn."

The car stopped abruptly at a light, a chirping from the front shattering the moment. "Your uncle, Ms. Griffin," the driver said, his polite voice splitting the veil Finn had raised, their temporary isolation already gone. "He wants you to know everything is ready for your guest."

Dana flushed and straightened. "Of course," she said, once more all business. "Why wouldn't it be?"

Shoving away a gnawing ache that he could neither define nor fully admit to himself, Finn turned and stared at the bright lights of the frozen city.

CHAPTER ELEVEN

Post Office Plaza
Cleveland, Ohio
4:00 a.m., Dec. 24

Dana tracked the iridescent green numbers on the Audi Q7's radio console as they flipped to 4:00 a.m. At that precise moment, the limo turned into the narrow street between the Ritz Carlton Hotel and the Post Office Plaza building. She'd been awake almost twenty-four hours, and the adrenaline jacking her system had left her alternately strung out and exhausted. Her bones jolted over every grain of salt on the bleak white streets, her skin shivered at every breath Finn took in the seat beside her.

The sudden whitewash of her pain had been impressive, but she got the feeling it wasn't all Finn had wanted with his little Mr. Invisible trick. He'd wanted to tell her something, something important. Something that made her heart pound and her nerves tingle with anticipation, with fear, with excitement—

And yet, all this was insane. If she was truly supposed to believe Finn, she was riding through downtown Cleveland, Ohio, with a Fallen angel, ready to save her uncle from…um, demons.

Max would be suffering a complete meltdown if he was here.

As they pulled up to the sidewalk, the doorman appeared, unreasonably cheerful for the early hour. The Audi driver handed off the keys to him while Dana and Finn mounted the steps to the Post Office Plaza building with two other men. They'd barely cleared the second flight of stairs into the lobby when Dana's phone buzzed. She scowled down at it, her headache returning in force. *Another damned cybersecurity breach.* That made six hits in three days.

"You're upset," Finn murmured as they moved toward the elevator bay. "About something different, though. Something new."

Dana snorted a laugh. "Give the man a prize. Somebody's been trying to hack into our system, unsuccessfully, so far," she said. "We've been having unusual activity all week." She looked up at him, an idea dawning that she just as quickly rejected. "No. There's no way it's related to tonight's attack," she said. "Those guys we met on the street weren't hacker material. They looked like they could barely spell."

Finn was saved from replying by the whoosh of elevator doors, and they filed into the metal box, accompanied by muscle and guns.

"Where's Lester?" Dana asked, and the guard nearest her turned slightly.

"You'll meet Mr. Morrow in the gallery," he said.

"Your uncle is a collector?" Finn asked, and she jumped. She hadn't realized he was standing so close to her.

"Amateur only," she said, her eyes fixed on the line of gradually lighting numbers. "He funds student archaeologist digs and occasionally picks up pieces. Or he gets word of an artifact about to go up for sale on the black market and steps in to collect it before anyone else gets a jump on it." Was that how he obtained the mysterious document Finn and this Bartholomew wanted so badly? At a dig site? Usually, Lester sent her out to collect the specimens — if he didn't, he shared the details of the recovery of every shard of pottery, every scrap of papyrus with her. But there'd been nothing recent about a document, she was sure of it.

The moment they reached the twenty-first floor, one of Lester's security guards peeled off, presumably to loiter somewhere else so as not to worry the few staff members working the graveyard shift. In all, Exeter and its sister companies held the top three floors within Post Office Plaza, and Lester's gallery was on the second of those floors, near his office. Walking more quickly, the remaining guard led them to the gallery room and keyed the security pad to unlock the doors. They strode into the center of the brightly lit room, which was unoccupied, and Dana did a double take.

Lester had been busy.

The room was long, relatively narrow, and windowless, lined with thick mahogany shelves. At odd intervals, space had been created to allow for the occasional piece of framed artwork, but most of Lester's collection usually fit easily on the shelves, each with its own tidy explanatory note card. In the center of the room, a conversational grouping of chairs and tables welcomed guests to enjoy the surroundings in comfort. Typically, the shelves were sparsely lined with gleaming bits of antiquities—cups, platters, vases, sculpture. But not tonight.

Tonight, Lester must have dragged out every box he had in storage to dump them out up here.

The room was filled to bursting with piles of historical baubles—every possible piece of dishware, weaponry, decoration, jewelry, or artwork that Lester must have kept over the last forty years or more, since he'd begun what he'd always affectionately termed his hobby. Looking around, Dana quickly reassessed his hobby as an obsession...and judging by its sheer volume, a more expensive one than she'd ever realized. She hoped it wasn't an illegal one as well. She could only wonder at the value of the document that had captured Finn's and this Bartholomew's attention.

"You've arrived."

They turned to greet Lester, who stood in the doorway, and Dana watched her uncle's entire face light up the moment he set eyes on Finn.

Here comes Santa Claus. Forget Lester Morrow's custom-made suit and expensive shoes, forget the snow-white hair and seen-it-all eyes. Her uncle was as giddy as a first grader on Christmas Eve, and it appeared his present had come early this year.

"Lester Morrow," Finn said beside her, his voice rumbling through the room.

Lester stopped short, his bushy eyebrows leaping up, a wide smile breaking out across his face, smoothing out some wrinkles, deepening others. Even his eyes were filled with delight. "Finn," he breathed, the word a benediction. "I knew you would come. I've waited so...so long." He gestured for the guards to leave, and shut the door behind them.

"You've added a few pieces, I see," Dana observed

118

drily as her uncle finished resetting the door locks, then came up behind them to take their coats, every bit the consummate host.

"I've pulled my collection back to me over the past few months. Everything I have is either here or on loan to the city library," Lester said to Finn. "When I learned you were here, I had the rest of it brought up from storage. Forgive me for not having time to set up all the information cards but…" He paused, rapt. "I expect you don't need an explanation for anything in my collection."

"No." Finn turned away from them and walked down the length of the room, to all appearances unmoved by the millennia of bling Lester had lugged up for his review. He passed the garish life-size Virgin Mary portrait without hesitating, so score one for his artistic integrity, but then he stopped, his attention caught by a pile of jewelry and pottery. Dana stepped closer to her uncle as Finn picked up a heavily carved Mayan vase and turned it over in his hands.

"From the Classic period," Lester supplied loudly, his voice grating on Dana's nerves. He sounded like a child too eager to please, and Dana was fast reaching the limits of her patience. She was tired, she was under-caffeinated, and she was annoyed with Lester for nearly getting them both killed over a pile of paperwork.

"Lester, we can probably cut to the chase here," she said, her voice low but sharp. "Whatever it is you've got for Finn, give it to him so he can be on his way. And the next time you stumble into something that brings the hounds of hell yapping at your heels, maybe tell me what's going on up front so I can arrange enough security to handle it."

She hadn't planned on explaining that the *literal*

hounds of hell had been in the mix tonight, but Lester jolted at her words with a defensiveness that was undeniable.

"Dana!" he hissed. "Please, be quiet!" To her complete surprise, his voice broke on the words, and his face went scarlet with embarrassment. He darted a glance to where Finn was poking through a treasure trove of Egyptian jewelry. When her uncle looked back at her, his eyes were shining with naked emotion, and only then could she see the desperation that practically consumed him. It was an unnerving, pitiable sight. A better person would have felt sorry for the man, but she didn't. Lester *knew* better. Dana opened her mouth to protest, but her uncle held up a trembling hand to stop her.

"I have waited so *long*," he said again, and his earnest words succeeded where his eyes could not. "You can't understand the importance of this—this meeting to me. It's all that I have worked for. All I've lived for, for more years than you would ever believe."

"Okay, well, Finn said you were *attacked* over this document that he wants from you. That that was the reason behind the thugs hitting us on Halloween. What are you even doing with something like that?"

"I know, I know." Lester sighed heavily, his look turning woebegone. "I never wanted you to learn how dangerous all this was. I'm so sorry, but this is critically important to me."

Even knowing that he was a master chameleon, the sight of her uncle's crestfallen face winged through Dana, shattering her irritation. *Dammit.* Lester Morrow might run a multinational company with enough perks to keep him in fast cars and well-cut suits—and, apparently, a lot of dusty relics—but he was still an old man. An old man who wanted his meeting with destiny. Dana grimaced, brushing his arm lightly in reassurance. The movement was eerily similar to the affectionate touch she'd given Willie at Flannery's Pub, and she felt the net of her obligations tightening around her.

"Well then, go ahead," she said, then glanced over to where Finn was standing. He was hefting a heavy gold bracelet and staring straight at her, his eyes a question. She nodded once, stepping away as Lester trotted up the swath of golden carpet to pay homage to his guest. Dana rubbed her temples, which were once again throbbing, then jerked as her cell phone buzzed in her pocket. She pulled it out, keeping Lester and Finn in plain view as she glanced at it.

Found breach. Griffin X server. Need you down here.

Dana's stomach twisted. Griffin X was her company's most secure server, holding clients' top files as a backup should disaster strike. "Hackproof," as Max liked to say, except he wouldn't be able to say that anymore. *Well, shit.* She wouldn't be any help down there if Max was already aware of the point of entry. It was simply a matter of following the trail. And she didn't particularly care for the vibe between Finn and Lester either. Her uncle was talking animatedly to Finn, pointing first to one trinket, then another. Finn kept nodding, but she noticed he wasn't letting go of the dull gold bracelet. She thumbed Reply and typed back.

Can't. Who?

There was a pause while Max typed, and Dana's eyes darted up first to Finn and Lester, then to the wet bar at the side of the room. The coffeemaker there was basic, more for show. No comparison to the setup she had down at her office, but it would do.

Her hand shook with the receipt of Max's reply, and

she glanced down again.

Exeter. Lester? Replaced 23 of own files since 12/21. Last transaction this morning finally tripped the wire.

Dana blew out a short breath. Lester replacing his own files shouldn't be a big deal. But to replace them on Griffin's private server took multiple approvals, approvals he didn't have. Getting around those security measures each time would be tricky, since the codes were switched every few hours. She glanced around at the motley collection of trinkets Lester had hurriedly pulled out of mothballs. If his last attempt at moving files was this morning, then that would probably have been while she and Finn were running for their lives. Time had grown too short, Lester had gotten sloppy. But he wasn't a stupid man, and even now, she felt his eyes on her. She looked up with a smile.

"Thank God," she said, clearing out her cache with a few keystrokes.

"Is there a problem?" Lester asked, coming halfway toward her and radiating concern, clearly torn between ensuring she kept her mouth shut and taking care of Finn.

"No problem at all," Dana said. "Max thought one of our servers had crashed, but it was probably only an electrical glitch. Everything is sailing along, all systems go." She looked at them brightly. "Well?"

Is it so difficult to get this exchange over with? How long would it take for the ceremonial handing over of the scroll so they could all go crawl into a pot of java somewhere?

"Dana, you must be exhausted," Lester said, as if hearing her thoughts. "Please, both of you, sit down." He shooed them both toward the chairs, and bustled over to the wet bar, punching buttons as the coffee machine whirred to life.

Dana gave thanks to God for her beloved uncle. The wise man, the kind man, the generous ma—

Finn carefully set the bracelet down on one of the small tables, then looked at Dana intently. "Your uncle has collected many impressive artifacts," he said quietly. "More than I would have expected. How much do you know of his work?"

She frowned at him, one eye on Lester. Could the man take any longer with a freaking mug of joe? "It's a hobby, Finn, nothing more," she said. "Lester doesn't visit the digs himself." She needed to distance Lester from the document, whatever it was, and convince Finn it had fallen into his hands almost by mistake. "Whatever it is he found, he's probably not aware of its importance. And most of the stuff here is fake, copies of items he's sent on to museums."

Finn looked unconvinced, then Lester arrived suddenly at Dana's elbow. "You take it with cream and sugar, don't you, dear?" he asked, and Dana squinted at him.

"Not since I was twelve, no," she grumbled. Still, coffee was coffee, and she slugged it down. The cloying sweetness seemed to coat her throat, but she wasn't about to argue. She needed the juice.

"You could use about an hour of rest, I think. Maybe six," Lester said, shaking his head. He turned his gaze on Finn. "You agree she should rest?"

Finn, to her surprise, shifted uneasily in his chair. "She should rest," he said, his words a flat agreement, not a show of solidarity.

"Well, I'm glad we got that cleared up," Dana said, not even bothering to keep the irritation out of her voice. Lester hadn't gotten Finn coffee, just her. Was her fatigue really showing that strongly? This was such a waste of her time, and everything seemed so hurried. Constricted. Finn and Lester gazed at each other with an undercurrent of intensity that bothered her on a soul-deep level. Apprehension skated through her, and instinctively, she pulled her phone out of her jacket and stared at it. Another message from Max had come through, words that made no sense written across the screen.

This won't make you happy.

Why was her phone in her hand?

Lester came over to her, holding his hand out for her phone. Not knowing why, she jerked it away and curled it into her body, as if she was a ten-year-old refusing to give up her favorite toy.

"Dana, you really should rest," Lester said soothingly. He reached out to squeeze her shoulder. As she winced at the contact, wanting to get away from him for no good reason, he looked at her more closely. "Is your leg bothering you?"

"My leg is fine. *You* are bothering me." She was angry, she was almost certain, but her thoughts skittered around her head, refusing to cooperate. She was angry...at Lester, she thought. For...a very good reason.

"Well, it's all worked out, Dana." Lester's voice cut across her scattered thoughts as he patted her arm. "He's here with me, finally." He nodded toward Finn, who was staring at her uncle with a decidedly grim expression. "Everything is going to be all right."

Certain details stood out sharply in her mind. Lester, patting her arm the same way Margaret had, as if she was a prized Chihuahua. Finn's furious gaze, almost primal in its intensity, completely at odds with his unconsciously elegant attire. Finn's hands, clenched together above the golden cuff. Her own nearly empty mug, with the dregs of the too-sweet coffee pooling in the bottom.

The numbness started in her hands and feet first, crawling up her skin, winding toward her heart.

My coffee, she thought. *The bastard spiked my coffee.*

She swung her head around toward Lester, the action seeming to take twice as long as it should.

"No," she breathed.

And fell into blackness.

CHAPTER TWELVE

Exeter Global Services
Post Office Plaza
Cleveland, Ohio
4:30 a.m., Dec. 24

Finn carefully unclenched his fists as he watched Dana slump bonelessly on the couch. He was here for Lester's list, he reminded himself. How the man treated his own flesh and blood should be irrelevant. "Was that necessary?" he asked.

"No, but it was convenient." Lester checked Dana's pulse first at her wrist, then at her neck, but he didn't try to pry her phone out of her hand. Probably wise. "My niece is very dedicated to me, and I wanted to continue our conversation without her learning too much of the more sensitive nature of my work. Such knowledge would only lead to unnecessary concern on her part, when she should focus on healing. I'd hoped she would leave of her own accord, but now I believe it is better if she sleeps under my watch. You'll forgive the subterfuge, I hope."

"What did you give her?"

"My personal physician's own creation, actually. A low-dose sedative, meant to act quickly but with a relatively short duration. Dana will awake unharmed in several hours and with much-needed rest. You can see that she has overtaxed herself." He beamed down at Dana, but his expression wasn't exactly protective. It was more the pride of ownership. *What's going on here?*

Finn sent a quick brush over Lester's mind — and was blocked. He scowled. Probably not surprising given the number of blessed artifacts in the room, but still, annoying.

"Don't worry," Lester continued as Finn glanced around, trying to identify the trinket causing the interference. Could be, Lester had it on him, tucked in a pocket for protection. Smart man. "She has nothing to fear within the confines of this room. It's been retrofitted to my exact specifications, from wall thickness to surveillance equipment to alarms that will light up the control boards of security firms from here to New York."

Finn raised his brows. "Including Griffin Security?"

"I've taken the precaution of removing Griffin from video access. We'll not be disturbed."

While Lester spoke, Finn's gaze dropped to the solid gold cuff he'd picked up, undistinguished from its fellows except for a faint string of etched glyphs around its edge. Lester had no doubt recovered it illegally on one of his unsanctioned "digs." But the old man couldn't know what he had. Humans rarely did when it came to arcane artifacts.

He picked up the ornate bracelet again, trying to

master his reactions. Unfortunately, Lester took the opportunity to move another step closer. It took every ounce of control Finn had not to take him by the throat and shake the life out of him.

Get over it, Finn thought grimly. Dana hadn't been harmed. She'd wake up without injury.

And he'd be gone with the archangel's precious list.

He swallowed, forcing the hand gripping the golden cuff to stop shaking.

"There is so much I wish to share with you yet," Lester said at his side. "Before you leave. I know you can't stay long."

Finn scowled. "How?"

Lester blinked several times, far too quickly. "I...well, you told me so." Before Finn could react to that, Lester briefly touched the sleeve of Finn's jacket, the gesture of a servant, then wheeled away from him, moving with determination. He stopped midway down the room, where a six-foot-tall copy of one of da Vinci's Madonna paintings hung in a heavy gilt frame, and punched a few buttons on the keypad beside it. The portrait swung open with an efficient click, the shadowy view of a stairway visible behind it.

"I know how this must look." Lester gave a quick, embarrassed nod to Finn, his face coloring. "A secret doorway hidden by a painting, the painting itself an allegory of my work for mankind. But I'm a sentimental old man, I'm afraid, with a penchant for drama. Come, then." He glanced nervously over his shoulder at Dana's sleeping form. "While I suspect Dana will sleep for a few hours, I've learned from past experience that I always overestimate the effect of drugs in her system."

Finn's body jerked with a visceral force. "You've drugged her before?"

Lester's face tensed a fraction at Finn's tone, but his smile was intended to soothe, and Finn knew his attempt at feigning detachment had failed. "I'm sure that must sound alarming, but she was only administered sleep aids while she was in the hospital," he said, his words too careful, too practiced. The cornflower-blue eyes crinkled, the mouth turned down a fraction, and in a blink, Lester was the soul of self-deprecation, the perfect image of the doting uncle all too aware of his own limitations.

Lester was hiding far too much.

For the first time since the archangel had asked him to retrieve the list of…whatever it was, Finn wondered why Lester had that list in the first place. What did it mean to him?

"Dana is quite a precious gift, you must understand," Lester said, unwittingly echoing Finn's earlier thoughts. "She gave me quite a scare when she was shot."

Finn lifted one brow. "Oh? Tell me about that night."

"Please, one moment." With another wary glance in Dana's direction, Lester pulled the door wide open. A flight of stairs curved away from the door in a tight spiral, the descent illuminated by a series of blue lights that cast no light beyond the doorway. Lester stepped in, then turned back to Finn, his eyes gleaming with an energy that seemed out of place in his weathered face. Keeping the weighted door open with a hand, he beckoned Finn to follow.

"Come with me," he said. "I'll explain everything."

Adrenaline kicking in hard, Finn left the cuff on the table and followed Lester down the curving steps, entering a room that was nearly twice the size of the gallery. Half the room was open space, concrete floor, and bare walls broken only by a single elevator door, its floor indicator set on L.

The rest of the room, past a reinforced-glass barricade, was almost completely given over to proof that mortals were diligently trying to live up to their potential. Finn felt a surge of wonder at what he saw. Despite all their doubt, their confusion, their outright refusal to connect with their own buried divinity, the restless minds of humans never failed to surprise him.

Screens lined the walls, all of them flashing bright displays of rapidly changing locations, and a sophisticated computer station curled around the room, gleaming with lights and yet more embedded screens, these streaming with rows of information. Against the far wall was a plateglass case filled with yet more artifacts: a battered spear, several chalices, a pair of silver gauntlets, and dainty reliquaries of smoked glass — all of them appearing far more precious than Lester's gallery stash. His prized possessions, Finn realized, secrets within secrets. Flanking the display case were shelves of weapons, lined up with almost as much pride as the riches under glass.

The juxtaposition of ancient artifacts and modern technology and weapons was not lost on Finn. Mankind was not leaving behind the mythology of their past, but seeking to incorporate it, belief informing science, science clarifying belief. What would another few hundred years bring to this race, he wondered, if they were left to develop on their own?

Assuming they didn't kill themselves first.

Something flickered within him, the barest memory. Then it was gone.

"My apologies." Lester said, noting Finn's

expression. He turned and pulled out a remote from his jacket, systematically punching the keys while screens flickered off. "I forget how jarring this must be if you're not used to it," he said.

Finn didn't speak as Lester shut down four of the six screens. The two that remained were scanning crowds visiting several different types of stone monuments — Stonehenge, Mayan and Egyptian pyramids, the ruins of the Parthenon. He had seen these places before — when they had been whole, unbroken, shining examples of wealth and beauty for civilization. For all of their advancements, time had passed brutally for humans, history ground under the heel of conquest.

"What are you looking for?" Finn asked.

"Nothing specific, I assure you. These are simply routine satellite feeds," Lester said. "I keep the system on around the clock." He spoke nervously as he moved about the room, cutting the power to other text-based screens. "Opening the door takes it out of standby mode, and I neglected to power it down when I was down here a short while ago. An old man's nerves, I daresay," he said, chuckling.

Finn raised his brows, aware that Lester's fussing was covering more than the man's idle chatter. Two of the cameras in the far corners of the room had been switched on, trained on the space in front of the glass. "You have the list here?" Finn asked, noting the elevator again. The indicator light gleamed behind the number 2. Someone was coming up.

"Of course, of course," Lester said, not denying that the document Finn had come for was a list. Still, his gaze was hyperfocused, and Finn tensed, his body settling into combat mode. He'd been told that Lester would be expecting him with open arms, but the human was nervous. On edge. And Finn knew mortals too well not to know what those signs meant.

"What's wrong, Lester?" he asked, keeping his voice casual. "What is it you need to tell me?"

Lester's face fell, his fingers curling around the remote. "I trust you implicitly, but I alone have been blessed with contact. None of the other members of the society has," he said. "First, the vision before solstice…now this. I cannot apologize enough, but our caution is part of the protocols established when our organization was founded. We simply must be sure."

Finn covered his surprise, balancing on the balls of his feet. What vision—what society? Something else the archangel had not warned him about. He was beginning to wonder how much he knew about Lester after all.

Lester flinched as if he'd been slapped as the elevator door swished open, and Finn turned to the sound of a half-dozen men pounding into the room— running straight at him, weapons drawn.

Finn read the attackers instantly. All six were human, which made things complicated. They were young, fit, almost too eager, with the air of men pent up too long waiting for a reason to fight. Four of them barreled straight for him; two more hung back with impressive armfuls of guns. To Finn, the men moved as if in slow motion, which made his job both easier and more difficult—easier to dispatch them, more difficult to keep from hurting them.

He connected with the first pair of attackers and lifted one by the force of his return blows, slinging him into the other man. The flanking pair ran into each other as he stepped forward, and they spun around, anger shimmering in their auras. His speed had surprised them, their eyes unable to track his movements, and he delivered a series of jabs before they could regroup. The crunch of bones grated on his nerves as he connected with his targets, but the exertion brought a refreshing rush to his senses.

The four assailants scrabbled back, resetting their positions. Two of the men seemed more muscular, brute-force men — typical bodyguards. But the others were leaner, though well muscled, light enough on their feet to demonstrate that they were versed in martial arts. And the men with the guns were lighter still, untested, fresh recruits not quite yet up to the task of hand-to-hand combat.

Finn braced himself as the men regrouped and raced toward him. *A test of my speed and strength, then,* he thought. *To prove I am something more than human.*

He grinned. *Fair enough.*

Two of the men circled behind him, and he allowed them to set up their position at his back. He crouched and turned as the first man leapt, punching the man sharply in the abdomen. He was careful not to break any ribs, but it was a close thing. The second man, he dispatched with a swift punch to the jaw. Then he launched himself past them to one of the gunmen, reaching forward to twist the rifle out of the man's hands.

The gunner didn't have martial arts knowledge and tried to resist, the sound of his breaking wrist causing Finn to wince. He yanked the gun up and back, pointing it away from the men, and unloaded a round into the far wall. Then he slapped it down into position again. He didn't know this weapon, but firing it was easier than it looked. He caught sight of the man to his right lunging forward, and thrust his foot out to the side with a sharp crack, taking the man down as he twisted and pinned the final gunner in the face with his rifle. Undaunted, the gunman maintained his position, aiming at a point two centimeters above Finn's nose. He didn't know that Finn could beat the bullet. He only believed that he — for the moment — had the upper hand.

But no arrogance flowed through his surprisingly bright aura. No fear. Just a calm certainty of success. Odd, for so young a man. Odd, and interesting.

"I'm not exactly sure how to use this weapon," Finn said. "But I think at this range, you don't want me to practice on you."

The kid facing him — and he was little more than a boy, maybe eighteen at best — narrowed his clear blue eyes as the first sparks of indignation surfaced within them. His aura shifted and suddenly became even brighter, clearer. It was almost as bright as Dana's had been in the heat of the street battle. Finn had thought then that it was merely the result of the adrenaline jacking through a mortal, but the other soldiers' auras were nowhere near this bright. He frowned, allowing his sensory net to expand. It crept forward, threading through the thoughts of the men on the ground, then pushed against an unexpected barrier. Almost as if —

"Drop the weapon, Timothy," Lester said sharply, cutting through his focus. "The rest of you, stand down."

Without hesitation, the young man named Timothy lowered his gun and assumed a ready stance, and only then did the others rise silently. They stood in formation, professionally stone-faced, awaiting Lester's command. Finn stepped back as well, straightening the sleeves of his dinner jacket before assessing their injuries.

A broken wrist. Damaged ribs. A quadriceps muscle

so deeply bruised that the reality of the hit wasn't even going to strike the man for another six hours. Finn could heal them, but he wouldn't put it past Lester to set the men on him again. And he had no patience for another test.

"We've spent eight hundred years in hiding," Lester said quietly beside him. "You must understand."

Finn turned to appraise Lester. He was no longer apologetic, he was relieved. And even more excited than before. *Hiding from what?*

Finn held up the assault rifle. "How do I use this?"

"Timothy," Lester said curtly. The second gunman strode forward, his mind remaining closed to Finn's touch. In quiet, succinct tones, he explained the operation of the rifle he referred to as an XM8-hybrid.

"These never made it into production," Lester commented after Timothy went through the firing process of the rifle without actually shooting it. There was a new inflection in Lester's voice, a hardness that Finn had missed before. *That was new,* he thought, Lester's persona slipping as his own excitement ratcheted up. "They were considered too hot, too untested. Politically unfeasible. But we were able to improve upon the prototype behind the scenes. We're pleased with the results." He looked up, surveying the damage to the far wall, and nodded.

Finn let his gaze linger on the man. The archangel would not be pleased to know that humans believed they could test the Fallen…or demons, for that matter. He wondered idly if he would include that in his report. A part of him appreciated the initiative Lester and his recruits were taking…a part of him recognized the danger of it.

"Go," Lester said as Timothy finished his

explanation and stepped back. The boy didn't ask for the gun back, and Finn didn't offer it. The room cleared almost as quickly as it had filled, and Finn stared hard at the blood on the floor. He'd connected with mortal flesh, breaking bones, opening skin. It was not why he'd come here.

Lester held up the remote again and pressed another button, and the entire wall of glass moved, allowing Finn full access to the computer consoles. There was a small conference table in front of the machines, a few heavy books stacked upon it. Lester pulled a chair out from the table, looking up when Finn didn't move.

"I wish we had more time," Lester said, pressing his fingers into the soft ebony leather of the chair.

Finn scowled at him, his nerves firing. There was too much going on here that he didn't understand. Danger hung behind every blinking light, with every nervous twitch of Lester's fingers. "How much time do you need to hand me a list of information?"

Lester took a deep breath and shook his head. He bowed slightly to Finn. "I'm afraid I've angered you," he said quietly. "And that was never my intention. Truly, we are blessed by your visitation. We stand ready to serve as God's right arm, exactly as you instructed."

Finn stiffened. "What were you told of me, and when?"

"It was a week—ten days ago. A dream. The most glorious dream you could ever imagine, telling me to send my emissary on solstice night to claim a special gift, and meanwhile, to make ready our most precious truth," Lester said, and his face lit up at the memory. "And then that night, after Dana confirmed she was on her way with the artifact without issue, I received another vision—that an angel of the Lord would come

136

to see all that we had prepared."

Solstice, Finn thought. Right. The veil was so very thin on solstice night, there would be no better time to impress such images upon a mortal. And Finn had been in Canada, saving Dana from possessed dire wolves…something that had been conveniently omitted from Lester's second vision. So someone else had been jerking Lester's chain—had to be Bartholomew.

"I was told that you would come for our soldiers," Lester continued, rapt. "That the fight for humanity's survival may finally be joined."

Finn blew out a long breath. "Soldiers," he said. Only Finn had beaten Bartholomew at his own game and gotten here first.

"We have been waiting so long for you." Lester repeated, the words some sort of mantra or prayer. His fingers gripped the chair again, digging into the expensive leather. "We will support you. But there are many who would try to kill you, if they knew who and what you were. I can tell you everything you need to know." Lester gestured to the chair beside him. "The army of God is yours to command."

This time, Finn sat with him, more heavily than he'd intended. Lester had assembled an army of God? To, what, fight the demons that'd recently come through the veil? They'd mobilized that quickly?

No. That was impossible.

"An army to fight who?" Finn asked.

Lester shrugged, his eyes drifting toward the computer consoles. "There are always those who believe that man should not aspire to God's service. They seek to destroy all that we have done, the lives that we have saved. Generations change, but still they come."

"And the men who attacked you and Dana eight weeks ago?"

Lester shook his head. "Despite what Dana said, I don't think they were a part of this. They never got the chance to explain what they wanted," he said with a wry smile. "But Dana proved her worth that night a hundredfold." His eyes shifted to Finn, then away again. "Did she, ah, tell you about it?"

"She told me enough. Four men in a parking garage. She was shot, the bullet shattering bone — "

Lester sat up sharply. "She *knew* her tibia was broken? How? What did she say specifically?" he demanded. Clearly, Lester hadn't given Dana an accurate rundown of her injuries — and she'd trusted her uncle enough not to question him. Finn schooled his features into ambivalence, suppressing emotions he wasn't used to feeling. Rage. Possession. The urge to defend.

"No. I could tell it, though, from touching her."

Lester seemed to accept this, and Finn pressed on. "There's no way she didn't realize how messed up she was, though, at least on some level. There were doctors, nurses, around her. Not to mention her own family..." Finn narrowed his eyes. "You paid them off. All of them. To lie to her about the fact that her bone had shattered. That's completely insane." And borderline criminal, he suspected. But mostly insane.

Lester sat back in his chair. "She'd never been badly injured before. It was the only opportunity we could test her healing process, and we didn't want her to know the extent of her injuries, for fear her mind might stall her recovery." He shook his head in wonder. "She surpassed all our expectations. She has come back stronger, with no trauma, no side effects. We even cut her painkillers during her rehabilitation, unknown to her. She barely even flinched."

And in that moment, Finn knew, even if he couldn't read the old man's mind. Lester's attitude toward Dana, his treatment of her and his disdain, were not the hallmarks of the close family bond that Lester affected. How many lies had he woven, and for how long? "She's not your niece," Finn said.

"She's so much *more* than my niece." Lester's face grew fierce. "She is destined to lead her people against our enemies. To fight the ultimate battle. And we, in turn, must protect those warriors," he said, waving to the screens which were skimming metropolitan centers. "We are their guardians who never sleep — their guides who are constantly seeking more of their brethren." At these words, his tone dipped into outrage. "The human populace is growing, but the numbers of these special souls are ever decreasing," he said. "It has grown more difficult to find them, not less so, with the passage of time."

Finn nodded, at last realizing what it was that he had come here for. What it was that the rogue Fallen wanted. What Michael the Archangel wanted as well. A list, yes. But a list of *people*. People who weren't Connected, apparently, but who were — better, somehow. Stronger, faster, able to heal more quickly, able to lead.

But so what? There were plenty of Connecteds roaming the earth already, and many of them had impressive skills all their own. What made this list so important?

He nudged Lester along. "So you've gathered their names for me, for — "

"For you and for God," Lester said. "Your children

will be ready."

Finn stopped, glanced back at him. *Children?* "Ah...they will?"

"Oh yes. The children of the first angels of the Lord to walk the earth, the lost that we have found," he said, totally missing how Finn's eyes popped wide.

"Children," he managed to respond, barely able to keep his voice steady as agony streaked through his skull, hammering at his brain. There was something here, something important, but he could barely draw breath to speak. "Of...angels."

Lester nodded, clearly relishing his role as teacher. He leaned toward the console, completely missing how Finn gripped the handles of his chair, struggling not to pass out from the pain that assaulted him from every side. "From the very beginning, thousands of years ago, there were some of your progeny who were more...special. More blessed than their peers. Though all the offspring of the Nephilim were strong, in each generation, there were one or two children blessed more fully with the gifts of his or her angelic forebears. They were stronger, taller, more sensitive, more discerning. Properly cared for, they became the geniuses or great athletes or fearsome warriors of their time. We—the Society of Orion—always knew your children walked among us. But humanity lost its way." Lester reached out to pull a gold-leafed book toward him. It wasn't a Bible after all, but an illuminated history text. "They were so special, you see. And in the darkest age of our world, special was not to be borne. But there *were* those of us who believed, who helped when no one else would help, even when our beliefs should have destroyed us. See?"

He opened up the history text to a violently

illuminated scene. The Sack of Rome, where the brightly clad Swiss Guard were overwhelmed by mercenaries. In the background, clearly distinguishable, was a man surrounded by a soft golden light, helping a veiled woman and a flock of children escape into a dark passage. Finn's throat closed at the engraved image, but before he could focus, Lester was shifting pages, thumbing backward in time through scores of illuminated panels. He pointed next to a picture of Joan of Arc, painted again with the mysterious glow that separated her from all who surrounded her. And then a picture of King Arthur's court, where some of the assembly were surrounded with gold halos, while others were not. The king himself was notably absent from the painting, but Lester didn't rest upon that scene. He quickly fanned through page after page of illuminated history.

"What is this book?" Finn asked, his mind frozen on the page representing the 1527 massacre at the Holy See. The shock of what he was seeing finally pierced his own thundering pain. There'd been so much death that day in Rome. So much desecration.

And Bartholomew had seen it. Bartholomew, who was now hunting for Lester and his list.

"Our history," Lester said. "When the Society of Orion was founded in 1223, we commissioned painters and historians immediately. There was already so much we had lost," Lester's fingers moved reverently along the heavy page, tracing the outside edge of its picture. "But we vowed to create a visual library to showcase the best that humanity had to offer."

He offered Finn a weary smile. "Orion was founded so that God might see our service to the children of his angels and forgive us when the final judgment came. Or, should he not be stirred from his wrath, that we might have our own protectors for the end times. Leader to leader, man to man, we have kept our pledge to protect the most sacred information of all." He reached under his collar and brought out a key on a long, well-worn chain. The artifact that had been protecting Lester from having his thoughts read, Finn realized in a flash.

"I was tapped to lead Orion at age thirty-five." He chuckled softly, gazing at the key. "The youngest leader ever, even since its founding at the dawn of the Inquisition. Before Orion came into being, the list had been kept by a small network of individuals unconnected but for their common knowledge of the children, unknown to their enemies."

He shook his head, then tucked the key away once more. "We have watched and we have prepared, and we have guarded the list, the location of each of these special souls in each new generation carefully preserved so that the Dawn Children could protect us from God's wrath. For what father would destroy the children of his own angels? And here you have come," he said, gazing again at Finn. "And we will give this list to you, in time, with all their identities, all their locations. So that together, we might save the world."

Finn shut his eyes against another flare of pain at the phrase "Dawn Children." But he couldn't focus on his own reactions anymore. He didn't know why Michael wanted this list, exactly, but he had a good idea of why Bartholomew did. Dana had stood firm against her demon and Possessed attackers, not only with Finn, but when she was protecting Lester. She'd taken down those demons too. Something no human should be able to do. Dana — and those like her — apparently *could* fight in a war against the demon horde. And if Bartholomew was intending to lead that horde into battle, the descendants of the Fallen were the only humans who could stop him. For all that they had no idea what they were.

Bartholomew wasn't looking for the list to exalt these children. He was looking for a murder map. And Dana was at its center.

"Those men you set upon me," Finn said stonily. "Not all of them were…"

"Dawn Children? No." Lester's face flushed. "Only Timothy Rourke. You remember him, I think."

Finn nodded. "The boy with the bright aura."

"One of our greatest achievements, besides Dana. A Dawn Child nurtured since birth to excel in the trade of warfare, trained on every type of urban assault weapon we could procure. Timothy is part of my private security detail, the most aggressive use of a Dawn Child the council had ever sanctioned after I'd positioned Dana to serve as my official security advisor. But with the boy…we could go further. Do more."

Finn didn't love the sound of that, but he kept his expression steady. "More how?"

"He learned so fast! Followed complex orders, thought strategically, and he always wanted to push the envelope. To attack, to drive, to kill, if I asked it of him." He swung his gaze to Finn. "Your army will be well trained. You'll see. God will see."

Finn could read the rest in the man's eyes. At the bidding of their keepers, the Dawn Children would be tasked with making Holy War. And Lester would be their leader.

"And how did you track down these, um, children, exactly?"

Lester leaned forward eagerly. "Bloodlines." He

pulled another book forward, this one equally old, and covered in a rich, dark leather that had aged to the sheen of fine wine. Opening it, he pushed it toward Finn, watching him eagerly as Finn scanned the lists of names, lines of genealogy arcing out, page after page. Some stopped, abruptly, others continued, and others were annotated as false starts. The names spanned countries, continents. Centuries. "We knew they existed, of course. They were gods and goddesses to the ancients. And we've never stopped searching for them." He paused, watching Finn closely as he quoted from Genesis. "'The Nephilim walked the earth in those days—and also afterward—when the sons of God went to the daughters of men and had children by them. They were the champions of old, men of renown,'" he said, then offered a quiet smile. "All we had to do was look for the heroes."

"And you found them."

Lester nodded. "There was so much death, at the beginning in particular. I shudder to think how many Dawn Children were killed before anyone even began keeping a census, and we will never know the full scope of our loss." His eyes drifted up toward Finn's, unable to hide his own censure. "They had so little chance of survival, despite their gifts," he whispered. "You had to be aware that humans were woefully unprepared for the grace of heaven's touch."

Finn grimaced. There was no way he could respond to that. "Yet you protected them—and the list."

"We have kept it safe for centuries. First on scrolls, then parchment, then paper." He gestured at the room surrounding them, bristling with machinery. "Now we have even better means of preserving it." He paused. "Even as it grows shorter, despite our best efforts to preserve the lines."

"How many are left?"

"Fifteen hundred," Lester said. "Fifteen hundred Children to save the world."

"You're in touch with all these families?"

Lester waved a weary hand. "It was never as easy as that, I'm afraid. We live in an enlightened age, where beliefs in the supernatural, of man's connection with the Spirit, are better accepted. But over the millennia, the knowledge that you — and your child — and your mother or father, or, when we are blessed, both — were descended from *actual angels* was not always an easy passage. We tracked the Children without their knowledge. For many years, that was enough. We helped to arrange marriages, matching them to other Children to ensure the purity of the line. Those whose lines were the most direct were taken without their knowledge from their own parents and fostered with members of our organization to ensure they grew up under the careful watch of Orion. They were kept healthy, directed, and ready to serve."

"You kidnapped them," Finn said as Lester cued the screens again.

"The end times are drawing near," the old man said firmly, and the screens filled again with images of the population centers of the world, followed by vast vistas of oceans, prairies, deserts. Then again, the stone monoliths of Stonehenge, the pyramid of Giza, the Mayan ball courts. "There have been many false hopes, but they are coming all the same."

Explosions filled the screens, illustrations of Armageddon, shattering stars, meteor showers, the great rivers and oceans of the world overflowing their banks as the world heated up. Maps were redrawn as cities submerged and ice caps melted. In different parts of the world, other landmasses formed, new territories for humans to conquer. Finn stared, transfixed.

Lester practically quivered with excitement. "These images represent the sum total of every Armageddon myth or speculation known to man. And visions beyond extraordinary, culled from the greatest minds on the planet." He chuckled. "Unsurprisingly, many of those visionaries are Dawn Children themselves, and they are completely unaware of it. It is incredible what we can see, what we can predict, what we know — or suspect." Lester shook his head. "'You do not know the date nor the hour,' it was claimed, and yet, we know both, somehow. Or, I should say, we know many, many possibilities. Some grim, some glorious. But as I said, all of them are coming."

"Yes," Finn said, his tone low, serious.

Lester turned quickly, beaming at him. "How long I have waited for those words, that confirmation," he said. "And the timing — well, there are many possibilities there as well. When the long-burning fuse of humanity finally reaches its end, our fifteen hundred Children stand to defend us from God's wrath. They are His own, after all. Protected, preserved, and made ready again for His love. And if He is unmoved, then they will be humanity's greatest warriors in the battles to come."

Finn glanced back to see Lester's eyes shining with conviction. "So how is it you came here?"

"To this workaday Midwestern city, far away from everything?" Lester asked with a grin. He leaned forward conspiratorially. "For the exact reason you ask. No one would look for the saviors of the world in Cleveland, Ohio. We have learned well the lessons of our forerunners. We are not proud. We draw no attention to ourselves. We hide, we wait, and we prepare." He exhaled with genuine pleasure. "And at last, you are here. I will share that information with my fellow society leaders and, with their blessing, give you your list."

Finn scowled. "I need the list now, Lester."

"And you shall get it," Lester assured him. "But we must be careful, always vigilant. We must protect the Children. First, there will be a short list I can provide you, then the full list before the clock strikes midnight. I know! I know the importance of the day. But the day is come, and you are here. We are ready at last. Everything is perfect."

"Yes, perfect," Finn said grimly, then he drew in a long breath. "In the meantime, tell me — show me everything."

CHAPTER THIRTEEN

Exeter Global Services
Cleveland, Ohio
9:15 a.m., Dec. 24

Dana's mouth felt like she'd eaten her own gym clothes and chased them down with a stiff shot of last season's running shoes. Her head throbbed, her body was stiff and unnaturally cool, and she could tell her heart rate was a few beats shy of full working order. Still, she was extraordinarily happy to be alive.

Much easier to kill her uncle that way.

She lay there a moment more without opening her eyes, in case Lester's cameras were trained on her. She was almost certain she was still in the Exeter gallery. It smelled the same, anyway, and the couch she was lying on was covered in identical soft, buttery upholstery. The room was dead silent, however — not the kind of silence that hinted at people watching you, waiting for you to twitch…but the silence of being ignored. Abandoned. Like you weren't worth watching in the first place.

Screw. That.

Slowly, carefully, Dana slitted open one eye. A quick sweep of the room indicated that Finn and Lester were no longer in it, but she didn't know where they'd gone or how long ago they'd left. The gallery's state-of-the-art directional lamps were blazing, but the light streaming through the tall windows indicated that it was well past sunrise. She flicked a glance to her watch. Almost 9:30 a.m. Aces. She'd been out for over four hours.

She tested her muscles, stretching out her body bit by bit. Everything seemed intact, and she felt remarkably good. Completely refreshed, actually. So, fine. She'd needed the rest.

Lester still had no right to drug her.

A sound from the middle of the room riveted her attention on the large painting of the Madonna, two baby boys, and a gentle-looking angel, seated in an idyllic rock-strewn setting. She scanned the picture for a moment, then her eyes shifted to the blinking keypad next to it. That particular security panel was keyed to a room-specific system and had been installed by Lester's private team after he'd brought more of his treasures together for safekeeping. Long used to her uncle's predilections for layers upon layers of security, Dana had never given the panel a second thought after Lester had explained its presence. But as she stared at it now, it shifted from red to green, and the painting swung open, clearly some sort of door.

Dana clamped her eyes shut right after Lester's polished ox-blood cordovans stepped into the room. She could convince her uncle that she was asleep, no question. But if Finn remained with him, she probably was in trouble. The man seemed to know every time her blood pressure changed.

"She'll be waking soon," Finn said, and Dana felt the telltale kick to her pulse. He knew she was awake, and he was letting her know he knew it. *Dammit.* She wanted them to keep talking. "How much of this information does she know?" he went on, and her heart did a slow flip. Finn was continuing the conversation for her benefit, and she had no idea why. Maybe he didn't appreciate Lester drugging her either.

"She knows nothing," Lester replied, his words low and dismissive. "And it'll stay that way. She tends to take threats to me very…personally." His tone softened at the end, and Dana could almost picture him smiling, that kind, gentle expression that had drawn so much business his way throughout the world. *Bastard.* "She can't interfere with my work at this point."

Breathing was such a strange thing, Dana thought, her mind racing to understand Lester's words. You paid no attention to it at all ninety-nine percent of the time. But the one time you needed to disappear into your own breath, it seemed to ring in your ears, scrape in your lungs, announce with a loud and rolling exhale that you were there.

"You must know that you have enemies, Mr. Morrow," Finn said. "What if they reach her after I leave?"

Enemies? Breathe in, breathe out. Finn had told her that Lester would be safe. What other enemies could her uncle have? Besides her, anyway?

Max's text messages came back to Dana in a rush. The security breach, Max's suspicions that someone at Exeter had been moving files. Lester's comments about his work and concerns over interference. Silently, Dana tried to redraw a picture of her uncle to fit with this new information, but her mind summarily rejected the effort. Something here was very, very wrong.

"Dana proved her skills to me eight weeks ago," Lester continued, pride surfacing in his voice. "She can take care of herself should the need become great. She is one of the purest Children."

Thanks, pal, Dana thought, schooling her features into placid slumber. But Lester was speaking again.

"I'll be back shortly, to escort you out," he said. "My day shift of personal security has arrived, and I don't think it would be wise—"

"I'll remain here," Finn said, cutting Lester off. The sound of footsteps over plush carpet approached Dana, then moved past her, as if she was one of Lester's trinkets left on a shelf. There was more murmured conversation, then a door opening and shutting. *Okay, then.* She needed to plan her next action, and that had to be centered on her getting back to her own office. Max would have a report for her by now. On the security breach. On Finn. On Bartholomew too, if she was lucky. But she had to lie quietly for a few more minutes. They both might have left, of course, but she wasn't taking any—

"He's gone," Finn said.

Dana opened her eyes and glared up at him as he stood a few feet away from her, his expression wary, as well it should be.

"Thanks for the news flash." She swung her feet around and sat up sharply, gritting her teeth against a sudden pop of pain in her head. "So he doesn't want anyone seeing you, huh? You planning on committing a crime I should know about?" She found her phone next to her on the couch and thumbed it awake. Instantly, it buzzed in annoyance. No doubt Max had been trying to reach her. Too bad he hadn't come up and pounded on the door.

"He's trying to watch us."

Dana's adrenaline jacked again as Finn sat beside her, his body far too close to hers on the leather couch. Before she could move away, he placed a hand on her leg.

Dana's eyes practically crossed at the contact, and her hand went limp. The phone fell to the plush carpet with a gentle thump.

Dear. Holy. God. She no longer needed Finn to dull the pain in her leg, so the force of his touch skittered into her nervous system with nowhere to go and nothing to do but apparently stimulate her adrenaline and endorphin centers. In one split second, she'd become a live wire of sensation, focusing on the heaviness of his hand on her leg.

"He is?" she managed, all too aware of the security cameras whirring in the corners of the room. "Why?"

"We don't have much time," Finn said quietly as Dana kept her head down, struggling for breath. "I've disabled the cameras, but he'll become aware of the transmission error in a few short minutes and return immediately. So listen to me. I had believed your...uncle's enemies would abandon him once the document is delivered. I no longer think that. If it is Bartholomew who is after you, he will want to be sure no one else ever learns what's in that document. And if he knows what you are, you won't be safe. What we need to do—"

"Hold on there, Sparky." Dana's head came up, all her senses fully back online. "Why won't I be safe? What's going on with you and Lester? Tell me. Now."

A flash of irritation darkened Finn's beautiful face,

but there was resignation there too. If she hadn't just been drugged by her own uncle, Dana would have laughed. On a need-to-know basis, she pretty much always needed to know, and Finn apparently had finally figured that out. She always had asked way too many questions, but it'd never slowed her down in the end.

It wouldn't today either. "Sorry. If you're in a hurry, the fastest way to get me on board is to spill everything."

"We don't have—"

"We've got thirty seconds. Go."

With a move so fast she couldn't process it, Finn reached out and grabbed Dana's hands, once more flooding her with a jolt of what had to be pure electricity. It wasn't an entirely relaxing experience. "You feel this?" he demanded. "The circuit of power?"

"Yeah, Taser Hands, I do," she gritted out. She pulled back, but he didn't let go.

"You shouldn't. The fact that you do makes you different from most humans, who would only feel the barest spark unless I forced the matter. Your circuits are wide open."

"Why?" Dana didn't think she was going to like the answer to that question.

She was right.

"The short version? You're a descendent of humans and Fallen angels. Yes, that was a thing," he said, cutting off her protest. "It's part of most religious mythology, up to and including Judeo-Christian teachings, which you very well know. What you don't know is that while most descendants of those pairings were better than average, some were significantly above average." He shook her hands. "You would be an example of that. Whenever you felt like you didn't belong, like you were different, whether that was a good or bad thing at the time—well, you were. You are. When you fully access your power, nothing can stop you. For artists, it's called being in the flow. For great strategists, it's winning whatever battle you set for yourself. For leaders, it's rallying the world to your side. For teachers, it's shining a light where before there was only darkness. For you, it's that time a thousand. You shouldn't wonder why you drifted into a security role, Dana. It's exactly where you should be...only there's an entire world out there for you to protect."

"I don't—you're wrong. I've never been that special," Dana whispered, blinking rapidly. She hadn't been either. "I would've noticed."

"You may not have, but others did. Up to and including your uncle. Who should have told you a long time ago."

She stared at him. "And my mother?"

"Ahh—probably not, actually. But neither of you should beat yourselves up too much for not figuring it out on your own. Funny thing about humans, they tend to believe the worst in themselves and those closest to them, not the best." His lips twisted. "Probably kept most of your kind alive."

"There're more out there like me?" Dana jerked a little straighter as she suddenly made the connection. "Of course there're more. That's why you're here. That's what's in the document, isn't it? These other people. And me too."

Finn grimaced. "Give the lady a prize," he said, echoing her own words from last night. "We can discuss the rest later, but right now, we've got something more important to fix." He drew a deep breath, as if fighting his own battle with what he had to say. "You have abilities that I can show you how to access, to help protect yourself—and others too. But you must ask me to show you." He leaned forward, and though his grip on her hands loosened, she somehow felt more transfixed by the look in his eyes, the gentler touch of his hands on her skin. Her heart started racing, and her skin heated up down to her toes. "That's kind of how it works between, um, what I am and what you are," Finn continued. "You have to ask."

Dana blinked at him through a haze of something that felt an awful lot like desire, but with an urgency to it that made it seem closer to fear. She cleared her throat. *I have to ask?* That shouldn't turn her on as much as it did. She should be focusing on her own safety, her seriously twisted family tree, the abilities Finn seemed to think she had...or maybe the whole Ancient Aliens vibe of having a great-grandsomething who had wings. Like that shouldn't be super creepy or anything.

It wasn't, somehow. But it should be.

She cleared her throat, trying to focus. "Fine. But we can deal with any threats to me tomorrow. Right now, I need to know more about this list."

"No, you don't, dammit. Listen to me." Moving too quickly for Dana to track, Finn tightened his hold again and pushed her back into the cushions of the couch until she was pressed hard against the soft, expensive leather. An entire constellation of stars seemed to burst inside her at his renewed contact, the twisting roil of her nerves practically vibrating with energy. Finn might not be her kind, exactly, but there was no question they were supposed to fit together, the sum of the two of them far greater than their separate parts.

Finn continued, anger rife in his voice as he leaned over her, reclaiming her focus. "Just because you don't understand the danger building against you doesn't mean it isn't there. You have enemies out there who are *not* normal humans. You think you can protect yourself from me? Even if you wanted to?"

He paused, suddenly reassessing where he was, where she was. He'd stretched her out again on the long couch, and now his body half covered hers, their combined weight sinking into the luxurious cushions. His face flushed with his attempt to control his own emotions, and he pulled himself back, letting her go, but his point had been made. "And especially if you didn't."

Dana sucked in a shallow breath, shivering uncontrollably. "Stay off me," she said, as sternly as she could manage, even as her body cried out for more contact, not less. She was swimming in an open electrical current, craving the pain and pleasure of this full-on connection. And at the very edge of her consciousness, the desire to reach for more beckoned, teasing her with the memory of its seductive power.

No — Yes. No. Her mind hung on to the tiniest thread of coherence, and that thread pounded with fear. Finn's body against hers wasn't like any other man's she'd ever felt. It wasn't just that he was big or solid. She'd known her share of strong men. She'd felt the weight of their bodies and the heat of their desire. But this was different. This was power and possibility, outrage, and need, and pure, unadulterated energy, so strong it threatened to consume her.

And she wanted it. Badly. *Yes.*

Finn reeled back as Dana had asked, but he knew that what he had to give couldn't wait.

"I can make you stronger yet, Dana," he said,

knowing his words sounded hopelessly archaic, but unable to explain more clearly while the panic surged within him. Dana needed the grace, the power that he could give her as a Fallen, and she needed it now. As the daughter of the angels who had walked the earth more than six thousand years ago, she'd be open to that grace in a way few humans would be.

But she had to ask for it. Despite his show of aggression, he couldn't force it upon her.

"You're special, Dana. You have a strength within you that can help you survive, succeed, achieve feats you can barely imagine, and protect yourself — above all, you *can* protect yourself. But you have to know how to trigger this strength. And you have to be able to trigger it in others too. Do you understand?"

"Not even remotely," she said tightly, glaring at him. Still, there was no denying the shift in her energy. She believed him, or she believed him enough, and she totally accepted his explanations, exactly the way she'd said she would. The answers he'd given her would hold for the moment, and that was all he could ask. "But okay. Do it. Do whatever it is you're saying you can do."

Finn swallowed, his own heart banging loud enough to be heard across the veil. He'd never touched a human with the intention of triggering their gifts before, but somehow, he knew what to do.

"You're sure?" he managed, struggling to refocus.

"Jesus! Yes," Dana snapped, her own face awash in desire and fear. "Get it over with already."

Finn shifted, moving closer to her, and Dana didn't shrink away. He felt his own body surge in reaction, but his jaw was clenched, his breath coming fast. "Pain can serve as a trigger," he said. "So can danger. So will outrage, if it's strong enough. Any extremity of emotion can place you in a position to reach into yourself and grab hold of this power that is yours by birth, a place of stillness beyond the storm." He leaned closer, and Dana hissed a short warning breath. "But first," he whispered into her ear, his lips grazing the soft, tender skin as she choked out a breath, "you have to endure the storm."

He shifted, dropping his head to her mouth to kiss her hard, the movement causing Dana to arch upward off the couch and into his body. A wave of heat billowed toward him, and he lifted his head again to meet her wild, crazed eyes, her lips parted from his kiss.

"Reach for it, Dana," he whispered. "You can. You must."

"What are you doing?" she gasped, but he only laughed low in his throat, the sound cruel, defiant even to his own ears.

"It's there, isn't it?" he purred, leaning down to nuzzle the side of her face, trailing a delicate path of kisses along her jaw, teasing the thin gold hoops at her earlobes. She shuddered beneath him again, her sigh turning into a low moan. "You feel it coming over you, a pressure, a storm of color and sensation. It makes you strong, Dana. It makes you who you are. It's a power that is yours to claim for your own."

"You mean lust?" Dana shot back, her words devolving into a groan. "Because that's pretty much—"

"Not lust. Not exactly." He met her gaze again, desperate for her to understand, no matter how hard she kept pushing back. "You have to surrender to it, Dana. Let it happen." There was so much power available to her, so much strength. If he could just get her to reach for it—

Suddenly, she did. She blinked, then stared at him wide-eyed, her gaze filled with awareness and power and something else, something he didn't recognize, that called out to him with an agony that caught him completely off guard—

Hope.

Wait, what? *Hope?*

In a flash of awareness that blasted across his circuits, Finn's own memory was flayed open, revealing images he was sure he'd never seen before and yet…they seemed vaguely familiar. Earth, spinning and twirling beneath him, nothing but streams of endlessly beautiful light, a glorious tapestry of millions of souls whose emotions were a mash-up of joy and pain and sorrow and fear and doubt and exhilaration—and one emotion no angel could ever understand, could ever feel. Because they had no need to feel it, for all that they could recognize it shining forth from the children of God in an endless fire.

Hope.

He gritted his teeth against the agony that pounded through him, trying to focus on Dana as the image winked out as quickly as it'd come, leaving nothing but pain. But it wasn't fully gone—he could almost remember. Remember! At least that one small fragment. Somehow, Dana had unlocked it within him, had shown him the path. She was even more of a key to his redemption than he realized…one he had to learn how to use in less than fifteen hours, before he lost her forever.

But Dana was shaking her head again, the tenuous hold she had on her belief already fraying. "I don't—" she said one last time, and true pain fried along Finn's circuits, frustration boiling through him. He had no choice if she said no…no choice!

Then she leaned forward and kissed him.

In a flash, Finn pulled her to him as if he was sealing both their fates, devouring her, claiming her, his body fusing with hers even through their clothes in a firestorm of heat that battered and swept him along, overflowing his senses. He poured into Dana the energy he knew would galvanize her power, setting her skin, her hair and eyes, bones and muscle, blood and marrow alive with heat and vitality — and, it couldn't be helped, a mindless, yearning, unending desire.

He drew back from her abruptly, and still she blazed. She stared at him, and he had no idea what she was seeing, but from the wide-eyed shock of her expression, he could only imagine.

"My God," she gasped. "What *are* you?" She reached out to him, and Finn pulled back farther, the light jumping between them taking on a raw, needy edge.

He held her out stiffly from him. "You can see me as a Fallen," he said. His mouth quirked. "Trust me, if you saw me in my other guises, it wouldn't be as pretty."

She blinked at him. "Your other —"

"We'll cover that later. What's important is that you can see yourself too. How you've changed. Look at your hands, your legs. Your body. Claim your reality. You don't have much time before they return."

He swung off her, backing away a few steps, and Dana raised her own shaking fingers to her eyes.

Finn knew what she was seeing. Her hands glowed with fire. Not a wasting flame, but white, healing, which he knew would fill her with a strength and purpose beyond anything she would have imagined possible. She looked up, and once again, she seemed to flinch.

"You're glowing too," she whispered.

"All part of the package." He gestured, and only

160

then did she look around the room. The illumination jumped and flashed from many of Lester's collected objets d'art—the relics, the vases, the statuary, the scrolls and parchments and bits of bone and blood held fast in golden cases. So many of them glowed, the room seemed to light up as if the stars of heaven had been caught and held in place.

"What is this?" she breathed.

"Your birthright." Finn held up the ancient gold cuff he'd taken from Lester's collection, covered in glyphs and stylized drawings. "You see the glow?" he asked, and she nodded, transfixed. "That glow shows you all that you are related to as the daughter of a long-ago Nephilim, Light Walker, Watcher, Crosser...so many names, but all the same thing."

"A Fallen," she said, clearly trying to wrap her head around the idea.

He nodded, watching her, waiting for her gaze to return to his. "If you're in your power, the glow you see will also show you what to fear."

His words seemed to shake her, and the glow dipped a little, ratcheting back. She looked bereft. "It's weakening," she said, and he nodded, lifting the bracelet higher.

"Focus on the cuff. It's the strongest item in this room due to its purpose and the fact that I'm holding it. You should be able to get a sense of its power, even as your connection to me fades." He tossed the bracelet toward her, and she caught it, the heat obviously searing her fingers so abruptly, she almost dropped it. "But the strength that is your birthright will never fully leave you, Dana. Not anymore. And now that you know it's within you, you can call it up yourself. However, if you wear that bracelet, your mind and your thoughts will stay your own." He quirked a smile. "Even from me."

She blinked, then stared down at the golden cuff in her hands and nodded. As her breath slowed and she steadied herself, the cuff appeared sharper, clearer than anything else in the room, even to Finn's eyes. As if it was in heavy focus, everything else dimming around it.

"You'll notice this about people who are — like you," Finn said. "And those like me, as well." He looked at her hard. "But in the short term, if you see *anyone* like me, Dana, especially after today...I suggest you run."

She gave him a grim smile. "I'll keep that in mind," she said.

"Put the cuff on." Finn looked away from her as she slid the cuff over her shaking hand, pulling her sleeve down over it. She straightened as he glanced again toward the security cameras.

"They're not back on yet," he said. "But they will be shortly. Lester is rebooting the surveillance system. You'll have another minute before it clears."

"Great." Dana wrapped her arms around herself tightly, her fingers finding the edge of the cuff. She pulled her hands away just as quickly, smoothing them down the front of her suit. "I thought you had a jammer," she said.

"It was a temporary solution," Finn said, looking away from her. "An apparent circuit failure. Anything more sophisticated would have caused an entirely different kind of alarm."

"Uh-huh. And did they teach you that in Fallen angel school, or — " Dana's buzzing phone cut off her retort, and she realized she'd let it fall to the couch again. She grabbed it and peered at the screen.

"It's Max."

"Good," Finn gritted out. His body had started

shaking, and he didn't know why. He felt haggard, drained.

"Um, we should go." Dana stuffed it into her pocket. "He's got information on your friend Bartholomew. He's found him."

Finn dropped his hands slowly, then forced himself to look at her. "After tonight, I don't expect to see you again," he said again, not sure why he did. "You've got to take care of yourself, right? Use your strength. All of it."

Dana nodded, but her face went carefully blank. "I'm good at taking care of myself."

"I know." He walked toward her, every step a struggle. He reached for her right hand, lifting it to expose her golden cuff. "This will protect you from harm from anyone like Bartholomew, though it's probably better that you keep that information from your uncle."

He curled both hands around the relic, his thumbs grazing two prominent glyphs. A curious sound seemed to rise within the room, a rushing hiss that filled all the empty spaces. She stared at him as if trying to memorize his every feature, but he could feel her fading away from him even as he stood not two inches away.

"Where are you going after tonight?" Dana asked, her sudden words surprising them both. "Where are you from?"

But Finn could only gaze at her, willing himself to hold it together. She glowed, a vessel made solely to hold a shaft of lightning that couldn't quite break free. "I'll go back where I belong," he murmured, the sound flowing out through the room as a sensory experience much more than something merely spoken. But he couldn't leave well enough alone — not yet, not now.

Maybe if he did one thing more with the unexpected energy that suffused his body in his guise as a Fallen, he *could* see her again. No matter where he was after all this was through. Maybe he could ensure that her light shone so brightly that it would pierce even the most eternal darkness.

He could do that, he thought. He would do that.

He reached for the bracelet on her wrist and held it tight. The space between them seemed charged with electricity, curving around him and the cuff he'd wrapped around her, his knuckles white against its smooth surface, gripping so fiercely that he feared he'd crush it.

"This is all I have to offer you," he whispered. "You were made to shine."

The power leapt up between them a final time, a current jolting on the razor edge of pain and pleasure. Something seemed to bloom inside Finn in response, a ragged, wild need —

And then it was gone, vanished.

Dana stumbled back a step, her eyes wild. "What the hell was *that*?" she managed, even as someone rapped powerfully on the door.

"Finn?" Her uncle's voice was strained ever so slightly past the edge of politeness. "Dana, the door is jammed. Are you two all right?"

Finn gestured her toward the door, his own heart impossibly heavy. "Consider it a gift."

CHAPTER FOURTEEN

Griffin Security main office
Post Office Plaza
Cleveland, Ohio
10:00 a.m., Dec. 24

"Max?" Dana called out, forcing her voice to sound strong, stable, and not at all as freaked out as every other part of her was. "Whaddya got for me?"

She entered the room as Max sat forward. He reached out to snag his most recent file directory printout, deftly missing the day's sculpture-in-progress of take-out coffee cups, drink stirrers, and binder clips. Scanning the page again, he looked from it to something on his screen.

"Plenty." Max spun around in his swivel chair as his office was breached. Then he stopped short, quickly rolling his chair back as he blinked from her to Finn. "Um…you okay, boss?"

Dana grimaced, not even wanting to know what she looked like. Because she felt like she'd just French-kissed a nuclear bomb.

If what Finn said was true, she was the great-grandsomething of angels. If what he'd done to her hadn't been an epic hallucination, she had enough energy inside her to light up a Third World country. If what he'd explained to her wasn't complete and utter bullshit, she had work to do. To find those who were like her, and then...

And then she didn't know. But first she needed to secure her, well, family, for lack of a better word.

Family. For the first time in far too long, she liked the sound of that.

"I'm good," she said, realizing that Max was still staring at her. "Finn, meet my technical security expert, Max Garrett. Max, I invited Finn to tag along for your report on this Bartholomew. He thinks he may know the guy." She headed for the coffee machine, grateful that Max did make an effort to keep a path clear to that brilliant addition to the office, if only to keep it regularly stocked.

She punched buttons while Max took another drag on his own coffee.

"What happened up at Lester's?" he asked. "You were out of contact for hours."

"I apparently was more tired than I thought I was." Dana's cheeks burned as she pulled her cup out of the machine. "I fell asleep."

Max blinked. "You did what?" he started, but snapped his mouth shut when she glared at him. "Well, your mom called here since you didn't respond to her directly," he said. "She wants you to meet her for breakfast at eleven o'clock at the Renaissance."

He grinned at Dana's succinct curse.

"Of course she does," Dana muttered. "That's

166

freaking perfect." She glanced up at the clock, but there was nothing for it. Lester had just drugged her to the gills but thought she'd woken up without a single suspicion. If she stood up her mother, her mother would contact Lester, and Dana needed the return of her uncle's attention like a hole in the head.

Better to keep playing the game.

And then, of course…

Dana grimaced, pushing her jumbled thoughts away. "Okay. I've got a change of clothes here, so let's forget about that for the moment." She flicked her gaze back to him. "You figure out who this Bartholomew is?"

"I think so," Max said, wheeling back a little bit, apparently to put some additional distance between him and Finn. "The boys in blue have a low-level watch out for one Bartholomew Petolya, no indication why, but they started the surveillance right after the dude officially moved to town on November first. My contact at the police department says they know where he lives, and everyone's been advised to keep an eye out on his comings and goings, but no one's supposed to give him any trouble. Apparently they're waiting for him to make the first move."

"Anything to tie him to the attack on Lester on Halloween night?" Dana asked.

Max shook his head. "They were pretty sure he was already living somewhere in the city at that point, but they weren't tailing him then."

"What's his current residence?" Finn sounded particularly intense, but Max was already backed up as far as he could go.

"Penthouse in the Summit Building, Warehouse District," he said. "Coupla blocks from here, most expensive digs in the city. I double-checked my other sources on the name, and if Petolya is our man, we've got our hands full. He's got mob connections all over the East Coast, plus a steady flow of recruits from both local venues and shipped in from Eastern Europe. Not a very nice group, from what I hear. Very low on the evolutionary scale. Petolya's been pretty well established in Philly for the past thirty years or so, with his hands in everything from racketeering to antiquities dealing, but he's apparently moving the operation to Cleveland."

"Philly…" Dana frowned. "Why do I—"

"The car in the street," Finn supplied. "Before we went to the cathedral."

"Right." She recalled the image perfectly. Had she always been able to do that? "Max, run a check on a Lexus sedan, maybe black, maybe dark gray, license plate number 074332. It was tailing me last night, and I'm curious if it's connected to this Petolya guy."

"Roger that." Max made a note. "I also looked into whether the dude's either sold any of these so-called antiquities to Lester or bought anything from him, but so far, no dice. Lester hasn't sold any of his junk since we started working with him, and his acquisitions seem to be all on-site." He flashed a grin. "Get it? Like, archaeological site?"

Dana rolled her eyes, but she couldn't help smiling in response. "What else?"

"Not much. Sometimes he uses intermediaries, but unlike most of these guys, he enjoys keeping a hand in the work, so he'll also meet with his business partners himself. Has a rep for brutal efficiency. Kind of a freak, from what I'm hearing, demons and occult stuff, that sort of thing." He looked back at Dana. "You want me to tip the police about a possible connection to Lester's attack?"

"Don't," Finn said from his corner. "I'll take care of this."

"But they already know something about the guy," Dana countered. "Otherwise, they wouldn't have a tail on him. And my dad worked for the police, back in the day. There might be information there we could use."

Finn's expression effectively dropped the room's temperature by fifteen degrees. "I only need to know where Bartholomew is," he said. "The rest is immaterial."

"Right. And I'm sure he's going to just be hanging out at his penthouse, waiting for you to show up," Dana said drily. "You want to waste your time roaming through the city for him, though, be my guest."

That shut Finn up for a second. Good.

It didn't last long. "When can you have the information?" Finn asked.

"By the time I'm done with breakfast." Dana turned back to Max. "Next question," she said. "How hard would it be to break into every single server Lester has, even the ones we don't technically have access to? If I wanted to get into Lester's business down to the roots of his hair, how long would that take you?"

Max tilted his head, considering. "Rough guess, a couple of hours. Won't know until I come across a firewall I didn't put up, though."

"Start hunting for one," she said. "But first tell me about the files Lester pulled. What were they?"

Max snorted in disgust. "*That*, I don't know. Here's an example of one of them." He moved his hands over the keys, and rows of data began filling the screen. "The data looks randomly generated, but I think it's some kind of code. I'm running it through a pattern finder.

I've got no idea how to sort it out, however, no clue what type of information we're even looking at. And these are only a handful that he didn't successfully delete. I suspect there are a bunch more that he did."

"Could be client notes or product research," Dana mused. *Or a list of names and addresses.*

"Could be Lester's secret recipe for chicken wings." Max lifted one shoulder, dropped it. "Whatever it is, he buried those files deep. I'm surprised *he* even found them again."

"And there's no difference in the file lengths? So we're talking exactly the same data?"

"Apparently. I'm trying to find other links between the files, maybe find a pattern that way. He's been doing this for a while, though. The first file showed up in late September, 2001."

"Right after nine-eleven," Dana murmured.

"Yup." He turned his attention back to Dana. "Then he faithfully added another new file every six months or so after that. Last update was late September, but that most recent file was accessed again in early November. And now, poof. As far as Lester believes, both the original 2001 file and all the backups are gone."

Dana shifted her gaze to Finn. "You think this is the same information he's going to give you?" she asked. "Would he have made that many copies of it?"

"It's possible," he said. "When did Lester start removing his files from the system?"

"Three days ago," Max said. "December twenty-first."

Finn grimaced. "So it all began on solstice. He said he received information then. In a dream."

Dana and Max exchanged a look. "Solstice," she repeated.

"On solstice, it's easier for extrasensory communication to take place. It's possible that someone reached out to advise Lester to destroy any duplicate files." Finn frowned, studying the screen behind Max.

"Wait a minute." Max looked particularly appropriate with his wide eyes and startled expression, since he was standing directly in front of a wall full of UFO headlines and posters. "You mean like telepathy or something? Like Lester had a vision or something to dump a bunch of files, and boom, he did it?"

"In a manner of speaking, yes."

"So now what?" Max asked, his voice hushed with excitement.

"So now we've got my uncle listening to instructions he got in a fucking dream." Dana growled, chucking her coffee cup into the recycling bin. "Sadly, that's not the most insane thing I've heard today. Okay, I've got to get changed. Show Finn all the files you've uncovered, Max, as well as everything you've got on this Bartholomew Petolya, and check on that car." She moved toward her private office, swiping her key again to gain entrance. "I'll be back as soon as possible."

Finn stared after Dana, then slowly turned his head to meet Max's gaze. The young man blinked rapidly, his gaze darting around, clearly wishing the office was a little bigger.

"Where do you want to start?" Max asked.

"First, there's something you forgot to mention to Dana," Finn said. "Something worrying you beyond your immediate focus on the files and your search on Bartholomew."

Max blinked. "What do you mean?" he asked,

shaking his head as if to clear it. "I told you everything—"

"What happened last night after the party, Max?" Finn asked quietly. "Did you receive a call from Dana?"

Max nodded, frowning. "I had work to do, so I clocked in here. I sent the night-shift guy home. Shocked the hell out of me when I got the distress call. I thought she'd long since gotten home. When she didn't follow up, I called the dispatcher over at the precinct house and waited." He frowned. "It kind of took a long time before I heard the sirens." He bit his lower lip. "Too long. They waited ten minutes—I'd forgotten that, because once she texted me later, I knew she was safe. Then she asked me to do a search on Bartholomew, and everything else sort of went poof."

"Who would have been the officers assigned to the call?" Finn asked.

"I—I don't know. We haven't gotten a call about it yet to debrief, so I don't know who showed up." Max glanced toward Dana's office. "That's kind of odd too. If the cruiser didn't actually find Dana, they should have called here to make sure it wasn't a false alarm." His eyes widened, and he straightened in his chair. "I can't believe I didn't think about that before. Why didn't they call?"

"What's your reputation with the police?"

"Solid," Max said. "And normally, they're super protective of Dana because of her dad. She knows all the beat cops and most of the older detectives and admin types. They take care of her."

"What about after the assault on Lester on Halloween?" Finn asked. "Did they take care of her then?"

Max sighed, rolling his shoulders. "Well, she was

out of it for a few days, so Lester handled the report. They couldn't find her attackers. And yeah, they stopped looking pretty quickly, you ask me. But Lester was certain it was a case of some trigger-happy thug startled by Dana pulling her own gun. Thank God she wasn't hurt worse."

"Her assailant blew apart her shinbone. I think she was hurt badly enough," Finn commented, and Max squinted at him.

"No, he didn't," he said. "The bullet went straight through muscle. Lester framed the X-rays for Dana's office." He chuckled without humor. "How else do you think she recovered so fast? She was up on her feet again within a week, walking around and bitching up a blue streak about it. Her calf looked like Swiss cheese, but Lester had a crack team on her, and she hung in there. I definitely don't think she's a hundred percent, but you'll never get her to admit it."

Finn blew out a sharp breath, and Max suddenly straightened, the pressure Finn had been exerting on his mind releasing. He blinked and looked around, clearly confused. "Um…what just happened?"

"She walked on her injured leg within one week?" Finn pressed him. "And you all thought that was reasonable?"

"What? Oh yeah. But she did. The docs had somehow got the extent of her injuries wrong, and her pain tolerance is insane, and—" Max halted as Finn held up a hand, glaring at the door to Dana's office.

"Give me a minute," he said.

Finn covered the few feet to Dana's office without pausing, placing his hand over the keycard unit and disarming it.

Dana looked up as he entered, her phone pressed to

173

her ear, and he stopped short. Now clad in a rich garnet sweater that molded to her body, she'd traded her silk for denim and her high heels for a low-slung pair of boots. The rich leather jacket she held in her left hand gleamed in the light of a wall of blinking computers, which also made her skin luminous and her large eyes impossibly green, and the gold cuff on her wrist peeked out from below her sweater, giving off its own subtle glow. The overall effect caught him completely off guard, and he felt his body respond, fast and hot.

No. Frustration knifed through him. If this was the kind of reaction mortals had to deal with all the time, it was no wonder so many of them went mad.

Dana, clearly unaware of her impact on him, tossed her jacket on the table and dropped her phone on it. "Okay, my mother has confirmed breakfast. For the first time in my adult life, she apparently can't wait to see me." She leaned against her desk, eyeing him with interest. The soft, knowing smile on her face made Finn's palms start to sweat. She was absolutely breathtaking.

"Your check bounced, I'm afraid," she said, her gaze never leaving his face. "But the real Dr. Lee Schaeffer — who was quite gracious about the donation, by the way — won't give up anything as to how his wallet and his checkbook found its way into your hands. Mom also can't quite explain how their raffle matron somehow managed to miss the fact that Schaeffer's ID photo looks absolutely nothing like you, even though IDs are required with any handwritten checks. Funny, isn't it?"

"I blend in," Finn said.

Dana raised her brows, but her change of clothing had shifted her attitude. Her clothing, and doubtless the strength he'd opened her up to too. She was relaxed, inviting, her gaze softening as she searched his eyes, her brow furrowing in the smallest of frowns.

"You want to tell me the rest of the story? What you wouldn't tell me before?" she asked quietly. "Are you in danger?" Concern radiated from her, her aura even stronger now that he knew what he was looking at.

She was worried about him.

That realization punched Finn low in the stomach, his hair-trigger physical responses firing even more emphatically, urging him to go to her, to take her into his arms. She, a Dawn Child being hunted by a rogue Fallen and an army of demons, feared for *his* safety. She had no way of knowing the irony of that.

He needed to tell her *something*. She needed to be prepared, ready. But how much was too much? He instinctively believed that there was safety in this Society of Orion that Lester had drawn around himself and Dana, but the man's casual indifference to Dana's injury, his willingness to drug her, to lie to her and to the people who cared for her the most, couldn't be ignored.

"There's more I have to explain to you, Dana," he said. "About Lester."

"Yeah, I've been thinking about that. Why do I suspect last night isn't the first time my dear uncle drugged me?"

She folded her arms over her chest again, but her entire body fairly hummed with electricity. The channel Finn had opened up within her, allowing her to tap her own power, was reacting to him. As she grew more used to it, accepted it, worked with it, the flow of energy within her would become even stronger. She would appear more radiant to others, more beautiful. She would *shine*.

A Dawn Child, Lester had called her. Even thinking the term made Finn's head pound again. Something about that term, those people, was important to what had happened to him. What he'd done.

How he'd sinned.

Finn blew out a breath, remembering Lester's urgency in showing him the complex infrastructure of Orion. Every screen, every new line of text had made his gut tighten. This was not some religious cult consulting horoscopes and stockpiling water against the coming end times. This was an organization spanning six continents and thousands of cities, so deeply embedded in society that some of its farthest flung branches probably didn't even know there *was* a society. From scientists to biologists, psychologists to theologians, archaeologists to adventure travelers, Orion had tapped every resource available to keep the Children safe and to prepare.

Dana was strong, but she was human. Fragile. Emotional. He didn't need to destroy her world, tell her the truth about her uncle, her family. He must only keep her safe until the archangel had the list. After that...he didn't know what would happen.

Finn looked around her office, her sanctuary, stiffening as his gaze fell on a framed newspaper clipping detailing the death of a Cleveland police officer. Walter Griffin. Dana's father. Perhaps not her biological father, given what Lester had told him, but the man who'd raised her from infancy and kept her safe.

"How long ago did your father die?" he asked.

If the question surprised Dana, she didn't betray it. "Almost fifteen years," she said.

He walked over to the clipping, the words leaping

out at him. Dana said something more, but her words faded as he took in the thin, typed lines, the impossible detail they included.

Griffin was shot twice in the head and four more times in the torso before managing to apprehend the assailants... Captain Griffin died at the scene... Assailants in custody.

Finn's bones began to ache.

An obituary ran alongside the newspaper account, but he paid no attention to it, his eyes riveted on the injury description, knowing that Dana had fallen silent, knowing she was watching him, her body keening with her own remembered pain. But what strength of will must it have taken for a man to move forward with six bullet holes in him? What effort must it have cost him to capture his attackers?

And most miraculous of all, Walter Griffin hadn't been a Dawn Child. He'd been a simple mortal, like the ones described in the news articles covering the wall above Max's desk. Miracle Grandmothers and Children Who'd Defied the Odds, ordinary people surviving cancers and natural disasters. Griffin was "only" human, yet he'd given Dana her first and best example of true mortal heroics. And he'd loved her. Somehow, Finn couldn't believe that the gruff-faced man staring out at him from the faded newspaper clipping was part of Lester's secret society. And if Walter didn't know the truth about Dana, that meant her mother *had* known.

So Dana was still living a lie.

But it was a lie that might yet keep her alive.

He grimaced. "Lester did drug you before. At least once that I know of. Probably more."

"Halloween," Dana muttered. Her gaze was fixed on a series of X-rays hung on the wall—none of them showing a shattered bone. Finn knew they were what she'd been shown of her own wounded leg, all part of the lies she'd been told about her own injuries. "I knew it. Why?"

"According to him, you were, ah, a little more hurt than he let anyone admit to you." At Dana's curse, he continued. "He wanted to see how fast you would heal, how quickly you would bounce back. How strong you were. If he'd told you the true nature of your injuries..."

"He was afraid I'd lock up." To his surprise, there was no outrage in Dana's voice. When he looked up, she shrugged. "He's not necessarily wrong. There were times when the only thing that got me through PT was my complete and total fury that I was feeling that much pain over a relatively minor gunshot wound. I'm not sure I would have pushed myself so hard..." She shook her head, glaring at the X-rays again. "Bastard."

Finn tightened his lips. If Lester was to be believed, far too many of Dana's ancestors had been hunted down, killed — or worse. It might not be an ideal situation, but the enormous machine that had fostered Dana was dedicated solely to keeping her alive, keeping her safe.

Perhaps her safety was enough.

"Your uncle believes your abilities go beyond simple strength," Finn said carefully. "He also thinks you're psychic."

Whatever Dana had expected him to say, that wasn't it. "Psychic," she snorted. "Lester — the same Lester who's currently trashing company data based on a *dream* — told you he thinks I have psychic powers?"

"Your leg is better, isn't it?" he said, and she stiffened slightly. A warm surge of affection curled through Finn at Dana's blatant skepticism. "That wasn't all me. Your belief helped you long before I showed up."

"No thanks to my family," she said bitterly. "You'd think if I had psychic powers, I would have been able to predict everyone turning into an asshole." She waved at the X-rays. "So these are all bullshit, I take it? Is that what you're trying to tell me?"

"Your uncle wanted to keep you strong," Finn said. He did too, if he was honest. He wanted to surround her with safety…but he would be leaving in less than fifteen hours. Possibly never to return, unless the archangel deemed it wise.

And if Michael had any idea what Finn was feeling right now, he wouldn't let him get close to Dana again. Ever.

Which meant that Finn could only arm Dana. Show her the strength she possessed. That knowledge would help her regardless of whether or not she knew about Orion. About Lester. About her own parents.

"Those X-rays were…yeah. They were bullshit," Finn said, pointing to the prints. "They were someone else's X-rays entirely."

"Someone else's," Dana repeated softly, but she didn't move, her gaze locked on the images.

"The bullet that struck you split your tibia, probably shattered it. It was impossible for me to tell merely by touching you. But your leg was definitely broken several times." He glanced at Dana, saw a half-formed denial dying on her lips. "Lester had you taken to a ward he had set up specially for you, treated you with private doctors and nurses, the security ironclad. No one on the outside knew the truth. Not Max, not your mother. No one."

"That's not possible," Dana said. "Maybe fifty years ago, but not anymore. That kind of thing doesn't happen these days."

Finn shrugged. "You don't have to believe me. If you have another X-ray done, you'll see that your bone is held together with a metal plate." He looked away again. "I'd suggest not letting your uncle know about the new scan."

That caught her attention. "Why?"

"Because he doesn't yet know the full extent of your abilities," Finn said, turning. "And he doesn't want you to know he lied. He saw you fight, and he saw you heal—but he knows the truth will alarm you, and he's not all that keen on you being alarmed."

Dana pursed her lips, her eyes dark and haunted as she stared at him. "What happened to me that night, Finn?" she asked. "I'm only remembering in bits and pieces."

Finn closed his eyes. He'd finally gotten the whole story after pushing the man, hard, and the images still chilled him. "Lester was attacked. You protected him. There was a shooter who thought he'd taken you out, but that wasn't the end of it. There were attackers on foot as well. Even with your damaged leg, you killed three of the assailants with your bare hands, in a blind rage, before Lester could fully register what was happening. By the time his backup security responded, it was all over."

"All over," Dana said quietly, nodding, though her eyes remained troubled. "There was, um, a lot of goopy black blood. I remember that now." She shuddered, her voice trailing away.

"Your uncle wants to protect you. To keep you safe." He deliberately stood apart from her, though he ached to take her in his arms. *Forbidden,* he reminded himself, but the voice was weaker, less sure. It was good that he'd be getting the list from Lester within a few short hours. He didn't think he'd be able to be around Dana much longer. "You have to believe that."

Dana shook herself, her laughter false and jarring. "Well, it's been a day of crazy things I'm supposed to believe, I guess," she said, picking up her jacket and holding it close to her, the movement too much like an embrace. Every nerve ending in his body screamed that she wanted to be held, to be protected, and the primal urge to be that protector rose up within Finn, a hurricane force.

He started forward just as Dana turned away, and stopped short as she threw her jacket over her shoulders, stuffing her arms into the heavy leather sleeves.

"I've gotta get going," she said, and millennia's worth of training and belief waged war with Finn's immediate need to take her in his arms.

No. There was nothing he could offer her that would last longer than one night.

He clenched his hands into fists, ashamed to realize that even having a single night with Dana Griffin — a few short hours — was beginning to seem worth it. "Yes," he said flatly. "You should go."

CHAPTER FIFTEEN

Renaissance Cleveland Hotel
Grand Lobby
Cleveland, Ohio
11:03 a.m., Dec. 24

Stay focused. Get through this meet, get back to the office, and then you can deal with all the insanity waiting for you there.

Some of it anyway. Dana didn't think she'd finish unwrapping this year's Christmas gifts of crazy anytime before Easter. There was simply too much to process, coming at her too fast, all of it connected to a man...angel...whatever the hell he was, who short-circuited her brain every time he came within five feet of her. And the touch of his hands on her skin...

Dana rolled her eyes. Of course, that was what she'd be focusing on. Not the list of men and women targeted for extinction. Not the fact that she apparently was either psychic or superpowered or, at a bare minimum, an excellent candidate for *American Gladiator*. No, all she wanted to think about was the way Finn looked at her, as if he could imprint her on his brain to remember her for all eternity...as if he'd never see her again after today.

An entire night garden of sadness bloomed deep inside Dana at those thoughts, and she quickly pushed them away.

"Stupid," she muttered. Straightening her shoulders, she drew in a deep breath, the canned air of the indoor mall redolent of candy canes, hot chocolate, and roasted chestnuts. After she cut through the Ritz's lobby to gain access to Tower City Center Mall, she weaved her way through last-minute Christmas shoppers toward the Renaissance Hotel, one of Cleveland's grandes dames of old-world luxury.

A few minutes later, she walked into the Renaissance's opulent lobby, unable to school her features away from the wistfulness she always felt in this majestic space. Of all the hotels downtown, she loved the Renaissance the most—its quiet, nostalgic elegance a beautiful counterpart to the clanking, cranking, nonstop action of the industrial city. She especially loved the hotel's lobby, with its enormous chandelier and stunning blue-and-gold trim, its gleaming grand piano and majestic marble fountain. Clevelanders and travelers alike gathered here at all hours, and it was no surprise that her mother had chosen it for their meeting. Being seen here at brunch was a critical component of any society matron's publicity schedule.

But coming to the Renaissance never reminded Dana of her mother as much as her father. Probably because he'd brought Dana here every Christmas when she was a little girl to show her the beautiful tree on Public Square and dazzle her with stories about what good things came to children who believed in Christmas. Later, when she'd thought herself too grown up for Santa Claus, he'd brought her here just to let her watch the little children who still did believe, to relive her own sweet memories in the light of their eyes.

The place gleamed with that sort of memory, she realized, her slightly skewed vision taking in the atmosphere of the lobby. It shone with a rarified light, the whisper of expectation shimmering at every turn. She'd have to come back here later...if only to catch sight of the hope in the children's eyes.

It certainly would be good to find something worth believing in again. After Finn's latest revelation — a revelation she knew had to be true — she didn't know who she could trust anymore. Everything about the man was a contradiction. She'd felt the connection between them — the spark of interest, the physical magnetism. She couldn't have imagined that. And yet, he hadn't made a second move toward her. He continued to play the role of the mysterious emissary, shadowy protector of her uncle and herself — even as he flat-out accused her uncle of lying to Dana, drugging her, and manipulating her for months...probably longer, if Dana was honest with herself. But that wasn't as important to Finn as the precious document he'd come for.

It made no sense. She knew he wanted to protect her. Yet he'd insisted she remain with Lester — and then shared with her information that proved her uncle was a liar. *Why?*

Yet more crazy for her to work out after she had brunch with Mother of the Year.

Dana glanced around the restaurant, finding her mark immediately. As usual, her mother's table was positioned at a strategic advantage to see and be seen by everyone in the room.

Claire Griffin's perfectly coiffed golden hair and slender, erect figure easily made her one of the most striking women in the restaurant, and Dana couldn't help feeling a twinge of remorse that she hadn't inherited any of her mother's willowy blonde elegance. It might have made things easier if they at least *looked* as if they belonged together. Worse, she knew without a shadow of a doubt that her mother would have no interest in dining with her this morning...except to get the gossip on Finn's tour de force last night. Nothing moved the woman so much as the idea of being in the know.

Still, Dana couldn't stay mad at her mother — she'd suffered too much loss herself. She'd never remarried after the death of Dana's father, and that had been fifteen long years ago. At first, Dana had thought her parents had simply had a love match, but her mother never spoke of her father — ever — at least not to Dana. So why she'd stayed single all these years remained a mystery.

"Hey, Mom," Dana said as she walked up to her. In her leather jacket and trousers, she felt decidedly underdressed compared to her mother's crimson silk dress and matching pumps, the ensemble perfectly setting off the heirloom pearls that were merely one highlight of her mother's exquisite collection of jewelry. She was definitely the belle of the ball, today, but then she'd been lovely last night as well — even though Dana had only seen her across the room. Claire had come from money before marrying Walter Griffin, and she'd spent that money lavishly to create the perfect image of the elegant matron...and doting mother.

"Dana!" Claire Griffin managed to infuse the name

with warm affection, but that didn't necessarily mean anything. Dana had seen her do that on a moment's notice with large donors to one of her myriad charity affiliations. "What have you found out about the check from Lee Schaeffer? Can we keep it?"

Shoving down an all too familiar pang of resentment, Dana leaned over and hugged her mother gingerly before sitting opposite in one of the embroidered side chairs, clearly playing court to her mother's position in a dominant wingbacked chair. "I doubt it, but I'm sure Lester will make a donation if that's what you need. Considering I was a last-minute addition to your fundraising pot, though, do you think that's really necessary?"

"Well, it did show considerable nerve," Claire huffed delicately, then eyed Dana over the rim of her coffee cup. "And using a stolen identity! It's absolutely absurd, unless this is all part of some grand scheme Lester concocted without telling anyone." She paused expectantly, but when Dana didn't speak, her mouth formed a little moue of distress. "Well, come on, Dana," she said. "You know that I need to be able to explain what happened to the gala committee. Even if we don't get the additional funds, you have to admit that the entire charade was somewhat coarse. And God forbid anyone outside the committee finds out it was all a hoax. I'd be a laughingstock!"

As she listened to her mother hold forth on a host of potential slights to her reputation, Dana felt the world gradually close in on her, cutting off her breath. How many similar complaints had she listened to over the years? How many more years of complaints would she be forced to endure? She'd long since understood why her father had kept his apartment in the city even after he'd married Claire and moved to the big house in the Heights. The woman was more than a little exhausting. Had she ever really loved Dana's father? Had he loved her back?

Unsettled, Dana swung her gaze out into the festive, glittering lobby. A faint glow hummed along the water fountain, the lights, and even a few of the people who appeared to be in particularly good spirits. But there was nothing like the radiance she'd seen in Lester's office.

"Oh, really, Dana," Claire sniffed. "Don't stare off into the distance that way. People will notice."

A waiter had placed ice waters and lime in front of them and poured more coffee. With consummate patience, Dana allowed herself to be drawn into her mother's world of social obligations and dramas largely of her own making. It made for an hour's worth of conversation, but as it finally drew to a close, Dana sipped the dregs of her coffee, watching her mother with the sight that Finn had somehow flipped on for her. The sight he said was part of Dana's advanced psychic powers that she'd never tapped.

She didn't know if she was happy with what she was seeing or not.

Claire Griffin was lit from within, but with an indifferent, muted glow. Her true light was probably buried under decades of bearing the weight of society's censure, Dana supposed. As well as her brother's? Now that was a question worth asking.

Dana leaned forward. "How close are you and Uncle Lester, Mom?"

A shadow passed over her mother's face so quickly, Dana might have imagined it. "Well, that's an odd question," Claire said frostily. "We've known each other our whole lives, of course. We've chaired more events together than I can count since he came back to Cleveland, and—"

"And when was that, actually? Right around the time that I was born, wasn't it?"

"Really, Dana, what is this about?" Claire's mouth had thinned, and Dana sensed the change in her demeanor. "I asked you here to discuss last night's events—"

"And I want to discuss this morning's," Dana said. Heat rose within her. "This morning, in his office, Uncle Lester gave me a coffee mug full of tranquilizers to knock me out."

Claire started to protest, and Dana held up her hand. "Please, listen. I know that he's lied to me," she said. "I don't really care. But have you known about those lies? For some reason, that's really important for me to know."

Her mother was sitting ramrod straight, her eyes wide. Dana had never taken that tone with her, and she clearly didn't appreciate it. But she was more startled than outraged for the moment, and Dana plunged on. "How much do you know about my injury in October?"

"Why, the same thing as you, Dana," Claire said crisply. "You were shot."

"Did I break a bone in that attack? Was I shot through the bone?"

Her mother's lips curled in distaste. "Well, of course not, dear. You couldn't have broken a bone without it showing up on the X-rays."

Lester hadn't told her anything, Dana thought. Or her mother was a damn fine actress. How sad that she really didn't know which was the truth.

"Okay, so where were you while I was undergoing

all my surgeries, then? Especially after they finished all the cutting. How did they explain to you what was happening to me?"

"Well…" Claire squirmed, but her frown seemed heartfelt. "Lester didn't call me right away. By the time I reached the hospital, they'd already operated, and you were completely passed out. Unresponsive. They — Lester — eventually sent me home. Said that he would keep watch over you. 'Keep watch,' those were his words. I went home until they called me to tell me you could be seen."

"And what condition was my leg in at that point? Could you see the cast?"

"There was no cast, Dana, just a heavy dressing of sorts. You didn't break any bones — "

"Did you see the wound itself, then? And how long was it after surgery that I regained consciousness?"

"I did *not* see the wound, thank you, no. I had no interest in doing that."

"So you don't know if it was broken or not."

"Oh, Dana, don't be ridiculous! You couldn't have been walking around in mere days if it had been broken."

Dana hesitated. "I've been given reason to believe that maybe things were a little bit worse than Lester let on. That's all. He's never done anything like that, has he?"

"Of course not," Claire said firmly. "Your uncle has done nothing but give you love and support since the day you were born. He would be mortified to hear you speak ill of him today."

"He drugged me today, Mom."

"You *think* he did. How do you know? How could you know? You've pushed yourself so hard to recover from your injuries. How do you know you didn't simply pass out?"

Dana shook her head, remembering the tang of the bitter coffee she'd swallowed. She hadn't imagined that. She hadn't simply decided to take a little nap on the couch while Finn and her uncle talked shop. But her mother's face was stony, and Dana knew she wouldn't get anywhere further with this line of questioning. Claire clearly thought of her only as a less than dutiful daughter. Not magical, not special, merely a pawn in an endless societal whirl. "Are you going home after this?" Dana asked at length.

"Of course," Claire said stiffly. "We have twenty people coming for Christmas dinner tomorrow, including yourself—and a guest, if you have one to bring."

"No, most of my friends have their own families to spend their Christmas with."

"Even your admirer? Whoever was impersonating Dr. Schaeffer?" Claire's eyes had gone bright again, and it was her turn to lean forward. "If Lester met with him, then he had to have approved of the man's unorthodox behavior, as hard as I find that to believe. Perhaps I should meet him as well. He went to great lengths to get time alone to talk to you, after all. Margaret said he was *insistent*."

"He won't be here tomorrow," Dana said, suddenly tired. The gap might be too broad between her and her mother, but that didn't change the reality of the men Dana had faced in the street last night. If Finn was right and they didn't leave Lester alone after he handed off his list, then her mother was as much a target as the rest of them. "Listen. You need to get out of the city as soon as you can. Do you have your driver downtown?"

"Of course, dear. But I have shopping —"

"Do it in Crocker Park," Dana said. "Lester has some business associates in town who've decided they're not happy with him. Last night, they decided to take out that anger on me. I don't want them to widen the net any further."

Her mother paused, studying her. She wasn't surprised, which sent Dana's radar pinging all over the place. "Does Lester know you were attacked?" Claire asked quietly.

"Yes, he does."

"And he let you out of his sight?"

Dana thought about that. Herself, in the long shadow of Finn as they'd left Exeter's offices. Lester looking on, his manner more excited than agitated, but definitely letting her go. "Mom, is there anything I should know about Lester that you're not telling me? People's lives are at stake here. Including yours."

Her mother's lips twisted. "You always did insist on being dramatic." She shook her head. "My life stopped being 'at stake' a long time ago." She signaled for the waiter, her manner cool. Unaffected. As if a mask of civility had slipped back into place, never to be unsettled. "I think breakfast was a bad idea. I think you should go home and get some rest."

She sat back, her audience with Dana clearly at an end. But as Dana moved to stand, her mother placed cool manicured fingers on her arm. "Dinner tomorrow is at one p.m., remember. If you plan to bring a guest, let me know by six p.m. tonight."

"Got it," Dana said, pulling her arm away.

Her mother favored her with a chilly smile. "And if you don't come, expect your uncle to come fetch you," she said, her eyes remote. "He's very good at getting people to do what he wants."

Dana didn't bother responding to that, merely turned sharply away and headed out of the restaurant, which had suddenly grown too stuffy. She found herself in back in the all too vacant mall multiplex, but it was hard to focus too much on the empty stores, given the fantastic Christmas décor and colorful street vendors...

And the cacophony of competing thoughts and emotions racketing around her brain.

Her phone buzzed, and she pulled it out of her pocket, then quickly hissed a curse as she read Max's text.

Dr. Doom gone. Said he found out what he needed.

How? she keyed back.

No clue. I was plowing through files, but he didn't watch. He sat and meditated or whatever, then poked through your WWE shrine in your office, checked out some vids. Then he told me to tell you he didn't need your help and split. Creepy as shit, not gonna lie.

"Dammit," Dana said again, keying back instructions to get a tail on Finn as soon as possible. Though good luck with that in Cleveland on Christmas Eve. Public Square would be jammed tight with people determined to celebrate the holiday in style. Even the mall's concourse was bustling, never mind that only half the complex's stores were open. You wouldn't know there was any vacancy in the plaza from all the pop-up kiosks and brightly colored displays. A couple of buskers played music at one end of the fountains and, nearer her, several tables had been set up with vendors selling calendars and stocking stuffers. There was even —

Dana pocketed her phone, frowning. A woman sat at one of the tables, shuffling a deck of cards. Dana'd never seen her before, but it wasn't the oddly colored deck that caught her eye, it was the woman herself.

She glowed bright enough to see from space.

As Dana fixed on her, the woman looked up. She was athletic looking, slender, but it was a little difficult to see that given the white-gold glow that surrounded her that stretched out about three feet. Underneath the halo, she was a pony-tailed brunette in a battered leather jacket and dark jeans stuffed into scuffed boots. And she was shuffling the cards like it was her job, even as she met Dana's gaze.

"Dana Griffin?" she called out with a grin. "And don't ask me how I know. I'm psychic."

"That's great. I'm not."

"Yeah? Is that why you're reacting to me as if I'm all bright and shiny?"

Dana's brows went up, and she pulled her bag higher on her shoulder as she walked closer to the woman. "You want to tell me why you're all bright and shiny?"

"Sure I do. If you tell me something I want to know."

Dana glanced around. No one was paying any attention to her, and she'd apparently lost Finn, who doubtless believed he had a line on an at least five-hundred-year-old bad guy. Given how her day was going, how much more crazy could talking to some strip mall card reader be?

She stepped forward, then slid into the chair opposite the woman. As she did, the glow around the reader dropped markedly. She was younger than she first appeared, nearer to Dana's age. "Who are you?"

The woman chuckled. "Probably a good question. Maybe not the best question, but you've earned it, at this point. I'm Sara Wilde. I collect artifacts. I—"

"You!" Dana's eyes flared wide. She recognized the glow now, only she hadn't seen it as a glow before. "It's electricity, isn't it, around you? You're the one generating all the electricity at the sites where we missed out on Lester's artifacts."

The woman didn't deny it, merely offered the roll of one shoulder. "And Lester would be..."

"My uncle. Collector of old, weird, random crazy."

"Like the Anunnaki relic you recovered from northern Canada three days ago?"

Dana narrowed her gaze. "Like that."

"You know it shouldn't have been there, right? It's not exactly the kind of thing that would've gotten carried over on a land bridge or something."

Dana shrugged. "I'm not an archaeologist. I'm security."

"Security." Sara lifted a skeptical brow. "Who just so happens to get sent out on jobs to pick up old, weird, random crazy. You ever think to ask about that?" She dropped the cards on the table. "Shuffle three times, then cut."

Dana picked up the cards, shuffling them with far less finesse than the woman had. "Is that my question? Why Lester is sending me out on those jobs?"

"Oh, I think you know that one already." The woman flashed a quick grin. "I figured you'd be asking for something more helpful. Like how you can find Finn."

Dana paused. Of course this woman was an associate of Finn's. How else would she know about the relic? "Who is he, exactly?" she asked.

"Also a good question, but not my story to tell. However, I happen to have a soft spot for anyone who's not being given full information, when actually they need it. That's happened to me more than a few times. So I'm going to help both you and Finn out."

"And in return?" Dana suddenly figured it out. "The relic. You want the Anunnaki relic."

"It shouldn't have been in Canada," Sara said again. "But it's pretty sweet, wherever it came from. You can get it?"

Dana thought of Max, and of Lester's chamber of secrets, all laid out for Finn to see. Had the relic been there? Probably. "Oh...I can get it."

"Then let me see how I can help you."

Dana cut the deck and Sara reassembled it, then picked it up, laying out the cards in quick succession. Dana wasn't familiar with Tarot, but she knew that was what she was looking at. The three cards had a moon in a dark sky above some weird, oversized creatures crawling out of the water, then a pope seated on his throne, then three young women dancing in a circle, all of them holding cups aloft. "Look, I don't see how —"

"First we got night, someplace people usually go to at night, maybe involving the occult or hidden secrets, maybe not," Sara said, cutting her off as she tapped the first card. "The Moon is all about secrets, so secret alcoves, hidden staircases, underground hideaways, that kind of thing."

"Okay..."

"This card should help clear it up." Sara touched the card with the pope. "The Hierophant. Given the givens you don't need to know about yet, this could be the cards jerking my chain, but I don't think so. So it's more likely a church, a cathedral, anything like that."

Dana made a face. "A church people go to at night on Christmas Eve?" she asked. "That doesn't really narrow it down. And Finn doesn't really seem to be much of a fan of churches."

Sara snorted. "Fair enough. Which takes us to card number three." She pointed to the dancing women. "That could mean a lot of things, but in this context, I'm going to go with booze." She looked up at Dana. "So a church that people go to at night, with booze."

Dana shook her head, then she stopped, blinking. "No. No, you have got to be kidding me."

Sara grinned. "You know a place?"

Dana coughed, barely able to keep from laughing. "I know a place. I can be there in fifteen minutes, actually. It's that close."

"Hang on, hang on." Sara deftly spread the remaining cards in a smooth arc, then drew one, and flipped it toward Dana. A guy standing at the foot of a pathway, beside two staffs driven into the ground. "This place you know, plan to be there at two o'clock. I wouldn't get there much before, or you'll screw up the reading. Finn could go elsewhere, whoever he's going to see could go elsewhere, a million things could go wrong. Life's a funny place. But you get there at two and, well, you'll find your man."

Dana stared at her a long minute as Sara grinned back at her. "Why are you telling me this?"

"Because as much as I know about what's going on in this world, there's still some important information that people are trying to keep from me, and that crap's got to end." She leaned forward, and for the first time, Dana caught sight of the pendant dangling from her neck. A delicately wrought set of old-fashioned measuring scales, gleaming in the harsh light of the mall. Sara gathered up the cards. "You go find your Finn, and you make your own decisions. To hell with people wanting to make them for you. Sound good?"

Dana found herself smiling as well. "Sounds good."

"Excellent." The woman squared the deck, then reached into her leather jacket and came out with a business card. "You need to find me again, you call, okay?"

"I will." Dana took the card with one hand as she fished in her pocket with the other. She pulled out her phone, hit a button, and put it up to her ear. She glanced at the card. Sara's name and number on one side, while on the other…

The call connected. "Max?" Dana said, returning her glance to Sara. "I'm sending over a friend for a special covert op, Sara Wilde. I need you to help her." She smiled at the rush of Max's reply that came back over the phone. "Oh, yeah. I think you're going to enjoy this."

CHAPTER SIXTEEN

The Church Nightclub
Theatre District
Cleveland, Ohio
2:00 p.m., Dec. 24

Finn was approaching the nightclub when a soft laugh drew his attention. He glanced to the side, then stared, grimacing at the surge of pleasure that stirred within him to see Dana standing there. He'd hated lying to her, hated leaving her. Hated even more that he cared about such things. She'd seriously harshed his mellow, and he didn't know if he'd ever get it back.

But he had bigger problems at the moment. "What are you doing here?"

"We've got some real trust issues to work through, you know that?" Dana stepped out from the wall, turned to look up at the building. "The Church, huh? Kind of funny, since you guys have an aversion to the place. He in there?"

"He is. Bartholomew apparently is a funny guy."

The nightclub didn't look all that prepossessing from the outside, its existence marked only by a shingle hanging out over the street, lettered in archaic script, long elegant letters announcing The Church, est. 2001.

"You know this club?" Finn asked her.

"Question of the hour. But yeah, I've been inside maybe twice, enough to figure out the layout, more or less. It's not really my scene."

"It looks abandoned."

"That's part of its shtick. The windows are draped with a heavy black crepe curtain that only comes up on certain nights of the year—Halloween, Mardi Gras, that kind of thing—so that passersby can be entertained by some of the more colorful exotic dancers the club retains as waitstaff."

"Nice."

"We aim to please here in Cleveland." She nodded to the door and the black silk wreath hanging on it, ruby-red holly berries glistening within its ebony embrace. "At least they have a Christmas wreath."

"And they're open." It wasn't a question. A tiny brass placard announced the fact.

"Yeah, well. The Church is always open. How they find the clientele to keep it hopping twenty-four seven, I have no clue. But it's been around long enough to have a track record—my dad told me about it. The police are never called here. The neighbors never complain. It's a regular donor to community events, and it welcomes the media whenever some stringer needs to write a story on the city's goth underground." She glanced at him. "So why are you waiting outside?"

"I can feel him in there," he said. "He's waiting for me...which doesn't make sense. They're not supposed to be able to track my activities."

Dana frowned. "They who? Demons? Or specifically Bartholomew?"

Finn's eyes widened. That's right, Bartholomew was a Fallen, not a demon. Of course he could track Finn. There was no end to the things he was learning about this being that he once was…in all cases, it was better than the being he'd become.

He wondered if Bartholomew had had anything to do with that too. There was too much about this job that resonated with him, too much that caused his skull to ache. Too much, as usual, the archangel hadn't told him.

"Let's go." Finn reached out and pulled the door wide.

They were almost immediately assailed by the heavy bass of house music, even though the main dance floor was down the corridor. Giving Dana a second to adjust her eyes to the gloom, Finn frowned into the face of the Japanese school girl in heavy kabuki makeup who smiled winsomely at them as they approached the stand.

"Twenty-dollar cover, each," the girl chirped.

Before Finn could move, Dana pulled out her wallet. "Twenty dollars? At two o'clock?"

"Donation to The Church," the girl said with a shrug, her English as flawless as her skin. Finn didn't wait for Dana to pay but pushed down the corridor, every sense tight.

The place was hopping. Easily a hundred of the faithful paid tribute to the kaleidoscope of lights and music that thundered out over the room, most of them barely dressed and the room itself warm enough to justify their lack of attire. He moved through the crowd, trying to look everywhere at once.

It was quite a scene. Immediately in front of them

cavorted two blondes, possibly twins, certainly made up to look that way with platinum hair sticking straight up in high ponytails and heavy orange eye shadow ringed with dark black liner. Their lips were garishly orange too, their white bodies writhing in even whiter, skintight dresses that ended a few inches below their asses. The women definitely outnumbered the men on the dance floor, but the men were scarier, a collection of leather-clad misfits with enough piercings to set off metal detectors five miles away. They writhed and hissed and moved around Finn and Dana like a sea full of eels.

Finn's gaze slid over the crowd, finally spotting a bouncer. He moved forward as a man knocked into him, scowling. "You here to drink or look around?" the waiter growled, offering him a tray of steaming blue drinks in test tubes. Finn waved him off. Around them, the lights pulsed wildly, the music growing more frenetic as they moved deeper into the Church's domain. It wasn't a single dance floor at all, but a collection of sitting rooms and parlors and open hallways, all draped in heavy black crepe and accented by schizophrenic lighting and horrible music. There appeared to be one bartender for every five patrons, and the alcohol was coming fast and furious.

"This seems early for so much alcohol," he suggested.

"Christmas Eve," Dana said, unperturbed. "Most of these folks will be entertaining family for the next forty-eight to seventy-two hours. There probably isn't enough alcohol in the world to prepare some people for that."

They moved into another room, this one thankfully less crowded but still thrumming with music and bodies. As Finn moved for the bouncer, the man stepped away, farther into the crowd. Irritation flashed through him. He had no time for this.

Another few steps and Finn was up in the guy's face. "I'm looking for Bartholomew Petolya," he said, and the man looked at him with the same dead-eyed glare that the hostess had perfected, but with significantly less makeup.

"Never heard of him," the man sneered, his expression hard and stupid in the frenetic, pulsing lights. And he stank of sweat, fear, and bubblegum.

Finn recognized the scent of the Possessed immediately. "This might help you remember."

He reached out and broke the man's arm.

Dana didn't even react at his side, but the man dropped to the floor, and Finn regretted the move for an instant as he felt the mortal's pain. Then he grinned hard at the outrage that spilled out of the man's eyes. The fastest way to break through a demon's hold on a human? Unexpected pain. As the man howled, the sound of the demon inside him getting yanked up on his toes was almost lost in the noise. Almost.

"I asked you a question," Finn said. "Where is Bartholomew Petolya?"

The demon wailed through the man's gaping lips. "He's not here, he's not here!"

"Try again," Finn said. "I can *smell* him, and he's not much better than you."

"*Fallen*," hissed the demon, the man's mouth twisting into a hideous snarl. "You'll die for that."

"Get him. Now." Finn reached to the man's thick neck and yanked the heavy medallion he wore tight, strangling him with it. "Or you'll die inside this skin sack as well."

The man started choking, his eyes fixed on Finn,

unable to tear himself away. Slowly, inexorably, as he approached death, the human came to the fore and the demon was temporarily overcome. The moment the man nearly passed out, Finn released the chain and kicked him forward into a group of writhing humans draped in red-and-green spandex. "Get Bartholomew," he ordered as the mortals scattered. "Now."

Half crawling, half running, the man fled, the demon within him outraged but unable to override the pain receptors that had triggered the human's survival response.

"That's probably not the best way to win friends and influence people," Dana commented, and he looked at her surveying the scene. "So far, the bouncers here are either blind or they've been told not to cross each other's territory. You've been picked up by two different men, and the bartender has his eye on you too. But none of them are making any move toward you."

"Not yet anyway." Finn reached out and took a drink off a passing waiter's tray. It looked like sludge and smelled worse, a steaming concoction that was closer to medieval grog than anything mortals should be drinking in this century. And it was spiked with more than alcohol. He set it on the counter beside him. "I need you to promise me that you'll leave when I tell you to."

She shot him a glance. "Is that going to be happening anytime soon? Because I wouldn't mind meeting Bartholomew. I've heard so much about him."

"You'll see him. But only so you'll recognize him, should you ever encounter any of his kind again," Finn said. "Pay attention to everything about him. He's a Fallen—stronger than a demon—but he's gone rogue, and he's not the only one out there, I fear. Memorize every detail. But don't come after me if I go down. And if you suddenly get a strong, Finn-flavored urge to get out of here, heed it." Finn glanced at her, his heart giving a hard knock to his rib cage. He couldn't help it. He was becoming what he most feared, tempted by a mortal he was destined never to see again.

Perhaps this was the archangel's true test of his willpower. If so, Finn was in big trouble.

As if sensing his dismay, Dana stepped toward him. *Too close, too close.* "I'll leave, but you have to promise me to take care of yourself," she said, looking up at him, searching his eyes. "Whatever business you have with Bartholomew, it's not worth getting killed over. There's the list to recover, right? You need that more than him."

Finn looked back at her, relishing her nearness before he redoubled his hold on his reactions. "I do need that," he agreed. "And I'll find you." He wasn't sure if it was the truth anymore or not, but he wanted it to be.

She nodded. "You do that." Then she glanced around. The crowd had begun to edge closer, but not by much, the stain of violence permeating the air around them. "You think they're going to come back with him, or ask you to come with them?"

"I think we're about to find out."

Men seemed to flow through the various doors of the club like ink, taking up their locations around the room as the music shifted and rolled, while at the same time, the crowd gradually got the picture that something important was going down in this room and that they should move their own parties elsewhere.

Finn assessed the figures before him. Intriguingly, most of them were Possessed, not demons in full glamour. The Possessed definitely seemed to be Bartholomew's preferred method of doing business.

They were also spoiling for a fight, and probably for more than one reason. None of these men were among the ones he had dealt with last night. It would be too soon to repossess those broken human bodies with fresh demons, no matter how hardy the stock. But the demons he hadn't destroyed would have found new hosts, and they would be eager to settle the score.

Within seconds, the room had emptied of any mortal whose body wasn't otherwise occupied. Even the bartender had abandoned her post.

Dana shifted beside him, and he reached out an arm to block her.

"Behind the bar," he said. "It'll be easier on me if I can deal with them my way. Remember, no matter how bad I appear to be losing, don't step in to help me out, okay?"

She looked ready to argue, but as the men rushed forward, she moved faster than he would have expected. She vaulted over the bar and spun around, both surprise and anger lighting her features. Surprise at her quick reactions, anger that she couldn't participate? Finn didn't know and frankly, didn't care. Dana would have to watch this particular show.

The men rushed him all at once. There was no artistry or testing involved, as with Lester's carefully staged production. It was a mob rush, the attack of wild dogs on a creature they wanted for their own. He would fight, for a while, then he would allow himself to be taken. He only wanted to get to Bartholomew.

But he had some steam to burn off before he got there.

His attackers engulfed him. The first thing he noticed was that they fought like animals, not men, tearing, ripping, fingers poking into his eyes and mouth, trying to get a purchase on his clothes, kicking and pummeling. They'd been possessed too long, their human hosts pushed deep into the background.

Behind him, Finn felt the horrified pressure of Dana's stare. He battled back to let her know that he remained conscious, then returned to the baying and howling men that surrounded him. The music cranked up, thundering throughout the room, such that any of the lost souls at the front of the establishment wouldn't know the thrashing that was going on in the rooms deep within The Church's dark center. As certain members of the Possessed got close, he looked into their eyes, selectively punching some of their demons back beyond the veil with an ease that surpassed even the Syx's legendary capabilities, the human hosts slumping in a daze without the demons to animate them. He used the pile of mortal bodies to clear a space for him to think, then deposited them carefully out of harm's way. They would be sore when they awakened, but they would be whole again.

He figured they'd appreciate the difference.

After his third demon expulsion, he thought he heard Dana cry out, an exhalation of sheer horror. Finn risked a look over toward her, to see her struggling with a man who was screaming obscenities at her as she pummeled him. This particular Possessed had more fight than most of them, and he wasn't giving up easily, but Dana seemed to grow stronger in her conviction the more he raged at her, her return anger directed not at the man but at the demon inside him. In terms of who'd win dominion over this particular human, Finn's money was on Dana.

Then a new group of attackers poured out of the hallway into the already packed room. As the first wave retreated and a second wave struck, Finn crashed to the floor, the weight of the demon scrum pressing him down into the alcohol-and-sweat-soaked floor. What seemed like hours passed, until he'd lost count of how many demons he'd allowed to pile on him, and how many had actually started to get in shots that were beginning to hurt.

Suddenly, the music stopped.

A single sound permeated his ears over the pounding of his heart. The sound of a man clapping.

Wincing, Finn rolled over, shoving off the demon soldiers that had gone mute and dormant around him, an army of rag dolls. He got to his feet, and came face-to-face with the rogue Fallen.

"And to think, I have imagined this day for centuries, only to have it surpass my wildest expectations," Bartholomew said, his voice a rich mixture of a dozen cultures. "Finally, I see my own kind once more."

Tall and rangy, the rogue Fallen had the warm skin tone and dark eyes of a Saudi prince, his hair and beard neatly trimmed, his manner commanding respect. He dressed expensively, his well-cut suit perfectly tailored over his large frame. Gold glinted at his cuffs and ears, and around his neck hung a similar medallion to the one the bouncer had worn. There must have been a sale running at the mall.

Either way, Bartholomew Petolya had left his guise as a holy man well behind him, leveraging his abilities of a Fallen to reenter society with a vengeance.

"I know your name is Finn. And you have brought the woman, I see." Bartholomew grinned. "We've been trying to get her for some time. So I can also thank you for that."

Finn stiffened, but Bartholomew raised a hand. "Be at peace," he said, gesturing one of his men to go behind the bar. "Indulge me."

The man grunted as he stepped behind the bar, moving over to where Dana's jacket lay crumpled. "She's not here," he said.

Finn turned. Dana's leather jacket lay over the shoulders of the slumped body of the man who'd attacked her, but she was nowhere to be seen. Hopefully, she'd run when she'd seen him go down under the pile.

Bartholomew sighed from the front of the room. "Mortals have such a tendency to go off script, don't they?" He signaled to two of his men, who left the room immediately. But Finn knew that Dana wasn't stupid. She wouldn't have escaped the room during a fight that she saw Finn was losing on purpose, only to let herself get captured by Bartholomew's men.

At least, not unless she had no other choice.

"But come now," Bartholomew said. "We have much to discuss. I find the fetid stench of this place to be something I can only endure on a limited basis. Let us walk a bit."

He gestured expansively, and Finn followed him out the door, into the cold white brilliance of the Cleveland winter's day.

The moment they cleared the door, it swung shut behind him, effectively closing in Bartholomew's other stooges. Bartholomew turned to him and smiled, and for the first time, Finn got a good look at his eyes.

There was...something wrong with his eyes. They flashed with madness and desire, but there was also an unholy purpose lighting their inner depths.

"You feeling okay, there, buddy?" Finn ventured.

He'd been beat up more than he'd expected by the demon scum inside, but he edged forward anyway, looking for an opening to attack the rogue Fallen.

"Finn, Finn, Finn," Bartholomew said, his face flushed with excitement. "There is so much I would teach you, so much that you should know." He flung out his arms wildly, claiming the street, the city, the planet for his own. "Catch me. I beg you."

CHAPTER SEVENTEEN

Cathedral of St. John the Evangelist
Cleveland, Ohio
2:30 p.m., Dec. 24

Dana entered the cathedral from the front this time, trotting up the wide stone stairs, pulling back one of the broad doors. The foyer was quiet, pristine, and she crossed quickly to the doors that led her to the cathedral's sweeping hall, looking for Father Franks.

She saw him almost immediately, instructing a small host of maintenance workers in placing white poinsettias on the altar and celebrant chairs. A dozen artificial trees had already been erected around the altar, and yet more workers were running extension cords between them, linking them to the already winking display around the nativity scene to the left of the altar.

Dana strode up the main aisle, the cobblestone floor uneven beneath her boots. She felt her blood thrumming against her temples and forced herself to hesitate as she reached the break in the rows of pews. Father Franks looked up, eyes going wide for a second before he nodded to her and went back to his instructions. Dana could only stare.

The priest was surrounded by a pulsing, incandescent golden glow. It was faint, certainly. Nothing compared to the white shimmer that had come off Finn. But it was indisputably there, as readily apparent as the priest's thick silver hair or the slight stoop to his shoulders as he leaned down to explain flower arrangements. Dana tried to train her eyes on the workers around him, and nothing came off them. But Father Franks glowed with a life, a vibrancy that was unmistakable in the magnificent sweep of the church.

Trying not to fidget, Dana turned her eyes to the beautiful stained glass windows detailing various scenes from the Bible—the Nativity, Jesus Teaching at the Temple, the Last Supper, and easily a dozen more. The cold light of the December day shone through the glass, scattering rich jewel-toned patterns across the gleaming, polished hardwood of the church pews and gilded plaster of the thick columns that held the roof aloft. The light threw the church into quiet brilliance, under the careful watch of hundreds of angels represented in paint and stone throughout the church.

Her father had known every stone of this place, calling it his sanctuary. She couldn't remember being here more than a dozen times in the past year, though. Including last night.

Then Father Franks was in front of her, startling her out of her reverie. "Dana," he said, and his eyes betrayed his concern as they searched hers. "What's wrong? Where's Finn?"

"He's...losing a fight. On purpose. And I need to talk to you," she said. "Now, and alone."

"Of course." Father Franks looked toward the beehive of activity around the altar, then gestured. "We can talk in my study."

They walked with purposeful strides toward the back of the cathedral, Dana grimacing as they passed the altar. She remembered Finn standing here, in the flickering candlelight, his eyes wide with wonder. She knew Franks remembered it too.

"You thought he was a demon." Dana's quiet words were cut off by Franks's hand on her arm.

"I did," he said. "While in truth, he's worse, in some ways. So much worse." He opened the cathedral door that led into the administrative portion of the church and gestured her through. Here, there were more people, but they moved through them quickly, heading deeper into the labyrinth of the Church's inner sanctum. "Where is he now?"

"Nightclub on Euclid, The Church." She shifted her gaze toward him. "Going down hard, but again...on purpose. Meanwhile, I think I saw — I know I saw — men with demons inside them, Father. Women too." She shuddered. "They looked...I can't even describe it."

"Faces contorting outside the frame of typical human bone structure, animalistic screams, your name repeated over and over?" Father asked, but his question didn't need an answer. "The tricks never change," he said. He unlocked his office and stepped inside. "Finn sent you here?"

The first thing she saw was Franks's desk, covered with file folders and notebooks. There was a computer on a side desk, but it sat gleaming and undisturbed. The good father probably only used it under duress. Lining the wall were dozens of framed newspaper clippings of church events, smiling parishioners, news about the pope.

She realized the priest was waiting for her response.

"Not exactly. He told me to stay safe, then the Possessed came in. A lot of them." She paused, looking around the small office. It had been years since she'd been here last. The room was a compact library, with books lining the walls from floor to ceiling, and four book-strewn leather chairs gathered in a conversational setting around a low table. A desk sat in the far corner, with the banker's light on, file folders and paperwork scattered across it. Sitting on top of the folders was a worn leather pouch, its edges frayed and nearly white with age. The pouch was open, and Dana could see a flask and crucifix edging out of the bag before Father Franks pushed the items back inside the casing with a tidy sweep of his hand.

"How many?" he asked, recalling her to herself.

"Maybe twenty. It was hard to see. The place is a techno club, lots of bright flashing lights. But they were there and they...were wrong." She shook her head. "I don't think Finn can be possessed," she said. "I wasn't so sure about myself. And once it seemed like Finn was deliberately giving himself up, I sensed very strongly that I should go." She forced a smile. "I don't think he wanted to add me to the casualty list."

"I appreciate that." Father Franks moved away from her as he opened up his closet, taking out purple and white vestments. A long, heavy jacket hung over the chair, ancient with age, and Franks tapped it as he walked by, assessing his supplies. Dana turned her attention to the walls of books he passed. Bibles of every stripe lined the shelves, along with works on archaeology, theology, Christology, and religious theory. And, oddly enough, an entire shelf devoted to angels, saints, and demons. All decidedly newer books, more than half of them dipping into secular perspectives. On a stand by the shelves, a lectern held up a thick, ancient Bible, its heavy pages opened to Revelations. "Did he kill the Possessed?"

"I think he was sending the demons out of some of them," Dana said. She didn't tell him about the man she'd encountered whose demon seemed to *recognize* her. She didn't remember much of what happened after that, until the man had slumped in her arms. "They seemed like they were breathing when he was done. Others...sort of exploded."

"Those would be the true demons, not Possessed." Franks said, though the admission clearly cost him. "Finn is a Fallen. He would save God's children if he could. The others he would consign to whatever hell they deserved." He donned the surplice over his black shirt and trousers. It fell only to his knees, with a long slit on either side. Demon hunters apparently needed to be able to run. The violet stole went on next.

Franks turned to look at Dana. "There are knives in the closet, four of them," he said, as he leaned over his desk. "Get them for me."

Dana turned and opened the closet, and hanging on the back of the wall were two sets of large ceremonial knives. She pulled them out, then frowned. "These aren't even sharp."

"They aren't meant to draw blood," he said. "Give me one, you keep the other. There's another long jacket in the closet. Put it on." He scowled at her. "Where's yours?"

"Draped over one of the bodies. I left it behind to give myself a head start." She pulled out the brown leather duster, cracked from weather and salt. "You should take better care of this," she said.

"It was your father's."

"I need — I need to talk to you about him too," Dana said, moving in beside Franks. He glanced down at her, and Dana focused on the floor, suddenly nervous. Now that the time was here, she didn't know what to say. She took a deep breath, held it, then let it out slowly, surprised at how her throat burned with the movement. "I need to know…if he knew about me." She looked up to see Franks staring at her with wide, unhappy eyes. "What I am."

Father Franks didn't change expression, but a wave of loss spilled off him as strong as if he'd been wounded in front of her. "Ah, sweet child. There's probably only one thing you truly need to know. And it is something you already know in your heart. Your father was an ordinary man, Dana, not like you. He married his wife, Claire, and eventually welcomed you into the world. He was a good man, a good policeman, and he loved you more than anything. But his burden was that he was plagued by demons. Or, rather, you were."

Dana's eyes popped. *"What?"*

"Yes," he said quietly. He nodded at the coat in her arms. "He came to me after they had first appeared, not knowing what he was seeing or why. Not knowing why they sought you out. For many years, he accepted it as his cross to bear, the pain that he witnessed, the constant vigilance. He believed you were special — and, of course, you are. He vowed to protect you. One day, he decided he could no longer merely protect you, however. He had to fight back. He came to me for help with that as well."

She swallowed, holding the coat tightly. She'd never seen it before, and now it represented everything about her father that she didn't know. "Did he win?"

"Not always, and not that last time," Father Franks said, and she stilled at the tone of his voice. Suddenly, Father Franks looked old. Old, weary, and resolute. His eyes were no longer gentle, they were cold. His shoulders didn't round over in gentle apology, his hands didn't shake. He picked up a small duffel bag and slung it over his shoulder. "But often enough. Come with me."

The back door to Franks's office led to a short staircase. The priest moved down it with surprising grace and pushed through another door into a basement room set up with weights, mats, and a punching bag.

"Demon hunting keep you in shape, Father?" Dana asked as they moved through it, the bright light shining through the windows letting her know they were near the parking lot. He threw the duffel on a card table and opened a large metal cabinet. More flasks went into the bag, along with stakes, an old Smith & Wesson, and bags of powder. She frowned at him. "What is all this stuff?" she asked. "We're not going after vampires."

Father Franks chuckled darkly. "People never give the Possessed much credit. They accuse them of having weak minds, a lack of faith." Into the bag went an embroidered veil, a Bible burned around the edges. "But it is those who are possessed that have the greatest faith of all. For if you are to allow a creature within you, you must first acknowledge that creature's right to *be* within you. Its strength, its dominance. You must cede your control of your own self-determination to something which you view as more powerful than yourself. This takes a very strong belief." He zipped up the bag and turned to look at Dana. "Put the coat on. You'll need to be able to maneuver with it on."

She did, and he pulled the knives out of their

sheaths. "You don't drive with the tip, as if to cut," he said. "Although you can if that is necessary. But the force of these blades is in laying them over your opponent's heart in a crossed pattern, the bottom one vertical, the top horizontal. Like this." He stepped up to her, placing the blades into position. "No matter what religion the mortal professes to believe, he will recognize that symbol. More importantly, the demon inside him will. Or, if it's not a possession at all but a demon appearing human—and there are more and more of those these days—you can be sure they'll know it as well."

"Got it." Dana felt the blades heavy on her chest and willed herself not to step away. But the religious relics felt odd in that position, a faint thread of violation worming through her. "So what's the other stuff for?"

"Symbols of the religion lost whenever the possession began. Even fallen-away believers have their own inviolate truths. For some, it's holy water, for others, a crucifix. Still others, a stake, silver bullets. An elixir of salt and wolfsbane. But for those believing that a demon has entered, something external must be introduced to bring it back out. That," he smiled, "and these." He held up a pair of heavy wire cutters. "To cut any medallion off them that's holding the demon in place, which is also a common trick."

"I've seen those medallions," Dana said, startled.

"I thought you might have." Franks returned the knives to their sheaths and buttoned up his jacket. Then he turned toward the door. "Finn is very likely no longer at the nightclub," he said. "The building is riddled with escape routes, and if Bartholomew wanted to speak with him alone, he has the whole city to work with."

"So do we," Dana said. She pulled a thin metal

device out of her back pocket, then hit a few key instructions. Instantly, a radar swept on.

"I took the precaution of planting a tracker on Finn." She frowned down at the system. "It looks like he's at..." She frowned. "The cemetery?"

CHAPTER EIGHTEEN

Erie Street Cemetery
Cleveland, Ohio
3:00 p.m., Dec. 24

Bartholomew clearly had been serious about his game of tag.

Before Finn could grab him, he'd taken off at a dash, not stopping until he reached the grandly arched opening to some kind of city park, which was dwarfed by the stadium across the street. He turned, as if to make sure Finn was following him. The lettering carved into the stone was clear in the harsh sunlight: Erie Street Cemetery. Bartholomew turned and ran lightly over the snow-encrusted surface of the sidewalk, his body fleet and agile.

Finn staggered along behind him, still far faster than mortals, but nowhere near reaching Bartholomew's speed. He'd not fully gotten used to being Fallen yet, while Bartholomew had had six thousand years of practice, and there was that small problem of recently having taken more than his share of a beating. He glanced around as he jogged down the long central roadway of the cemetery. Trees dotted the landscape, the precious real estate otherwise taken up with row upon row of tombstones, most of them easily over a hundred years old.

Figures that Bartholomew would choose a cemetery. To a being that lived forever, a cemetery was like Disneyland. A glimpse into an experience they would probably never know.

Finn felt the change in the air as Bartholomew stopped, pivoted. He stopped as well, cautious. Not sure how to play this.

The Fallen laughed. "You haven't gotten used to the weight of the atmosphere yet, have you? You will. When I finally accepted what my role was on this earth. It became...far easier."

"You left the church in Lyon. Why?"

"You've been speaking to Father Franks, I see. I knew there was something about the man that was important—knew it. But I couldn't decide exactly what. That's the problem with the Fallen's perspective. You'll know what I mean, if you live long enough. You can see, if you look hard enough, entire lifetimes. Not merely the path, but every step along the path. Franks was a vital key to my future, I knew it in my bones, but I didn't understand how, back then. It was only after the good father made his way to this city that he met Walter Griffin. A man who'd spent so much time in the presence of the light, I mistook him for the light himself. It took me years to realize my mistake, but still proved to be vitally important to me."

Finn frowned at him, and Bartholomew came up closer to him, just out of reach. "You're no match for me,

Finn. You aren't strong enough. It's best if you acknowledge that."

Finn's anger filled the small space between them. "What do you want with Lester Morrow?" he asked.

"Ahh... my dear Lester. Had I known how close I was to his operation fifteen years ago, when my pets killed Walter, I would have made much better use of my time in this pit. But it took me finding Lester along the trail of his own greed to realize what he was, what he might have. And honestly, I have to thank you for that. Were it not for you being sent here by your precious archangel, I might still believe that Lester was merely a minor player in this game. But he isn't, is he? He's the ringleader. And Dana is his star attraction."

Finn shifted. "How do you know anything about who sent me?"

Bartholomew ignored the question to ask another of his own. "Tell me, Finn, how will it feel when you're asked to leave your precious Dana Griffin behind, knowing that merely for having met you, she's become a target? If you thought she was in trouble before, rest assured. You've all but ensured her death."

He sighed. "Too bad I can't let you stay to help her." And he launched into Finn.

This time, however, Finn was ready. In some ways, he'd been ready for more than six thousand years.

Finn took the weight of Bartholomew's attack as a storm of absolution, the feeling of power and thrust knocking him backward but not down. As his fist connected with the rogue Fallen's temple, the crunch of bone against bone exceptionally gratifying.

But Bartholomew had been fighting on this plane for far longer than Finn, at least in this present form. He jerked his head back from Finn's punch, then came at

Finn with fists pounding in explosive, percussive bursts, his movements fueled by rage and fire and more hatred than Finn would have thought possible. He was the most dangerous of breeds, the madman who thought himself sane. The self-righteous zealot who thought himself justified.

And in questioning what might happen to Dana after he'd left her to face life as a newly awakened Dawn Child, he'd opened up a hole inside Finn that might never be refilled.

Bartholomew dragged in a breath, and Finn followed it with a crack to the jaw with his elbow, his body pressing forward as he pushed Bartholomew down to the snow-covered ground. They scrambled there, neither one getting the upper hand for some time until Finn finally threw Bartholomew over onto his back.

"And what do you gain from this list?" Finn seethed as Bartholomew scrambled up to face him. "Why are they so important to you? There're simply not that many of them."

Bartholomew laughed, a sharp, guttural sound. "Even a handful of the Dawn Children are enough, properly trained." His eyes blazed with feral intensity. "Which is why I won't give them that chance."

"You are *filth*." Finn surged forward and crashed into Bartholomew again, the rogue Fallen falling into the snow face-first, rolling to the side to avoid Finn's lunge.

"Maybe," he gritted out, as he wobbled once more to his feet, circling Finn to the right. "But at least I know what will happen to mortals when they are subject to the rule of Fallen and demons. At least that rule will be straightforward. As it stands, these people are *slaves*.

They know so little. They can't even protect themselves. They deserve to know their fate, not be led by the nose to slaughter."

"They'll never allow themselves to be ruled by the legion," Finn spat, both of them glaring at each other, lungs heaving.

"And how long do you think they'll last with so many new demons free to roam the earth? A year? A week? Either way, they will be ruled. It's the natural order. Because the legion know what the humans do not. Earth is *dying*, its people losing hope day by day. Soon only demonkind will thrive here, and humans will serve them like dogs."

No. Finn blew out a long breath, keeping silent, not willing to countenance Bartholomew's words with agreement or denials. "And the Dawn Children?"

"Would only delay the inevitable, if they don't accept my rule. But they will, or they will die. The time has come to act."

"Then act," Finn said, but Bartholomew only laughed at his ready stance.

"I would never tire of this," he said. "But I've made promises to the horde that I must keep. You've taken them out one too many times, I'm afraid. They have a bit of a score to settle, and I have generously offered to even their odds."

Finn frowned at him. Evening the odds didn't sound good.

"You're new to being a Fallen, you're weak, and now you've been properly tenderized," Bartholomew continued. "It's not every day that fresh Syx is on the menu. And no one is hungrier than a demon who's forced to hide in a meat sack to evade capture from the deadliest enforcers on the planet."

Bartholomew threw his hands high, and light burst forth at Finn's face, blinding him as a new wave of noise pounded into the clearing. Finn whirled around, his eyes on fire. The men from the nightclub were back — and more on top of that — but here there were no shadows and throbbing music to distract anyone from the task at hand. A task which, apparently, was him.

Nevertheless, with his eyes dazed, Finn could rely only on his auxiliary sensory skills, which laid out each of the humans in front of him like a blueprint, their faces obscured while their very souls were revealed.

All of them had been possessed. He could see the demons straining inside the bodies of their mortal hosts, could feel their palpable need to burst through the flesh of the mortals and take physical form. He could sense their anguish, their hatred for what they had been forced to endure since the Syx had begun their work in this plane. And he could sense it all pressing toward him. Heavy upon him, seeking to crush, to destroy.

They wanted to send a message — to his team, to the archangel. And he was the canvas for that message.

"Leave enough of him for identification," Bartholomew said from somewhere on his right. Then he was gone.

Finn turned, first to the right, then the left, trying to see what the demons saw, willing himself to keep standing. As he staggered to the side, he heard the voices starting up, calling out his name. The creatures within urged their humans forward, the whites of their eyes showing. Their faces contorted into the angry face of the mob. All around him, the sky was little more than a white blur, and Finn reeled as the first pipe came down upon his shoulders, hard enough to drop him to the ground again. He crouched, trying to protect his internal organs.

He couldn't win this fight, he realized. Whatever Bartholomew had done to his eyes, his body as a newborn Fallen, it was too much. All Finn needed to do now was get away. Not fight, not kick back, just make a hole and go into it, through the swirling snow, through the biting wind, through the agony of the thudding torture that was filling his mind with numbing blindness.

But he wouldn't get that chance, he didn't think. He'd been stupid. Prideful. He hadn't planned on another attack of the horde. He hadn't expected to ever be weak.

He thought of everything he'd done to this point, everything he'd seen.

All of it felt lost to him. An empty pit in his stomach.

He'd been sent here on a madman's course, to procure a list of souls the rogue Fallen wanted to execute — or worse. But what would the archangel do with that list? Would his treatment of the Dawn Children be any better?

A kernel of truth Finn would not be able to fully explore, unless he got away from the Possessed and their clubs.

Finn tasted blood in his mouth as another beam struck him square in the jaw, the screams of the demons morphing into the guttural howls he knew so much better. They piled on him anew, and they were too much...too much.

He crashed down to the ground as a screech of tires sounded in the street beyond the cemetery walls, a car thudding over stone barricades.

"Finn!" Dana screamed as a wave of searing-white heat sealed his eyes for good.

Chapter Nineteen

Erie Street Cemetery
Cleveland, Ohio
3:45 p.m., Dec. 24

Dana grabbed the door handle to propel herself out of the car as Father Franks started shouting. "Not yet!" he yelled. "We'll go through."

The priest's Fiat easily cleared the narrow gates of the cemetery's opening, and he gunned every one of its cylinders to blast up the pathway, wheels spinning in the crusted snow and ice.

A mob had assembled, beating the tar out of someone at their center, someone who had to be Finn. Light poured off the place—not the dirty light she'd seen back at the nightclub, but raw, red, and filled with rage. The possessed demons had come out to play this time, their entities barely contained within their human skins.

"Saints in heaven," Franks breathed as he revved the car. "They're not even paying attention."

"Well, clear them out of the way," Dana said. "Try not to hit Finn."

The priest gunned it and laid on the horn, but the throng of demons persisted, some of them peeling off to come and pound on their vehicle. Dana flinched back, grabbing for her phone. "We need to dial 911."

Franks laughed harshly, then looked at her with eyes gone wild with adrenaline and purpose.

"The police can't help us. They won't come until this is done, even if you'd sent them an engraved invitation. Last night proved that." He turned and pulled out his bag, squinting to see the faces of the demons as they open-mouth screamed into their windshield. He rifled through his duffel, pulling out rosaries, crucifixes, and flasks. "We're going to go old school on this one," he said, flashing her a grim smile. "Get ready for the smell."

They plunged out of the car and into the fray. Dana had more space than Franks, and she frowned as they pressed in closer to him, then realized it was her cuff holding them back. "Stay with me!" she shouted, but the priest couldn't hear her, his face contorting as he spoke words of Latin she couldn't hope to imitate.

Okay, she thought. Father Franks had made a good start.

And if what she'd experienced with the Possessed who'd attacked her in the club…she'd be able to finish the job.

Uncorking a flask, she held it up like a prize, making certain that the demons' eyes were trained on it, their pupils dilating as they realized what it meant. She splashed it in a wide circle, and the skin of the infidels immediately started smoking, their screams of rage sounding a little extra-burnt. Then she raced forward

227

with a rosary wrapped around each fist, her arms working quickly.

Whenever exactly the shift within her happened, she couldn't have said.

One moment, she was biting, tearing, scratching—feeling pain, yes, though that pain was obliterated by the keening surge of adrenaline that filled her ears and made her heart pound in her chest. Then she floated above the pain, above the rage, watching her body move with purpose and beauty that transcended reality as she beat and pummeled the demon-possessed humans into submission. She felt the burn beneath her effort, but above all else, she felt the smooth slash of energy that carried her forward as dark blood spilled with every punch.

She cast a glance at Franks, who was using a crucifix as a makeshift dagger. Flipping the topmost of her own supply of crucifixes into her hand, she emulated his gesture, then plunged the base of the crucifix into the nearest Possessed.

The man screamed as the crucifix caught fire, and he peeled off her, racing through the crowd. Suddenly, Franks was beside her, his face alight with grim triumph.

"His faith was strong!" the priest yelled, preparing to bury another holy shiv into a possessed man's shoulder. "Finn is next to the mausoleum—looks bad."

"Thanks!" Dana beat her way over to the short, squat building of harsh stone and saw Finn on the ground. His face was ash white and crisscrossed with gashes that looked like they came from both knives and nails. His body was hunched into a small knot, and he looked well on his way to dead. But the melee around him wouldn't quit. Dana suspected that thirty minutes after he died, the first of the demons might realize that perhaps he wasn't going to get up after all.

After dispatching another possessed mortal with a right hook graced with large red-hued rosary beads, Dana landed a right hook that nearly shattered another man's jaw. Her hand burned in protest, but then, finally, she was at Finn's side.

"Get off him," she yelled, yanking a creature off him. She smelled the acrid scent of burning clothes behind her. Whipping around, she was shocked to see half the demon possessed screeching and dancing around as if on fire, Father Franks stalking through the group with a fierce grin on his face.

"We have to get him out of here," he called.

She nodded, falling to her knees to revive Finn while Franks brandished an oddly shaped cross of heavy wood and spikes. To this particular brand of Possessed, it seemed to be the right button to push. Salivating and trembling, they howled at Franks, enraged, and Dana was glad that the priest stood in front of her.

"Finn!" she shouted over the din. She slapped his face once, twice. "Finn!"

On the third swipe, he moved, faster than her eye could track. He grabbed her wrist hard enough to break it, and she was caught, transfixed by the anger and pain in his eyes.

"Finn!" Franks's powerful voice thundered between them, and Finn looked with wild eyes at them both, then shook his head, abruptly coming back to reality. Between the two of them, they hauled Finn up and half carried, half dragged him to Father Franks's Fiat. Dana coughed and spit, not sure what Franks had splashed on their clothes, but it smelled a lot like garlic mixed with sulfur.

Barely able to get him into Father Franks's compact car, Dana piled in next to him. "Go to my apartment—freight elevators," she shouted as Father Franks gunned it down the narrow road to escape the cemetery. Finn had started flailing again, but more weakly this time, and the words coming out of his mouth sounded unlike any language Dana had ever heard. He remained in the throes of a battle, she realized. A battle that had taken over his body and mind.

"Hold on," she whispered, her hands straining to keep his arms in close to his body. "We're almost out of here, just hold on."

They crunched back over the brine-soaked access road back onto Ninth Street, a crowd beginning to form as the smoke and screeches burst into a sudden, whooshing conflagration over the cemetery. And, finally, minutes later, Dana could hear sirens shattering the brutally cold day.

The pain bore Finn up on a tide of howling rage, his body flayed, his bones separating, each of his organs exploding, then everything smashed back together again for the process to begin anew. He'd never known agony such as this. The feasting and delighted glee of his attackers had turned his guts to water, the sense of his power leaching away giving him the first true taste of oblivion.

When he'd first realized he had been condemned as a demon, he'd thought he'd known what it meant to be betrayed, destroyed, humiliated. He'd thought he would never feel anything so horrific again.

He'd been wrong.

The Possessed humans ruled by the Fallen were, if

possible, more vicious than true demons. It was as if the presence of the demon within them made the humans connect with their own basest instincts, the instincts Finn had always known — *known!* — were within them, that he'd always feared would come to the fore to harm each other, to defile God's holy work, to destroy...

Finn froze, allowing the demons in his mind to crowd in closer, biting and ripping. He *had* known, he realized. Back before he'd committed his sin, when he was an angel, consecrated by the Father. He'd known and he'd refused to help the mortals advance their destructive way.

He had *refused!*

A blast of pain so sharp it made him gasp detonated in his head. Suddenly, before him stood the Archangel Michael, glowing in holy radiance, and behind that great warrior of God lay the kingdom of heaven, too bright and beautiful for Finn to fully comprehend, for all that he knew where he was, knew it with crystal clear memory, because he'd *been* here before. And the archangel had been with him.

"What is this?" he cried, the agony of his long-ago failure surging up to ring its hollow dirge against his broken bones.

"You wanted to know your sin, demon," the archangel intoned. "You are looking at it."

Finn writhed and twisted, trapped in the net of shadow attackers that had followed him into his delirium, but his eyes could see, his ears could hear the vision that the archangel showed him. He saw himself, vibrant and full and true, every inch of him radiating disdain as he stared out over — what? In his current state, Finn couldn't see what lay beyond the precipice, at the very edge of God's great kingdom, but he could imagine what it had to have been.

Earth.

"You were one of the most glorious angels the Father ever created, Finnamti Kingau, the Far-Seer," said the archangel." You were born to teach, to guide. To gather up the willing and the bold and take them further than they could ever go on their own. But you were *too* far-seeing." Michael's tone hardened. "You knew what the creations of the Father were capable of, the poison, doubt, and fear that lay within them. You knew what they would face, how they would fail. And that they *would* fail, over and over again, in ever-expanding ways."

"I couldn't help them do that," Finn moaned, twisting in agony. *This beautiful, glorious creation of the Father, riven and ruined by the lowest and meanest of mortals, when they could have been more — so much more. Far greater in their truest incarnation than even —*

"Enough." The archangel's sharp rebuke slammed into Finn, tumbling him back into the thorned and ripping claws of his attackers. "It was not your place to be defiant, to refuse the call to guide. You'd convinced yourself that the worst of humanity was inevitable, and you would not go. The Father would not force you. But that didn't mean your skills, your talents, your strength could not be made to serve."

"I don't understand." As Finn spoke, he dropped his guard. Screaming with excitement, a demon pierced his chest clear through and twisted his claw, ripping his way out, and Finn fairly radiated with the agony of what should have been a death blow — would have been a death blow had he still been a demon. But he was Fallen, which he was coming to understand was code for "able to endure a *sick* amount of pain."

"You didn't need to understand," the archangel retorted. Finn didn't know if he was angry over Finn's fresh confusion or his long-ago refusal to teach the mortals. "Where so many of your fellows were eager to walk among God's children, to savor the new reality their leap across the veil would bring them, you resisted, you rejected, you refused. All because you didn't believe in the ultimate grace of His creation. You lacked *faith*—even as an exalted angel, nearest to His light. You committed your sin before you walked the earth as a Fallen…so you *never* walked the earth as one."

"But you said—" Finn gasped, weakly battering back another onslaught of the Possessed, humans who were by far the most obvious case in point that he'd been absolutely right all those millennia ago. "You said the Father would not force any service upon us if we were not willing…"

"The Father didn't," Michael said, his tone implacable. "I did."

"*What?*" Finn's mind was fracturing, every separate assault from the Possessed attacking him a new betrayal, a new affront.

Michael's condemnation kept on coming, his words driving new nails into Finn's flesh. "I could not abide you refusing any task set to you by the Father. Because if you were the first of His chosen to do it, you would not be the last. As God's highest warrior, I could not, *would* not let that stand."

"But—"

"You didn't Fall from the blessed realms of heaven, demon," the archangel cut him off coldly. "You were pushed."

CHAPTER TWENTY

Chesterfield Apartments
Penthouse
Cleveland, Ohio
4:20 p.m., Dec. 24

Dana watched as Father Franks carefully folded his stole and surplice, both of them soaked through with sweat and blood. He placed them into his half-empty duffel bag and zipped it shut, his hands resting on the salt-and-snow-crusted case as he spoke words of benediction over it. Watching him, Dana sagged against the doorframe, her eyes going from the somber-eyed priest to Finn spasming on her bed.

Random, discordant thoughts assailed her. It was the first time she'd had a man in her apartment in years — certainly the first time she'd ever had two. And she couldn't remember the last time she'd had a man in her bed. Or…or whatever Finn was.

Her apartment was much the same as it had been the day her father had died and left it to her…after his father had left it to him, and his father before. She never would have been able to afford this place otherwise. Books lined floor-to-ceiling bookshelves and tall windows looked out on two sides of her penthouse block to the cold and heartless city below. Her furniture was neither modern nor antique—it was simply old and sturdy. Only the bed was relatively new, a large wooden sleigh bed, an extra-long California king. And still Finn dwarfed it.

Now he lay quiet, the tremors that had racked his body finally subsiding into shivering twitches. Father Franks had prayed over him despite Dana's significant concern that the action would do more harm than good. But Franks had to return to the church, to finalize preparations for Midnight Mass and ensure that his congregation was safe. With so many demons afoot and the priest's own interaction with them to forestall their attack on Finn, it was all too reasonable that they would seek retribution. And according to the priest, even a demon would enter a church if its motivation was strong enough.

Beside Finn, he'd left a mini kit of his exorcism tools. He pointed to it. "You're going to need to carry that with you," he said, and Dana shuddered.

"Father, I don't know any of the Latin, and I'm not a consecrated priest. I wouldn't know the first thing about exorcising anything that might be crawling around inside someone."

"You've already done more of it than any priest I know," Franks said. "Besides, if I'm able to reach you in a time of need, I'd rather you have the tools on you than hope I'm carrying mine."

"Fair enough." Risking the few moments away from Finn's side, she crossed to Franks and walked with him through the apartment's living room/kitchen combination and out to the miniature foyer.

"This place is decorated exactly the same way your Father had it," Franks said, looking down at her. In addition to the exhaustion, there was reproof in his eyes. "You can't live in his shadow forever, Dana. If this day shows you nothing else, you must accept that."

"He made this place safe for me, Father," she said with a sigh. "Forgive me for valuing that particular aspect of it today. I'll rearrange the furniture some other time."

"Dana…" Franks paused. "Your father was a very special man. A good man. And his belief in God was devout. He carried himself with faith and integrity. That path remains open to you, no matter what's happening now, no matter who you've been—or choose to become."

Dana patted his shoulder. "You always have a way of helping the unchurched find their way back into the fold, don't you?"

"Not always," Franks said grimly. And with a last look that held more emptiness than Dana had ever seen in him, he walked out, shutting the door quietly behind him.

Dana went to the kitchen to pull a huge carafe of water out of the refrigerator. She winced as she inventoried the rest of the contents: cans of Guinness draught that had been in there since before her injury, wilting lettuce, sad excuses for vegetables, and a slightly questionable block of cheese. She ate on the go, stopping into corner delis and convenience stores, wolfing down diner pie and burnt coffee. She didn't need to be a gourmet cook in her apartment. It was enough that it was safe. Shutting the refrigerator door, she opened the freezer and pulled out a bottle of black cherry vodka. She had rubbing alcohol already set up in the makeshift first aid station she'd assembled out of sheer fidgetiness while Franks had worked on Finn's absolution, but the vodka wasn't for Finn—it was for her.

Grabbing a jar of almonds from the counter, the only definitively safe food in the apartment other than condiments and alcohol, she moved back toward the bedroom, forcing herself to reenter the room.

Everything Finn owned reeked of smoke and violation. She'd stuffed most of their clothes into the washer except the sweaters, which she currently had banging around in the dryer with tennis balls and a fistful of dryer sheets. She'd quickly changed into jeans and a cardigan sweater, pulling her wrecked hair back into a ponytail, refusing to look at herself in the mirror, knowing what she would find in her eyes. Fear. Loss. And a totally baseless hope.

Now, her arms full of supplies, she hesitantly approached Finn, her mind running over the instructions that Franks had given her.

With these tools, your father could assist the oppressed by the simple act of laying on of hands.

Dana had never seen her father do that; he certainly hadn't ever offered to heal her wounds that way. But her father was a true believer, a churchgoer with a capital C. Dana was lucky to nod in reverence to the cathedral as she walked by it. She'd simply never had that level of belief…in anything.

Still, Franks had seemed fairly convinced that she could offer Finn help. And his breathing had grown more ragged, his breath rattling in his throat. Pulling the notebook paper Franks had left for her closer to her, Dana took a deep breath and pulled the sheet down slightly from Finn's chin.

A broad expanse of chest peeked out, the skin completely free of hair — not even a dusting at the point where men typically had the slightest indication of a trail, a path of possibility leading down to —

Don't think about that. Dana bit her lip and, before she could lose her nerve, pressed her hands down squarely on Finn's chest, her thumbs interlaced.

Sensation rocketed through her, and she drew in a shuddering breath, her eyes darting to the scrawled prayer Franks had recommended. "Omnipotent and eternal God," she began, her voice already faltering. This was never going to work. "The everlasting Salvation of those who believe, hear us on behalf of Thy sick servant, Finn, for whom we beg the aid of Thy pitying mercy — "

"Stop."

Dana jerked her head up, her mouth dropping as she looked into Finn's clear, tormented eyes. She moved to pull her hands off his chest, but his, as always, were faster. In less than a second, his hands folded over hers, holding them tight. Even broken and bleeding, the speed with which Finn could move nearly blinded her.

"I'm sorry, I'm sorry," Dana said hurriedly. "Father said that those words — the prayer for healing — would help. That my father had used them and — "

Finn's laugh was low and looked like it pained him. "Dana, you're far stronger than your father was. The energy in your hands would have made you a great healer, had you chosen that path. Merely resting your hands on me, on any of the sick, with intent, will bring relief."

"Oh." Dana swallowed. "Then, ah, you're okay? After whatever it was they did to you?"

"I wouldn't go that far. Bartholomew has an extreme advantage over me, in that he fully understands what a Fallen's body is capable of in this plane and what it isn't. I don't want to know how he came by the information of what injuries would cause me the most pain, even though we are destined to heal. But I'll be okay, eventually."

She frowned. "You've been cut."

"And that'll heal as well. Within a day, here, I think. Without help. Sooner, yes, with the aid you would offer." He flattened her palms on his chest, and Dana drew in a sharp breath. He moved his hands slightly over hers, caressing her fingers as he held them trapped against his skin. She felt the warmth of him, the smooth skin overlying thick, corded muscle, and her own body tightened in response. "How did you find me?" he asked.

"Transmitter," she managed, and he smiled, the sight bringing its own healing to her. But on the edge of that was a thin, curling sense of need that seemed to start in her core and extend throughout her bloodstream, twining around her breasts and coiling between her legs. Her breath was coming fitfully between her lips, her lungs laboring even as her body ached to lean toward him.

"Of course," he murmured, and his eyes turned to the collection of tools and bottles that she had arranged beside the bed. "Um…so you were going to play doctor?"

"I don't know. I—I wanted to help." Completely mortified, Dana yanked her hands away. This time, Finn let her retreat but followed her until he was seated upright, face-to-face with her on the bed.

"You have great strength within you, Dana," he

said, the words almost an intonation, but while he tried to remain stoic, he couldn't stop the grin that teased at the corner of his mouth. "But I don't think the fastest way to mend me will be with alcohol, scissors, and gauze."

"Then what should I do?" she demanded, irritated. "You're hurt. Injured." Finn's body was so close to her that she could feel the heat radiating off it, and she was painfully aware that under the soft Egyptian cotton sheets, he was completely naked.

"Well, I'm not *dead*, it would seem," he parried, and he shifted his hips, the evidence of his erection clear and unmistakable. "In fact, I'm predicting a full recovery." He moved more forcefully, rolling up on his knees as she perched on the edge of the bed, trapped in her own awkwardness. "So I take that as a good start, don't you?"

She looked at him, unable to stop her smile. "I do."

"Excellent. And if you're looking for suggestions for next steps…" he murmured, and leaned down to kiss her.

Dana resisted for only a moment, her own body screaming for release even as she knew she should allow him to rest, to recover, to do…whatever the hell it was he needed to do. But her skin was on fire where he curled his hand around her nape, fanning out her long hair over her shoulders as if he'd never felt the contours of a woman before. Finn stopped, breathing in deeply, then tilted her back enough so that he could look down at himself. The sheets had fallen away from his body, pooling in a luxurious pile at his hips. His gaze traveled back to her belly, then her breasts, then her face, which had to be flame red with embarrassment at this point. Why was all this so *difficult*? she thought, disgusted with herself. All she had to do was dive at him, and he'd do the rest, she was almost certain.

I mean, sure, he's a Fallen angel and all, and I've never had sex with a Fallen angel, but what does that matter in the end? It can't be all that different, can it? He's got a clean bill of health certified by heaven, I'm on birth control, he wants it, I definitely want it, and—

"I'm pretty sure what happens next requires fewer clothes." Finn's voice cut across Dana's thoughts, and she jerked in surprise.

"Of course! Of course it does," she blurted. "But I— I'm a mess. I should shower, I should—my body, I—"

She quivered in his hands as he continued to rub her shoulders, his laughter light and impossibly intimate. He lifted a hand to brush his thumb pad over her lips, pulling her lower lip down as he explored its texture. Then he leaned in, taking that lip into his mouth, his heavy groan sending a ripple of pleasure through his body that reached hers as well.

"Dana," he rumbled softly. "I honestly can't remember the last time I've had sex, but at my best guess it's been at least six thousand years. And in all those millennia, I've never felt so desperate to feel a woman in my arms as I do right now with you. It's everything I can do not to drag you into this bed and rip your clothes off before you take your next breath. So I don't so much give a shit about whether or not you've taken a shower in the last few hours."

"Oh," Dana whispered. "Well…that covers that, I guess."

"We good, then?" he asked, his voice quiet, almost gentle.

"We're, ah—we're good."

"Good."

Then his hands were at the neckline of her sweater, and despite his threat of ripping the garments free, he instead eased his fingers slowly along the shallow scoop of its neckline, pressing over the delicate collarbone. The touch of his hands there made Dana's head fall back, and Finn quickly moved into the space she had bared for him, his teeth gently scraping along her neck, his tongue rough against her hot skin, his own breathing sounding as shattered as hers.

She felt his fingers slip beneath the collar of her sweater, and the heat between her legs intensified. Despite her best efforts she suddenly felt awkward again, clumsy in the presence of — well, the presence of —

"Finn," she managed.

"Let me," he said, his words hoarse. He bunched up her sweater to bare her bra and followed the line of the delicate silk band around to the hook in place. He thumbed it loose.

"And how is it you're so good at removing a bra if you haven't had sex since the Stone Age?" Dana asked wryly, and he looked at her, his eyes now as hot as his body.

"Fallen angels come fully equipped with a particular set of skills." He grinned, then his gaze searched hers. "If you're uncomfortable — "

"I'm not."

An instant later, Dana's bra and sweater were suddenly gone, tossed to the far wall of the room. Gently, Finn moved his hands over the mounds of her breasts, kneading them in wonderment, his eyes widening as the nipples pebbled and hardened in his hands. He spread his fingers wide, claiming each breast for his own, then, as promised, followed the path his fingers had taken with the questing insistence of his mouth, his lips at once gentle and fearless, seeking to touch, to tease, to take her as much as she would let him, and to come around and take her again.

Dana shuddered against him, her hands pressing up against his arms, his shoulders, pulling him to her, unwilling—unable to stop the tide of her emotions as they rolled through her. Her need increased even as Finn leaned down farther, his curious hands tracing the curve of her waist where it flared out to meet the hard edge of her jeans.

He slid his fingers underneath the waistband, and Dana let out a sharp hiss.

"I, uh—I haven't been with anyone. In a while. Like a long while," she said lamely, the enormity of what they were doing suddenly hitting her.

Finn chuckled. "I think I'll beat you in that game."

She swallowed, her tension ratcheting higher as he moved to unclasp her jeans. Finn wasn't your ordinary one-night stand. He wasn't even your ordinary once-in-a-lifetime stand. But her heart was thudding despite her awkwardness, and she found it was her hands that were brushing his away, dragging the zipper down bit by bit as Finn's breathing grew more labored and his body bucked over hers, his gaze tracking the trajectory of her fingers.

Then the zipper got stuck.

"Um…" Dana yanked, then yanked again. *Is this seriously happening?*

"Now you're just teasing me." Finn's laugh was clear and bright, and a heartbeat later, he thrust her hands away, peeling her jeans down her legs as she pressed herself back into the pillows, her body burning for him, her brain in the process of significant meltdown.

"Sweet fire in heaven," he breathed. "You're beautiful."

She grimaced. "Well, I wouldn't go that far."

"I would." Finn's brilliant blue eyes were alight with a glow that would have unnerved Dana if he'd given her even a moment to reconsider. Instead, he traced a trail of kisses down her stomach, over the soft curve of her belly, suckling her hipbones hard as her body strained toward him. His eyes swept her body, coming to rest on her legs, including the heavily grafted right shin, which he laid his hands upon, soothing coolness warring against the heat he was inspiring throughout the rest of her body.

"Such beauty, everlasting," Finn said, moving to her feet, drawing his hands along them and then moving back up her legs to where she was burning for him, practically whimpering, her body convulsing as he explored her inch by inch. As he moved closer to her core, however, his movements shifted, his pace slowing, his already gentle touch becoming impossibly light, teasing her, tempting her. He brushed his fingers over the vee between her thighs, and Dana let out a sharp gasp, but he didn't dip farther, his fingers instead trailing over her as if she were a puzzle he wasn't yet sure he wanted to figure out.

"What are you doing?" she asked in mounting panic, her body betraying her with wet heat that elicited a growl of wonder and frustration from him, Finn's fingers dipping far too gently into the musky dampness, just enough to pull her out of her skin. "Please, don't—don't stop. Not yet, not—"

"Dana," Finn whispered, and the brush of his lips over her thigh made her tremble in anticipation. "Tell me what it is you want. Whatever it is, I'll give it to you."

Something in his voice rumbled through her, her mind going blank with a sudden fear and mad, ravening joy. He was giving her something — a gift, a moment, she didn't know what. But her mind and body were tumbling over with emotions, her senses overwhelmed and her body naturally curling into his, shutting off all thought, all realization of anything but the need that poured from her and invited him into her, to claim her for his own.

He hadn't made a move toward her, she realized dimly. He was watching — waiting — for a word, a sign, an indication that this was what she wanted. Distantly, she wondered if he hadn't been with a woman in so long that he'd forgotten the way of it. More distantly, the faintest cry of alarm reminding her that he was *a freaking Fallen angel and she did not want to screw this up for him!*

Was she the first, then?

Instead of mortifying her, the idea enflamed her, her body experiencing a rush of heat that blanked her mind of any thought save for him taking her to completion, him exploring feelings that he might never have felt before, her body as his playground — and his to be hers as well. To claim him, first and forever.

Her mind tipped over into a cauldron of sensation, where rational thought had no more place.

"Please, Finn, use your mouth — your tongue — your…your cock, I don't care," she burst out, the words foreign and unnerving in her own ears. "Please just keep going and don't stop until I — there, there," she begged. She dragged his hand over where her body burned for him, splaying his fingers against the sensitive engorged skin. Too late, she thought of how she must sound, the wanton plea in her voice, her body slack and open to him, and she moved to surge up, to take it back, to make it right—to somehow undo what she had started.

Finn's left hand on her belly stopped her, pushed her back.

While his right hand spread her wide.

CHAPTER TWENTY-ONE

Chesterfield Apartments
Cleveland, Ohio
4:55 p.m., Dec. 24

Finn drew his tongue along the sensitive folds of Dana's clit, then dipped into her, his brain damn near short-circuiting. To become a Fallen who toyed with a human female was supposed to be a crime, yet the thought of leaving Dana without bringing her to satiation, the thought of leaving her body before he himself had reached fulfillment, was completely impossible to him.

He suckled at her wet heat, and Dana arched off the bed, her mouth making unintelligible sounds of urgency, of passion, of need.

Yes. This was what he'd ached for, Finn thought, never realizing it had lain so close. This was what he'd forgotten.

This was what had caused the best of his kind to crave the fall, to endure a life of ostracism from heaven for the touch of a mortal who brought his entire being alive, whose blood burned for his touch, and whose body craved his hands as if it had been made especially for him.

He tasted her more deeply, bringing his hands around her to cup her against him, the movement again making her legs fall wide and causing his shaft to stiffen. He groaned, shifting in the tangle of sheets wrapped around them both. She was so hesitant, for all her strength — so unsure of what he would do to her.

And he himself had no real idea of what he could do.

He drew his hand into a fist and grazed Dana at the point where the folds disappeared into smooth, nearly hairless skin, then, as she gasped, he applied more pressure, his tongue returning to taste her as she writhed in the sheets beneath him, trembling and calling his name.

He paced himself with the ebb and flow of her movements, winding her tighter as the minutes slid by, then easing her back, then repeating the cycle over and over again, with only the shuddering of her breath to guide him. Her soft whimpers turned to panting, then to unintelligible words, and then suddenly she convulsed, her arms flinging out as if she'd been exposed to an electric shock. She nearly shot off the bed and into his arms, throwing him back into the sheets, her body scrambling over his, her breath coming hard and fast.

"*Finn*," she panted, and she leaned into him, straddling his hips, the full weight of her lean, muscular frame pressing him down. Her eyes were hazed with satisfaction, and she glided along his cock, stopping when it was snugged up against the vee of her thighs. The opening there was warm and wet, impossibly inviting, and she leaned down close to his face, her gaze heavy on his lips, her mouth open. He could think of nothing else, suddenly, than the image of lifting her up and onto his shaft, pressing deeply into her and making her his.

All at once, she seemed to recall herself, like a door being opened onto a forbidden room. "I want — " she began, her eyes clearing as she seemed to realize where she was and what she was doing. "I just want — "

"Kiss me," Finn whispered to her, and her face grew flushed with heat. She dropped her mouth to his slowly, as he had to hers, tasting him, touching him, drawing her tongue along his lips before dipping it hesitantly into his mouth, then pushing in with more force, her mouth and hips moving in a cadence that explained to Finn how the mortal body was made to move, and to move together with another.

She dragged herself down him and as the pressure of her left his cock, he nearly cursed in frustration. But she was pure, liquid heat, moving along his chest to his abs, nuzzling his hipbones, her hands squeezing on his hips and kneading the muscles of his thighs as she slowly, inexorably worked her way down, her mouth widening into a smile as she moved the tangled sheets from between them and his heavy cock sprang free.

"You have to tell me what you like," she said softly. "I want you to feel all this, everywhere." As she spoke, she moved her lips gently over the tip of his shaft, her mouth soft and pliant against the silken head, her tongue darting out to graze it with exquisite roughness, and Finn shook as Dana had done, unable to control his convulsions. Slowly, she drew her tongue up his length and took just the tip of him in her mouth, for only a second, before shifting again and letting her tongue drift down all the way, until she teased at the heavy sac beneath.

"You're so...good," Dana said in husky, soft tones, her cool fingers slipping under him to cradle his sac in her palm. With her other hand, she circled his cock, her grip becoming hard as her mouth came down again, this time taking him deep into her wet mouth as she moved in a rhythmic cadence, her mouth a combination of heat and wetness and firm grip and the softest touch on his balls.

Finn fisted his hands into the sheets. He couldn't think; he could barely breathe.

"You like this, yes?" she asked, again her lips dancing over the tip of his shaft, then moving to the sensitive skin deep inside his thighs, playing there. "You want me to keep going?"

He gasped out a response that seemed to please her, because she bent to him again,

sliding down the bed until her face was level with his rigid cock. She took it into her mouth, stretching her lips over its length as he went absolutely still beneath her. She plunged down once, twice, and he groaned. He could feel his temperature soar beneath her hands, the tremors thrumming through his legs.

Finn endured the sweet slide of Dana's mouth over him one more time as his brain threatened to jump out of his skull.

She moved up again, her mouth opening over the tip, laving him with terrifying tenderness. Her tongue slid sweet and silky around, over, down, and again. He felt himself begin to shake.

"Dana," he gritted out, and she looked up at him. He had been shoved all the way to the back of the bed, devastated by the effect of her mouth, her hands, even the long soft caress of her hair as it draped over his quivering thighs. The pressure began to build up within him anew, demanding release, and he felt an unbearably intense need to complete what he had begun with her and claim her for his own.

Thousands of years of training, of knowledge pounded through him, his heart thundering powerfully, his mind racing, his blood surging. But his truth no longer lay in doctrines and oaths and ancient edicts. It lay within his need to serve and be with Dana. Not humanity. Not even the Dawn Children. Not a cause greater than himself or less than it should be. But the simple need to reach out and gather a woman close to himself, to claim her as his own and to dedicate his every waking breath to her safety.

Dana clearly felt the shift within him, and her own body shook with uncontrolled need before she looked up to meet his gaze.

"Is there, ah, something else I can do for you?" she asked in a husky voice, her shy stab at humor affecting him even more. She was off-balance, unsure, and it was one of the most intimate and open expressions he had ever seen. And he had done this to her. With his body, with his touch.

With his heart.

"Dana," he breathed and clasped her to him, pulling her up onto him more fully as he covered her mouth with his. Dana sank against him, sinuous and warm beneath him as his hands moved down her body, marking every curve and ridge, cataloguing every indentation and rise. "I want more," he said, his words a plea as much as a command.

"How?" she asked, and he looked at her with confusion.

"There are many ways of making love, Finn," she said throatily, and her eyes were heavy and hot. She reached out, her hand stroking his quivering cock, and he felt the urge to explode immediately, without waiting to join with her.

"As long as it's soon, Dana, I don't think it'll matter so much."

"Then let me watch," she said softly. She kissed him long and hard, then nipped at his lower lip, bringing him back into focus. He opened his eyes, not aware he'd closed them, but when he reached for her, she placed heavy hands on his shoulders.

"No," she whispered. "Let me this time."

This time. Under her hands, he moved easily, pressing deeply into the sheets. She stretched him out and straddled him, the shape of her neatly fitting against his, causing new sparks of awe and delight to shoot through his bloodstream. His heavy cock bucked up against her, and she ground against his groin, slick and hot, her hands moving to steady herself on his shoulders.

"Just lie there for a second, okay?" she asked, and she pressed against him, her perfect breasts heavy against his chest and her face dropping to score a row of hot kisses against his neck. She touched her teeth to his skin, dragging her mouth along his collarbone and up the column of his neck. She kissed along his jawline as he lay there, trembling, and her eyes flashed with pride and triumph as she felt him shaking beneath her. "You want inside me?" she whispered. "Because I want that. I want to feel you deep inside me, all of you. Would you like that?"

Finn groaned, unable to stand it anymore. With a movement that felt as natural to him as breathing, he reached for Dana, lifting her high, settling her down on his erection in one smooth thrust, sheathing her tightly over him. They both gasped at the impact, and Dana reared up, forcing her hips down as her legs bent to keep her steady.

"Oh," Dana breathed in sharply.

He stilled for a moment, staring at her as her lips parted and her eyelids drooped.

"You're good," she said, color coming back into her cheeks. "It just—it's all good," she murmured, her eyes closing in concentration. She bit her lip, then slowly, excruciatingly slowly, began to move on top of him.

Finn felt her close around him, constricting against his shaft, and he groaned low in his throat. His eyes were filled with the perfection of her. Her long neck, her rounded breasts that swung with each thrust of her hips. The curve of her waist as she moved and bucked on top of him. The long rush of hair that tumbled over her shoulders. She was beautiful. Mortal.

His.

Dana reached up and ran her hands along her waist, then brought them up, curving her fingers to touch her breasts, teasing out the nipples as if to put them on display for him, and Finn felt the release build within him, knew that this would be the final time.

"Dana," he gritted out, and she laughed with pure abandon, feeling it too.

"I want to see your eyes, Finn," she said, and he tensed, unable to deny her, but unable to keep what he knew would happen to his eyes from her if she kept looking at him like that. He ground up into her, his hands suddenly on her waist, her hips, pulling her down upon him even as the blood rushed into his ears and his chest expanded, his heart surging against his rib cage and his body building toward a crescendo he could neither avoid nor fully understand. He shifted his hands inward, his hands arching Dana outward again, his thumbs applying pressure that caused her to gasp even as he refused to let go, forcing her to ride the storm with him, bringing her up on the same gust of sensation that was threatening to utterly consume him.

A shift, a movement, a moment later, and Finn felt the explosion deep within. Dana gasped on top of him, clearly shocked as she watched his irises change inexorably, the reflection of the bright and brilliant blue orbs clear in her own eyes.

"Finn!" she whispered, but she was too lost in the maelstrom of sensation to fully get the words out, and he pulled her close, enveloping her in an embrace that would last for far less than a lifetime. She was his. For as long as he could have her.

Finn closed his eyes as the primal forces of their bodies took over.

Time was now his enemy, but he could no longer fight the pull of extreme exhaustion that was weighing him down. Exhaustion and — something else. Peace. An abiding sense of rightness. A flood of emotions that coursed over his defenses and pulled him toward a world he had never wanted, never known, never imagined.

For the first time in his immortal life, Finn the Far-Seer fell asleep in the arms of a woman he loved.

CHAPTER TWENTY-TWO

Cathedral of St. John the Evangelist
Cleveland, Ohio
6:00 p.m., Dec. 24

"Why did you tell Lester to meet you here?" Dana asked, and Finn slid her a look. She was too keyed up, too anxious, scanning the front of the church as they waited for Lester to join them. "I thought you didn't like this place."

"I knew it would make him feel safe."

"Yeah, well that's one of us." She glanced up, peering toward the rafters as she shoved her fists into her pockets. "I've always hated the angels in this church." Her harsh black coat matched her darkening mood, but there was nothing for it. They'd been awakened far too quickly by Lester's text, telling them he was ready to meet for what he termed "the first delivery." They'd had time only to shower—a long shower, admittedly, tangled in each other's arms—and then come to the church. There'd been no time to talk about anything but the barest of logistics.

Dana sighed. "I mean, I've been in here hundreds of times, and I know the story. They're the angels of St. John's vision of the Revelations. You know that, right? Death, destruction, carnage, oblivion. Not a happy group."

He glanced up as well. "They were here to usher in the end of the world. That wasn't a happy job."

"Still, they're angels. It wasn't like their heads'll be on the chopping block."

Finn didn't comment. Instead he allowed his eyes to drift to the myriad pinpoint white Christmas lights fusing into a shimmering canopy over the broad open space in front of the altar, which was filled with Christmas trees and white poinsettias. The shrine to the Bethlehem scene was set off in the distance, also surrounded by poinsettias and tiny white lights, giving the whole display a fairy-tale appearance. The church was gleaming with brilliance, the darkened stained glass windows appearing to be the only shadow in the building. He glanced over to the pictures of Jesus, surrounded on all sides by his apostles and yet more angels.

The church, in fact, was filled with angels. They watched over the nave and sacristy, were carved into the wooden screen and pieced together in stained glass that was currently dull as lead, but in the middle of the day would enflame the church with brilliant fiery color. Where there weren't angels, there were admonitions detailed in beautiful vignettes and symbols, all just out of view of the casual observer. Tucked into the eaves were pictures dire enough to make an angel frown too, images pulled from the pages of Revelations, meant to press a flock into service in whatever way possible. Fear apparently was a popular choice.

"The mortal quest for understanding its origins created a great deal of art," he murmured.

"And a great deal of death."

They stopped, as Lester entered the building, walking up the long corridor with Father Franks. Finn could feel Morrow's energy, excitement. The man had something for him, without question. Good.

But...not everything, he sensed. No more than the short list, as Lester had promised. He reached out and touched Lester's thoughts, skimming them lightly, which was all he could manage with whatever ward Lester still carried on him. A hundred names alone. That wasn't going to be enough.

Lester walked up to Finn and handed over the envelope with a flourish. He was a strong, proud, and driven man, filled with passion for his purpose. And he was jerking Finn around.

"The rest?" Finn asked, his voice hard.

"There remain others to convince," Lester said, his smile placating. "I need one...maybe two hours. I didn't want you to wait any longer while we got the others onboard. It is, after all, Christmas Eve."

Finn scowled, but another flick through Lester's thoughts revealed his truth, his heart. "Where are the rest of the people on the list?"

"Safer than they ever have been," Lester beamed. As he did, Finn came up against a new block in his thoughts as unexpected as it was strong. The block of a zealot, he realized — something against which even an angel had no sway.

What was the man hiding?

"We should meet at Exeter," Lester said, unaware of Finn's attempt to rifle through his thoughts. "It's safer, and I'll be finished with my last call at eight o'clock. I can see you there at eight fifteen."

Finn nodded, though the idea of waiting any longer ground against his nerves. Lester, however, was looking at Dana, and his eyes traveled between the two of them, noting Dana's clothing, her stance, and perhaps even the energy that wound within her.

"You've told her," he said to Finn. "About who she is. What she is."

"Some," he said. "But she needs to hear the rest from you. All of it."

"Hello, I'm standing right here," Dana said testily, her scowl for both of them. "But Finn's right. It's time. I need to know."

"It is time," Lester agreed, sighing. "It's well past time, perhaps."

He lifted his gaze to stare at the wall above Dana, where a saint's image watched them with dubious concern. And he began in a ponderous, preacher-like tone.

"Before God created man, He created angels," he said. "The angels were made in the image of God, true stars of heaven. Some of this order believed themselves to be equal to Him, above Him even, and these were cast out of heaven."

Dana glanced at Finn. "Um, I'm aware of grade school catechism—"

Lester held up a hand. "But some who were cast out had sinned in no way, not at first. These were the Fallen, the Nephilim, whose role was to watch over humanity. They were better, brighter, stronger...the heroes of the ancient world. And though many sinned and found themselves among the demon horde, some did not. Some of those angels fell in love with the daughters of

Men and begat children. In turn, some of those children were like their forebears — and they walked the earth like gods. They were called the Dawn Children."

Dana tensed, but Lester continued on. "Much of the change wrought by the Nephilim was good. They directed mortals to create some of the ancient wonders of the world — the Egyptian pyramids. The temples of the Mayans. The gardens of Babylon. They imparted their wisdom and their skills — which they retained from their divine state. Some Nephilim, in truth, were considered gods themselves — Zeus, Osiris, Quetzalcoatl — and their feminine equivalents. Some of their children became the rulers of men. Taller, stronger, possessing great powers. The stories of Hercules and Achilles came from these legendary men and women. The rulers of Egypt and the Mayans. The warriors of the Celts."

Despite herself, Dana was clearly intrigued. "Those were all earth-bound angels?"

"It can't be proven, of course. What in life can be proven when it is a question of faith as much as fact? But what is known is that God unleashed a terrible flood upon the earth at some point in the birth of history. And according to some texts, that flood was intended to wash away this apparent scourge of Nephilim and their young."

"So God wasn't completely a fan, I take it."

"A fair assumption."

"And therefore Noah wasn't a Dawn Child."

"I wouldn't say that." Lester's smile was absent, a teacher lost in the magic of his story. "The loss of so many great minds was devastating to early man, but according to further texts, the Nephilim were not fully destroyed in the flood. No, it took the coming of the

Jews to Canaan to wipe the immortals out entirely."

"Another hit from God," Dana murmured. "Not a good track record."

"And yet...and yet..." Lester looked over at her. "The Dawn Children were not completely destroyed. They flourished in every culture. Sparta, Greece, Egypt, Rome, across Europe and in the highlands of Scotland. The mountains of South America. These children did not die. They were the heroes of their time, the scholars, brilliant souls caught in human bodies which, more often than not, were taller, stronger, and healed faster than those of their peers."

"And you know this how?"

"A group of believers researching ancient biblical texts and other creationism stories banded together in the twelve hundreds, initially as part of the Knights Templar." Lester was watching her now, and her expression made him smile. "Yes, those knights. In working through the genealogy, certain patterns emerged. Each generation gave birth to only one child. The children were gifted — whether in beauty, intelligence, strength, or a special skill. And in nearly every generation, the children of this line had made their mark through service to their fellow man."

"Well, forgive me for mentioning this, but the Knights Templar also didn't turn out all that well, as I recall."

"Yes," Lester said. "When they banded together for one of their greatest acts, to protect the pilgrims to the Holy Land, synergies began to happen. They pooled their wealth, and they accrued great power. They built churches that were in their own way as clear a marker upon the earth as the temples and pyramids of the Greeks, the Egyptians, the Mayans. They did not rule man, but they grew in prominence and stature quickly. Too quickly, as it turned out. When their order was betrayed and destroyed, it became clear that special souls like the Dawn Children could be as much a target of human jealousy as of a possible curse from God. At that time, it was decided that they should be found, nurtured, and protected as well as they could be. Surely, God would be merciful, the thinking went. Surely, these humans who had the blood of angels running through their veins would not face the wrath of the Creator, so many generations after the sins of his children. Still others felt that God was not decrying the existence of the Nephilim and their offspring at all. That the devastations brought upon this special race were the result of human failings alone, not divine anger. But either way, they had to be protected."

"So that's what you're part of, this group of people who are dedicated to protecting Dawn Children?"

"Yes."

"And that's what I am?"

His smile was brilliant. "Yes. You are one of the Children we are dedicated to protecting. Third in line of purest blood, in fact."

"Purest…" Finn winced as the full impact of Lester's statement hit Dana. "Wait. You're *breeding* us?"

"Nothing so crass as what you think," Lester said. "There are fifteen hundred families that have been identified, spread out over the whole world. There used to be hundreds of thousands before the Great Flood, and then tens of thousands before the Dark Ages settled across Europe and before European invaders wiped out entire civilizations with their diseases."

"Fifteen hundred families left," Dana said. "I get how you might think that God isn't on your side."

"Your side too," Lester said quietly. "The same hand that wrote about the defilement of the human race through the intervention of the Nephilim also wrote vividly—luridly—about the end times for humanity. Much of humanity will be destroyed, its warriors all gone, unable to stand against the tide of retribution that will be loosed upon them."

"Warriors," Dana said.

Lester didn't bother to nod. "The identified families understood the importance of keeping the line as strong as possible. Marriages were arranged, children were fostered if they were found in dangerous environments. We have never attracted notice for our work." He shifted his glance toward Finn. "Until recently."

"Uh-huh. Recently as in today, or recently as in two months ago?"

"Do you not understand the importance of this, Dana? You're one of the Dawn Children. You have been blessed by God."

"Well, great," she said. "So now I know that I'm on your list. And presumably, so does someone else, since I've been jumped twice in the last day. Where does that leave us?"

Lester snapped his gaze back to her from the stained glass window he'd been studying. "Only that we need to keep you protected. Finn can only stay a short while longer. Then we have to make your care our first priority. As it has always been." His voice grew harder. "Since the moment you were born and given to Walter and Claire to be raised.

Dana blinked at him. "What do you mean, 'given to,'" she asked slowly.

Lester's expression shifted, becoming both calculating and cloying at once, Finn thought. Dana didn't react to it. Perhaps in some corner of her mind, she knew. Perhaps she'd always known. "Your biological parents were not a safe environment for you." Lester said.

"According to who?"

"Not all Dawn Children were moved for the good of humanity. Some turned to darker paths, and those were the ones who struck fear into the hearts of mankind. They were the ones who were hunted and shunned. They remain the ones against whom we maintain constant vigilance. They were the ones that called down rage upon all of the Children, and for good reason. They started wars and ended lives. They ruled without care or consideration. They manipulated humans in any way they could. But they carried the line of angels, and so they had to be watched. Monitored. Even protected, no matter that they were not redeemable."

"My birth parents weren't redeemable, then? Or did you simply not want to go to the trouble?" Dana's words were cold, almost automatic, and Finn fought the urge to reach for her. This was her truth, and she would face it her own way, he knew. But the moment she reached for him...

"Your parents were already committed to the side of darkness," Lester said quietly. "We knew it was only a matter of time before you would be as well. And with someone so strong, with such a bloodline as yours, we couldn't allow that to happen. Not to you, and not to humanity."

"Where are they now?" Dana asked, and Lester sighed, hunching his shoulders. "Are they dead?" she snapped, a hint of hysteria in her voice. "Did you kill them?"

"No!" Lester said, appearing truly shocked at the

question. "They aren't dead. They abandoned their city, however, and are off the grid. We don't know where they are."

"Then how do you know if they're alive?" Dana asked, and Lester smiled.

"Your parents aren't the easiest people to kill," Lester said. "They were alive when they left you behind. And you were blessed with adoptive parents who loved you, cared for you..."

"One of them, anyway."

"And sacrificed their lives for you that you might live in safety," Lester retorted, his tone cutting. "Your birth parents never *once* looked for you, Dana. We expected them to, planned for it. We assigned additional security and gave your adoptive parents enough money to live in luxury, without any need or want. But it wasn't easy. It could never have been a normal life for them, the life they'd dreamed of when they were planning their wedding, for all that they didn't know the full story." He shrugged. "Your pain is understandable, but imagine learning that your life must irrevocably change — that you have no choice or hope for it to improve, and that you might one day be betrayed, all because of a child who desperately needed protection. They gave you that protection. Willingly."

Lester smiled, his eyes feverish, and Finn couldn't help suspecting that he might have had a hand in that "willingness."

"Think on that, on all that has been done to keep you safe," Lester said, his voice crisp, resolute. "I must go to make my final calls, and get the approvals I need," he said loftily. "Be ready at eight fifteen. I'll come for you."

CHAPTER TWENTY-THREE

Exeter Global Services
Cleveland, Ohio
8:30 p.m., Dec. 24

"Where the hell is Lester?" Dana wrapped her arms around her body. She was cold. She was constantly cold, it seemed, especially since Lester had dropped his little bomb at the cathedral.

Her parents had gone to the dark side, he'd said. He'd ranked them up there with criminals. Warmongers. Defilers of all that was right and good in the world. His words came back to her, crushing in on her throat, her lungs, robbing her of breath.

She should call Claire—she knew she should, and yet—what would she say? *Hi, Mom, I know you've been lying to me all this time, but that's okay, Dad was too?*

Dana rubbed her forehead and paced back toward her desk. They were all in her satellite office with Lester's workspace, Max working outside the door on a computer he'd hacked into. Finn was watching her cautiously, too cautiously, as if she might break at any minute. She scowled at him as Max poked his head through the doorway. "We're making progress out here," he said. "The partial list you got from Lester is helping a lot, so is having access to Exeter's files from inside Lester's own system. But I should probably ask — when's he due to show up?"

"Any minute, and I'm not sure we're going to have much warning. How long will it take you to get out and make it look like you're doing nothing but taking up space?"

Max tilted his head, considering. "Couple of minutes, tops. I'll be at the ready for emergency stoppage the minute you say the word. Hey — " His face lit up. "We've got his goons at the front door too. They'll sound the alert when he comes in, won't they? That'll help."

"Yes, it will." Dana pulled out her cell phone to contact Lester's chief bodyguard as Max returned to his work, leaving Finn and her alone. The place was crawling with security, posted at odd intervals up and down the cube rows. Lester had sent all his shift-work staff home other than the guards — at 8:00 p.m. on Christmas Eve, he knew no work was going to get done. And considering who he was housing in his private office, the fewer people who knew about the activities of Exeter, the better.

After relaying directions that she figured had about an eighty percent chance of being followed, she pocketed her phone and looked at Finn. "Are you going to say anything or just stand there staring at me?" she asked him as she glanced at the paperwork on Lester's desk. It was the next year's planning for Exeter's security upgrades, which she'd had couriered over early, because it was one of the few things she could get done even from her home. She'd spent hours on the document, tracing Lester's activities for the past year, calculating his expenses in services and personnel, trying to guesstimate what the new year would have in store.

She frowned down at the stack of pages. Just yesterday, this information had seemed the most important thing in the world to her. She'd needed to get the document on Lester's desk, then return to sort through her emails, maybe even addressing the end-of-year budgeting process that should have been done six weeks ago.

Now it seemed as if it was paperwork from someone else's life, far, far away. "I wish I understood why this is happening," she muttered.

At this, Finn decided to rouse himself. "You've had a significant shock, Dana. You need time to process it."

"Yeah, well, I don't have any time to process it," she snapped, shoving her papers out of their tidy pile and into a scattered heap on the desk. "You saw Lester. He's off his nut. He's dangerous, and I don't think you realize that. You're leaving in a little over three hours, and for what? So I can cope with the fact that I'm the only Dawn Child out there who knows what we are, what might become of us? How am I going to protect them if I can't explain to them why?"

"That's why Lester is—"

"Lester is wrong," Dana cut him off. "It's one thing to protect a group from harm. It's another to lie to them their entire lives, orchestrating their every move because they're your special puppets. When I think of all the times he was there for me, watching over me, I want to throw up. I wasn't a favorite niece of his," she said, self-disgust threatening to choke her. "I was a favorite pet."

"The Society of Orion correctly identified the children who were the most at risk given their genetic makeup and life circumstances," Finn said reasonably. "If Lester had known you were likely going to die or be turned by your birth parents, it is not at all unreasonable that the society would intercede. Imagine where you would be if he hadn't found them—found you?"

"Yeah, Lester's a real humanitarian. What was I thinking?" Dana glanced at him, but her eyes sheared away before she could make real contact. "Do you know? Who my parents really are?"

"No, I don't," he said. Finn's voice was warm, comforting, but there was too much distance between them. Something that she'd need to get used to, she supposed. "Your adoptive father and mother were there for you, though. That's more than many mortal children can say."

"Yeah, but Walter did more than I ever have for others, and he wasn't one of the chosen elite," she said bitterly. "He was simply a man trying to do his best...and doing far more than he should've been able to do. God! My mother doesn't even realize what her own husband did in his free time. Can you imagine the level of deception that has to exist in order for Orion to even survive? I can't even wrap my head around it." She shook herself, tension riddling her. "I've gotta go see what Max is up to."

"Max will tell us when he's found something," Finn said. "I think you need to take some time to assimilate what you've learned about yourself." He waited a beat. "And about me."

She looked at him, and her blood pressure spiked.

"All I need to know is that you're leaving in a few hours," she said warningly. "That helps put everything back into perspective."

"Perhaps for you. I, however, have one or two more things that I need, if that's all right." He got up, smooth as silk in his dark clothing, and moved over to the office door. He stuck his head out and spoke to Max, but Dana couldn't understand the words. She caught the sound of Max's affirmative, however, and Finn pulled back inside the door before she could challenge it. He pushed the door shut, resting his hand on the knob for a brief second before pulling it away.

"I don't have time for a fireside chat."

"Neither do I," Finn said. And he took one step toward Dana, then another.

Unexpected heat flared deep in her belly as she stared at him. "Um, are you going to be okay?" she asked as he moved toward her. "You—you said something in your sleep that I couldn't understand, but it didn't sound good. Something about—about forgetting. Not wanting to forget." She was scooting back from him as she spoke, suddenly unsure, and Finn's grin, hard and bitter in the harsh fluorescent lights, stopped her.

"There's a great deal I'm not going to be able keep, Dana," he said quietly. "Not beyond this night. I would ask, then, for something else to remember."

Dana could practically feel her pupils dilating. "Oh," she whispered. "I'd like that too."

"Yo, Dana, Finn!" Max's voice came through the door, urgent and excited, a moment later he pounded on the wood for emphasis. "Sorry to interrupt, but stop whatever you're doing and come out here. You're really going to want to see this."

It'd been nearly five minutes since Max had interrupted what Finn had been pretty damned sure would've been the second most transcendental experience of his existence, and Finn still wanted to kill the man.

Instead, he watched Dana stare at the computer screen, the lines of strange symbols and glyphs slowly moving into intelligible language.

It was a list of names, dates, and locations, each with an additional code that Max had already tracked to another portion of Lester's vast computer system, and was working with an experimental decoder to unlock. Lester had never shown up, never called. But with any luck, Finn thought, they wouldn't need him anymore.

"That file is massive as compared to this one," Max said. "Unless he's encoded actual DNA in there, the only thing it can be is a multimedia file — photos, scans, that sort of thing." He was clicking through the last commands on the file search command, glancing over to watch the progress of the main list. "I've cross-referenced it with the list Lester gave you," he said, "and the names match up at the very end of each cycle. There's no doubt about what this is."

"A genealogy tree," Dana murmured. "What's the earliest date on record?"

"Unknown seems to be a favorite one on a lot of them," Max said. "Earliest known is a couple of centuries BC. I don't think they did so well on record keeping back then, or it wasn't a big enough deal to track down ancient census lists."

"Primarily Middle Eastern?" she asked, scanning over the spooling rows of names and dates.

"All over the place. But the Middle Eastern trails are among the oldest." He sobered. "Of course, those tended to end the earliest too."

"End?" Dana frowned and looked at him. "How many trails do you have here? All told?"

"Over five thousand," Max said. "Lists with open-ended results is fourteen hundred ninety-six, but a lot of those are pretty much gobbledygook."

She nodded, and Finn watched the play of emotions on her face. "Call up my name, please," Dana said.

Max started typing furiously. "I knew it," he nearly cackled. "I totally knew it."

A noise sounded behind him, and he turned, searching the brightly lit room full of cubicles for movement. And first, nothing stirred, and then…

No. He was imagining things.

"Has Morrow reported in?" Finn asked, his eyes narrowing on the far doors. Guards stood there, and this was only the innermost set of doors. Lester had constructed his office floor to specific requirements, he'd told Finn. Requirements that included three lines of interior walls, each with fireproof doors. Fireproof, bulletproof, and blast proof, Max had confirmed. They were safe inside Lester's little fortress, he'd made sure of it. Finn looked down at Max, who was watching him with curiosity. "What did you say?"

"I just got word this second. Lester is on his way. He said all systems were go for the list, he'd gotten the last approvals," Max reported. "He has his own men with him, he told me to tell you, Dana. A half dozen, I think. I don't think he'll get into any trouble."

"Oh, I doubt that," Dana said thinly. She glanced up at Finn as Max turned back to the monitors. "What do you make of this?"

He looked at the screen that was populating with Dana's family tree. He recognized none of the names, but beneath her two parents—both indicated as Dawn Children—her name had been inscribed in the same bright blue font color as her sire's. Everyone above that trio was recorded in dull gray font. He looked back at her, and her smile faltered.

"I think that means they're still alive," she said. "My biological parents."

"This could be an old list," Finn warned. "There's no telling when it was last modified."

A knock came at the door, and Finn turned—then lifted his brows in surprise.

"Sir."

Finn looked down at the same young man who had held a gun on him not sixteen hours earlier, his expression open and unmarked by guile, his eyes a soulful blue. Beside him, Dana stiffened.

"Who are you?" she asked.

"Timothy Rourke, ma'am," he said with a curt nod, his attention straying only for a moment from Finn. "Sir, there's something coming up through the elevator shafts."

Max piped up. "You have visual in the elevators?"

"We do," Timothy said. "But it doesn't make sense. There's something there—but not there."

"Demons," Finn said curtly. "Not Possessed, but actual demons. They can cast an illusion, take on different looks if they want, or no look at all."

Everyone in the room stared at him. "But…the surveillance system tracks heat signatures too," Max offered.

Finn shrugged. "Great with humans. Not so much with demons."

Tim squared his shoulders. "Well, I can sense that something is coming, and I want to move you into Mr. Morrow's secure room. He left us with specific instructions that none of you were to be harmed, and so I ask you—"

"What do you *think* is coming up, Mr. Rourke?" Dana asked coolly, her eyes challenging the young guard. "Did Morrow prepare you for this?"

"Not exactly," he said carefully. He flashed a smile and looked all of twelve years old. The effect wasn't wasted on Dana. Even now, she was standing more at ease, her head canted forward, her eyes gentle in the face of the boy's feigned nervousness. A master manipulator, Finn thought. "Morrow doesn't know I'm pushing the panic button here. But I suspect that what's out there isn't going to be pretty, and I'd rather you be smart and alive than cocky and dead."

"Sounds like good reasoning to me," Max put in, and Finn fought a smile. The tech specialist had been eyeing the rifles and guns they had been sporting, and his mind had clearly been turning. "I really don't want to lose what we have here, Dana, if we can avoid it. Even if it's a false alarm and not demons crawling up the elevator ducts, we need to protect the data."

Dana shook her head. "Fine. But where else are we vulnerable? They're going to have to get humans in here too, I'm thinking. That was more Bartholomew's MO, not full-on demons. Where would they come in?"

"The freight elevators," Finn said in tandem with Max.

Finn glared at the teenager. "Tell three guards to meet me at the side wall of elevators. Those are the freight ones, right?"

"Yes," Max said, flinching away when Rourke

scowled at him. "Hey, hey, hey, back it down, buddy. I've lugged plenty of computer stuff up those elevators. I know the layout." He turned to Finn and Dana. "It's an open floor space there. Nothing to hide behind for either party."

Dana moved over, frowning, and stopped in her tracks. "What are these, Max?" she asked, and Finn stepped in for a closer look as well. The pictures currently flashing up on the screen weren't randomly scattered photos — there was a pattern to them, a familiarity, which apparently made a more than passing impact on Dana.

Finn moved a step right, but as he did so, he heard it again. A low, guttural, scraping noise, overridden by dozens of feet stomping in unison, the rush and tumble of voices sounding like only one thing.

Demons.

He turned to Dana. "They're here," he said.

She grimaced. "How many of them and where?"

Rourke's earpiece crackled, and he tapped it, instantly wincing at the loud burst of static that hit him. "Report!" he said sternly, and the voices came back clear and steady through the rain of machine noise.

"We have visual," someone said, and Max looked up, instantly changing the screens over. From lines of text with ancient secrets, he moved to a thumbnail scan of all computer surveillance images — there were more than thirty of them.

Lester apparently didn't believe in taking chances.

"There they are," Max said, but the words were weak.

Finn stepped in immediately when he saw what was slinking its way down the corridors. At least thirty demons, armed to the hilt, fresh into a possession and ravening with hunger.

"I'm going to have to take them," he said to Dana, and she shot up in response.

"Not alone. How many men do we have, Rourke?" she asked.

"Eight total. Six within the building, two guarding the perimeter with on-foot surveillance."

"Try to reach them if you can—" Dana began.

"We can't wait for that," Finn interrupted her, shaking his head. Bartholomew wouldn't underestimate the humans again. "Rourke, how long have you been working with Lester's combat unit?"

"Three years," Rourke said, and Finn took his rifle out of his hands before he could blink, sighting through it.

"Where can we get more of these?" he asked.

"Weaponry cabinets are on each level." Rourke spoke quickly as he turned, and Finn could already hear the cries of the men on the outermost doors. Lester's façade was bulletproof glass, but a wall of glass seemed like pale security against a demon.

"We've got an eye-witness sighting," Max called out. "And from the looks of it, a couple of seriously freaked-out security guards."

"This isn't your average group of punks," Finn said. "Their leader will kill his own men if he has to."

"Bartholomew will be with them?" Dana asked, and Finn nodded.

"Oh, I don't think he'd miss this." He tore Rourke's earpiece-mic unit out and held it up to shout into it. "Aim for their legs, their arms—any extremity. Do *not* shoot to kill. Do you understand me? Unless—" He shot a look at Rourke. "Are there any more as good as you?"

Rourke frowned, shook his head. "No."

"Then do *not* shoot to kill. There's no point. Wait for us to do that."

The man on the other end of the line bristled. "Who the hell are—"

Rourke pulled the mic out of Finn's hands. "Lester called. He's put Finn in interim control of security. Do what he says," he said. "What's the status of the intruders?"

"Well, they're not doing much of anything," the man said. "They seem to be getting louder, though, their words—I can't understand a goddamn thing they're saying."

Finn nodded. "They'll keep doing that until they've built up enough of a field to crash the glass. Physical bravery is beyond them, but hive mind rules."

Dana stared at Finn. "What are they here for? We don't have the full list yet."

"Apparently, they don't know that," Finn said. "You need to stay safe."

"Bullshit. I'm going with you." She pulled on her own rifle, flipping off the safety. "Rourke, we need someone to stay with Max."

"Max is going to be just fine packing up all this prize data and getting the hell out of here," Max interjected tartly. He pushed a small tech gadget at her. "Put this in your ear. I'll radio you my location and you can come pick up what's left of me, if something goes south."

"On second thought—" Dana pulled her Glock out of her shoulder harness, and handed it to Max, butt out, trading it for the comm unit. "I know you know how to fire one of these things. I'm hoping that we can keep them out of here, but if anything gets too close, blast first and radio us second. You say the word, we'll come back for you."

"Roger that," Max said faintly, looking down at the gun. "You know, on second thought…maybe I'll call in some backup. I got some guys who owe me…God knows we've got enough weapons here to spare."

"Do that," Dana said sharply. "But tell them to be careful."

Over the radio, they heard another scream, and then the sound of crashing glass.

CHAPTER TWENTY-FOUR

Exeter Global Services
Cleveland, Ohio
9:20 p.m., Dec. 24

Dana, Finn, and Rourke ran through the doors just as
fire opened up in the lobby area of Exeter, the level of
firepower more than overmatching the guards. Dana
watched as two of Lester's men were blasted completely
out of their stations against the far wall, their bulletproof
vests buckling but not breaking under the blast of
automatic gunfire. The three of them dove for the
nearest cubicle walls as the leader of Bartholomew's
attack crew paused and held up a gauntleted fist, an
eerie false silence falling upon the room.

Slightly ahead of her and to her right, she could see
Rourke. There was something funny about him, like he
was lit from within. Not as bright as Finn was,
but...something. She wondered if Finn had given him a
ward for demons when he'd handed him back his gear.

She sure the hell hoped so.

Dana crawled forward, her gun out, and lifted her head slightly to get a better view of the creatures.

Bartholomew hadn't been so careful this time, after all. There were easily twenty men, but they were freshly possessed, looking more like the creatures she'd seen on the street than the men in the nightclub. Each human wore a medallion, but their eyes were wild, their bodies shifting and quivering, as if the demon had been shoved into them unawares and was now desperately trying to get out. They fanned out in a slow perimeter sweep of the room, and Dana blinked to see them there, among the tidy cubes that sported pictures of spouses, children, and dogs, castle-of-the-month calendars, and Browns bobbleheads. The men were large, rough looking, and to a one looked like thugs. These men had not been handpicked for anything other than their ability to kill, and it was showing. Their eyes goggled and whirled, even as their focus on the head of their little pack was unwavering.

Now this was a man who had once been intelligent, Dana thought. Eastern European, like most of the rest of them, but his eyes were hard, not wild. He moved easily with the demon inside him, rough and grisly, but cunning. He'd be the one to watch.

She glanced around. Were any of these men actual demons displaying glamour, not Possessed? She would need to learn how to tell them apart eventually. Not today.

"Finn," the man called out, and Dana was surprised to hear his voice. It didn't match his body but cut through the heavy silence with elegant superiority. "We know that Morrow has given you a list—at least a partial one. What you don't know is that he's dead."

Dana stiffened, but she couldn't turn to look at Finn.

279

Dead? But he had his bodyguards with him!

"We don't wish to harm your woman. At least, no more than you've harmed her already. We only want the list of the Children. Ten, a hundred, a thousand, they deserve what we can offer them. A choice of eternal servitude and restriction, or a choice of freedom."

The demon waited a moment, and when no action was forthcoming, he made a curt motion with one of his hands. Two additional guards were shoved forward out of the mix of Possessed. They had been slashed across the face but were otherwise unharmed. At the leader's gesture, they were forced up onto a table at the front of the room, in front of the monthly call-center statistics board that Lester had posted for the troops. They stood there, resolute, as the sign blinked through the numbers for calls held, calls dropped, and calls transferred.

"You want to see the start of the human carnage at your hands, Fallen? Or do you want to give me the list and let the Dawn Children choose for themselves?"

Dana could feel Finn near her, her heightened sensitivities reaching out to him. He shifted, and she could picture his face. Agonized over the loss of mortal life, a life they could not get back, while he, immortal, would live on through their suffering. She closed her eyes. *No,* she thought at him. *Don't do this, don't listen to the empty promises of one who would take so much, and give back so little.*

"As you wish," the Possessed said, and he dropped his arm. Instantly, the creatures around him opened fire on one of the guards, only one, while the other flinched but remained standing, his brother-in-arms crashing over the table with a sickening crunch, collapsing to the ground. As one, the horde roared with satisfaction at the kill, their mouths gritted into horrible masks, their nostrils flaring. Dana could hear Finn hissing in distress.

"That was not enough to convince you, I see? There are two more like that outside. And I think if we look hard enough, we can find a few more." Dana couldn't see what he had done, but a whizzing missile flew by her head, crashing into the pod beside her. Instantly, the tightly knit cluster of computer stations, monitors, printers, and high-tech Wi-Fi routers exploded, throwing her backward into the rubble.

"Dana!" Max hissed in her ear, and she slapped her hand against her temple to shield the noise. As if anyone could hear over the exploding circuitry, a million dollars' worth of workstations going up in flames around them. "What the fuck is going on out there?"

"Finn!" roared the main demon, and Dana scrambled forward, pulling her gun. The demon now stood on the table with the remaining guard, a man he held up by the collar. Someone had lashed the man's hands together with computer wire, his feet as well, but his mouth was free. As the smoke cleared around him, the demon chuckled.

"Tell Finn who you are, Mr. Green."

"Mike Green, security guard, sir," he said, and Dana closed her eyes. *Oh no.* This was not a trained professional. This was one of the men the building had hired.

"And how did you come to be involved this evening?"

"I'm on duty, sir. I heard the sound of men running, and I followed. I pulled Christmas Eve so..." He swallowed. "So I could be home with my family on Christmas Day. Tomorrow, sir."

Dana winced, her throat closing up. If she could get close enough...

"Uh, Dana, you need to know this, and you need to know it now." It was Max's voice again, only he sounded deadly calm. "You've got a problem out there."

"We've got several of them," she hissed back. The crackling of a computer monitor beside her covered her talking, as did the man speaking above the din, a knife to his neck drawing blood as the creatures surrounded him. He had a daughter, only two years old. He'd missed Christmas at home the year before because of the job. He just—he just wanted to go home.

Dana drew her arm level, and Max would not shut up. "The kid you have in there with you," he hissed. "Rourke. You gotta get him out of—"

Then the demon started shouting again.

"He is going to *die*, Finn, a human! A child of God. And his family will lay his death at your feet, an entire generation marked by your blind faith in those who would see humans as bound as he is, their lives utterly destroyed. A pity," he said, and he raised his arm, the Possessed around him growling in renewed excitement. "You seem like a good man, Mr. Green," he said, and his voice was all the more chilling for his cool rationality. "My condolences to your family."

"No!" Two voices screamed out at the same time, Green's and a man much closer to Dana, his voice young and strident, his eyes flaring wide with rage. In the space of a second, faster than Dana's eye could track, Rourke raised his gun and opened fire on the demon on the table. The demon fell back off the table, definitely wounded, while the other Possessed turned in snarling fury, their guns drawing down.

Explosions shattered around her. Across the room, Rourke gave a startled cry.

"Son of a *bitch*!" Dana gritted out, rolling to the right, Max's voice pounding into her ears.

"He's a Dawn Child, Dana," he shouted. "He's one of your own. You can't let him die!"

Dana's eyes widened in shock as she burst into the cubicle corridor, both hands on her Glock, firing low and hard while running forward. She reached Rourke within the space of two breaths, moving faster than she would have thought possible. With the full impact of her urgency guiding her steps and her mind totally focused, she could see the aura around him burning bright with purpose and fire. Throwing Rourke roughly over her shoulder, she crouched and ran as Finn rose up behind her, laying waste to the first line of demons even as more poured into the room from every doorway, as if a hive of the bastards had opened upon them.

She ran into a darkened conference room as the battle raged outside, and laid Rourke down on the ground as carefully as she could, then ripped open his shirt. As she saw the bloody mess of his body, she drew back in horror. These were not Rourke's first wounds, but they were likely to prove his last.

Feet thundered by the conference room door, and Dana jerked her head up, shocked by the look of the new men. These were not demons, and they weren't the police. They were pale, resolute, and snugging serious metal against T-shirts emblazoned with every nerd icon known to man. And they looked like they could handle their weapons.

Max's reinforcements.

"Ahh—" The voice drew Dana's attention down, and she pulled herself closer to Rourke, cradling his head in her arms.

"It's okay, it's okay, Timothy. You're going to be all

right."

"It's Tim," he said with a faint smile. "And you're a terrible liar."

"No, no, you're wrong. I'm serious." She pressed down on the worst of the wounds, but he was bleeding from too many places, and she couldn't press enough to hold his body together. "Sometimes," she said, "sometimes if you focus the right way, you can actually heal yourself from bullet wounds." She licked her lips, shocked to find tears were coursing down her face. "You've had that experience, right, Tim?"

She remembered Max's words, knew he was listening to her, knew he could hear the death rattle of Tim's breathing, rough and ragged over the mic. "You look like you've gone through quite a lot already, and you made it through."

Around them, the carnage reigned. However many Possessed Finn had taken down by wounding or killing them, the body count had to be growing. Glass was blown out and smoke billowed upward into the sky. "Hold on, Tim, help's coming," she said. "The police will see the smoke. We'll get you out of here and into a hospital faster than you can believe.

"You moved...too fast," he said, and his eyes were searching hers, eyes that were clear and blue and far too young to be asked to see so much. "You moved like I do, when I — when I'm mad enough."

She grinned through her tears. "That's right, Tim," she said. "I moved like you did. I'm very much like you are, even though we never met before today."

He nodded, wincing as he coughed. "I wish I could have met you...before today."

Dana's stomach twisted at the small drop of blood that formed at the side of his mouth. Dammit, where were those sirens? She had to lean down to catch his next words. " — name?" he asked.

"Dana. My name is Dana Griffin, and you better remember it, because I'm going to be coming after you for a job just as soon as you get better, do you hear that?"

"Work — for Lester."

"Well, Lester doesn't take care of you nearly well enough," Dana said. "I will." She paused, beginning to tremble as much as Tim had when he'd first fallen. But she was more concerned now because Tim was resting easily, sinking to a place from which she could not pull him back. "Do you have any family, Tim? A mom or dad? A sister I can call to come visit you in the hospital?"

"No," he said, and again the soft, sad smile. "Lester…was all the family I had. Parents…died a long time ago. He a-dopted me," he managed. "Paid for — everything."

Cold shock washed over Dana. This boy was her. Her all over again. She pulled Tim close. "Well, you have a really big family now, Tim," she said. "Fifteen hundred brothers and sisters that you never met. And I'm going to tell them all about you."

She couldn't dash the tears from her eyes, so she let them fall onto his face in a gentle rain. "I'm going to tell them how brave you were, how fast you moved to save someone so that they could go home and spend Christmas with their family."

"I'd seen…Green around. Good man."

"And you're a good man too, Tim," Dana whispered. He smiled at that.

An explosion sounded outside the room, and Dana and Tim crouched together, their hearts hammering loud enough to compete with the noise. Shouting and more explosions followed as Max's reinforcements roared after more demons. And finally, in the distance were the sirens.

But Tim was already fading from her, his aura dimming around him like a soft and spectral fire. "Tim, I want you to know that we will keep them safe," she said, and her voice broke as he opened his eyes again. "We were meant to do great things, you know," she said. "I'm not going to let you down."

"And you'll remember…?"

"Yes," Dana burst out, on the verge of crying again. "Everyone will know of the sacrifice you made and why you made it. You'll be the first to the fight."

"First—is good," Tim said, and he settled again, smiling up at her while she bit her lip to steady herself. "I always wanted to have a big family," he said.

"Me too," she said softly.

But Tim could no longer hear her.

CHAPTER TWENTY-FIVE

Exeter Global Services
Cleveland, Ohio
10:00 p.m., Dec. 24

Finn moved forward rapidly, using his rifle as much as a tool to disarm his attackers as to incapacitate them. As he fought, he kept one eye on the conference room where he'd seen Dana disappear with the young guard. He needed to get over there—right after he cleared a path for escape for both of them. The attack had been fairly self-contained, but it was only a matter of time before the fire alarms were set off or someone tripped battery-powered security systems. The men who'd shown up to help dispatch the Possessed were doing so with a ruthlessness that reminded him of the single-minded focus of video game players, but they were fast running out of prey. Even now, many of the Possessed were racing through the corridors, no longer set on attacking as much as escape.

Still, there would be plenty for the police to

question. And he and Dana needed to be out of there before they showed up.

He ran for Dana's conference room, but before he could reach it, another wave of the battle surged in front of him, spilling from another chamber. Finn plunged into the melee of the Possessed, the line between death and destruction blurring with every hit, every kick, every broken bone. Within minutes, more of the Possessed had dropped, and others screamed as they fled, their minds focusing only on escape.

Finn straightened, turning to where he could barely see Dana lying slumped and bleeding in the conference room, when the sound of slow, lazy clapping stopped him in his tracks.

"Bravo," Bartholomew said, and Finn pivoted toward him. The rogue Fallen looked none the worse for wear for the attack, his evening wear barely creased as he picked up the gun that had been lying by his side. "You've proven yourself to be quite a worthy opponent, Finn. I've enjoyed fighting you, but like all good things, this too must come to an end. You're displaying a lamentable fondness for mortals, and that, my friend, is the surest way to get yourself killed."

"Your men were massacred tonight," Finn seethed. "You led them here to be slaughtered."

"Not quite the truth, but close enough." Bartholomew shook his head. "The list is here, Finn. Lester doesn't have it after all—and believe me, I pressed him hard. Strange how he could block me mentally, but that's a temporary problem. And once you're gone, there will be no one to stop me from finding the list…and exacting retribution. I've established an outpost in this city, and I have standards to uphold."

"I wasn't the one gunning down your troops," Finn said, realizing suddenly that Bartholomew didn't know that Dana was in the next room—Dana and a second Dawn Child.

"Locals." Bartholomew curled his lip. "They'll pay for that in time. You can expect no additional help from them, though it was an inspired choice."

"I didn't call them."

Bartholomew raised his brows. "Then you'll allow me to give my congratulations to Ms. Griffin, or one of her associates," he said. He cast a glance heavenward, a slight smile on his face. "Assuming she survives the night, she'll prove to be quite an asset to my cause, I suspect."

"Not gonna happen, dickhead."

"And you'll stop me how, exactly?" Bartholomew sneered. "If you want to, have at me, but you'll need to be quick about it. In a few short hours, you'll be gone—and I'll still be here. When that happens, I'll simply come in and scoop up the mortal, and we'll all go on our way."

"No, you won't," Finn said. "I'll kill you first."

"You know...I almost think you would," Bartholomew said.

He opened fire into Finn's chest.

Finn crashed backward from the bullets, even as he rolled down and under, shifting left at the last minute, the speed of his movements allowing him to miss the full thrust of the assault. Bartholomew had simply guessed wrong, he realized, as he watched the trail of bullet holes spring up in a lazy J to the right, continuing on to shoot out the windows. Cold, bracing air rushed in.

Bartholomew took one step forward, then another.

"I know your woman is somewhere close, maybe even watching for you. She'll be alone someday, Finn. When you're long gone and forgotten, she'll be alone and at risk. And, once again, I'll still be here, waiting and watching. There are too many demons ready to be commanded. The Dawn Children cannot stand against us. They will join us, or they will die. After that, nothing will stop us."

"She doesn't have the list," Finn said.

"Ahh, but she's *seen* it, hasn't she? At least part of it. And she's a Dawn Child. Her mind was not made to forget."

Bartholomew took another step, the angle of his approach taking him over to the bank of windows that looked out over the city. "I haven't had the opportunity to turn a Dawn Child in quite a few centuries," he said, his eyes scanning the room. "You really want to leave her to me?"

Finn leaned against the wall, pressing his hand on his wounds. He could heal quickly, but he'd lost a great deal of blood, and blood was not regenerated so quickly for Fallen as it was for the Syx, it appeared. He needed time to complete the process.

He turned his head, noting another downed human not three feet away. His body was out of Bartholomew's sight line — as was access to his rifle. Finn leaned over to the man as Bartholomew continued his rant. Whether the man was dead or simply passed out, Finn couldn't take the time to determine. He lifted the rifle and pulled himself upright.

"What would you have me do, Bartholomew?" he asked. "We weren't made to rule the humans, any more than we were made to kill them. Have you forgotten so much of your promises that you've forgotten that?"

"You're a child," Bartholomew spat. "I made no *promises* that retain any power over me."

He took a step away, and the sounds of fighting drew closer. The new men were battling back the Possessed, but they couldn't ignore that time was passing. Soon there would be sirens blaring, the sound of armed, official men rushing up the stairs to the floor, the cacophony of fire trucks on their way.

"It's over, Bartholomew," Finn gritted out. "For once, face the consequences of your actions."

"You won't kill me," Bartholomew sneered. "I'm all you know of being a Fallen. That makes me much more valuable to you alive than dead." He brought the gun around, his head tilting up as he heard the sound of glass crashing, screams of rage filling the echoing chambers. "Whereas, if you're planning on giving the list to your precious archangel, you're more important to me dead than alive."

Finn shifted his gun a little. "I understand. But it turns out I mainly want to hand you over alive so the archangel can beat the shit out of you. He's even better at it than I am." Then he shot Bartholomew in the leg.

The rogue Fallen wheeled back, his eyes going from Finn to the far door, which was now being battered with a round of machine gun fire. Max's attack squad must have realized he was here, and they were coming to finish the job. But guns fired by humans wouldn't work on Bartholomew. Only Finn could harm him.

"I have more information than you could possibly imagine, Fallen. Information you want. Information you truly need. But you'll only get this one chance."

Finn hesitated, and his heart beat with agony at the choice. To go after Bartholomew now was surely the sounder course. He would catch him, especially with a wounded leg. There was so much he could not know—so much he needed to know. He would be giving Bartholomew to the archangel on a platter, and that would count for a lot.

And yet—he steeled himself from looking back toward the room where Dana lay, possibly passed out from blood loss, at risk from both the Possessed and the police, once they showed up, whose showering rain of bullets might just as easily kill her as her attackers.

He couldn't leave her. Not until he had to.

He'd made his choice.

Bartholomew knew it the same moment he did. "So, that's the way of it, Fallen," he said, his tone rich with contempt. "You failed."

At that moment, the door burst open, and a screaming torrent of bullets blasted through the room.

Moving faster than human eyes could track, Bartholomew tucked the assault rifle close to his body and jumped out the window, bullets peppering the wall harmlessly in his wake.

CHAPTER TWENTY-SIX

Exeter Global Services
Cleveland, Ohio
10:30 p.m., Dec. 24

Dana sat inside the conference room, her body half covering Timothy Rourke's still form. When warm hands circled her shoulders, she went rigid, shoving up with one hand to fend off her attacker while she twisted away.

"Dana," Finn said sharply, forcing her to refocus. "It's me. It's Finn." He pulled her bodily off Rourke, and while she knew with one part of her brain who he was, why he was there, and that he was a friend, she couldn't help the violence of her response, her arms flailing wide as he sought to hold her close.

"Finn," she managed, drawing in a deep breath. "He was — he was a — "

Finn cut her off. "You're hurt," he said, his voice going deadly calm. "How many places — where?"

Dana looked down at her arm with dull eyes, a

dripping stain spreading beneath her. "Bullet to the shoulder is only a graze," she said. "Knife stab to my upper left leg I can't even feel anymore." She held up her left hand. "I think I broke a finger or something."

"Dislocated," Finn said, curving his hands over it. She winced for a moment as the joints moved back into place, then welcomed the soothing warmth that washed through her. He lifted her face again, and her mouth worked as she struggled to get the words out. "He's dead," she said miserably. "I couldn't save him. I didn't know how to — to get him to save himself."

Finn looked down at Timothy, and she watched as he counted the bullet holes, his mouth going grim. "I can't save him either," he said quietly. "You gave him what he needed, here."

"I couldn't do *anything*," she whispered, her eyes drifting down to Timothy's impossibly young face. "I didn't know how."

"You gave him arms to lie in. That's more than most get. Now come on," he said brusquely. "We have to get out of here."

"What do you mean?" Dana looked around wildly even as she forced herself to her feet. "Where's Max?"

"Gone," Finn said. "Same as his geek squad. I assume he'll contact you, but the police have arrived and they'll keep us here for a lot longer than I can afford to wait." He looked at her. "We need to leave."

They ran out into the main area just as feet thundered down the hallway, official-sounding boots accompanied by low-pitched shouts. As they ran past Lester's office, she stopped.

"Shit," she muttered. The door stood ajar, and it would have served as a reasonable hiding place. "Max?" she asked as she pushed her way inside. There was no one there and she stood for a moment, not quite sure why she'd come in here.

"Dana," Finn growled, and she nodded, heading back to him. She no sooner crossed the threshold than she swooned.

"Whoa!" Finn grabbed her, holding her close while she fought to remain upright.

"Sorry, I—I can manage myself." She shook her head to clear it...that didn't help.

"I know. You'll stabilize shortly. The weakness is the result of blood loss. But we have to keep moving."

She shot him a look. "You up for giving me a transfusion?" she said wryly.

"Don't think it hasn't been tried."

Dana shuddered as they moved through the room, past mounds of destroyed computer circuitry and crushed monitors. Her gaze swept what was left of Lester's pristine call center. There was easily a hundred thousand dollars' worth of damage, more if the sprinkler system finally kicked on and soaked the remaining equipment and furniture.

"Where's the rest of Lester's security team?" she asked. "If a full-scale attack was leveled on his office, he should have disaster recovery already in here."

Finn looked out one window, then backed away from it as sirens cut through the air. "If the alert goes through Lester, they could be waiting for authorization."

"No, he wouldn't have set it up that way," Dana said, shaking her head. "Lester could be here, incapacitated. He'd want to be sure that help was on the way."

"Well, it's not coming fast enough. We're going to take an alternate exit," Finn said, and they moved through the room to Lester's gallery. The door was locked, but Finn put his hand over the alarm panel, and the circuits immediately shorted out. The door swung open, and they moved through it, Finn shoving the door back in place. With every step, as Finn had promised, Dana stabilized, while Finn reached out to pick up a few pieces along the way.

"What are you getting, souvenirs?" Dana demanded as he overrode the computer circuitry on the painting and that door swung open as well. They thundered down the steps, and she gasped as they ran into the computer room.

"What the hell is this?" she demanded.

Finn moved immediately over to the elevator shaft, the doors opening with a soft sigh when he punched the Down button.

"Nothing you have time to look at—come on!" He pulled her into the elevator shaft, and they plummeted downward.

The elevators opened deep within the Post Office Plaza parking garage, but it was comparatively quiet even as the patrol cars roamed above them. They moved through the darkness, winding their way back toward the street level. Despite her initial rush of energy, Dana felt her breath coming more heavily as they finally resurfaced far down on Huron, and she stopped, doubling over as Finn came back to her.

"I'm going to have to carry you," he said, and she nodded, too tired to protest.

"Where will we go?" she asked, but then she was in his arms, the buildings moving by at breakneck speed. She thought she saw the gleaming lights of the Winking Lizard Tavern, but they vanished as they plunged ahead, turning a sharp right. In hardly any time, Finn slowed his run to a trot, then down to a quick stride, Dana blinking as she peeled her face away from his chest to see where they were.

The twinkling Christmas lights of Flannery's Pub surrounded her. Without putting her down, Finn walked inside.

The Christmas Eve crowd flooded away from them, and Dana struggled in his arms, forcing Finn to put her down again, though her knees shook and her feet seemed too small to support her legs. The first thing she saw was Bob's arrested face, staring at them in owl-eyed fascination for a half moment before rushing toward them. Then her gaze canted right, and the line of old men at the bar captured her attention, most of all Willie, who stared at her in shock.

"Dana, what happened? Are you hurt? Should I call the police?" Bob sputtered, and Dana quickly shook her head.

"No—really," she began, and Finn finished her thought.

"Do you have a back room here? Someplace she can rest in private?"

"Absolutely, we have an office in the back. Come this way," Bob said. He raised his voice. "Everything's okay, folks, nothing but a friend of ours shaken up after Christmas shopping who needs a place to relax." Laughter greeted his announcement, and the crowd shuffled aside. Dana hunched down tightly to hide the blood stains on her dark clothes.

They moved into a short corridor and pushed through an "Employees Only" door, and Bob pulled out a set of keys to the management office.

"There's a couch in here, and I can get you something to drink." He looked at Dana with hard eyes.

"You need a first aid kit or something?" he asked.

"Yeah, that'd be good." Finn had already stood again, watching at the door. "You think we were followed?"

"No," Finn said. "But when the police canvass the area for questioning, they're going to come here."

"They'll be tied up in the building for a while," Dana said, and Bob shook his head.

"Most of the folks here tonight, they know Dana," he said. "The Dana they know doesn't show up in a dead faint, carried by a giant. They'll know *someone* came here and appeared to be hurt, but they won't know much else than that."

"What about you?" Dana asked. "You can't lie to the police, Bob."

He stood up. "The Dana I know doesn't ever show up in a faint either," he said with a grin. "We take care of our own, doll."

Finn came back over to her as Bob produced the first aid kit. "I'll need a minute," he said. "If you have brandy—scotch, anything—that would probably be good."

"You got it."

Bob left, and Finn opened up the kit, pulling out the gauze and tape.

Dana frowned. "I think the bleeding has already stopped," she said as he eased her out of her jacket, unzipping her tunic to expose her shoulder. She glanced down at it, and sure enough, the wound was already sealed over, raw and angry but no longer bleeding.

"This is for show," Finn said, pressing the gauze over the wound. Dana closed her eyes momentarily as another flood of warmth consumed her. It was almost worth getting shot for as good as she felt when Finn touched her. Almost.

She opened her eyes to find him staring at her, his eyes dark and intent. "You have to take better care of yourself," he said softly, and she smiled, her heart filling her chest, pressing against her rib cage and forming a solid lump in her throat.

"I'll be okay," she said quietly.

"You have to be," he breathed. "You have to protect the others like you, to be strong no matter what comes."

She nodded, but the look in his eyes had her heart starting to thump awkwardly. "You'll be there to protect us too," she said quietly. "You can't leave us."

Finn curved his hands over hers. "I'm a danger to you."

"That's not true," Dana said, searching his eyes. "We can help you, like you help us. You've already taught me so much — think of what you can teach the rest of us. You can teach us what to expect, prepare us for battle. We won't be able to do it without you." Finn's face remained grim, and she laid one hand along his face, her next words bubbling up unexpectedly. "Please don't leave me, Finn," she whispered. "I can't face this without you. I don't want to."

"I'll never leave you, not really. I'll protect you, wherever I am."

Her smile was wry. "Not exactly the answer I was hoping for."

He laughed, the sound breaking her tension, and she turned her head away, forcing herself not to cry. "Here." He handed her medicinal wipe packets. "Your face —" he said, gesturing to the bathroom.

Dana started up. "What?" she asked, and he pointed to the small bathroom attached to the office. She moved into it quickly. "Well, for the love of God, why didn't you tell me?" she sputtered, aghast to see her face tracked with tears, smoke, and — yes, undeniably — smears of blood. It was a good thing no one got a good look at her up front, although, arguably, she looked even less like her usual self.

Haunted green eyes stared out of deep-set sockets, her skin pale under its thick covering of grime. She started with the wipes, her hands shaking as she opened the packet.

"How long until the tremors stop?" she called out, as Finn moved through the office.

"Thirty —" He paused. "Perhaps ninety minutes. The bar stays open past midnight, even on Christmas Eve. You should stay here until then. Keep safe, out of sight. If you can get a change of clothes, that would be good."

"I can call Max —" Dana frowned, patting her ear. Her earbud had fallen out, probably somewhere along Prospect during their run, and she had no idea where her phone was. "I'll call him from the house line, I guess. Or someone else's phone."

She abandoned the medicinal wipes, threading her fingers through her hair to lift it off her face. With her bandaged shoulder bulky underneath her jacket, she looked exactly like what Bob had called her, a victim of overeager mall walkers.

"Okay," she said, coming out of the bathroom. "So what is our —"

She stopped, the room seeming to telescope out in front of her. Finn wasn't there.

"Finn?" she said nervously, the sound echoing in the empty room. "Finn!" She lurched toward the door of the office and yanked it open.

Willie stood in front of the door, his fingers

nervously scrunching the edges of his fedora. She sucked in a ragged breath, trying to keep her composure, when inside she knew what had happened. She looked at Willie. "Where did he go?" she asked, and he shook his head.

"He came out to the bar, but Bob was busy, down at the other end, some of the young ones having too much to drink," Willie said in his whiskey-ravaged voice. "He told me to come back here. That he had to leave. Then he was gone. Like he hadn't even been there." Willie's eyes flared wide, their mercurial cloudy blue reaching out to her. He was frightened, and Dana faltered, moving forward, her heart breaking even as she knew she had to be strong—because that was what people expected her to be, because that was what she was.

There would be time for crying later.

"It's okay, Willie," she said, pulling him into a hug. The old man stiffened, then his arms went around her, shaky and unsure. And she remembered the words he had said the night before, speaking to her about her father. She gently pulled away, looking down at him. "You knew my dad wasn't really my dad, didn't you?"

Willie straightened, looking betrayed. "I never said that," he said, his tone challenging. "I never said—"

Dana shook her head. "It's okay. I know it now too." All the wind seemed to go out of the slight man's sails, and he slumped down, patting her hand awkwardly.

"He would tell me the most wonderful stories, Dana, stories to keep an old man company, stories to make you believe in things."

"I'm sure he did." Dana smiled. "Why don't you come in to the office here, and keep me company?"

They had just moved back through the doors when Dana saw it, a folded piece of stationery square in the middle of the manager's desk. It had her name on it, and she picked it up with shaking hands, turning it over. Bob came bursting through the exterior doors, and she turned quickly, putting the letter inside her jacket pocket.

"Irish coffees for—hey, there, Willie, what are you doing back here?" he said.

"Keeping me company," Dana said, patting the man on the shoulder while she took the drink into her hands. It was scorching hot, both from its temperature and its alcohol content, and she downed it in a single gulp. She was the master healer, after all. Her throat would mend itself.

She wasn't so sure about her heart.

Don't. Think. About. That.

Dana refocused on Bob. "How late are you open tonight, Bob? I don't want to be in your way."

"It's no problem at all. We're open until midnight, maybe later if the crowd sustains itself, and then I can drive you home, and you too, Willie," he said with a smile as the old man looked at him hopefully. But Bob's smile belied the concern in his eyes. "Are you sure you're okay, Dana? I can call one of my EMT friends to come here, check you out—"

"I'm good, Bob, really—"

Dana's words were cut off by a buzz against her chest. Setting down her empty glass with a thud, she pushed her hand into her jacket and pulled out her phone, praying that it would be Finn or Max.

She frowned. It was Lester. *Lester!* She knew that bastard hadn't been killed. He'd merely left them all to fry.

She tapped on her phone and shoved it against her ear. "Lester," she said, managing to keep her voice steady. "Where are you now, and what are you doing?"

"Good evening, Dana," Lester said, his voice strangely lyrical, as if he was on the verge of laughter he couldn't quite release. "I need you to do something for me."

She straightened, sending a worried look at Bob. Where was Max when she needed him? Come to think of it, where was Finn? "Um...are you okay?" she asked. "Do you know about the attack at your office? We were worried about you. You never showed."

"I was busy, I'm afraid." And for the first time, Dana heard the sound of muffled complaint in the background, a feminine sound — not really a voice as much as a mewling gasp, a high-pitched shivery sound that reminded her of...something. She couldn't remember what, but it was familiar, right on the edge of her memory.

"Right, well, what do you need?" Dana asked, reaching inside her jacket to finger the letter Finn had left behind. She jerked her hand away as tears began to well up. She wouldn't be able to read it anytime soon. She knew it wouldn't help. Not yet.

"I need you to come to the rooftop of St. John's right away."

"Oka—what?" Dana quirked her brows, aware that Willie and Bob were staring at her. "Lester, Midnight Mass is going on there. What in God's name are you doing on the roof?"

In response, Lester's voice was cold and sure, shivering over the cell lines. "Claire, perhaps you can explain to your daughter what she needs to do?"

Dana's brain stuttered over his words as two identical sounds came together at once. Her mother's racking, heartfelt, but nearly silent sobs at her father's funeral, and the whimper of stifled misery she'd heard in the background.

"Dana, no!" she heard, her mother's words cut off with a smack, and she felt for her Glock before Lester's voice came back over the phone.

"I have your mother, Dana—you might not think of her as such anymore, but I *am* hoping for her sake you do. If you want her to live, you'll be at the church within the next fifteen minutes. Alone." He breathed with unbridled enjoyment, and Claire's whimpers intensified. Dana could imagine him tightening his grip on her arm, her hair. "Please don't disappoint me."

"She's your sister!" Dana protested, the desire to reach for the power that Finn had opened up within her suddenly bright and sharp. She welcomed it, relished it. She stood straighter, preparing to bolt. "Lester, what's going on? Why are you doing this?"

He sighed, almost sounding remorseful. "I told him you were the answer. That's all I said. So now, all they want is you. And I'm going to give you to them."

He clicked off the phone.

Chapter Twenty-Seven

Cathedral of St. John the Evangelist
Cleveland, Ohio
11:00 p.m., Dec. 24

Finn pulled the key out of his pocket, forcing his hand to steady as he pushed it into the lock. Every step away from Dana had been excruciating, every step toward the cathedral maddening. But he had gotten here in time.

He fell into the corridor, his entry scattering a small group of white-gowned children. "I need Father Franks," he managed, pulling himself up. He couldn't help their fright at his appearance. The aura around the church had intensified, as it did on any major holy day. But this was no ordinary holy day. If the archangel was to be believed, a portal straight to heaven would open up at the apex of Christmas Eve, a mere hour away.

"Finn." In full vestments, Father Franks stepped toward him, then looked hard at the children surrounding them. "Tell Father Andrews that I'm dealing with a matter of church business, Jamie. I won't be in line with you all."

"But the bishop is here!" the boy said, his eyes round. He couldn't be more than ten years old, his shock at the priest's change in plans written in his red-flushed cheeks.

"The bishop will understand most of all, Jamie," Father Franks said with a smile that had the boy nodding. "So move along and let him know, then get yourself in line."

"Yes, Father," the boy said, turning away at a run.

Franks gestured Finn up the corridor. "Three hundred and sixty-five days in a year and you have to choose this one for your showdown," he muttered, and despite himself, Finn laughed. Franks passed him, then led him to a small corridor off the main area, turning a key inside the lock. As if recalling himself, he peered up at Finn as he let him in the room.

"If Dana gave you the key to the church, she knows you're here, I take it?"

Finn moved inside, peering around the small room. "She doesn't know I'm here. She doesn't know where I am." He turned and stared at Franks. "It has to stay that way, for her sake."

"Where is she?" Franks asked sharply. "Bartholomew can't be following her, can he?"

"No," Finn said. "I left her specific instructions to stay where she was—Flannery's Pub. She'll be safe there, no matter what may befall me."

"You're not going back to her," Father Franks said.

"No. What's coming will come, but it isn't my battle, no matter how much I want it to be." His heart ached with the admission.

"'And I will make the sky above you like iron and the ground beneath you like bronze.'" Father Franks said quietly. "What will you do?" Finn shook his head, glaring at him, and Franks pressed him. "What does your heart cry out for you to do?"

"Emotion is a human failing, Father," Finn said. "Your race has ever condemned itself by acting out of passion and pride, not logic."

"Yet we're still here, toiling along after all these thousands of years," Franks said, unperturbed. "You can't discount that we're trying to right our many wrongs."

Finn sighed, sensing the waves of quiet pain rolling off the priest now more than ever, as if Christmas Eve merely magnified the priest's suffering. "Father," he said, not unkindly. "How long has it been since you lost hope?"

Franks stiffened beside him. "I don't know what you're talking about," he retorted, and Finn shook his head.

"Yes, you do. You couldn't speak with such compassion to your flock unless you knew the depths of their doubt, fighting against it yourself. You couldn't hold Dana so closely in your heart. You couldn't have been a friend to Walter and rested easily with the paradox that Dana's very existence brought into your life. Even I—especially I—do not fit within your worldview."

He waited, knowing the many paths the priest could take. But Father Franks was first and foremost a man of truth. "Walter was a shining light in the darkness. A gift of angels. You would have seen it were he alive today. He was my friend. Dana, by her nature, was darker, quieter." He laughed, his eyes widening. "And so she should have been, given her biological parents' gift of heritage to her."

"Walter knew?"

"A little," Franks said. "Enough. But Walter… If any man was sent from God, he was it. When he died so senselessly, so stupidly, I told my congregation that God had readied heaven to take him early. But I couldn't believe that. God wouldn't have left us so bereft, not when the need was so great."

"Fifteen years is a long time to harbor doubt and continue your service to the church."

"My service grew more sharply defined after that," Franks said. "Administrative work, caretaking of the cathedral."

"Exorcisms."

Franks looked at his large, worn hands, calloused and creased from a lifetime of service to his fellow man. "I seemed to retain the capacity for that, which should have given me solace." His lips twisted. "It didn't."

He turned to Finn, but as Finn looked up, Franks blanched and took a step back.

It had started, apparently. Though Franks was a devout man, he couldn't have expected the change in Finn. Angels in heaven were different from what people thought they were, Fallen included, when they were close enough to the sacred realm. There was a reason for all that white light people reported in their near-death experiences.

"Don't be alarmed," Finn said as Franks struggled to adjust to the change in his eyes, his skin. "There's a portal opening at midnight, and I—for the moment—am a Fallen. To be this close, that I might reach out and touch the hand of God…" He shook his head, smiling grimly. "As a Fallen, I change."

"Then I will pray for you and stand with you, Finn. Now and ever."

"I…thank you." Finn swallowed. Humans never ceased to amaze him, and once again he was laid low by their spirit, their generosity of nature. Their innate desire to save, not squander, the gift that had been given to them.

They turned as lights flashed into the parking lot, raking across the room. Finn felt his heart surge, the proximity of the portal opening making him hyperaware of one other of his kind drawing near. He growled deep in his throat, and Franks moved to him. "Bartholomew is here," he said. "I don't expect him to be alone."

Franks stiffened. "He would bring his Possessed to a house of God on Christmas Eve?"

"There's no end to what he would do," Finn said. "Where is there access to the roof?"

"Up the hallway, there's a door to the parking lot. It'll be locked—" Finn's look cut him off. "Then that's the way he'll get up there. There's no external fire escape."

"Then that's where I'll be. Bartholomew will likely send men up before and after him. If I can get to him in the stairwell, stop him from whatever he is seeking to do…it will be enough." He looked at the priest. "You have a choice here as well. I'm not sure what good you can do following me, but you have a huge congregation to protect in the main part of the church."

"Should I get them evacuated?" Franks said.

"There's no need," he said. "No harm will befall them from what happens tonight, not directly. Whatever is done will be undone to the eyes of mortals." He gave Franks a lopsided smile. "And who knows, perhaps their prayers will help."

"Then I'll make sure none of them come into this

building." Franks held up his keys. "That, at least, I can do."

They headed out, parting outside Franks's study. Finn waited until the priest strode out of sight before he turned, slipping like a wraith toward the back of the building.

He would wait in the shadows for Bartholomew to arrive...then the Fallen would be his.

Chapter Twenty-Eight

Cathedral of St. John the Evangelist
Cleveland, Ohio
11:15 p.m., Dec. 24

Dana forced herself to breathe in, breathe out as she scraped herself up the back staircase to the roof. With her keys mysteriously missing, she'd left Flannery's on foot and raced over to the cathedral, slipping into the crowd of churchgoers and heading down to the basement. From there, it was a simple matter of crossing the rabbit warren of interconnected rooms and going up the backstairs. Any locked doors she encountered, she simply picked her way through or kicked open. The church clearly was not intended to keep the determined out.

But now that she'd reached the roof, she saw Lester standing there, talking to himself while he held her mother in his arms.

Her mother. Dana shivered despite herself. Claire wasn't her mother, not in the biological sense. So much of what she'd experienced made so much more sense. Claire's distance from Dana, particularly after Walter's death, her distrust. Where Walter at least had fostered a sense of kinship with her, Claire could claim no such bond. She had only this child, forced upon her at the whim of her domineering older brother, the same way her husband had been introduced to her, no doubt. The cool, calculating act of a businessman warrior out to save the world.

And now Lester had lost his mind. Dana wondered if he'd ever really had hold of it. The pressure of running a multinational society of kidnappers and religious zealots would have been wearing on the most disciplined of brains. And he'd always struck her as a borderline obsessive personality. All these years, she had admired that in him. It had made them seem similar in a way, an attention to detail, a focus on work, a dedication to serve.

She'd been so dedicated, in fact, that she hadn't recognized she'd been lied to all her life.

Dana curled her lip and readied her gun. She couldn't risk a shot the way Lester was holding her mother, but if he lapsed in his concentration, he was hers.

"Lester!" she shouted as she walked out on the roof, the wind howling around her and carrying her words away. Lester must have heard them, though, because he turned toward the sound of her voice.

"Come closer!" he yelled, and Claire shook violently in his arms, her trembling now uncontrollable.

"Put her down!" Dana said to him. "I'm here just like you asked of me. You don't need her anymore."

Lester ignored her, and she kept walking closer, keeping her voice loud but low-pitched, controlled.

"Come on, Lester. I came as quickly as I could."

"You're lucky there's still time!" he growled. "If you'd taken any longer, your mother would be dead."

He was already clearly upset with Claire, holding her far too tightly and far too close to the edge of the roof. Her mother's mouth was covered with duct tape, which also bound her hands. If he threw Claire off the building, she wouldn't be able to blunt her fall, even if she knew how. She would be dead or paralyzed on impact.

Dana scanned the rooftop. It was clear of debris, nothing she could use to catch Lester's attention. She had her gun, but that wouldn't help much, since he had Claire pulled up against him as a human shield. He'd shoot her or toss her, either option easily accomplished before Dana could reach him. The wind was swirling around them, tearing at their clothes as she approached, and she tried again. "We're all good, Uncle Lester. You have what you wanted. I'm here."

"Not quite," Lester said. He cocked his gun and pointed it at Claire's head. "But you're almost right."

Claire stiffened, her eyes wide and pleading, the whites around them showing clearly in the blaze of light from the church. Beneath them, through the church walls, the thundering sound of the chorus could be heard.

"I thought you would figure it out sooner, you know. That somehow you'd learn my secret. Part of me wanted you to find out so that I could finally explain everything I'd done to bring you to this point, everything you were in the big picture. But you never had a good enough reason to understand what was inside you. Now you do, and it's almost too late for me to enjoy it." He sobered, his mouth turning down at the corners, and he looked over Claire's shoulder. "I did what was best for humanity."

"I know you did," Dana said. "And I want to help you do more. Tell me how I can do that, Lester."

"You're everything to me, you see. You are the beginning and the end, all in one package. One of the strongest Dawn Children we've ever tracked, the genes of a superspecies brought together in one place. And more than that is in you: the hope for a new beginning for our people." Lester smiled broadly. "And they've come for you, for what you are and who you are. I will lead our people to the promised land, and you'll be my greatest gift. My greatest sacrifice."

Even Claire had stilled, her wide, horrified eyes staring at her brother. For the first time, Dana wondered how well Claire knew her brother. All these years, Dana's life had been filled with lies. Apparently, Claire's had too.

Dana tightened her hand around her gun. "How am I to be your gift, Lester?" Dana asked, hoping to keep him focused on her and not on her mother. "How do you want me to sacrifice for you?"

"Put the gun down," Lester said, his voice surging with power. "Get on your knees. And roll up your sleeves. There's something I'd like to show you."

Dana did as she was asked, her eyes narrowing on Lester. Her arms were unmarked but for the thin, circular scar in her right forearm, all that was left of Lester's wonder drug. Now she stared at it, a sick dread pooling in her gut. She'd trusted Lester so much—with her body, with her life. And now…

"That's right," Lester said. "You were a miracle, you healed so quickly and so well. So it was only fitting that we entrust the miracle of our future to you. And in the process, give me portable, biddable, and virtually indestructible access to the list. Which, as you can see, has come in quite handy for me."

Dana forced her head up. The wind had picked up strength, and she leaned into it, struggling to keep her arms straight. "The list—?" she began, but this was Lester's moment, and he wasn't going to let her steal it.

"Of course," he said, screwing the gun deeper into Claire's temple. "Courtesy of a tiny microchip surgically implanted next to your bone, wrapped in an ancient seal invisible to most scanners if you don't know what you're looking for, virtually undetectable, even, as it turns out, to demons and Fallen angels. I'm just so grateful that Bartholomew came to me before I gave the full list to Finn. I'd never imagined there would be two angels of God to come to stand for his Children. Bartholomew's was an offer I could not refuse."

Dana kept her gaze steady. "What kind of offer, Lester?"

"Finn would have protected you—and that was good. But Bartholomew will do better. He'll create the army I've long dreamed of. He'll use you to your highest potential."

He'll kill us, you mean.

Dana shivered and rubbed the scar, searching for the alien chip in her body for which so many people had already died, but Lester's voice rang out above her, louder even than Claire's terrified whimperings.

"Finn's search was over before he even realized it had begun, Dana. You *are* the list."

From his vantage point by the stairs, where he'd been waiting for what felt like hours, Finn forced himself not to move as a dozen of the Possessed ran past him, their breathing heavy and harsh in the darkness. They were fully armed, their bodies tightly bound in protective vests and combat gear, and he smiled despite himself. Bartholomew was no longer taking any chances. He figured the police were working the scene at Lester's office, with the demon-possessed humans no doubt writhing away in protective custody or strapped onto hospital gurneys like a true nightmare before Christmas.

Then, just as he'd hoped, Bartholomew turned the corner. He had a man with him, a Possessed, whose sunken eyes and hollow cheeks marked him as one who'd already served under the mantle of possession for too long. Bartholomew's skin and eyes were bright, gleaming with his proximity to the portal as he came up the stairs, and Finn didn't wait for him to draw even.

He stepped out of his hiding place and booted Bartholomew in the shoulder, driving him down the stairs on top of his man. They fell to the first-floor landing, Finn clambering down the stairs after them, dispatching the hollow-eyed Possessed with a quick rap of his gun butt to his head, his arms swinging around to crack his forehead as well. Bartholomew was immediately up, squaring off against him, when Finn became aware of the men that stood behind him.

"Take the backstairs," Bartholomew said quietly. "I'll handle this."

The men retreated down the staircase, and Bartholomew and Finn squared off. "I didn't expect to see you here," the rogue Fallen said, his words flowing like silk over Finn's raw nerves. "You have to know the portal will open over the church tonight. Nothing like a sanctified meeting of the faithful to get the energy fields humming."

"Why are you here?" Finn asked, and Bartholomew lifted his brows.

"You don't know? Well, this is a grand surprise, then. But, sadly, still one I have no time for."

Bartholomew whipped his gun around and fired. Finn leapt over him, the bullets missing him as he fell on Bartholomew like the colorfully dressed wrestlers he'd seen in Dana's videos. Bartholomew collapsed to the floor, completely surprised, and Finn head-locked him.

"Why the *fuck* are you here?" he demanded again, twisting his arm tighter when Bartholomew didn't speak at first.

Bartholomew grinned at him, though anger burned in his eyes. "You're getting so good at being a Fallen," he said. "Such a shame it'll all be ending for you soon."

With that, Bartholomew brought his powerful hands up and around and punched Finn in the kidneys, taking advantage of Finn's momentary break in concentration to shove him to the side. He hurtled over Finn and started climbing, but Finn reached out and grabbed his ankles, yanking him back down the stairs.

Bartholomew came up swinging, and the battle raged anew. They beat and pummeled themselves up the stairs, closer and closer to the rooftop opening, and Finn realized that Bartholomew's rooftop reinforcements were only a heartbeat away. He couldn't go through that door without the rogue Fallen, that was for sure.

He turned and delivered a punishing flash of punches to Bartholomew's face and head, battering his perfect smile and drawing an arc of blood and spittle from his mouth as he slammed him once, twice against the concrete wall.

"Good news," Finn said. "It looks like I have more use for you than I thought."

He pulled Bartholomew's body up and draped it in front of him, cracking open the door as he used Bartholomew like a human shield. As he did so, he heard an older woman's muffled, heart-rending scream from the rooftop and a voice that he'd hear in his dreams for however many more centuries he walked the earth.

"He'll kill us all. Can't you see that? He already killed Tim!" Dana cried out, and Finn pushed through the door.

Several images struck him at once.

Dana, on her knees at the edge of the roof, her bare arms held out in front of her, palms up. She stared at her uncle in horror, her entire body trembling with pent-up energy, like a bomb ready to explode.

Lester, a gun trained on an older well-dressed woman whose golden hair was yanked back from her head and whose mouth and arms were duct-taped.

Fully twenty-four men, all of them Possessed, poised between Finn, Bartholomew, and the mortals, their maws open, their eyes wild, like a mob without its leader. Some of them were also looking up.

Bartholomew stiffened in his grasp as they both looked up as well.

At that moment, the canopy of stars above them rent in two with a thunderous boom, and Bartholomew and Finn were split, light exploding between them. The demon-possessed mortals fell away, then quickly circled back, the rage of their possessors against their sworn enemy overriding their human hosts' very basic need for survival.

The battle was joined.

CHAPTER TWENTY-NINE

Cathedral of St. John the Evangelist
Cleveland, Ohio
11:30 p.m., Dec. 24

"No!" Lester screamed. "It's too soon!"

Dana rolled to the side as the heavens tore apart above her. She scrambled up again, closer to Lester, forcing her full attention on him as the Possessed roared around her. She saw his body go rigid, his eyes wild, and she forced herself to ignore the melee around her.

Time seemed to stop. All she needed to do was focus on Lester, on getting her mother safe. The list didn't matter. The Possessed didn't matter. All that mattered was the woman in front of her, paralyzed with fear. A human. In that moment, all humans, held against their will by forces that would seek to control and punish them simply for being what they were.

No.

"Lester," Dana called, her voice sharp, demanding. "I'm here. Let Mom go."

"No," Lester turned on Dana and his face was contorted in rage. "The list is consecrated for the sword of God alone, and I have chosen Bartholomew to wield it as his sword. It must be him. You see what's around us! No servants of Satan must claim it for their own."

"So we'll give it to him," Dana said, edging closer, her voice pitched to calm him. "We'll give him the list, and you'll let your sister go. Can you promise me that?"

He watched her, his eyes going crafty. "He'll make me a general of the new army," he said, and Dana nodded.

"Absolutely. You're giving him what they want, what you prepared me for all these years."

"You understand." Lester's eyes burned with a fever, and she looked into them, seeing the madness that was kept barely at bay by the man's overriding passion. He believed, truly *believed* that he would lead the Dawn Children to save humanity. Nothing was more important than that, and Dana swallowed. Religious zealotry was perhaps the strongest motivator of all.

"I understand," Dana said. She took another step toward him. "So you can let your sister go."

"Not yet!" Lester howled, looking skyward again, but for only a moment, not giving Dana time to spring. Claire was dangerously close to the precipice and looked on the verge of swooning. "When the gates of heaven open at midnight, Bartholomew will have the power to summon his army to him. An army he alone can lead. And then—only then will I give him the Children to fight by his side."

"And how will that work, exactly?" Dana asked. "You've got a chip reader up here or something?"

"You will see. You all will see."

Lester had started rocking, even with Claire in his

grip, and Dana sucked in a breath. "I guess we'll see, then," she muttered.

Lester's eyes swept the carnage behind them, and his chin came up, his eyes wide. "It's time," he said softly.

The mist around the church turned to fire.

The newest thunderclap that came from the heavens was so strong that Dana was dropped flat on the rooftop, the noise rattling her bones. Lester remained frozen, seeming not to hear it. The battle around her intensified, but as she tried to make sense of the chaos, she knew something was different. Smoke billowed out all around them, and an unmistakable heat was building in the air. But heat from what?

None of the others seemed to notice, and Dana swallowed, even as Lester's smile grew beatific, his gun hand starting to quiver against Claire's temple.

"The time has come, as Bartholomew promised. God will hear his cry, and you'll be forged in the fires of his Holy War!" Lester declared, and the wind roared even higher, as if goaded by his words.

Dana stumbled forward toward the edge of the roof and looked down. Surrounding the church, below the thin layer of streets and cars and people, lurked a pit of molten fire that apparently, no one else could see. It roiled below an increasingly busier street as a few people who, Good Catholics that they were, escaped the church before the mass was well and truly complete. They bustled to their cars, clearly unaware, but there was no mistaking the fiery pit beneath them. She felt its pull, drawing her down.

This was where she would be forged as a weapon, Lester said. A place of fire and desolation. Was that what her future held? All her tomorrows? Could God really be so cruel?

But what was her alternative? To lie down before Bartholomew and let him strike her — strike them all — dead?

She swung her head back, her gaze skittering wildly over the roaring Possessed that chanted around Finn and Bartholemew, apparently locked in, well, immortal combat.

She couldn't let Bartholomew win. Hers was one life, but within her, she held fifteen hundred souls. They knew only a hundred names so far, but Max would find more. He'd know what to do. Maybe Finn could help too. She thought he would, for her.

But she couldn't risk Bartholomew — or anyone — taking this list from her to do with it what they would. The Dawn Children deserved to be more than fodder for Bartholomew and his Possessed, and they deserved more than what the Society of Orion had in store for them. They deserved a chance, no matter the cost.

"Lester, you're right. It's time," Dana said, forcing a smile to her face as she moved toward him. "I can hear God's call."

"You can?" Lester gasped, whirling around. "I will be a general in his army. And you will be his sword!"

"That's right," she said, stepping toward him. "I can see Him, his fiery angels, ready to reclaim his creation. There!" She lifted a hand, pointing, and Lester turned excitedly.

Dana bounded forward the last few steps, her arm swinging in a roundhouse that connected with the side of her uncle's skull. He went reeling in one direction, while she threw Claire down to another, her mother now passed out cold.

The list was still inside her, though. The list that

needed to be kept from Bartholomew and his demon horde above all else.

The bells of Christmas began to ring, and Dana leapt toward the edge of the roof.

CHAPTER THIRTY

Cathedral of St. John the Evangelist
Cleveland, Ohio
12:00 a.m., Dec. 25

Finn heard Lester's insane litany of his and the Dawn Children's place in the war as if it was delivered on the night wind. He heard Dana's careful response, her course of action plain in her voice as she finally surged forward, cutting Lester down, thrusting her mother aside.

But she didn't step away from the edge of the roof, from the fiery pit that Finn knew had opened up all around the church, the destiny of the demon horde that howled upon the rooftop. Instead, she homed in on it, apparently oblivious to the danger as the Possessed closer to her realized that she was no longer in the thrall of the human but had once again begun acting on her own.

That was what they'd been summoned for — to stop this from happening. They wouldn't let her go.

"No!" he shouted.

Even as he rushed forward, Finn was thrown to the rooftop as another thundering crash boomed above the cathedral of St. John the Evangelist. The howling wind mingled with the clanging bells of the cathedral, announcing the end of Midnight Mass and the official birth of the Christ child. The surge of joy and belief lifting up from the congregation was almost tangible, fueling the flames of the fiery pit and creating a thinning of the veil. He could almost see God's angels on the other side — true angels, he thought, glowing with holy fire. What he'd once been, all those millennia ago. What he could never be again.

There were more than he expected.

He fought his way through the crowd, determined not to lose sight of Dana. Lester and Claire were no longer in his line of sight, but Dana was moving closer to the edge of the roof, not away from it. She couldn't know what she was about to jump into. The pits that masked the portal to heaven were every mortal's incarnation of hell itself, and for good reason: they represented the faithful's greatest, most primal fear.

And Dana was facing it.

The demons raced for the rooftop's edge, suddenly realizing that Dana was about to deprive them of their prize.

Finn thrust one Possessed out of his way, then another. As soon as a pathway opened up in front of him, however, he could see he was too late. Dana was determined to do whatever it took to protect the fifteen hundred lives that even now slumbered in unknowing anticipation of the greatest battle mankind would ever face. If the list fell into the hands of Bartholomew and the demons, she would betray them. If it fell into the hands of the Society of Orion, she would destroy them. In death, her body burned to dust, she would save them.

She leapt off the edge of the roof and plunged toward the pit.

No!

Finn burst forward, and both demons and Possessed surged away from him, giving him another few moments of renewed speed and anger. And then he found himself at the edge of the rooftop, crouching at its edge as he looked down into the darkness. Time stopped, frozen as he perched there, a madness that seemed almost distantly familiar rushing through him, pouring into his bloodstream as the world went red, then white. He couldn't imagine how this had looked to Dana. Whatever her worst nightmare had been, she had seen it.

And she had leapt. One meaningless human who'd played her part for God. Who'd sacrificed all she had. He should honor her for that sacrifice, use it as inspiration. Find the other Dawn Children, deliver the partial list he'd recovered to the archangel, and let Dana give her life for what she believed in, a life that was, after all, hers to give. A life that she thought could only be worth so much…

Because he hadn't told her any differently.

"No!" Finn raged again, and for the first time in his immortal existence, tears rushed to his eyes and spilled over, pouring down his face. "No."

He leapt after her.

Dana knew she was falling into flames, but the rush of boiling heat was something she could never have imagined. Something brutal slashed her as she fell, her body on fire, her eyes clenched shut even as her mouth tore open in a scream she no longer had the voice or oxygen to sustain. She had leapt to her death without knowing where she was falling, conscious only that with this one act, she would save the lives of fifteen hundred souls, men and women who deserved the right to live their lives in secrecy, protected both from those who would own them and those who would turn them…and those who would kill them.

Her heart cried out for Finn as her clothes burned away from her body, the terrible lashing flames scalding her with liquid heat. Her eyes were fixed open, and a terrifying wasteland exploded in front of her.

Dana was in hell.

She fell to the ground with a thudding agony, the wind whipping around her, her hands on fire as the pressure forced her down, the ground opening before her with nightmarish visions of people crawling out of subterranean caverns, picking their way out of superheated slime, their faces in anguish, their eyes filled with agony. The screams of children and babies rocked her, crying out, their hands reaching toward her — too many to help, too many to save, too many to heal in a world where she had never been forced to believe.

She couldn't save them all. She couldn't save any one of them. She had *failed*.

Dana stumbled back from their grasping hands, but they caught and held her fast, her body convulsing. The chip in her arm suddenly seemed to burn with cold venom, forcing her arm close to her chest, pulsing against her bone, sending rivers of agony through her. Then the ground opened again and she was falling into white light, soft and beatific.

And far more frightening.

Dana's lungs began to labor. There was no air here, there was no life, and she knew she had somehow not died at all. She flinched away from the light, the welcoming flash of deceptive beauty, the outstretched hands of men whose faces were covered in hoods and whose eyes watched her darkly through the veil. She reared back, stretching hopelessly away. Surely she could not survive this, surely her body would be destroyed before they could reach her.

Surely she would not betray the saviors of mankind.

A blast of heat opened above her once more, and Dana felt her body caught up against a man's, strong and certain, hauling her back up through the white light, back into the hellish nowhere filled with darkness and despair. *Finn.* She writhed in his grasp as he tried to pull her toward the heat, her body finally succumbing to the impossible pressures of this place. She would die here, and she must die. She must do this for the men and women left on Earth. It was the only way she would know for sure.

But she'd be damned if Finn died alongside her.

Finn yanked her up, his face hard as he yelled at her soundlessly. Something was terribly wrong with his eyes. They glowed like white-hot coals, boring into hers as if memorizing her face for all eternity. He pulled her up farther, into the blasting heat, and the coiling darkness converged on her. She strained away from him, desperate for him to leave her, to escape, and cried out in silent horror at his stricken expression.

There was no more air to be had, and her lungs collapsed like tinfoil, crushed in the heat and oppression.

Finn's mouth covered hers.

Dana's eyes popped open, knowing that the breath he was giving her was keeping him from breathing, knowing that his body had already started to deteriorate. He poured all the energy of healing he had as a Fallen into her, but to his own detriment. His nerves began to crackle with the force of the energy exuding from him, and his strong arms around her body weren't enough to sustain them both. He couldn't die for her, not in this hellhole, not like this.

And yet he was. As much as she struggled and writhed against him, Finn used her energy, her focus to lift them both upward, through the fire and clouds, through the smoke and grasping hands that he shoved away as he climbed, pulling her up, covering her mouth in a saving kiss, then straining ever upward to bring her back to Earth. She could see it now, far above them, a precipice of light that shone with grace and beauty where around them there was only nightmarish scenes of waste and dereliction.

Dana's body reacted where her soul would not, stretching upward, helping with his trek. He whipped his head down toward hers, reacting with fierce joy, grabbing her shoulders with such an electrifying jolt that she felt the energy whip through her body, leaping within her, forcing her upward. His smile meant everything to her suddenly, the joy in his wild eyes overcoming her fear at the mania that drove him. She could do this, she *would* do this with him, and she grasped his arms and began to pull him up as well, his joy turning to frenzy as they clawed their way back up through the clouds and heat.

Finally, though, he began to flag. He pushed rather than pulled, his own body slipping farther and farther down into darkness even as he shoved her higher, so high that she could no longer touch him with her fingers. As she grasped toward him, reaching down, he shoved her mercilessly back up, the heat beginning to crowd his face, to crumple it in, the lack of oxygen turning her eyes dizzy and making her heart hammer. With one last surge, he propelled himself up, and she gasped — yes! He threw himself against her and gave her the very last breath of life he had, driving his energy into her, his madness, his hope, his desperation —

His love.

Dana's eyes flew wide as Finn pulled away, his face a mask of loss and misery. He shoved against her, and she went up again, finally feeling the rush of air back into her lungs as light cascaded around her, the natural pull of life reclaiming her as its own.

"No," she begged, but Finn was too far away for her to reach, and he plummeted back down into the pit of hell, a million hands grabbing for him, drawing him away from her, damning her forever.

He was gone. Blackness closed around her.

"No!" she cried again, a conflagration raging around her as she flung her last conscious energy out to him, her heart crushed in two.

Finn drifted in darkness, the pain filling his lungs with fire and his bones with lead.

But that was nothing compared to the terror that had overtaken his mind.

True madness, he thought, and his hand crept up, touching his lips where he'd kissed Dana — he felt he'd been drifting here for too long, that his last sight of her had been not moments ago, but years, an aching, mindless space that stretched into eternity while he was caught between the planes, lost to both sides.

Unable to enter his own world and face his own death. Unable to conjure the strength to return to Earth.

He would die here, utterly alone.

Finn drew in a ragged breath, throwing his head back. His body was burned beyond recognition, the skin giving way to muscle, the muscle giving way to bone and blood. He burned in retribution for sin, or he burned from not knowing his sin. It no longer mattered which.

And he burned most of all for the loss of his human.

He could not shut his eyes, his lids fused to his head, his mouth chattering in the heat that seared him so strongly that it became cold, an aching wash of agony he could neither hide from nor fully embrace. He wanted to die — but never die. For to burn alive for eternity and have the memory of Dana would be more valuable to him than to die and lose any bit of her smile, her glance, the feel of her hair against his fingers and the touch of her body on his. His heart swelled and made him gag with pain, his head throbbing with the weight of his memories, and yet he couldn't forget her, not even for one moment.

He had sent her back to Earth, where she would lead as one of her own kind, where she would take the list that was within her and prepare the world for what might come. And Finn would wait until eternity was done with him, and in the explosion of the planets and solar system, he would join once more with her.

It was worth the pain, the aching loss and loneliness. She was more to him than life, than death, than immortality.

She was his very heart.

"Far-Seer."

The name was spoken with such grace, such boundless love, that for a moment, Finn couldn't process the actual sounds, could only revel in the all-consuming power of the music of it, uttered in a thousand voices at once. He cracked open his eyes, struggling to see in the blast of light that came at him from all sides.

"Far-Seer, blessed angel." The words rushed over and through and around him, filling Finn with an energy so profound, he cried out, his body suffused with both wonder and joy.

This was the portal, he realized suddenly. Not the pit of fire that hid it, not the endless well of despair. This was the portal to heaven itself, and the gates were open for him.

He opened his eyes more fully, trying to form any words at all.

"Your gifts are full and precious to my Children, and you have suffered long to protect them. Suffered, and did not believe. But believe *now*, and you may have anything you desire. To stay not only among the broken and the lost souls of this world, but among their brightest jewels of hope. You are bound by the contract of your brothers, yes, but if they succeed, then you will stay with the Children of the Dawn. You will teach them, suffer with them. Live and grow with them. Or…I would offer you another path."

Finn stared, and in that moment, all his memories returned to him. His joy, his oneness with the light of heaven, his connection with all that is and was and had ever been. The overwhelming sense of belonging, of family, of endless love and boundless knowing. Everything he had ever yearned for without realizing it, mourned without remembering it. A place once more in the heavens, as he had been created for.

The voice poured over him in a cascade of light.

"You may leave your contract with the Syx. You have earned that right, and you finally believe enough to take that step. You may return to the light to add your grace to the fire of heaven, brightening the beacon for My children to find and follow. It is a role you served in well, and a role that gladly awaits you. You are forgiven, Far-Seer. You are claimed. You are a Child of God forevermore. And so, the choice is yours. Ask, and it will be given."

Finn gasped, speaking the ancient words he'd forgotten until this moment, the high words of a language that could kindle the embers of the universe. He reached out, and the light reached back to him, welcoming him in, gathering him close, promising him all that he'd ever wanted, all that he'd ever craved, all that he'd once believed and could still imagine, except—

He stopped.

The universe bowed out around him, allowing him to circle, to see, to use the gift and the curse that was his own to bear. He turned his gaze back to Earth, and so much of it was what he had seen before. The pain, the devastation, the fire and the flood. The breaking of the faithful—and not merely those who believed in God, but those who believed in anything, who strove to lift themselves and their loved ones to the next plane of existence. Their lot was bleak, and getting bleaker. The tides of despair crashing over the earth, wave upon wave. Darkness everywhere, thickening, growing, spreading...

Except where it didn't. There was one and then another burst of brightness, tiny stars that gleamed forth, determinedly pushing back the shadows, burning in the murk. They could never overtake the dark, it seemed impossible, and yet...these stars hadn't been there when he'd first gazed down upon the earth all those millennia ago. He hadn't put them there. God hadn't put them there.

Humans had made these lights to guide themselves by, mortals who believed they might find their way. Even when all was lost. Even when they had no reason for...

Hope.

Could he — would he — surely he couldn't turn his back on heaven, not now. Not when it was there for him to grasp, to hold, to add his light to in a shining beacon of glory.

Surely he...

He spun around, his arms flung out, stretching for the impossible truth of what he felt, when something different brushed against him. Something soft, almost ephemeral.

A human hand.

"Dana!" Finn gasped in the language of the stars, recognizing the long, slim, graceful fingers, the wide strength of the palm, the gleaming golden cuff. He gazed at it with soft amazement, his mouth working with utter disbelief...and also joy.

And also...hope.

"You are my angel, my precious child." The resonant words of all creation swirled around Finn, filled him up, made him whole. "Ask, and it will be given."

His heart swelling full enough to burst...Finn reached for Dana's hand.

The moment their fingers touched, he roared in

agony. Electricity fired through him like a wasting fire, exploding what was left of his body from within, with far more devastation than anything he could have sustained from without. And it was pulling him, bringing him up through fire and smoke and currents and pain, his head tilting back in anguish even as his body reformed around itself, his skin regenerating, his brain refusing. As the spiraling light erupted within himself once again, the new kind of madness took hold, spreading out through his body and fusing with the world around him.

He burst into consciousness in a horrific rush, the wind in a vicious gale around him again, the fire only in his mind. Darkness coursed around him, leaving nothing but his own screams and the quickly fading memory of a glory so true, so huge, so incredible that it had crowded out all else. He thought—he thought he saw Dana, impossibly brilliant, but he couldn't focus, couldn't see. The universe writhed and twisted around him, taking new form to accommodate him, both the demon he was and the Fallen he could become, but it was too much…too much!

Fire consumed him.

CHAPTER THIRTY-ONE

St. Vincent Charity Hospital
Cleveland, Ohio
9:10 a.m., Dec. 25

Dana opened her eyes with a painful flicker, then screwed them shut, the bright light harsh against her eyes. She drew in a rough, crackling breath and gagged, her mouth viciously dry.

She reached up to touch it, startled when her hand felt heavy, unwieldy. What…what was wrong with her hands?

"I wouldn't do that, Dana," The voice brushed over her softly, but she struggled against it, its lulling tones forcing her back into the numbing sleep that could not happen. Not now, not when she had to escape — escape.

"Hush, Dana," Franks said with greater urgency. "Don't make them think they need to put you under again. The sooner you can get yourself together, the sooner we can get out of here."

She stilled, suddenly aware of more than the

heaviness in her hands. They were wrapped in bulky bandages, and the entire room smelled like sunburned antiseptic. But she was here. She was...safe.

Although her mind couldn't quite acknowledge that reality, her eyes began to sting, the salt of her tears apparently abrading whatever was left of the soft tissue around her lids. She opened her eyes, her stomach pitching a bit as she heard the clicking noise of her lids lifting over her corneas.

Her eyes ached with the brightness of the room, the affront of Father Franks standing hunched over her bed, his hands shaking as he smoothed the hair out of her face with gentle hands. She felt her lips tighten into a moderately painful smile. She could practically feel her pupils dilating against the bright sunlight, and she tried to speak, her voice rough and raspy as her lips stung with the movement. "Hi," she managed.

"Hello, my dear, sweet child," Father Franks said softly, his scowl deepening the lines on his face that she'd never really seen before. She'd never considered him old before. She'd never considered him anything but — there. Solid, secure, protected by God. But his dark eyes were sunken as he watched her, tears leaking out at the corners. "We didn't know when you would be back with us. Thank you for beating our expectations."

With shaking hands, he lifted a water bottle toward her face, angling the straw between her lips. She drank as deeply as she could, but swallowing was more difficult than she had realized, and she winced as he dabbed a fine linen handkerchief at her mouth. Her skin felt tight, stretched too thin over her face, and her hands...

She stared down in horror at the mummified bandages encasing her fingers. "Where am I?" she asked. She remained blessedly numb, but all the information her fear was holding off pressed against her, clamoring to be known. "What happened to me?"

"St. Vincent's," Father Franks said. "Your mother is safe. She's heavily sedated and will be for days, I'm afraid, but she's doing well." He cleared his throat. "And you were admitted with burns to your hands, and some heat damage to your skin, nothing more. You started out...horribly burned. Your clothes disintegrated, nothing but a gold cuff on you. Which I have."

He shuddered, clenching and unclenching his own hands. "By the time we brought you here, however, you were remarkably recovered. We were able to say it was a boiler accident."

"The church?"

"There was nothing," Franks said, though she couldn't really follow what he was saying. "No fire, no pit, no nothing that you and I both saw with our own eyes. It was as if last night never happened. None of the congregation reported seeing anything but a particularly beautiful starlit sky." He drew in a heavy breath. "The Possessed and demons—all of them disappeared the moment the fire vanished. Just...poof. Bartholomew too. Lester, I'm afraid, isn't doing so well."

She frowned at him, his words still an incomprehensible cascade. "Lester?"

And it all came rushing back.

She jolted upright in her bed, her eyes going wild as the machines around her went crazy and her arms strained against the tubes keeping her in place.

"What *is* this shit?" she growled.

"Pain medication only, Dana. Your hands were

badly burned, but they're healing. Dammit, Dana, they're going to come—"

A nurse slammed into the room. "What's going on in here?"

"Call the doctor, Nurse Tilly," Franks said. "It appears our patient is awake."

"Miss Griffin, you can't be out of bed, you'll hurt yourself—stop!"

Dana threw her legs over the bed, her head spinning. She lost the rest of the conversation between Franks and the nurse, the unendurable need to retch overcoming her. She coughed heavily but didn't throw up, though she spit into her hand, her mind slewing sideways at the thick, wet sludge that came out of her mouth, as if she'd directly inhaled exhaust fumes for the past three days straight.

"Jesus," she muttered, grabbing a towel off the table before anyone else could see it. Her body had started shaking uncontrollably, the combination of the cool refrigerated air on her skin and her own adrenaline jacking her recovery process into overdrive. She looked down at herself even as Franks hustled the nurse out of the room, demanding for a Dr. Milton to be sent for right away even as the woman called for orderlies to come to the room.

She looked…remarkably whole, she thought.

Her hands were bandaged heavily, the thick gauze covered with loose gloves of some breathable fabric, giving her a seal hard enough to tap through. She peeked under one of the edges of the fabric and shuddered. Not quite healed yet.

She closed her eyes with an audible click and stiffened.

Eyelids weren't supposed to click.

Dana stood and unsteadily moved over to the bathroom, her feet unnaturally heavy on the cold floor. She shuffled into the bathroom, looking down at her bandaged hands for a moment until she glanced up at her face.

Her own face stared back at her, the skin red and tight, but intact. Only her eyes had changed. They...they almost seemed to glow, a little.

Dana gripped the sides of the sink, her body giving over to tremors as the memories she'd been holding off crashed down around her. The fall into the hellish pit, the farther fall into what could have been heaven but, so much more likely, was the den of evil that spelled the end of all mankind. Finn, dropping beside her, plunging to her rescue, pulling her back and pushing her up, sacrificing everything he had to save her, to make her live. He would want her to be strong. She knew it, even as her arms buckled over the cold porcelain sink, as tears tracked down over skin that was far too tight for comfort, but at least not covered in gauze.

But she didn't want to be strong.

She was here, and he was gone.

All she could recall was that she had reached for him, begging for him to look up, though his face and body were a nightmarish fright and his eyes were harsh with a light that seemed to burn from within him. He was still Finn, and she couldn't imagine life without him.

She couldn't imagine life at all.

She pulled away from the sink, her hand going up to touch the skin around her eyes. They looked out at her from the mirror, haunted. Angrily, she turned her arm over, her heavily bandaged hand jabbing at the skin of her right arm. It was unbroken. Whatever doctor

Franks had allowed to treat her, they hadn't taken the chip. The Children were safe, and now they could be found again.

If the list hadn't melted inside her.

She shook her head, turning away from the sink. Max would know what to —

She stopped cold. "Max," she murmured, and her fear mounted inside her again. She came out of the bathroom even as Franks came back in.

"I've brought you a change of clothes, Dana," he said. "You'll be released after another review of your progress, and you can visit your mother. She won't be going home yet, but you won't have to spend Christmas here."

"Where's Max?" she demanded, and Franks blanched.

"We haven't heard from him," he said. "But that could simply mean that he's —"

"No, he'd die before he didn't check in," Dana said, wincing at her unintentional meaning. "We have to find him, Father. He's out there. I have to go." She looked at her hands, and the specter of her last visit to the hospital overtook her. "What did they do to me?" she demanded, her voice cracking.

"Nothing. You're safe." Father Franks grasped her shoulders, holding her tight. "Your hands were damaged because, apparently, you held on to the equivalent of a live wire. It's going to take time for those to heal, more time than the rest of you. Your face is already nearly healed and we left your eyes," he swallowed, "untreated, to keep the curious from lifting your bandages before we can get you the hell out of here."

She looked at him, not comprehending. "You let

them *touch* me?"

"Yes, I let them touch you. My God, Dana if you had any idea what you looked like when you crawled back over the edge of the roof. By the time I reached you, there was no one left, Possessed or otherwise, but the entire place looked like a bomb had gone off on it, the church was surrounded by fire, and then—" He shook his head. "And then, suddenly, it wasn't. It was all back to normal. You and your mother—"

"Lester," Dana cut him off. "What happened to him?"

Father Franks sighed heavily. "He was admitted as well," he said hesitantly. "The psych ward, for the moment. They say it's only precautionary, but... I don't know how far he's gone."

"Pretty damn far, Father," Dana said coldly. The ache in her chest yawned wide again, her body shaking. "I want out of here." She turned away from Franks's kind eyes, staring blindly at the side of the room. "I just want..." She blinked. "What the hell is that?"

An enormous planter of poinsettias festooned the side table, threatening to collapse it. Franks sighed behind her. "I know, Dana. I know. They were delivered this morning," he said, and she turned back to him sharply, her heart swelling at the emotion in his voice. "No name, no card."

Dad.

"But...how?'

The priest shook his head, as mystified as she was, though his eyes were overbright, tears threatening at the edges. "That...I don't know. I don't think I'll ever know, but the Lord works in mysterious ways. We need to get you someplace more private, however. The police don't know you're here yet, but that's not going to last for long."

Dana struggled to focus, not to lose herself in the cocoon of despair. Father Franks was right. She had work to do. They all did. She tapped her wrist with a heavily bandaged hand. "This is a chip full of data we need to dig out of me, like right now. How are we going to do that?" she asked. She scowled down at her forearm, palpating the skin. There was definitely still something there.

"One thing at a time." Franks looked up as the door opened, looking no doubt at the doctor who was going to check her hands.

"It's about damned time," Franks said, but Dana didn't turn around.

"I *don't* want him touching me," she said, not bothering to look up.

She heard another deep sigh — not Franks, this time. "I am sorry, Dana," Finn whispered in a rasping voice, and she froze. "I never wanted you to be harmed."

"Finn!" Dana's head came up, and she spun around, careening into Finn as he met her halfway, her arms wrapping around him despite the awkward bandages, though his skin also felt too warm beneath her touch. But the pain was nothing against the roar of emotions welling up inside her, racking her with sobs. She couldn't believe it, he couldn't be here.

"It's all right, Dana, you'll be all right. I tried to protect you, tried to — but there was so much — "

"You're here!" she gasped, pulling back from him, trying to read his eyes. They glowed an almost incandescent blue. "But, how? I thought you couldn't stay. I thought you wouldn't — "

"I couldn't. I wouldn't." Finn nodded, giving her a rueful smile that healed her more than any doctor could.

"But then I met you."

"I lost your note to me," she said, miserable with the sudden memory. "It—it burned. Everything burned, I couldn't save it."

He frowned at her. "My note?" he asked, then his eyes widened. "Oh, the—"

"Coming through, coming through!"

The clatter in the hallway had them both turning, and Dana blinked, straightening in alarm as a woman of truly Amazonian proportions strode into the room. She was easily six foot four, dressed in a starched white nurse's uniform straight out of the 1950s, complete with crisp white cap over her dark brown bobbed hair. The uniform fit the woman's impressive proportions as if it'd been custom-tailored for her, down to the white stockings and—

Dana stared. Did they make platform nursing clogs?

The nurse tapped the oversized clipboard she held as another woman rolled a wheelchair in. The second female was also tall, though nowhere near as tall as the nurse, and dressed in the more standard white medical coat and black slacks. She had keen eyes, a face that betrayed no secrets, and her light brown hair was cut short and businesslike. And given the disapproving frown on her face, she looked like she meant business too.

"Good morning, Dana," she said, her gaze flicking to Dana's hands, then her position against Finn. "I'm Dr. Sells. You should be in bed."

Father Franks stepped forward. "I'm sorry, when were you assigned? I've met Dana's doctors."

The woman turned to him, while the statuesque nurse tapped her clipboard. "Father Franks, Catholic priest, exorcist. Not a Dawn Child, not a Connected in the traditional sense, but definitely somebody to pay attention to going forward, especially now that we've gone all Day of the Demon," she said. "Props to you, Padre. You rocked it in the cemetery, from all accounts."

Dana's eyes popped wide as Franks turned on the woman. "Excuse me?"

"Sorry, I know introductions are in order, but we don't have a lot of time." She held out her hand. "Nikki Dawes. An absolute pleasure. Really. I'm a huge fan."

The priest reached out, and Nikki pumped his hand enthusiastically, her grin going broader. "Yup, definitely something going on we need to study more, Padre." She turned to the doctor. "This is Dr. Margaret Sells. She has a clinic for people whose needs go a little beyond your typical Doc in a Box. And we should probably be getting you to said clinic, stat, Dana. Especially since you've apparently got Genealogy.com, the Dawn Children edition, stuck in your arm."

Sells strode forward to Dana, gently peeled her left hand away from where she held Finn in an ungainly hug. "Have you scanned it since last night? Is the data intact?"

A pang of fear arrowed through Dana. "I haven't," she said. "It may be destroyed."

"If it is, we'll recover it. We're good at that," Sells said reassuringly. She pointed to the wheelchair. "But we do need to get you someplace you can heal more satisfactorily."

"But who—who are you?"

"They're friends," Finn answered for Sells, and Dana looked up at him. He smiled at her, his expression bemused, as if he was still surprised to be standing in the same room with her. She understood the feeling. "I work with them in Las Vegas."

"Las Vegas?" Father Franks bleated. "I can't possibly—"

"We cleared it with your bishop already, Daddy-o," Nikki chimed in. She winked as he stared at her. "Said you bowed out of the service last night due to heart trouble. We may have exaggerated your health concerns the tiniest bit, but you've got the clearance to take some R&R for as long as you need it. Apparently, someone in charge thinks you work way too hard as it is. But we had a nice long conversation regarding your exorcism activities, and trust me. Given the givens, we're all ears about that topic these days."

"I…" Father Franks stared at Nikki, clearly flummoxed. "I don't know what to say."

Finn chuckled. "Nikki has that effect on people."

Dr. Sells continued briskly. "We've set up a suite of rooms in my clinic to ensure your privacy and allow us to scan and extract the chip while preserving its data. We've taken the liberty of transporting your vice president of cybersecurity—"

Dana blinked. "My what?"

Nikki scanned her clipboard. "Max Garrett?" she said, and Dana hiccupped a laugh. Max had given himself a promotion. Which was fine by her. He deserved a corner office for all he'd done this week.

Sells continued. "He's on his way to Las Vegas now, and we're preparing a tech room to his specifications to set up a new headquarters for the Dawn Children. They were…exacting."

"I bet they were." Dana snorted. Still, relief surged through her. *Max is okay.*

"So all that's left is you," Sells said, not unkindly. "I understand you've been through a very challenging twenty-four hours, but we should be going before our arrangements pick up any additional notice."

"Ah, Dr. Sells?" Another nurse dressed in a far more traditional attire appeared at the door. She blinked at Nikki a moment before Sells turned to her. "We need some signatures, and you'll be cleared."

Sells nodded curtly and moved toward the door, and Dana pointed at the chair with one of her bandaged mitts. "I don't need that. My legs aren't burned." She frowned down at herself. "Though...shouldn't they be?"

But they weren't. The skin beneath her hospital gown was pink and smooth...a little too pink and smooth, come to think of it. "Well, that whole healing thing is getting faster all the time, I guess."

Nikki snorted. "Oh, I'm going to enjoy getting to know you too, sugar buns. But let me go park this wheelchair first. Be back in a jiff. Pops, mind coming with? So, so many questions I want to ask you."

Franks flinched in surprise as he realized Nikki was addressing him, then shook his head, flushing with embarrassment. He was clearly as overwhelmed as Dana was. "Of course...of course," he said, hurrying out after Nikki.

When they left, Dana stared at the door, then up at Finn.

"What exactly is happening, Finn?" she asked.

"Too much at once, I can tell you that." Finn sighed. "But the short version of the story is...you have an entire group of people who want to help you, Dana. To support you and others like you, to help you do what you were born to do. To be your family."

"Family," Dana echoed, her heart thudding. She swallowed. "And what about you?"

Finn turned her toward him, and the emotion

shining in his eyes was almost more than she could bear.

"I had the chance to leave you, to return to a place I'd wanted so long, the desire had been etched into my bones. It was my right to return. I'd passed the test. I'd...I'd been forgiven." He smiled lopsidedly. "I even forgave myself, I guess."

"But you didn't go. Something happened...you're here," she whispered, and then nearly choked on a sob as a tear slid down Finn's cheek.

"I'm here. Because once my eyes were truly open, once I understood, I knew my real purpose in this universe wasn't high above this earth, as glorious and as beautiful and as magical as that realm really and truly is."

"It's not?"

He shook his head. "Some people spend their whole lives not knowing what they were meant to do. As it turns out, it only took me six thousand years and twenty-four hours to learn that my place was here. With you. Teaching you and your kind, helping you learn your true potential. Watching you grow. And..." He swallowed, and now Dana could feel her own tears falling, trickling down her too-smooth face. "And being your family, Dana. Through storm and fire and pain and...and one day, if you're willing, love."

"Finn—" she began, but her throat closed up, the words too much for her to say.

"My beautiful, brightest star of hope," Finn whispered. He opened up his arms, and she went into them, the tears falling faster as he wrapped his arms around her. "That note I left you was all I thought I could offer you, the barest pinpoint of light in a universe I longed to open for your eyes. But now...everything's changed."

Dana exhaled a long, shuddering breath, nodding against him. "It's changed," she said. It wasn't a question. It was a...a promise, she thought. Almost a benediction.

Finn brushed a light kiss over her hair. "Tomorrow, the world will be waiting for us. The archangel, the Syx, the Children. Today, I simply want to hold you." He rested his cheek gently against her head, still holding her tight. "And to convince you that for now, forever and always, a lifetime without end, I will never let you go."

Dana closed her eyes, and for the first time in longer than she could remember, truly believed.

~~~

DEMON BEWITCHED
Coming next from Jenn Stark!

You say witch like it's a bad thing...

Former fallen angel, current smokin' hot enforcer, and all-around demon most likely to get the girl, Stefan of the Syx knows women better than they know themselves. He should, because once upon a time, one of them caused his brutal damnation.

All these millennia later, however, Stefan still can't resist a pretty smile. So when he learns his chance at redemption entails pairing up with a gorgeous redheaded spitfire, he's ready to rock—until the other pitchfork drops. Because the bold, impulsive Cressida Frain's not only a woman, she's a witch. And a hookup between witches and demons is one of the few hard stops in Stefan's book of Go.

Unfortunately, this is one offer Stefan can't refuse. To

keep her new position as high priestess for her coven, Cressida must lead her people in an ultimate showdown against evil. To help her succeed, Stefan must allow Cressida to take him, break him and bind him to her — body and soul. But neither of them are prepared for what happens next...

It's out of the cauldron and into the fire when you're a *Demon Bewitched.*

Find out more about all Jenn's books, and sign up for her mailing list for sneak peeks, inside information and giveaways at jennstark.com!

ACKNOWLEDGMENTS

Demon Forsaken was a very special book to me, as it allowed me to bring to life a story I first conceived as an idea called *24 Hours to Midnight*. Thank you to everyone who read early versions of that story — you can see glimmers of it here, though Finn had his way with it! My ongoing thanks goes to Elizabeth Bemis for her fantastic work on my books and my site — and my gorgeous covers. My editorial team of Linda Ingmanson and Toni Lee were absolute champions on this book. As always, any mistakes in the book are most definitely my own. My thanks to Edeena Cross for her careful beta read, and to Sabra Harp, who helps remind me of everything I've forgotten. Special thanks too, to Geoffrey, for encouraging me to go where angels fear to tread. It's most definitely been a leap worth taking.

ABOUT JENN STARK

Jenn Stark is an award-winning author of paranormal romance and urban fantasy. She lives and writes in Ohio. . . and she definitely loves to write. In addition to her Immortal Vegas and Wilde Justice urban fantasy series and Demon Enforcers paranormal romance series, she is also author Jennifer McGowan, whose Maids of Honor series of Young Adult Elizabethan spy romances are published by Simon & Schuster, and author Jennifer Chance, whose Rule Breakers series of New Adult contemporary romances are published by Random House/LoveSwept and whose modern royals series, Gowns & Crowns, is now available.

When she's not creating fictional trouble for herself, you can find Jenn online at jennstark.com, follow her on Twitter @jennstark, and visit her Facebook author page at facebook.com/authorjennstark.